I0764439

Valdar the Oft-Born

A Saga of Seven Ages

by George Griffith

With an Introduction by
Darrell C. Richardson

Cover Design
By Dean Richardson

INTRODUCTION

George Griffith, though almost forgotten today, was one of the most popular writers of his own time. He was a contemporary of the great British writers H. Rider Haggard, H. G. Wells, and A. Conan Doyle. His books were written between 1890 and 1915. Twenty-five of his titles are listed in *The Checklist of Fantastic Literature.*

H. Rider Haggard's first book was published in 1882, and his last in 1930. Subtracting several books which appeared under different titles in England, Haggard has 45 different books recorded in *The Checklist of Fantastic Literature.*

H. Rider Haggard was the master of the tale of high adventure. His marvelous stories of Africa, Ancient Egypt, lost lands and lost races make him one of the great adventure writers of all time. Most of his yarns contained an element of fantasy and some of his books had traces of science-fiction. Although he will be remembered for *She* and *King Solomon's Mines* — the epic series about the African hunter, Allan Quartermain, represents his very best work. There are 15 books in this series.

H. G. Wells rightly deserves the title: Father of Modern Science-Fiction. His fame in the genre is secure. He just about invented every main type of science-fiction known. He is in a class all by himself, though he may owe a modest debt to Jules Verne.

H. G. Wells' literary career covers a longer period than either Griffith or Haggard, beginning about 1885 and closing in 1941. There are 34 different works of fantasy and science-fiction listed in *The Checklist of Fantastic Literature.*

A. Conan Doyle started writing in 1890, when his medical career was faltering, and continued to write until about 1930. Eighteen of his books are represented in *The Checklist of Fantastic Literature.* He wrote many other books not classified as science-fiction or fantasy, like the other writers mentioned here.

A. Conan Doyle created one of the best-known characters of fiction in history — Sherlock Holmes. But he also wrote excellent historical novels in the tradition of Sir Walter Scott. Furthermore, his stories such as *The Lost World, The Maracot Deep,* and *The Poison Belt* place him in the front rank of the great pioneers of science-fiction and the off-trail story.

Where does George Griffith fit in among his famous contemporaries?

In his own time, Griffith was one of the most widely read writers in England. He was one of the true pioneers in the field of "The Scientific Romance."

Writing about the appearance of a Griffith serial in THE ARGOSY, Sam Moskowitz records: "*The Lake of Gold*" (December 1902 — July 1903) by British author George Griffith, whose sales of science-fiction novels would exceed those of H. G. Wells in hard covers, was the only appearance of that fabulously popular author in a magazine edited in the United States."

Valdar the Oft-Born, though one of the most popular books written by Griffith, is now one of his most sought-after and scarce titles. The book is subtitled "A Saga of Seven Ages." In his dedication he called it a "Dream of the Changing Ages." It is a tale of re-incarnation. But the story is not built on the usual doctrine of re-incarnation. It is the type of re-incarnation found in H. Rider Haggard's *The Wanderer's Necklace* (1914) and *The Wonderful Adventures of Phra the Phoenician* (1890) by Edwin Lester Arnold.

Valdar the Asa, son of Odin the Father of Ages, awakens from the first of his many death-sleeps near Armen, City of the Sword. He soon leads these people into battle against the hosts of Nimrod and the City of Babel. He falls in love with the Lady Ilma, Queen of these ancient people.

Valdar lives for several thousand years in this great saga. He stands face to face with some of the great men and women of history. At intervals of time, he goes into his death-sleep. His body does not die and he awakens several centuries later *in his same body* ready to live another life. His great sword and his gold chain-mail always survives with him.

Strangely enough, he finds the Lady Ilma living in each of the seven ages. She, unlike her lover, is re-incarnated every several generations. Though her physical appearance remains similar, she does not go into a death-sleep ready for another life. Nor does she always remember incidents from her previous lives.

Valdar, after a 2000-year sleep, faces Tiglath, the Tiger Lord of Asshur. He walks the streets of ancient Nineveh. As this mighty epic unfolds he stands at the throne of Solomon and discovers Balkis, Queen of the South, to be his lost Ilma. Later, he is the lover of Cleopatra, and a friend of Caesar. He is present at Calvary. He rides with Mohammed and Zoraida. He leads the Sea Wolves of the Northland. He saves the life of Richard the Lion Hearted in the Crusades. He is of service to Queen Elizabeth. He is a prisoner of the Spanish Inquisition. Finally, he fights in one of the last great battles against Napoleon.

From the first page to the last *Valdar the Oft-Born* is full of red-blooded action and fantastic adventure. But Griffith has also woven into this epic story his vast knowledge of ancient lands and peoples.

— Darrell C. Richardson

CONTENTS.

Valdar

A Saga of Seven Ages

Prologue

THE great city sleeps at last—so far as it ever does sleep, this London of the English, this latest Babylon of the World-Lords, for the Eastern stars are paling in the whitening blue of a mid-winter dawn, and the earth is waiting, as a new-wed bride waits the coming of her chosen one, for the rising of the sun that comes from the south, for the re-birth of Baldr the Good, as we used to say in those old times of which I shall have to tell, I, Valdar the Asa, son of Odin the Father of Ages, the Thunderer, Giver of Victory.

Many and strange will be the things that I shall tell of before I have finished the task which I have begun to-night at the turning-point of the sun in obedience to the bidding of the Nornir, the three immortal sister-maidens who measure out the fates of men as they run from the past through the present into the future, Urd, Verdandi, and Skuld, to whom all things are known that have been, that are, and that will be. For I, who write these words, sitting at the northward-facing window of my upper chamber in Babylon the New, looking towards the stars that circle over what was my earliest home in the unremembered ages before the beginning of time—I, Valdar the Oft-born, though in outward seeming but a man little different from the thousands that I pass daily in your crowded streets, have clasped hands with men whose dust is the sport of the winds that blew over lands whose very names are forgotten, lost in the twilight mists of the Morning of Time, men who were dead before the story of Man began to be written. I have dwelt in cities out of whose ruins have been built other cities which now themselves are ruins, and I have seen in the height of their power and splendour, kings whose names, carved deep in everlasting stone, are now the only relics of their memory. I have stood on the roofs of palaces and temples where now the desert sands lie level, and joined in the wine-warmed chorus of roystering songs where now the lonely jackal yelps, and the owl of the wilderness blinks at the moon.

The kings and the warriors who to you are but names blazoned upon the scroll of History, have been my captains and boon companions-in-arms, my friends or my enemies as the Fates willed it. I have looked upon their faces with the same eyes that are now looking down upon this written page. I have loved them and hated them, feasted and fought with them, as you have done with the men of to-day and yesterday. I have gazed into the eyes of women whose love-glance has set empires ablaze, and I have heard the words of immortal wisdom fall from the lips of the sages and prophets who have revealed the Divine to men, and founded the religions of the world. I have seen the fickle tide of empire ebb and flow from East to West, and West to East again, and I have joined in the triumph-songs of victorious armies marching home from conquest over lands where now the desert winds whistle among broken ruins, or where the ploughman shouts to his horses as they drag the peaceful steel through the turning furrows.

Now you who read these seemingly wild words will ask how it came to pass that any being in mortal shape, whether of the kindred of Gods or men, should have fallen under the ban of so strange a-fate as this, and why he should have been singled out, among all the myriads who have lived and died and been forgotten, to live on and remember as a living man what others can only read as a story that seems like a dream of past ages, peopled with phantoms which move to and fro like shadows cast on a screen, or like vague figures limned in uncertain light on the dark background of the night of Time.

The question is justly asked—read on and you shall learn the answer. And if it shall seem to you only as the telling of a strange vision, the creation of a dreamer's phantasy, well, what is that to me or to you, since I have a tale to tell, and you, perchance, are in the mood to hear it?

And remember, too, even while you doubt, that truth ere now has often come to men in wondrous guises, and has been received or rejected according to their wisdom or their folly.

The myths of to-day were the faiths of yesterday, and the dreams of one age have been the deeds of the next. I, who write this, have seen men and women flung as prey to the wild beasts of the arena that their agonies might make a spectacle for the holiday-idlers of Imperial Rome, and I have watched other men and women writhing in the flames of the Holy Inquisition for professing that faith whose denial you hold to be a deadly sin. Need I point the moral finer? Surely not, for I ask you to hear the tale that I have to tell only with the ears of interest. This is all I am concerned with, for I am but he who tells the story, the channel through which the stream flows, and whether the waters are lost in the desert sands or fertilise the fields of future harvests, matters but little to their source or the bed over which they run—so read on if you will.

CHAPTER I

A STRANGER IN THE WORLD

Out of the night of unconsciousness came a faint, uncertain thrill of feeling. Through the black darkness of oblivion trembled a thin, faint ray of light which kissed my eyelids, closed for who shall say how long a sleep, and bade them open once again.

A shudder as of returning life—first a cold tremor quivering through stiffened limbs, and then in ever quicker succeeding waves to and fro from heart to brain and back again, and so spreading over the whole of my naked body as the ripples spread outward when a stone is thrown into smooth water, so ebbed and flowed the returning life-tide, ever stronger in the flow than the ebb, till, drawing a deep gasping labouring breath, I gathered my limbs under me and sprang to my feet and looked about me.

This is what I remember of the first of the many awakenings from the death-sleep that I have known since then, and so I, who then knew my fate but dimly, set out upon that long pilgrimage which began on an undated morning which, by the reckoning of you who read, was more than five thousand years ago.

As I rose to my feet, fronting the west, I drew another deep breath, and strained my still stiffened body and aching limbs to the full of my stature, stretching my arms wide apart as I did so. At the same moment a waft of warm air struck my shoulders, a swift flood of light streamed out of the brightening Heaven behind me, and over the bare sheet of rock on which I stood there fell in front of me a long shadow, the shadow of that mystic Shape which I have since seen symbolised in all the religions of the world, the Hammer of Odin, the Sword of Bel, and the Cross of Calvary.

I was standing on a bare expanse of grey-brown rock, and on all sides of me stretched endless successions of wild ranges of broken hills clothed in dense shaggy woods, which sloped steeply away into dark deep valleys in which the shadows of the passing night still brooded. For all I could see I was the sole inhabitant of some primeval world, alone and, but for the strength of my limbs, helpless, naked before the awful face of the All-Mother Nature.

But though I thought I was alone I was not, for soon a low hoarse cry behind me made me turn again, and I saw striding out of the dense pine growth that encircled the rock on which I stood, five stalwart figures of men clad in tunics of rich dark fur, with sandalled feet, bare arms and legs, and long black hair bound back from their brows with broad fillets of yellow hide. Each carried a bow and a quiver of arrows on his back, and the right hand of each grasped a long bright two-edged sword.

For a moment they stood and stared at me as though struck dumb by amazement. Then with swift, stealthy motion four of them ran forward and placed themselves on all sides of me, and the fifth, whose head-fillet I could now see was of gold, and whose scabbard belt was a broad chain of silver links, strode forward to within three paces of me, and spoke to me not unkindly in a musical unknown tongue, yet still keeping the point of his shining blade towards me.

I looked him in the eyes, spreading my unarmed hands with the opened palms towards him; and, shaking my head, said in a language that seemed half strange and yet my own:

"Your speech says nothing to me. Who are you?"

Then his brows came together, and a look of bewildered wonder sprang into his questioning eyes. He glanced round to his comrades and made a sign to them, still keeping his swordpoint on a level with my breast. I heard their swords rattle into their scabbards, and then the four sprang softly and swiftly forward and seized me by the arms and shoulders.

As I felt their grip a strange new spirit took possession of me, and the blood surged hot from my heart to my head. I felt the muscles gather themselves up into knots and cords over my breast and neck, and then I wrenched my arms upwards, and flung them back to right and left, and as I did so the four strong men that held me reeled away from me and fell prone, like little children, to the earth.

As I drew myself up again to my full height, which I now marked was a good span higher than the stature of the man in front of me, he uttered a low, sharp cry, and crouched as though he would spring at me, as many a time I have seen since then the lion and the tiger crouching at bay for the last deadly leap. Another instant and the keen steel would have been buried in my body, but, before he sprang, I, moved by some impulse that then I had no knowledge of, put forth my left hand against the point of the sword, and held my right out open towards him.

Our eyes met for a moment, and I saw a kindlier light spring into his, then a flush that must have been one of shame rose into his swarthy cheeks. He lowered the swordpoint and loosed his hold upon the hilt, and as the steel rang upon the rock his right hand met mine in the long warm grip that has been the sign of faith and friendship between man and man since the world began, and when the clasp had loosed again I was no longer friendless in the world.

By this time his four comrades had risen to their feet again, and were standing a few paces off, muttering to each other, and scowling half in anger and half in shame at what had happened to them at the hands of an unarmed man.

They had seen in me that which yet I did not know in myself, which I was not to know until many a long year of toil and strife, of lonely puzzling thought and swift, brief revelations shining through the smoke and dust of the battle-storm, and at last they bowed their faces and turned their eyes away from me as though they dared no longer to look upon me.

Seeing this, he who had clasped hands with me smiled again at me, and then, laughing, spoke some words to them, and taking my right hand laid it with the open palm upon his breast. His words and the sign were understood at once, and the four came forward, bowing themselves awkwardly as though unused to make obeisance, and he took them one by one and placed my hand upon their breasts, each one saying two or three words as he did so. Then he pointed his finger to himself and said slowly in a clear tone:

"Arax!"

And after that he pointed to me, raising his brows, and looking at me with an expression that said as plainly as words in my own language could have said:

"Arax is my name. What is yours?"

I was silent for a space, for I had no name, and though I understood his question I could not answer it. Then a word came into my mouth and I uttered it. It was *Terai*, which in my unknown tongue meant a stranger, or one who is newly arrived. He repeated it two or three times like a child who is learning a new lesson, making his comrades repeat it after him. Then when he had picked up his sword and sheathed it, he took me by the hand again, and led me from the rock towards the spot where he and his comrades had come out of the wood. From here a narrow path wound downwards into the valley, and into this we passed together, the four following us in single file, until the gloom of the forest, through which the stream ran as under an arch, gave place to a brighter light, and the path opened out into a little mountain glade, by one side of which, nestling under the tall, straight pines, lay a little log-built, moss-roofed hut, of which the door stood half open.

Into this Arax led me, followed by two of the others, one of whom struck fire from something he held in his hand, and with it lighted a pine torch which he stuck in a metal socket in the wall. As the torch burned clear I looked about me, and saw hanging on the walls of the hut bows and sheaves of arrows, axes, spears, and other weapons of the chase, whose names and uses I was soon to learn.

In one corner hung two or three skins, one of which Arax took down, and, spreading it open before me, showed me that it was a tunic of furs such as he wore himself. Then he made motions, by which I soon understood that he wished to clothe me in it, and this I let him do, awkwardly enough. Next he took a belt of dressed hide and put it round my waist, and after that he took the golden fillet from his own head and placed it on mine, parting my thick long hair aside from my face as he did so, and, lastly, he found a pair of sandals, and, motioning me to sit down, bound them firmly, but easily, upon my feet.

When he had finished making this, my first toilet on the earth, I heard a crackling sound outside the hut, and then there came through the open door a savoury smell that was strange to my nostrils and which woke still stranger feelings within me. I looked towards the door and then at him, smiling I knew not why, and he, nodding and laughing back at me, took me by the arm and led me out of the hut into the glade, where I found a fire of sticks burning brightly, and one of Arax's comrades cutting steaks of flesh from some newly-killed animal, the other roasting them over the flames. A third was rolling little cakes of meal and water on a flattened strip of bark, and soon the fourth came from behind the hut, bearing in his two hands a great bowl of foaming new-drawn milk.

Then we six—I and my five strangely-found friends and comrades—sat down on the green sward of that lonely mountain glade, and I ate my first meal on earth. It was the first time that I had felt hunger and thirst, and the first time I had assuaged them.

When at length we had finished, Arax rose to his feet, and put his hand on my shoulder and pointed over the hills away to the westward, and then at the path we had come by, signifying to me that we had a long journey before us. I nodded to show that I understood him, and then his followers trampled out the fire, took what little we had left uneaten of the animal into the hut, and when these simple offices were ended we started out again on our way, walking one after the other, Arax going before me with two of his companions in front and the other two behind me.

So we journeyed on through the forest paths, scaling mountains and dipping into valleys, while the sun rose higher and higher over our heads and began to shine in our faces until we scaled the last ridge, and from its top I looked down on to a wide, pleasant valley, out of the midst of which rose a great steep hill of bare, rugged rock, on the top of which I saw the afternoon sunlight falling on the white battlemented walls and low massive towers of the stronghold that was to be my first home on earth.

As soon as we had drawn breath on the summit of the ridge, Arax pointed towards the fortress, and said:

"Armen!"

Then, drawing his sword, he held it erect before him, pointing first at the city and then at the blade with gestures that I did not then understand, but which I was soon to learn meant that the stronghold on the mountain was Armen, City of the Sword. Then we struck into the path again downwards towards the valley, and when the sinking sun was but a short space above the tops of the western mountains, we were scaling the steep winding path which led up the rock to the chief or southern gate of the city.

As we passed under the deep portal between the great twin towers of the gateway, I saw on either hand of me a long line of men clad and armed as the followers of Arax were, and as we entered the short, broad street that led from the gateway to the central citadel a thousand swords on either hand flashed from their scabbards and went aloft in the bright evening air.

Arax now took me by the arm, and led me out of the little courtyard, into which the gates opened, into an ample well-furnished chamber in one of the wings of the citadel, out of which three other rooms opened. The walls of this chamber were of smooth stone, and hung with weapons of war and the chase, and trophies of armour and shields, heads of bears and boars, and the antlers of many a lordly stag that had fallen to his arrows.

Here Arax clapped his hands, and two men in grey woollen tunics, with clean-shaven faces and close-cut hair, came in and took away from the table two great flagons of silver. When they came back one carried the flagons full of dark red wine, and the other carried a trencher of hammered silver, on which were fresh-cooked meat, cakes of baked meal, and fruits. They set them on the table, and left the room backwards, bending their heads towards us as they went. Then Arax took a flagon and filled two goblets of beaten gold, giving one to me and taking the other himself, and so I and the first friend I had made on earth pledged each other in a deep draught of that good gift of the Gods which has been the symbol of kindliness and good-fellowship through all the ages.

Then we sat down to the table and ate together, and, after, he took me to an inner room, and there made me change my rough jacket of furs for a longer tunic of fine white linen embroidered with coloured threads. He put a belt of silver round my waist and a chain of gold about my neck, and then over my shoulders he hung a cloak of blue woollen stuff, held together with bronze clasps, and when he at last seemed satisfied with me he dressed himself somewhat similarly, save that he hung a sword on his hip, but, as before, gave me none. Then he pointed to a couch of furs against the wall, as though bidding me lie down and rest, and, nodding farewell, went out of the room and left me alone to think of the strange things that had happened since the morning, and to wonder what was to come next.

It was beginning to grow dark when I heard voices and footsteps, and saw a glow of light shining through the doorway of the central room. Arax came in, followed by a man carrying a lighted torch, and, seeing that I was awake, signed to me to follow him. In the central room there were six other men dressed like Arax, but not so richly, and three others, that I afterwards found to be servants, unarmed and carrying the torches.

Arax took me by the right hand, and said something to the men, to which they replied by each laying his hand on his sword-hilt and bowing his head towards me. Then Arax said something else in a sharper tone, and the attendants with the torches moved towards the door and stood in two lines through which we passed out into the courtyard.

From here we went under a deep archway and up a broad flight of stone steps, at the top of which were two great doors of bronze. On either side stood two men with torches, and on the topmost step before the doors was a man richly dressed and fully armed, holding in his right hand a naked sword, which, as we ascended, he brought up with the hilt to his own breast, and the point directed to ours.

As he did so, Arax, mounting two steps ahead of us, stopped in front of him, drew his sword, and made a rapid sign; then he kissed the cross-hilt, and dropped the point towards the floor. The steel-clad guard did the same, then turned and struck three blows on the door with the hilt of his weapon. Instantly they swung apart, and through them came a flood of bright red light, through which my dazzled eyes could see nothing for a time save dimly-moving figures and waving weapons.

When my eyes could see clearly again I beheld a scene which, amidst all the brave and wondrous scenes through which I have passed since then, stands out as fresh on my memory as does a man's first look upon the face of the woman he is to love. I was in a great stone-built hall, with an arched roof of mighty rafters of cedar, curved and peaked, and carved with wondrously strange devices. The walls were hung with shields and helmets and weapons and trophies of the chase and war, and along them stood two files of men, each holding a blazing torch aloft.

Down the centre of the hall were ranged two double files of warriors in mail and helmet, the inner of them holding their naked blades aloft with the points touching, and over these the outer rows held their long spears with points crossed. Between these walls of warriors, and under this long arch of steel, Arax and I went forward alone till we had traversed three parts of the great hall's length.

Then he halted, and signed to me to do the same; then there came another thunderous shout, a mighty clash of steel, and the swift orderly tread of many feet. The sword-arch vanished, the living walls opened out and fell back, leaving the floor of the hall clear, and in the midst of this I stood alone, ten paces from the foot of a throne raised on wide stone steps nearly half my own height above the floor, and behind this, raised as high again above it, was a great square altar hewn out of a single mass of rock.

At each end of it burnt in a golden dish a fire that sent up long pale flames and light feathery clouds of scented smoke, and from the midst of the altar rose upright a great cross-handled two-edged sword, whose shining blade flashed bluely in the flames of the two fires. At the right hand end of the altar stood facing the hall, an aged priest with snowy hair and beard, clad in a long white garment which reached from his shoulders to his feet.

All this, strange as it was, is easily described, but how shall my poor words tell of her who sat on the throne-seat with her hands clasping its two arms, and leaning forward looking me full in the face with a glance that dazzled me more than the glare of all the torches had done? Amidst all the crowd of her dusky black-haired warriors she sat, the only woman in the hall, pale as a lily and white as the first snow that falls on the mountain tops.

But I could see nothing save the loveliness that dazzled me and the wondering look in the two great starry eyes that were fixed on mine, and the sheen of the altar lights that played on the long waving tresses of red-gold hair that flowed out from under the glittering tiara of steel and gems which crowned her. Then, while I stood there chained and dumb-smitten by the magic of that fair presence, she turned her still wondering eyes to Arax, who had left me and was standing by the side of her throne. I saw her red lips part, and caught the sheen of her white, shining teeth through them as she spoke to him.

Where had I heard that wondrous voice before?—I, who was a stranger upon earth—I who, before that morning, had never gazed upon a human face? Yet, like a man waking from his sleep, and looking back upon some delightful vision of the night, I stood before her, striving to recall something that my dimly waking consciousness sought to grasp and could not. Then she ceased speaking, and, like the snapping of a thread, my brief waking dream ended, and I was recalled to the present by the familiar voice of Arax.

Still standing on the step of the throne, he faced the assembled warriors and began speaking in loud, clear, even tones, telling them, as I learnt afterwards, where and how he had found me. As he ceased a murmur of wonder ran up and down the shining lines of those who filled the two sides of the hall, and when he had finished the priest came to the front of the altar and spoke, I still standing in the midst of the floor with hungry, wondering eyes fixed on the face of her who sat on the throne. The priest said but a few words, and when he ended with a gesture that he made with both hands towards the queen—for such I surely knew she must be—the throats of the warriors gave forth their thunderous shout again, and with a whirring ring every sword leapt from its sheath, pointed for a moment towards the altar, and then sank and came to a rest across the breast of him who carried it.

As the shout died away Arax came down the steps of the throne, and, taking me by the hand, led me to it, and I think it no shame to tell that I trembled like a coward going to his death as I drew nearer to that fair face and the twin stars that shone out from under that steely diadem.

Moved by what impulse I know not, I, who had never bent my knee before, bent it now unasked at the foot of her throne, and as I did so she held out a little white hand with one great jewel gleaming on the forefinger, and my own hand, the strongest in all that great warrior-filled hall, shook like a wind-swayed leaf as I touched it. The worship that every man's heart holds for the beauty of woman bade me kiss it, and I did, and as its soft, warm flesh touched my lips my tongue was loosened, and, still kneeling before her, I looked up, half dazzled yet, upon her bewildering loveliness and said, in my own tongue, forgetting in the strange passion of the moment that she could not understand me:

"Where I have come from I know not, nor yet even who or what I am, but out of some far-off world beyond the stars I have seen those eyes of yours looking into mine, and by such a light as shines not in this new world where I am I have seen the vision of your loveliness. Your voice has spoken to me in my own tongue, though now it speaks in another, and my hand has clasped yours, though you know it not, and I but dimly guess it."

The words came ever hotter and faster through my lips, and by the time I had done speaking she had snatched her hand from mine, and had shrunk back into the depths of her ample throne-seat, her two hands clasped to her diademed brow, her lips apart, and her eyes staring at me half in wonder, half in terror. An angry murmur, quickly swelling into a deep, hoarse roar, rolled up the hall behind me, and through it I heard the sharp rattle of steel against steel as a thousand swords leapt anew from their scabbards.

I sprang to my feet, and, turning, confronted a thousand wrathful faces and a thousand gleaming blades with every point turned towards me. Then the sharp cry of a clear, sweet voice rang out, imperiously dominating the hoarse murmur that still rolled round the hall, and this was followed by another far different. All the angry eyes were turned away from me in that moment, the swords were lowered, and the warriors shrank back into the ranks they had broken.

I turned again and saw on my left hand the queen standing erect beside her throne, a tall white shape of more than queenly grace and majesty, and on my right the old priest with trembling footsteps descending the high altar steps towards me.

Then happened the strangest of all the strange things that I had seen that day. Five paces from me he prostrated himself at my feet, and then, rising on his knees and spreading out his hands towards me, said in my own tongue, but with the halting difficulty of one who speaks in a language that is not his own :

"Hail, Son of the Stars! Welcome in the name of those who have long expected thee on the earth! The Gods have at length granted the prayers of their servants, and the day of glory is at hand for Armen and the Children of the Sword."

For the while I stood speechless and spellbound by the wonder of it all until the priest rose from his knees, and, mounting the altar steps behind the throne, stretched forth his hand towards the throng of warriors, and spoke to them a few brief, earnest words in their own tongue. As he ceased the swords flashed out of their scabbards once more, and again, as they waved them high in the air, the warriors gave forth that deep-toned shout with which they had greeted my homage to their queen. Then as the shout died away in a rolling echo amidst the timbers of the roof, the priest went on, this time speaking to me in my own tongue, and this is what he said:

"Thou who art a stranger among men, who knowest not whence thou has come nor whither thou goest, if thou art he whom the Children of the Sword have long expected, that Son of the Stars of whom it was foretold that he should lead the sons of Armen to victory, thou whose speech is that in which, in the olden times, the Sons of the Gods wooed the daughters of men before sin came upon the earth—that tongue which is now forgotten save by those who serve at the altars of the Unnameable—if thou art truly he whom Armen hath long awaited, then, in token of thy mission, mount hither and take this sword from its place.

"But ere thou shalt dare the ordeal, hear the warning that was spoken of old, and still stands written in our Sacred Book, that he who lays his hand upon the Sword of Armen and fails to wrench it from the rock in which half of its hilt is buried shall be bound with chains of iron and laid upon the altar, and there he shall die the death that has been decreed to the blasphemer. Therefore, if thou art afraid of death, say so, and go forth unharmed, but let us see thy face no more!"

Greatly as I wondered at this strange speech, it yet woke within me an impulse which made me speak words that seemed to come not from myself, but rather as though some being wiser and mightier than I were speaking through my lips; so I said :

"I know not aught of that death of which thou speakest, nor yet of any fear that I can have of that which has no meaning for me, nor will I take the sword from where it stands at thy bidding only. But if she who stands yonder before me should bid me take it, then, though it were buried in the very heart and centre of yonder stone, I would pluck it forth and lay it at her feet to win one more kindly look from her eyes."

"He who knows not death nor the fear of death must surely be something more than man, yet he who would brave death for a woman's smile is very man indeed!" said the priest, smiling somewhat sadly upon me. And then, turning to the queen, he spoke to her a few words in the language of Armen. As she listened to them her cheek grew pale and rosy red by turns, her eyes wandered as though in bewilderment from him to me, and then, as he ceased speaking, she came down the steps of the throne towards me, and held out her hand.

I took it, and, amidst a silence in which our footfalls rang clear upon the stones, she led me up to the topmost step before the altar, and stood there beside me, pointing to the half-buried hilt of the sword. On the other side of me stood the priest, and he, laying his hand upon the altar, said :

"Now, Child of the Earth, or Son of the Stars, whichever thou art, the Queen of Armen, our Lady of the Sword, in whose service a hundred thousand warriors, such as thou seest down yonder, have sworn to hold their lives as worthless, bids thee take the Sacred Blade and wield it if thou canst. Art thou content?"

"Yes," I said; "and may my right arm wither to the shoulder if it fails me!"

Then I put out my hand across the altar and gripped the sword-hilt, of which there was just enough between the stone and the cross-guard for me to get my hand round it. As my grasp closed upon it there came over me the same impulse that had caused me to fling the four companions of Arax prone upon the rock; but there was something more than that, for I still held the queen's hand in my left, and I felt it flutter in my clasp as I stretched out my right arm over the altar.

I took one look into her upturned eyes as my grip tightened on the sword-hilt, then I shook it till the blade swung back and forth, quivering in the light of the altar fires, and then with one mighty wrench I tore it from the riven stone, waved it thrice above my head in the strange ecstasy of a new-found joy, and then, dropping on my knee, I laid it at the feet of her who was henceforth to be its mistress and mine.

As I did so the priest prostrated himself beside me, and every warrior in the hall knelt down where he stood, and, with the cross-hilt of his sword pressed against his brow, hailed me, the stranger from the stars—as all believed me to be from that moment forth—Lord of the Naked Sword and leader of the hosts of Armen. Then they rose to their feet and shouted a thunderous welcome to me, and the priest, rising, too, stood before me with down-bent head, and said:

"It is not fitting that my lord should kneel even at the feet of our Lady Ilma, to whom alone all the sons of Armen bend the knee; therefore let my lord rise, and with her own hands she shall gird on the sword which in thine shall bring victory over the enemies of Armen."

So saying, he turned and went into a chamber behind the altar, and came back bearing across his outspread hands a broad chain belt, with flat, thick links of beaten gold, and this, as I stood up, he clasped about my middle, and Ilma, lifting the heavy sword with both hands from the ground where I had laid it at her feet, hung it at my side, and then, bending down, blessed the golden cross-hilt with a kiss whose memory has made that keen, strong blade bite deeper and truer than any other weapon I ever wielded in all the thousand fights through which I have hewn my way to victory or death since then.

Then I turned and faced the now orderly ranks of the warriors, whose looks had changed from wrath and suspicion to respect and homage, no longer weaponless, but belted and sword-girded like the best of them. Then Ardo the priest spoke to them for me, and told them how I had done the marvel they had seen only at the bidding of their queen, and so braved death to win a smile from her lips and a look of kindness from her eyes; and that when I had laid the sword at her feet I had done so in token of service and devotion to her and Armen.

When he had done, the thunder-shout of the warriors again shook the cedar beams of the roof, and as this died away Ilma spoke to them also, and they listened to her like little children. What she said I did not know till long afterwards, but, just as music speaks alike to men of many languages, so her voice and gestures told me that she was speaking to them of me and of herself.

Then when the clash of blades and the roar of cheers that followed her speech had spent their last echoes in the roof, Arax made a sign, and instantly the ranks stretched out and came together, and, quicker than I can write it, the arch of steel was built up again from the steps of the throne to the door. And now Ilma came down from her throne-seat, and, bending her royal head in salutation as she went by me, passed from my sight down the long shining arch of steel, followed by Arax.

As her white form vanished beneath it, the torches burnt dimmer, and the altar flames shone paler, and the great hall looked as drear as a mountain valley after the moon has set in the night. I was standing with my eyes still fixed upon the great doors that had clanged behind her, when I felt Ardo's hand laid lightly on my arm, and, as I turned to him, he bent his head and said:

"If my lord will follow me, he shall learn much that perchance he is wishing to know."

"Ay, that I am," said I, "for this day's doings have been the strangest I shall ever see, and I have more questions to ask than thou wilt have patience to answer, so lead on and let me begin."

"Let my lord follow, and all my knowledge shall be his."

And, saying this, Ardo made a motion with his hand towards a small door in the side wall, through which I followed him as the warriors were filing out of the great doors at the end. He led me into a little chamber, plainly furnished, and lighted by a lamp of curious shape, whose flame was pale like those of the altar fires. There was a couch covered with furs against one of the walls, and on this I reclined, while he sat himself in a great carved chair of cedar, and so we talked.

"Tell me first," I said, "where am I, and what is this strange land to which I have come so strangely?"

"It is Armen, the Land of the Sword, and its people call themselves the Children of the Sword, for by the sword they won it in the ages that are gone, and by the sword they will keep it. For many generations that naked blade which you wear at your side has been the emblem of their faith and the visible symbol of their God."

"And," I asked, with quicker-beating pulse and words that came hesitatingly from my lips, "now tell me who is she who rules in Armen? Who is this daughter of the Gods whom you call your Lady of the Sword?"

"A daughter of the Gods she is in truth, for she came to us as strangely as you, my lord, have done. One day, nearly twenty summers ago, Arax, our king, the father of him who found you on the mountains this morning, was fighting the children of Asshur, of whom I will tell my lord more anon, when there came to him, through the press of the battle, smiting down and hurling aside all who opposed them, a little band of men of huge stature, the Anakim, Sons of the Desert, as they are called in the speech of the South, and one of these said to the king, 'Arax of Armen, hast thou time for love in the midst of war, and is thine arm as strong to protect the weak as it is to strike down the mighty?'"

"And Arax the king replied, 'My strength would be but little boon to me or my people if it were not.' Then said the stranger: 'Here is weakness for thee to protect. Take it, for it is written that if thou and it come alive out of the battle thou shalt give a queen to Armen who is of the kindred of the Gods, and who shall rule thy people after thee till he whom thou art expecting shall come from the stars and lead Armen to victory over the mightiest of her enemies.'

"So saying, the son of Anak laid a laughing woman-child across the king's knees as he sat on his horse, and then like a whirlwind he and his fellows were gone, bursting through the Ninevites as a torrent breaks through a bank of sand, and that moment the tide of battle, which had been going against Armen, changed.

"When the king returned in victory to the city, he gave the little maid to his wife, and put the matter before me. That night I read in the stars that the words of the son of Anak should come true, and so I told the king that if he would please the Gods he would make this maid his daughter, and train her up so that she should rule over Armen as it was written she should do, setting aside his own son Arax in obedience to the command of the Gods.

"It was a hard thing for a father to do, but when our Lady Ilma grew to maidenhood, different to all the dark-haired daughters of Armen, and so fair and winsome that men's hearts turned to fire at the sight of her, young Arax himself went to his father in the great hall one day, and there before the altar swore by the Naked Sword that the prophesy should be fulfilled, and that he would stand aside for his sister, as he has ever believed her to be, and guard her with his life and the life of every man in Armen until that should come to pass which my lord has seen to-day."

"And now," said I, "tell me how you alone understood the tongue I speak, and whether it is spoken by any people in the world.

"The tongue that my lord speaks," said Ardo, "is no longer spoken on earth save by a few priests of the holy mysteries of that inner religion of which the faiths and the idols of the common herd are but the faint and imperfect symbols. It was the language spoken in the days of the Golden Age on earth, before men sinned, and the Deluge destroyed them all save the family of one just man who had learned this language, and transmitted it as a holy and precious secret, so that the holiest of things might be recorded in it, and saved from the corruption and perversion of the vulgar. I am one of those to whom the knowledge has been handed down, and when I heard my lord speak in the mystic tongue I knew that the hope of Armen was about to be accomplished.

"Now as to these enemies of whom I have spoken, they are ruled by a proud and mighty king whose name is Nimrod. He is descended, as all other men are, from him I have told you of, but he and his fathers before him have lost the true faith, and worship the symbols themselves instead of that which they stand for, and so his heart has become swollen with pride, and he has made his forefathers into Gods that his people may believe him a son of the stars.

"On a river that flows out of the mountains of the South far away over boundless plains to a wilderness of water without shores that men call the sea, he has built himself a mighty city which was founded by his father Ninus, and is called Nineveh after him. This city he has made the centre of the mightiest nation on earth, and year after year, so surely as the changing seasons come round, he leads his armies forth east and west and south and north, conquering all who go out to do battle against them for their freedom and their homes.

"And now only Armen remains free and unconquered, throned on her shaggy mountains, and fenced in by the hundred thousand blades wielded by the Children of the Sword. Year after year we have gone out to meet them, and so surely as we have done so Nimrod has seen his armies hurled upon our rock-built outposts only to be flung back broken like water dashed against a rock. So far we have done nothing but defend our land and our home and fling the invaders back. But now that the time has come, and the hope of Armen is accomplished, you, my lord, as it is written on the face of the Heavens, shall lead the Children of the Sword into their own land, and within the walls of Nineveh itself you shall plant the emblem of our faith over the altars of Bel and Shamash. This I have read in the stars, and what is written in the shining pages of the Book of Heaven must surely come to pass."

While the old priest was speaking these last words I felt the blood grow hotter and flow swifter through my veins. A strange fire burnt in my breast and weird, fierce music sang in my brain. I felt a pride in my strength, and a glory in that kinship with the Gods of which they had told me.

The next day I rose to begin my new life in Armen, and there for many days I dwelt, learning, at first from old Ardo, and afterwards from sweeter lips than his, the language of my new country, and the hidden kinship that there was between it and my own, a priceless knowledge which, once gained, made my forgotten tongue the key to every other language that I was to speak in many nations in the ages that were to come.

In this time I also learnt from the greatest champions and most skilful warriors of Armen all the subtlest arts of that grim and terrible trade which I have followed in so many lands through so many changing centuries since then. I learnt to wield sword and battle-axe with such skill and strength that soon the stoutest man in Armen could not stand before me. They made me bows, too, for battle and the chase, which no other hands but mine could bend, and with them I learnt to send my arrows true to the mark a hundred paces beyond the farthest flight of any other shaft in Armen.

The best skilled smiths in the land wrought me a shirt of mail of links so wondrous fine and close that it sat upon me like a vest of silk, and yet it was so thick and tough that the keenest blades and the sharpest arrows were blunted and broken against it. They made me, too, a white-plumed helm of steel and gold, that would have sat heavily on any brow but mine, and my spears overtopped all others by a good three spans. The whole land was ransacked till they found a black charger, matchless in strength and beauty, and when I once got at home on his broad, strong back, I sat him as though he and I were one, and mastered every feat of horsemanship that the best riders in Armen could teach me.

Of Ilma, too, you will think that I should say something before my story takes me farther afield, yet what shall I say that you, who surely have loved and been loved, have not already guessed.

She went with me to mimic war and martial exercise in her scythed war-chariot, or mounted on her milk-white, desert-born mare, clothed from head to knee in linked steel, and armed as befitted the queen and mistress of a warlike race whose God was a sword and whose chief delight was battle; and together, too, we scoured the plains and threaded the forest in search of game lordly enough for our weapons.

And now that you have pictured us living such a life as this in those far-off days, when the world was young and blood was hotter and manners simpler than they are now, is there any need for me to tell you what sweet lesson I learnt for the first time from her eyes, or how it came about that a smile and a kindly word from her lips soon grew dearer to me than all my new-dreamt dreams of glory, or how I came to long for the time when I could flesh my still virgin sword on the enemies who had striven so long and so bitterly to tear her from her throne, and—as was the fate of all women of a conquered land who were beautiful in those days—carry her away to slavery and degradation in the palaces of Nimrod or his captains?

Well I knew, too, that if I came back in victory my reward would be the dearest treasure that Armen had to give or the whole world held, and she, too, knew it, for was not her fate as well as mine involved in the prophecy that had foretold my coming? She knew it, and the knowledge never brought a frown to her brow or a shadow into her eyes; and so, though no word of love had passed between us, or, as I had sworn to myself, should pass till my own hands had brought about the fulfilment of the prophecy, the cup of my gladness was full with the strong, bright wine of that glorious new life of mine; and in all the world, from Nimrod on the throne of Nineveh to the untamable wanderers of the Desert, there was no man so happy as the stranger who had come, nameless and naked into the world, to find a home and share a throne in Armen.

So the autumn and the winter passed away like a dream of youth and love and gladness, and then, with the first days of spring, there came hard-riding messengers from the South, bringing news of an Embassy from Nineveh, demanding tribute of earth and water from Armen in token of submission to the will of the Great King and the master of the legions of Asshur.

CHAPTER II

THE FLESHING OF THE SACRED STEEL

THE news had been expected, for every spring the same demand had come to Armen since the first battle had been fought, ten years before. Already the main bulk of our legions were on the road, pressing forward to the South under the lead of our stoutest captains, and when four days later the black-bearded, long-robed envoys of Asshur came to the citadel to propose the terms on which their master would give us peace, only the ten thousand swordsmen that formed, as I have said, the royal body-guard remained in Armen, saving only the garrisons of the towns.

We received them in the great hall of the citadel, Ilma seated on her throne, and Arax and I standing to the left and right of her, full armed, save that I had restored the sacred sword to its place on the altar for the time being. The envoys approached us, as all were compelled to do who came to the throne of the Lady of the Sword, walking between the two files of swordsmen, and under the steel arch of the naked blades.

There were four of them, grim, stalwart-looking warriors enough, splendidly dressed and armed, and walking with a haughty carriage well befitting the servants of the Great King who, but for our own land, was master of the East. But when they saw me standing there by Ilma's throne, my white-plumed golden casque overtopping Arax's by a good two spans, they looked up in wonder that had something of awe in it, and all the time that they were speaking, delivering the message of their master, I saw their glances ever wandering back to me, scanning my stature and my armour, and wondering at the golden locks, the like of which they had never seen on a man's head before.

Their message was brief, but sharp and stern. By their lips Nimrod demanded tribute of earth and water, the surrender of our southern outposts, the sending of a hundred hostages of noble blood to Nineveh, and the payment every year of a tribute in gold and silver, slaves, and cattle that would have been worth more than a hundred thousand pounds of your modern money.

For this he would cease his warfare against us, and leave Armen in peace. But if we refused the terms, then the armies of the Great King should overrun our lands as flooded rivers overrun their banks, and fire and sword should rage through Armen till its cities were made heaps of, its fields a wilderness, and its name wiped from the earth. These were the words of the Great King, and this was the way they were answered. First Ilma spoke, and said:

"The sons of Asshur have brought words like these before, but the Children of the Sword still hold their land, and I still reign in Armen. That is all I have to say, but there stands one here beside me who, in my name and the name of my people, shall give you the answer that you are to take back to Nimrod, your master."

As she ceased speaking she looked up at me, and I, turning my back without a word on the envoys, mounted the altar steps and took the sacred sword from its resting place. Then, descending to the floor in front of the throne, I said to the servants of Nimrod:

"Who is the strongest man among you, and who carries the stoutest blade?"

Then the chief of them, shifting uneasily on his feet, and looking out of the corners of his eyes on the great sword that my right hand held as lightly as though it had been a lath of wood, said:

"We came not here to fight, but to parley, and Armen has ever respected the lives of envoys. Let my lord remember that we are but four among many thousands."

"I have not asked my lord to fight," I said, adopting his own style of speech. "I ask you but to draw your sword and hold it at arm's length in your firmest grip. Then you shall take our answer back unharmed to your master, but if you fear to show a naked blade here in our presence we shall think that there is a stain upon it that the sons of Asshur are ashamed to show to their foes."

"The sword of Asshur has no stain save of the blood of her enemies and of those who refuse the yoke of the Great

King," he cried, flushing with rage at my words, and the same instant his sword sprang from his scabbard. The next, as he raised it before me, the mighty blade I held flashed high in the air above him, and then like a lightning bolt it fell and shore his blade in half as cleanly as though it had been a green reed. The hilt fell from his hand, and the two fragments clashed on the stone floor. Then as they stood before me, trembling with fear and rage, I pointed with my own blade to the two pieces of his, and said:

"There is the answer of Armen to Nimrod! Take it back with you, and tell him what you have seen, and tell him, too, that I, Terai, the Son of the Stars, am coming with a hundred thousand swords from Armen into the land of Nineveh, and that they shall hew his legions in pieces, even as this blade of mine has cut yours in twain. Armen has spoken! To-morrow you shall be taken in safety to our southern borders, and after that look to yourselves, and let Nimrod do likewise."

As proudly as they had entered the hall, just so crestfallen and bewildered did the messengers of the Great King leave it. The next day a strong guard took them back to their own land, and at the same hour Ilma and Arax and I started southward at the head of our ten thousand swordsmen.

For seven days we travelled on with all speed possible for so great a host, leaving all the strong places secure behind us, until at last couriers met us on the frontier telling us that half a day's journey to the west where our southernmost mountains sloped down into a wide plain, which had ever been the debatable ground between Armen and Nineveh, twenty thousand of our men were holding their own against twice their number of the legions of Nimrod.

The sun had set nearly five hours when we had this news, and instantly the trumpets rang out the alarm, the camp fires were trampled down, and within an hour the whole host was hurrying westward, in long columns of horse and foot, down the sloping mountain paths that led to the plain. I led the main body, riding by the side of Ilma's chariot, and long and sweet to me was the converse that we held on the deeds that were to be done by sunrise.

No human words could tell you what I thought and what I felt as I rode by the side of Ilma's chariot into the first of the thousand fights that I have fought since that memorable morning. I, who had never drawn a sword in anger, or shed a drop of human blood, was there riding into battle against the veteran legions of Nineveh, the virtual leader and champion of the only host they had never conquered. Think of that and of her who was to be the prize of victory, and you will understand what I say.

Fast as we were moving, I thought those clouds of dust would never be near enough for us to tell whether they hid friend or foe, or both, but still the moment came when we saw through them the flash of weapons and the glint of armour and the glow of gay uniforms and flaunting standards.

Three bow-shots off we halted, and Arax, dismounting, took his place beside Ilma in her chariot to cover her with his shield while she got ready the bow and shafts that she could use with such terrible skill. A hundred other chariots were ranged about her, and in front of them I, at the head of two thousand horsemen, waited for the moment for the first charge to be made. Then Ilma waved her hand to me, and I answered by flashing my great blade above my head in the light of the new-risen sun, and then the trumpets sounded and we moved forward.

We were advancing on the flanks of Asshur, and as we came on their trumpets blared, hoarse shouts ran from lip to lip, and the flank swung round, throwing out wings to right and left, and from those wings came showers of arrows whistling and singing through the air, but only falling half spent upon our armour, or burying their heads in the sand in front of us. The distance was a good fifty paces too far for the bows of Asshur to drive their shafts.

As soon as I saw this I threw up my hand and shouted for a halt, and the cry went back through all the wondering ranks as I stopped my horse and alighted. Then I took my longest and strongest bow from my bow-bearer and strung it, and, fitting a shaft to the string, I strode out to the front of the host, and, taking aim at a tall figure on horseback in the centre of the Assyrian line, I drew the shaft to the head and sent it singing on its way of death. It struck the Assyrian full in the centre of his chest, and his arms went up and he went down amidst a mighty shout of rage and terror from his men.

As for me, a mist swam before my eyes for a moment, and my hand trembled as I fitted the second arrow, for I had taken my first life. But, for all that, the second shaft flew far and straight as the other, and again and again I sped shaft after shaft into their close ranks, while theirs still fell short and harmless about us.

They had never seen such archery before, for my arrows pierced them front and back, and by the time my last shaft was sped the stoutest hearts in their line were fluttering with the fear that the bow which had driven them had been drawn by a hand of more than mortal strength.

This was what I had reckoned on, and, as soon as I heard their shout of fear, I threw my bow to the bearer again, flung myself into the saddle, and, waving the sacred sword above my head, shouted the battle-cry of Armen, and rode at a gallop straight on the central line of Asshur.

Behind me as I rode I heard the thunder of thousands of hoofs, the rattle of arms and trappings, and the wild yells of my own men, screaming with delight at the feat they had seen, and before me I saw like a wall the silent, sullen hosts of Asshur. I charged straight for the spot into which I had shot my arrows. As I swept up I saw a score of corpses lying transfixed on the ground, and then came the crash.

I felt a rain of swift, hammering blows upon my shield and helmet, and I saw my great blade, I know not how, cleave its way through the brazen helm of a tall warrior in front of me. Helm and head split to the neck under that mighty stroke, and at the same moment my horse reared and leapt forward; then down went man and horse under his hoofs, and there I was in the midst of the main battle of Asshur, with my teeth hard clenched and my breath coming hot and fast, slashing out hard and true, and at every stroke widening the circle of dead and dying that lay about me.

I was mad, drunk with the strong new wine of battle—no longer a man as I had been half an hour before, but a destroying fiend with blood of flame and heart of storm possessed by but a single thought—to kill and kill and kill as long as a living foe stood before me. Even the image of Ilma herself was blotted out by the blood-mist that was swimming before my eyes.

But soon I heard the roaring shouts of triumph behind me. The ring of foemen that was shrinking back out of reach of the dripping point of my blade broke of a sudden and melted away; the battle-cry of Armen rang loud on either hand, and as I glanced to right and left I saw the long swords rise and fall, and the white mail of my comrades burst like a shining sea through the dark, riven ranks of Asshur. Then I leapt my horse forward again, and away we went, hacking and hewing at the remnants of the broken columns, riding down horse and foot alike, and trampling them in the bloody sand as a herd of wild bulls might trample down a cornfield.

Then we turned, and rode to right and left to crush the two wings between ourselves and our comrades on the flanks, and as we did so I heard another cheer, the thunder of more hoofs and the rolling of wheels, and down the broad red road that we had made swept Ilma and her hundred chariots at full gallop on to the rear of the now broken host of Asshur. As she passed me she waved her hand to me, and I replied with a shout and a sweep of the blade that was now red from point to hilt. Then she passed, and I and my gallant horsemen fell to work once more.

That one wild charge of ours decided the day; but it was not until we joined our strength to that of the army which had withstood the ceaseless attacks of the Ninevites for a whole day, that what had been a battle became a slaughter. Once our wings touched, the seeming miracle that I had wrought inspired the whole army with that exultant confidence that makes one man with it equal to three without it, and then we hemmed them in with our long, sinewy lines of horse and foot, and crushed them in back and front, one upon the other, till they were no longer an army, but a rabble.

That night the waters of the Tigris ran red with the blood which our brave fellows washed from their armour and their wounds, but there was not a man in all the thirty thousand that had come alive out of the battle who did not lie down to sleep longing for the morning to light us on our way to Nineveh.

You may well believe that my first care, when at last my arm was weary of slaughter and the battle-madness had died out of my blood, was for her from whose lips I had now good right to hear the praise that would be my dearest reward. So, with all my gallant finery battered and bruised and soiled, and all of my skin that was to be seen covered with blood and dust and sweat, I went to Ilma's tent to ask how she fared.

Faithful Arax stood by the door in no better plight than I, for like me he would neither wash nor dress his wounds till our lady's convenience had been served; and, even as we clasped hands and I asked my anxious question, the tent-flap fell aside, and she who but a couple of hours ago I had seen clad in steel, charging in her scythed chariot through the ragged rabble that at sunrise had been the army of Asshur—her cheeks burning and her eyes flaming with the divine frenzy of battle, and her red-gold hair streaming out like an oriflamme behind her—now came forth robed and coifed in soft white linen, with a cloak of silver fur as fleecy as swansdown hanging from her shoulders, as calm and sweet and stately as though she had just stepped down from her throne in Armen.

"Welcome, my lord, and bringer of victory! Truly this has been a day of glory for Armen and for you. But what is this? Your wounds are still undressed, and you have not even removed your armour. And you, too, Arax? Here you are on guard at my tent before you have taken a moment's care for yourself. Nay, I am well, you see, and unharmed, thanks to you, Arax, and your good shield, and I will not speak another word with either of you till you have taken off your armour and cared for your wounds, so go to your tents forthwith, for it is the Queen who bids you"

An hour later, when the moon was climbing up into the southern sky among the brightening stars, we were back, clean washed and clad in our linen tunics and woollen cloaks, and found our men spreading long tables by the river bank and setting them out bravely with flagons and goblets and dishes of gold and silver that we had found in the Assyrian camp.

Then we found that our lady, ever thoughtful for us, had ordered a feast to be prepared for her captains, and when it was ready she came and sat at the head of the longest table, with Arax on her left hand and me on her right, and we had the greatest leaders of Nimrod's host that had survived their shame brought out and made them serve us on their knees with their own wine in their own drinking cups, for a conquered foe got but scant courtesy in those rough-and-ready days, and might think himself well favoured if he got out of a defeat with his life and a whole skin.

We made gloriously merry that night, and crowned the first victory of Armen with many a brimming goblet of the red wine of Eshcol, drunk from Assyrian gold, and, though we had marched half the night before and fought the whole livelong day, the moon was sinking into the west before the last of us left the tables; but, late as we kept it up, when the trumpets rang out at sunrise there was not a man of us who was not already awake, wondering when the signal to break camp and march would be given.

First there was an hour's talk among the leaders while tents were being struck and waggons loaded, and during that we decided to keep southward along the river, with the broad, swift stream on our left flank, and our clouds of light horse scouting and foraging to the west and protecting our right. So we formed up and journeyed on for a day and a night without halting more than was necessary to rest our chargers and beasts of draught. Not an enemy did we see, not a footman nor a horseman of all the hosts that our captive had told us would bar our way into the land of Nineveh.

On the morning of the fourth day after the battle, when another night's march and another sunrise would show us the walls of the Great City, we saw a single horseman, wearing the fur tunic and leathern helmet of the light horse of Armen, ride at full gallop up to the eastern bank, and wave his spear as though he were beckoning us. With one mighty splash a hundred of my own men leapt their horses into the river. and swam across to get the news of our other army.

When they brought it back it was brief enough, but to the point. A day's journey to the southward and eastward, on the other side of the river, the man army of Asshur, under the command of the Great King himself, was drawn up barring the way to Nineveh. On our own side ten thousand tributary troops were marching under Tukul, one of his most skilful captains, to drive us across the river to be destroyed by the Great King when he had crushed our other forces. No news of our victory in the north had reached Nineveh, for all the fugitives had been intercepted and killed by Nimrod's order.

It took but brief debate to show what was best to be done in such a case. Nimrod had manifestly been grievously deceived as to our real strength, and for once the Great King might be caught napping. I, with ten thousand horsemen armed with bow and spear and sword, would cross the river, leaving Arax and our lady with twenty thousand horse and foot and the hundred war-chariots to break up Tukul's force, and chase it to the walls of Nineveh. We would send a message to our main army of the east to attack the king's position as soon as the moon rose, trusting to us to join the battle at the right moment. Then, as the scout rode away with our message, I went to take leave of Ilma.

"May the Gods speed you well, my lord, and send you in victory to the walls of Nineveh!" she said, as she put her two hands in mine, and I raised them to my lips. "We shall meet there or never, for there is nothing but victory or death for us and Armen now."

"Then it must be victory," I said, "and it shall be. Armen has too much need of us, and I have too much need of you, sweet Ilma, for the stars to break their promise now."

"Then may it be to Armen and to you, my lord, as it would be if my wishes and the will of the Gods were one!" she answered, looking down with shyly veiled eyes, as self-confessed of love as the simplest maiden in her land. If an army had not been standing by I should have taken my leave differently, but as it was I only said:

"The Gods themselves could not refuse a prayer so sweetly spoken. Farewell till victory joins our hands again!"

Then I knelt before her, and she put her hands upon my helm and blessed it—a pretty custom that we had in those days—and then I rose and swung myself upon my horse. At the same moment my ten thousand horsemen moved forward to the river bank. There was neither bridge nor ford, but what did that matter to my gallant mountaineers, or the horses that could breast a torrent as well as they could leap a fallen tree?

The Assyrians never seemed to dream that we were so near, for we lay there unmolested till night fell, and then, under cover of the hills and the darkness, we went away, steaming like a host of grey shadows over the heights and across the plain that lay between the two ranges. We had just gained the gap when a scout came riding hard towards us to tell me that the whole army of Nimrod lay camped on the farther slope some two leagues away, and that a shallow river flowing southward guarded its flank. So we halted where we were, keeping a sharp look-out, and waited for the moon to rise.

CHAPTER III

FROM VICTORY TO DEATH

I WOULD gladly dwell on all the gallant feats of arms that were done under the light of the moon and the stars that night; how we watched our time, and, when the battle was raging so hotly on the front that there were neither men nor moments to spare to keep watch for the unexpected, burst in five solid columns, each two thousand strong, upon the weakened flank of Asshur, and raised the battle-cry of Armen so loud and fierce and high above the roar and clash of the battle that the Assyrians for the moment lost their heads and believed themselves surrounded.

Again and again I rode at the head of my troop through the shrieking, swaying, struggling rout of men, grappled in the death-grip, shouting for Nimrod to come forth and do battle with me for his crown and his kingdom. But I never found him, for the Great King had fled, and he who had never turned his back upon an enemy before had already galloped away with his body-guard to make ready for what he saw might well be the death-struggle of his empire under the walls of Nineveh.

Sunrise found me at the head of my troop again, riding for the river with our main army in order of march, advancing on Nineveh about ten furlongs to the eastward. I saw nothing of Ilma's army. The whole of the western bank of the river as far as the eye could reach shewed not a sign of like, and so we concluded that she and Arax had either passed on and were already under the walls of Nineveh, or that they had gone westward in pursuit of Tukul's force. Soon we sent out a couple of swift riders to the eastward to tell the army that a halt was to be made ten furlongs from the city walls unless the march was opposed by another army from Nineveh, in which case news was to be sent to me at once. I also detached two hundred horse to swim the Tigris and find out where Ilma and Arax were with their army, and bid them join us on the banks of the river, at that distance from Nineveh.

Then we rode on with scouts thrown out far ahead of us so there might be no riding unawares into reach of the army that we knew we should find waiting for us under the walls of the Great City, which by noon we saw in all its earliest glory and freshest beauty lying on both sides of the Tigris before us.

But, wonderful as was this our first sight of the first Great City that stood in the Land Between the Waters, all its marvels were as nothing in comparison with that which stood two furlongs from the eastern gate. It has been called a tower of some two hundred cubits in height by those who had never seen either itself or the smallest fragment of its ruins. Your historians and explorers of the lands which were once Asshur and Chaldea have pointed to ruin after ruin of structures that were old when it had vanished, and said this or that is all that is left of that great Tower of Babel which Nimrod and his people of Nineveh built to rise beyond the clouds and mock the forbearance of Him who had said that He would no more drown the world, and set His bow in the clouds in token of His promise.

Like one man we reined in our horses, struck dumb with awe and wonder at the sight, and even we, who within ten short days had broken in pieces two of the armies of Asshur and put the Great King himself to flight, looking at each other as though asking whether the Gods themselves would not descend and fight against us rather than permit the conquest of the people that had raised such miracles in brick and stone as these were.

But the dream lasted only for a few moments, for under the walls of Nineveh and round the mighty base of the Tower of Bel we saw the flash of armour and the glint of weapons gleaming like the foam of sunlit waves along the base of sea-worn cliffs, and as we moved forward again our scouts came riding in from east and west to tell us that two great armies were drawn up before the city on both sides of the river, and that, having slain Tukul and dispersed his forces, Ilma and Arax had turned back up the river to a ford that an Assyrian had told them of in purchase of his life and freedom and fifty pounds weight of gold, and would cross there and join their battle with ours against the Great King and his army.

This, by dint of hard marching, they accomplished by noon, and then our united host, numbering close on eighty thousand horse and foot, was drawn up in a long, deep, glittering array, about six furlongs from the eastern wall of Nineveh, and about four from the shining, serried legions of Asshur, standing at bay under the battlements of their haughty city.

The sun had never shone upon such a gallant sight on earth before. There were the two vast hosts, the one flushed with victory and aflame with triumph, and the other grim, silent, and terrible with the knowledge that this was the last stand that Asshur could make, and that they must either conquer us or shut themselves up in the city to watch us laying the fields and gardens and vineyards waste, and making ready to starve Nineveh and all her thousands into submission.

Now, when I, sitting on my charger by Ilma's chariot in the midst of our host, looked upon all these glories, my heart swelled with a strange, joyous pride in my breast, and I turned to her and said:

"Did ever man fight for a prize like this in the world before? Here are the greatest city, the proudest empire, and the mightiest host on earth hanging in the balance of the hazard of war. Will our Lady of the Sword bid me go forth and do battle for it alone?"

"Alone!" said she, looking up at me with wide open eyes and a sudden pallor that at the moment I loved better than her rosiest blushes. "Alone! You, one man, against all that mighty host! Nay, my lord, Son of the Stars as you are, and terrible as you have proved yourself in battle, I might as well bid you fall on your own sword as do that, and you shall never hear such mad words from me."

"Nay, nay," I said, laughingly. "If you thought that is what I meant, then indeed you thought me drunken with the strong wine of battle and triumph. What I meant was this. Here we are before the walls of Nineveh, with the ruins of two of the armies of Asshur behind us, and the last of her hosts in front. So far I have met no champion of Asshur worthy to stand before the sacred steel of Armen. Now Nimrod is the mightiest hunter and greatest warrior in all his kingdom. Shall I send a herald to him and bid him come forth and fight me, bow to bow, and spear to spear, and sword to sword, here between the two hosts, and let Armen or Nineveh be the prize of victory?"

She looked down and was silent for a space in which I could have counted twenty. I saw her bosom heave and fall under the supple links of her steel cuirass, and the colour come and go in her cheeks in swift succeeding waves of rosy red and milky white. Then she looked up, and stretching out her right hand towards me said, with pale cheeks and trembling lips, and yet in a voice that was bravely firm:

"The words of my lord are worthy of him. Send the challenge, and if Nimrod refuses it all the children of Armen shall be taught to call him craven for ever. If he falls, you will have won a prize worthy of your valour, and if you fall then the hope of Armen will be dead, and we shall have nothing more to wish or strive for. As for me, Arax has a keen sword and a strong hand, and my lord can ascend to the stars, knowing that I, at least, shall never be the prize of the Great King."

"It is said!" I cried, swinging myself out of the saddle. "Arax, you are the brother of our Queen and the Chief Governor in Armen, and so not even the Great King can refuse to hear a message that you bring. Will you be my herald and take my challenge to him?"

"Ay, that I will!" said Arax. "And with a light heart, too, for, unless the Gods themselves stop the fight, there can be but one end to it. If Nimrod will only come out and fight with you between the two hosts we shall feast to-night in Nineveh, and his captains shall serve us on their knees."

"Spoken like yourself, my gallant Arax!" I said. "Now peel a willow wand while I look to my armour and make my message ready. Then let the front lower its weapons and let the trumpets sound a truce."

So it was done, and when all was ready our host divided at the centre, leaving a long, wide lane hedged with a forest of spears, and down this Arax rode with a single trumpeter in front of him, bearing the peeled willow aloft in token of truce and parley. And this was the message that he took:

"Terai of Armen sends greeting to Nimrod, the Great King, and bids him for the sake of his honour as a king and a warrior, and the safety of his city and people, come forth and decide the hazard of to-day by single combat in the space between the hosts. Each shall be mounted and armed with bow and spear, sword and shield. Each shall have three arrows, and, if these are spent and neither falls, then the spear and sword shall decide the day, and the prize of victory shall be Armen or Nineveh, as the Gods may decide."

Then of a sudden there went up a shout from the ranks of Asshur, and we saw the front open, and Arax come forth at a gallop, waving something above his head. A cheer rolled along our own front as he swept down the lane and pulled his horse up sharp on its haunches by Ilma's chariot. In his hand he bore, instead of the willow, a headless arrow whose feathers had been steeped in blood.

"I bring the battle-sign of Asshur," he said, laughing, and casting it at my feet as an enemy might have cast a challenge. "And these are the words of the Great King: 'Nimrod of Nineveh sends greeting to Terai of Armen, and bids him come forth with what speed he may that the shame that he has put upon Asshur may be wiped out in the blood of his own veins.'"

"Good!" I cried, picking up the arrow and breaking it in two. "A right kingly and gallant answer. Now let us see if we cannot make the Lion of Asshur break his fangs on the Sword of Armen."

As I spoke they brought up my horse, and Ilma, white as any lily, descended from her chariot and bade me draw my sword. I drew it, and she took it and thrice she pressed those pretty lips of hers against the hilt before she gave it back to me, saying:

"There is my blessing! All my hopes go with it, and all that the love of woman can give to the valour and strength of man. Let my lord go forth in strength, and may the Gods send him back in victory to ask all that Armen and its Queen can give him!"

I dropped on my knee before her, and she laid her hands on the two sides of my golden helm, according to our custom. And then I took them and pressed them both to my lips, and as I rose to my feet I said:

"Never has man fought, or will fight, at a sweeter bidding or for a nobler prize. Farewell, sweet Ilma, till we meet again, either here in victory or beyond the stars in Paradise!"

When I swung myself into the saddle and looked to heaven for an instant the sun grew dull and the sky grey with mist. Then a deep, roaring shout rolled up and down our lines, echoed by another that rang from a hundred thousand Assyrian throats, and in an instant the lover had vanished and only the man and the warrior remained. My brain was cool, my eyes clear, and my muscles strung to battle-pitch as I rode slowly down the lane between the two halves of our cheering host out into the battle ground beyond, and as I cleared the lines I looked ahead and saw emerging from a similar lane that divided the shouting hosts of Asshur the stateliest soldier-shape that it has ever been my good fortune to meet in battle.

Helmed, like myself, with gold and steel, clad in mail from head to knee, glittering with gems and blazing with scarlet, the Great King rode forth, mounted on a charger as white as the snows on Elburz. We halted and saluted, and then he swerved to the left and I to the right, and so we passed at a gallop down the long lines of our cheering hosts.

I had not ridden a furlong before someone yelled at me from the ranks, and down I went along my horse's neck just as a well-sped arrow hissed through the air a foot above my back.

"Thanks, friend!" I laughed, as I saw the shaft bury half its length in the soil in front of me. Still I sped on till the shouts of Asshur rose to a yell, for they thought that I was riding away from the second shaft. So I was, for the next fell short, and the third came fluttering through the air so slowly that I caught it in my leather gauntlet and broke it in two. Then it was the turn of Armen to scream with delight, for now I had my three shafts and the Great King had none.

So I pulled up my horse and jumped to the ground beside him. I fitted a shaft to the string and waited till Nimrod turned to ride me down, as he must do now unless he fled before me altogether. I saw him turn a good two furlongs off and come at me, head down and shield aloft, like a thunderbolt. Then I drew the arrow by the head and let it fly. Both hosts held their breath as the shaft sang through the air. It struck Nimrod's brazen shield a span below the rim, pierced it as though it had been stretched linen, and struck the earth a good fifty paces beyond.

Then you should have heard the yell that went up from Armen as I pulled the second to the head and let it go when Nimrod was but a hundred paces away from me. It struck the shield square in the central boss, and shivered to fragments against the solid steel. But even before it struck, my third was in its place. I drew it to the head like the others, and, pointing it full at the noonday sun, let fly. It soared away beyond sight into the sky and no man ever saw where it fell.

In another instant I was in the saddle and, swerving out of Nimrod's path, I let him thunder by. Then my shield went up and my spear went down, and as he reined round I stroked my stallion's neck with my spear-hand and spoke to him and away we went, swift and straight as one of my own shafts. No horse was ever foaled and no rider ever sat in saddle that could have withstood such a charge as that.

We met with a crash and a clash that rang loud along the whole line. Each spear struck true to the centre of each shield and splintered to the haft, but mine was the longer by a foot, and so I got in the first blow. For one brief moment we swayed to and fro, horse to horse and man to man, and then I felt myself going forward. With all that was left of my spear I dealt Nimrod's horse a blow across the eyes that blinded it, and then down it went, and the armour of the Great King clashed upon the ground.

Then went up a scream of triumph from Armen and a wailing howl of rage from Asshur, but what both hosts expected never happened. Already my sword had leapt from its scabbard and was flashing high in the sunlight, for I was fighting for too great a stake to give away the advantage I had gained. Another moment and Nimrod must have yielded or died, but before the blade fell my own horse sprang back, as though a fire had burst up under his breast, and stood shivering and sweating ten paces from the fallen King.

At the same instant there rose from both the hosts and from the thronging thousands that swarmed upon the city wall such a cry as human voice had never uttered and human ears had never heard in the world before. I looked about me to see what it meant, and saw a sight that fixed the eyes in my head and froze my blood with horror.

The great flamed-crowned tower was swaying to and fro like a palm tree in a storm, and the battlements of Nineveh were falling in a shower of bricks and dust outward from the walls. Then, like a stricken pine, the mighty fabric of Bel tottered to its base, and fell with its whole length along the line of Asshur. The earth leapt and shook beneath my feet, vast clouds of dust rolled up where once had stood as gallant an army as as ever went to war, and out of them came such shrieks and yells of agony and terror that their echo rings still in my ears across the gulf of fifty centuries.

Then a sudden and awful fear burst the bonds of the horror that held me, and with one thought in my brain and one dear word upon my dry, trembling lips, I drove my spurs into my horse's flanks and galloped for the centre of our line. When I reached the place where the lane had been, I found that already discipline had given way to confusion, the ranks were broken, horses were stamping and shivering with terror, or rushing furiously to and fro with pale and wild-eyed riders on their backs. Great gaping cracks were opening in the solid earth and closing again, swallowing men and horses by hundreds. All thought of battle, all hope of victory and empire died in that awful moment, and Armen and Asshur stood, alike paralysed with terror on the quaking earth that was yawning into vast graves in every direction. As for me I cared no jot for life itself, or anything that the Gods could give me, saving only her whose name I shouted above the fearful chorus of sounds about me.

At last I saw her standing, white and trembling, on the brink of a dark gulf that had just opened at her feet. I swung my horse round, and as I shouted her name again she turned and ran towards me with outstretched hands.

I stooped as I passed her, caught her by the belt, and, as she clung to my arm, swung her to the saddle in front of me.

Then I drove my spurs into my horse again and away we went, for now I had got all that earth or the Gods could give me, and I cared not who lived or died behind us.

My charger, whinnying with terror, swept over the quaking ground like the blast of a storm. A chasm opened in front of us, but I put him at it and shouted to him, and he took it in as gallant a leap as ever horse made from that day to this. And so we sped on and on, whither I know not, saving that it was away from the doomed city, and all the terrors that were multiplying about it.

As I looked up I saw the blue sky change to dun red above me, the sun glared dully like a disc of blood out of the west, and all round, as far as eye could reach, red masses of flying sand rolled and tossed like the billows of some vast fiery ocean leaping up from earth to heaven. Then I knew that before us and on every side of us there was a fate from which there was no escape. I let the reins fall on my horse's neck, and, gathering Ilma up in my arms, I woke her from her trance of terror with the first kiss I had ever pressed upon her lips. She opened her eyes, and the blood came back in rosy waves to her cheeks, then it faded out again, and she freed one arm from my clasp and pointed to the horizon, and said:

"There comes the fire-wind, Terai! There is no escape from that, but the Gods are good, for they will let us die together. Alas for Armen and her gallant sons, those whom the earthquake spares the fire-wind will slay!"

"Die!" I cried, in the agony and revolt of my soul. "Nay, by the Gods, we cannot die! What! have I come from the stars and conquered the Great King and won you, my darling and my queen, to be choked like a trader's camel in a sandstorm? Nay, I will ride through it as I have ridden through the hosts of Asshur, and on the other side we shall find sunlight and safety."

"Nay, my lord and my love," she answered with sweet sadness. "There is no other side of that fiery sea for us. We shall die in the midst of it, and the death will be one of slow torment and long madness. But no, my dagger is keen, and death from your hand will be sweeter than life from another's. Promise me, Terai, that the burning sand shall not choke me and drive me mad."

Just then Tigrol, my horse, reared up, screaming with fear, and I felt a rush of hot, stinging atoms on my face and bare forearms. A blast of burning wind roared past, and through it Ilma whispered in my ear:

"Quick, Terai, quick—the dagger—in my belt."

As she spoke my poor horse stopped shuddering, and then, turning his tail to the wind as his instinct told him, went down on his haunches. I saw then that the end was very near, and, with Ilma in my arms, slipped to the ground. The first blast had passed and we had a brief breathing space. That was a wave, and behind it was coming the ocean. My gallant Tigrol had borne us bravely, and so I pulled him round across the wind and with a swift slash of my sword severed his spine at the neck and spared him his last agony. Then I turned to Ilma and saw that she had unhooked the shoulder straps of her steel corselet and dropped it to her feet.

She took the dagger from its sheath in the belt and came towards me smiling with it in her hand. As I put my arm about her there burst upon us another roaring blast of hot, suffocating wind, and the whirling sand-waves shut out sun and sky with their dun red curtain. Impelled by some fond instinct, I drew her down with me behind poor Tigrol's body, and there we lay in the shallow shelter on the burning sand—as strange a bridal bed as love has ever hallowed.

The storm roared on, and the sand began to stream in swift, wreathing sheets across Tigrol's body, and heap up round us, building the grave that would remain nameless for ever. I took the dagger from Ilma's willing hand, and then I laid my lips on hers and put the point to her breast. I felt just one sigh of her sweet breath, one faint flutter of her lips, and then as the death-film dimmed the love-light in her eyes my own heart burst with its surcharge of rage and sorrow. One last blast roared in my dying ears as my head fell down beside my darling's, and then the whirling sand drew its burning shroud over us as we lay side by side and hand in hand—dead, but not divided.

CHAPTER IV

THE TIGER—LORD OF ASSHUR

A GUST of cool night wind blowing across my bare face awakened me, and I looked up to see the full moon floating serenely in the zenith, and the stars, glorious in their white radiance, hanging like lamps of burning crystal in the sky. And Ilma! Was she awake, too? If not I must rouse her, since the storm and the burning had passed, and calm and coolness had come, I must——

No, by the Gods, that could never be! Fool, madman, murderer that I was, I had killed her, and that sweet, pure body of hers was lying beside me cold and lifeless in the sand, with her own dagger buried to the hilt in her breast, driven there by my own murderous hand! Where was she? I would gaze once more upon her white loveliness, now, alas, whiter than ever in the waxen pallor of death, and then, by my own hand, I would pay the penalty of my madness, and with the same dagger I would open a way to the only refuge that was possible for my bitter sorrow and despair.

Where was she? I turned on my side, flinging off the sand which the night wind had not yet blown away from my limbs, and looked down, expecting to see the curving mound of sand that would tell me where to look for her body. But the sand sloped smoothly away on all sides almost level with the desert. Still, had we not lain down side by side in that sad, strange, burning bridal bed of ours, and must she not be beside me still? The sand had only covered her, and beneath that grey, smooth surface I must find her sleeping the sleep of endless calm into which my hand had plunged her.

So I rose to my knees and thrust my hands down into the soft, yielding sand, but there was nothing there. In a sudden agony of fear and wonder, I thrust them deeper still, and flung the sand passionately to right and left, scooping a long, deep hollow in front of me. Still there was nothing but the loose grey grains of dry sand, which ran away between my fingers as I dug.

Then at last my right hand struck something hard. I clutched it, and, with the cloud of an awful fear falling upon my soul, I drew it out and looked at it. It was the golden hilt of Ilma's dagger, and from it there projected an inch or two of rotten red-rusted steel. Then a wild, wailing cry, half of grief, half of horror, broke from my lips, and like one possessed by an evil spirit I dug on breathlessly, fiercely, at what that sickening fear at my heart told me was now only the empty grave where once,—and who knew how long ago (?) my dead darling had lain.

I scooped away the sand all round the spot where I had found the dagger-hilt, running every handful through my fingers so that nothing might escape me, and ere long I came upon little morsels of something white, that crumbled away to powder as I tried to take hold of them. Then a little bank of sand above one end of the hollow that I had made gave way and fell down, and out of it rolled a grey-white skull, and even as I looked horror-frozen on the ghastly grinning jaws my senses reeled into unconsciousness, and I fell forward with outstretched arms over the poor handful of dust that was all that death had left of my sweet Ilma and Armen's peerless queen.

When I woke again the sun was shooting his first beams across the level plain, and I dragged myself to my feet and looked at myself. At my feet lay my helmet of steel and gold almost as bright as it had been when I set it on my brows to go forth to combat with Nimrod, but the leather chin strap had vanished. As for myself, I was clad simply in my shirt of steel mail, though the sacred sword of Armen still rested by my side. But the leathern scabbard that had protected it was gone, and the blade hung, naked and shining with undimmed lustre, supported by the cross hilt in the belt. Not a vestige of other clothing was left me. My linen vest and the leather shirt I wore under my mail, my sandals and the cross-garters that had held them to my feet, were gone. Nothing that was not either gold or steel remained to me. Then as I stood facing the new risen sun there broke upon my soul the first glimmer of the great and awful truth that I was only to learn in its fulness after many another falling asleep and many another such an awakening as this.

The first stage of my pilgrimage had been passed, and another one was beginning. Behind me lay the wrecks of my lost glories and my lost love. Before me lay the unknown, blank as the smooth wind-swept sands at my feet. There I stood, once more a stranger in the world, with no possessions save my helmet, my shirt of mail, and my sword, and in my heart the memory of all that I had loved and lost.

The sun was, as I have said, just showing above the horizon, and far away, sharply outlined against the bright eastern sky, I saw something that stirred my half-awakened blood to quicker flow, for it told me that I was not alone upon the earth nor even upon the desert. Between me and the sun stretched a long, slowly-moving line of laden camels, of men on foot, and men on horseback, and they were coming towards me out of the south-east.

I found Ilma's cuirass entire where she had dropped it close by our resting-place, and I spread that out on the sand and laid my treasures on it. But the greatest treasure of all, her golden dagger-hilt with the fragment of the blade rusted by her own dear blood, I laid apart by itself, for no need should tempt me to barter that. Then, with my sword, I cut the gold furnishings off my helmet, and, adding those to the heap, rolled all up in the pliant folds of the chain mail. Then, when I had reverently smoothed down the sand that covered Ilma's dust, I gathered up my possessions and started out towards the caravan, doubtful how a visitor who came in such strange guise would be received, yet driven to take what risk there might be by the stress of hunger and thirst.

I had approached within a furlong of the caravan when they saw me, and two horsemen left the line and galloped towards me. They were men of swarthy complexion, well sized, and dressed in white flowing robes, and armed with spears and short swords. I must have presented a strange and sorry figure as they reined up and saw me standing there on the desert, naked but for my shirt of mail and helmet, my skin grey and my hair matted and dull with dust.

They looked at me, as indeed they may well have done, as though I had been some visitant from another world, and after they had stared their fill, one of them said in a strange yet half familiar tongue:

"Who are you, friend, and whence come you in so strange a garb? Not from Nineveh, I take it, or, if so, then you are sadly behind the fashion, and grievously in want of some of our good Tyrian dyed-stuffs."

As I said, his speech was strange, but I understood it, and I answered, laughing, as well as I could:

"Nevertheless, friend, I am from Nineveh, or at least from before its walls, for the last sight that my eyes looked on was the ruin of the great city and the fall of the great tower ——"

Now, by Bel and Ashtaroth!" broke in the other in a voice of ridicule before I could finish. "Thy lips surely are lying to us, for the tower of Bel fell two thousand years ago, unless the traditions lie, too, and Nineveh is no ruin, but the stateliest city out of Egypt. What tongue is that thou art speaking?"

"A tongue in which I can tell thee," I said, hotly, with my hand on my sword-hilt, "that neither thou, whoever thou art, nor the greatest man in yonder train can say that I am lying without having his own lie thrust down his throat. It may be that my tale is a strange one, for I have slept yonder in the sand I know not how long, and have but just awakened. Yet what I tell thee is true, true as the steel of this good blade that I will prove it with."

"Steel! What is that?" said the other, imitating the word with difficulty. "Peace, Melkar! thy tongue is ever readier than thy sword, and to thee every strange tale is a lie. Canst thou not see the man is alone and looks weary, and perchance hungry and athirst? Whether he speaks truth or falsehood, he speaks it like a man, and in a tongue which, if I mistake not, is good old Turanian, a better speech than the mongrel dialect thou hast picked up on the wharves of Tyre and the decks of thy father's galleys."

He who said this was the elder of the two, and I noticed that his speech was finer and clearer and more like my own than the other's, so I turned my back on the other and said:

"Whether my tale be true or false, good sir, it will keep to another time. For the present I pray you take me as I am, a man friendless and alone, hungry and athirst, and yet having the wherewithal to buy meat and drink, and a sword to protect his own."

As I spoke I opened Ilma's corselet and showed the jewels and scraps of gold inside it.

"Whatever age I have awakened in," I went on, "I suppose gold has not lost its magic yet."

"Thou art right, friend," said the elder man, laughing and stroking his black beard. "We are traders, and know right well what gold can do, and if thou hast it, well, thou art welcome. Meat and drink thou canst have for the asking, but what else thou needest thou must buy. I am Zurim of Tyre, a Phœnician trader, and my goods are in yonder caravan on the way from Arbela to Nineveh, which I hope we shall see, not a ruin as thou hast said, but in all her wealth and pride and glory, before three more suns have set. Come back with us to the caravan, and we will serve you with what we have. As for this loose-tongued fellow, forget what he has said, for there is ever more speed than wisdom in his speech."

I have so many great things to tell of, that I must needs give but brief space to my coming into the caravan, and tell in as few words as may be how the merchants and guards crowded about me, wondering much at my strange appearance and speech, but even more at what seemed stranger far to them, the white metal of my sword and armour. I found them to be a company of traders belonging to a nation who had even then made the name of Phœnician famous wherever armies marched or fleets sailed. They gave me meat and drink hospitably enough, and sold me a tunic and sandals and a good cloak of woollen stuff, dyed sapphire blue in Tyre, for the fair weight of my scraps of gold I learnt from them that the very name of Armen was forgotten, and the destruction of Babel and the old Nineveh I had marched against had become a vague tradition, and Nimrod a legend, and that the new Nineveh to which we were journeying was ruled over by a mighty king named Tiglath-Pileser, a style which in English speech means "the Tiger-Lord of Asshur." Then, most momentous of all my discoveries, I learnt that in the centuries of my long slumber the art of hardening forged iron into steel had been utterly forgotten, and that thus I was the only man alive who possessed a secret that might well be worth an empire to me.

The night we reached the city we camped in a wide space of open ground set apart for traders round a well outside the main eastern gate, and, while the Phœnicians were unpacking their wares, and making them ready to take into the markets at sunrise, I amused myself furbishing up my sword and helmet and mail, and guessing at what might befall me on the morrow in the city of the Tiger Lord.

Of course, we were not without visitors to the camp, and among them were a good sprinkling of soldiers and officers in Tiglath's army, gaily dressed, lightly armed, swaggering coxcombs they appeared to my stern, old-world eyes, but still, according to all reports, well-trained and disciplined, and justly held in terror by such enemies as they met. You may well believe that my stature—I stood a good head over the tallest of them—my fair, flowing locks, and my strange white mail and sword, did not long pass unnoticed among them, and very soon one of them came and greeted me with that fellowship that has ever sprung from the brotherhood of arms, and asked me my name and country in what sounded to me like a corrupted dialect of the old language we had spoken before, as the Phœnicians had told me, the tongues of men had been confounded when Babel fell. When I gave him back his greeting in my old-world speech, he stared at me and fell straightway to asking me questions which I answered as my invention served me, and told him as much of my history as I thought fit, and that not by any means all truth, for I had no fancy to be the staring-stock of the whole city by the next morning.

Then at last he up and asked me point blank if I would not give my big limbs and long sword to the service of the Great King, as he called him, and win glory and booty and perhaps a province, in the armies of Asshur, in which, he told me, he himself was a captain of ten thousand, and to this I answered, and told him that for the present I had no master and wanted none, that I was travelling to see the world and its cities, and meant to take my own way of doing it.

"But what if my lord the king hath need of thee, and commands thee to follow his banner?" he asked, with a sudden haughtiness that stirred my ready blood and made me feel like felling him to the earth for his insolence.

"Then," I said, slowly, laying my hand on his shoulder and gripping it so that he winced in spite of himself, "I should tell thy master that I had no need of him and that I would not come."

"An answer that would leave thee wriggling on a sharp stake outside the city gate before thou wert an hour older," he answered, with a smile that was pleasanter than his words, "and that is a sight that I should grieve greatly to see, for, wherever thou comest from, thou art the goodliest son of Anak I have ever seen, and I would sooner see this grip of thine on the throat of an enemy of Asshur than feel it on my own shoulder. So, as the Great King hath already heard of thee, be not surprised if thou shouldst receive a summons to the presence in the morning, and, I pray thee, speak him fairly, for no man ever did otherwise and lived."

"If he sends to me as one king should to another——"

"What? Art thou then a king in thine old land?" he broke in upon my thoughtless speech, recoiling a pace as he spoke.

"Ay, a king both in my own land and here," I answered, laughing my mistake away, "king of a good blade and a strong arm, and such kingdom as they can hew out for me. Can thy master give me more than that in exchange for my freedom?"

"Spoken like a soldier!" he said, "and to-morrow will prove thy words. But now the city gates are closing, and I have a guard to keep to-night. Thou wilt see me again soon after sunrise."

With that he took his leave, and true enough the sun had hardly got his disk above the plain before he was at the door of my tent with an escort of gaily-dressed warriors clad in polished bronze armour with garnishings of brass, and with cloaks of bright blue cloth hanging from their shoulders. When I came out he showed me a signet ring set with a blue stone, and told me that he bore the commands of the Great King to bid me to his presence in the throne-room. The message was courteous enough, seeing whom it came from, and it was courteously given, so without more ado, for I was already dressed and armed, I said:

"My lord the king is gracious to the stranger without his gates. Lead on, brother of the sword, I follow."

He gave an order to his men, who had been staring at me with all their eyes meanwhile, and they divided into two files, and between these I walked beside my acquaintance of overnight through the great gate guarded by monsters wondrously carved in stone, two with bodies of bulls, wings of eagles, and heads of men, and two with human forms and heads of eagles.

From the inside of the gate a wide, smooth paved street ran in a straight line to the western wall, many furlongs away, lined with stately buildings and shady gardens, and along this we marched till we came to the foot of a vast terraced pyramid, up which flight after flight of broad marble steps led to a huge gateway through an avenue of stone monsters, like those at the gate.

We ascended the steps and passed through the gate into a wide lofty gallery, whose flat roof was supported by rows of fluted pillars covered with plates of hammered gold and silver. Between these, slender palms and ferns, and trees heavy with fruit or fragrant with flower, seemed to grow out of the marble floor, and between them the crystal waters of a score of fountains fell with a soft musical splash into their silver basins. At the other end of this gallery was another square doorway hung with heavy silken curtains of royal scarlet, and guarded by two double files of splendidly-accoutred warriors of the king's own troop.

As we passed between them my guide held up the signet ring. Every head was bowed before it, the curtains swept asunder, and I found myself in a vast pillared hall, whose splendours no words of mine could describe. My escort were lying prostrate beside me, with their foreheads touching the shining pavement of many coloured marbles, and in front of me, a good twenty paces away, rose above a score of low white steps a great golden throne, on which sat, gazing at me with black piercing eyes, the splendid figure of him who was justly styled the Tiger-Lord of Asshur. On the right hand of the throne stood a shaven white-robed priest of Bel, and—my hand trembles even now with shame and rage as I write it—seated on a low-cushioned stool, leaning back against the other side of the throne, the king's left hand toying idly with her red-gold hair, was Ilma, white and sweet and beautiful as of yore, but——

A sudden, unreasoning frenzy seized me. What was it to me that the man on the throne was a king, the despot-lord of millions? White hot with fury at the hateful sight, I left my escort grovelling where they had fallen at the door and strode forward to the steps of the throne. I stopped five paces from them, and stood staring blindly at the pair. Then I heard a voice that sent a shiver through my burning veins say:

"I see that thou art truly a stranger, as I have been told. From what far country dost thou come that thou knowest not that it is death on the stake to look upon the face of a throned king of Asshur till thou art bidden? Still, I will give thine ignorance grace this once; prostrate thyself and live, for thou art too good food for Merodach for those limbs of thine to rot on a stake in the sun."

Heedless of the seeming madness of my words, I clapped my hands to the hilt of my sword, and, looking Tiglath full in the eyes, said:

"I am a stranger and the king's guest, for he has bidden me to his house. For the rest, the eyes that have looked in the face of the mighty Nimrod on the field of battle will scarce be dazzled by the countenance of the Tiger Lord on his throne."

"By the Gods, thou art as mad as thou art insolent!" said Tiglath, still in his cold cruel voice, though a deep red flush rose from his curled black beard to his angry eyes. "Knowest thou not that Nimrod went to the stars two thousand years ago, while thou hast not yet seen thirty? Must I tell thee that the guard yonder are but waiting a word from me to cover thy face and lead thee forth to death?"

At this my proud blood burnt hotter than ever, and reckless as I was of life or death with that vile sight before me, I answered:

"Thou hast many legions, but there is no man in them who could do that. Call thy slaves yonder and let them try."

He looked at me and laughed, while the priest and the girl gazed wide-eyed with wonder upon me. Then he made a sign with his right hand, his left still toying with the girl's hair, and I heard a shuffling and then a tramp of feet behind me. I turned and saw the guard advancing with spears at the ready, the captain with drawn sword beside them. Counting him there were eleven of them. For want of a better buckler I tore off my cloak and wrapped it round my left arm, and just as they came at me with levelled spears I pulled my sword out of my belt.

When the spear-heads were within a foot of my breast they halted, and the captain ordered me to yield myself to him in the name of the Great King. For all answer I gave a downward swinging stroke with my blade and sent it shearing through a good half-dozen of the shafts as though they had been reeds. The points clattered on the marble pavement as I dashed the hafts aside, and made a long sweeping slash across the row of faces in front of me.

The good steel bit its way through flesh and bone and helmet straps, and as I saw the blood spurt forth the old battle-madness came upon me. The long forgotten battle-cry of Armen rang from my throat, and I slashed out right and left, cut and thrust, sending a man down at every blow with cloven skull or breast and harness pierced through and through, till the two or three that were left turned and fled from me, yelling with fear under their master's eyes. All but one, I should have said, for the captain had crept behind me in the *mêlée*, and as I stopped in my pursuit stabbed at me in the back with his iron sword. The blow was a shrewd one, and for the moment knocked half the breath out of my body, but my mail held true and the blade turned and doubled up under the force of the stroke.

Just as I turned on him I heard the king cry in a voice that shook with wrath:

"A coward's blow, Zercal! I will flay thee alive for it if thou hast killed him. By Bel and Asshur, no, he is not even wounded! What marvel is this?"

Even while Tiglath was speaking I had turned upon the trembling wretch who stood staring at the crumpled blade in his hand, dropping my sword into my belt as I did so, for I would not soil it with such base blood as his. I took him by the throat and said in a loud voice so that the king might hear:

"Fool, and coward to boot! did I not tell thee last night that there is no weapon in Nineveh that can harm me? Thou hast thought to bring me to my death. Now I will take thee to thine."

So saying, I gripped him tighter by the throat with one hand and took him by the belt with the other, and lifted him up and carried him to his staring, wondering master. Then, swinging him high above my head, I cried:

"Take thy slave, O King, I do not fight with dogs."

And with that I dashed him down upon the steps with such a will that his skull split open, and his armour burst asunder, and his blood and brains splashed upon the feet of the Tiger Lord, and stained the white robe of the shrinking, shivering girl who cowered beside him.

CHAPTER V

A MYSTERY OF THE FLESH

When I flung Zercal down and dashed his brains out against the steps of the throne, I believed myself that my last hour had come, and that I should be overpowered, and carried out to torture and death. But I cared nothing for this, nothing for the new life whose first days had shown the bitter, shameful sight that was still before my eyes, and I waited in hot defiance for the signal that was never given. It was death to enter the royal presence without orders, so the guard stood wondering at the door, but did not dare to pass it, and the king, instead of calling them in, looked up at me with a grim smile on his swarthy face and said, quietly:

"Bravely done, friend! Thine heart is as stout and thine arm is as strong as thy tongue is bold. Truly thou are fit to stand before kings, even the Lord of Asshur. Now tell me thy name and country, and say what that wondrous sword and mail of thine are made of."

The surprise of such friendly and unexpected words, and the mildness with which they were spoken, brought me somewhat to my senses, and, stepping back a pace, I said, still haughtily, but without any passion in my voice:

"In the days that are forgotten I was called Terai of Armen, and I came from the stars to lead the hosts of Armen to victory against Nineveh, and, in the hour of our triumph, at the very moment when Nimrod went down under my spear, the earth shook and opened, and Nineveh, and the Tower of Bel were mingled in ruin. I rode away with"—and here, do what I would, I could not help lowering my eyes to that fair flesh-and-blood spectre at the king's feet—"with one who was dearest to me of all our gallant host, and the fire-wind met us and the sand-storm overwhelmed us—and four days ago I woke.

"That is my story, which I see the king smiles at for a madman's tale. So be it. I ask no man for belief; I would to the Gods I had none myself! As for my sword and mail, they were forged in Armen many ages ago by arts that the Gods gave when the world was young and have since taken back to themselves. What their nature is the king has seen for himself."

"A tale of marvel plainly told," said Tiglath, half doubting and half believing, when I had finished. "For the first part I say nothing. Amrac here, who is High Priest of Bel in Nineveh, shall speak with thee of that later. But touching the sword and mail. From what I hear thou art far from rich. I will give thee the revenues of a province and the command of ten thousand in my armies in exchange for them. What sayest thou?"

"That the king can slay me and so have them for nothing, but that all the wealth of Asshur will not buy them from me," I said, slowly, looking the Tiger Lord full in the eyes the while. "They are all I have, but they are priceless, for the Gods gave them and the Gods alone can take them away. But I have another coat of mail," I went on, struck by a sudden thought that my good genius must have put into my heart, "and I will give it to thee, and make thee, too, a sword of this metal, if thou wilt give me——"

"What?" cried Tiglath, his eagerness at last getting the better of his dignity. "I am loth to slay a man like thee, so name thy price and thou shalt have it, even to the half of my kingdom."

"The king's word is passed!" I said, "My price is the girl at thy feet, two good horses, and freedom to depart when my task is done."

"I would sooner thou hadst asked for my richest province," said Tiglath, looking down at the girl, who was now staring from him to me with wide frightened eyes, "for the maid is fair, and Hiram of Tyre sent her to me but yesterday as a keepsake to remind me of my sojourn in Arvad. Still, as thou sayest, the king's word is passed, and what is said must be done. Bring me the coat of mail and take her to thy tent. The rest shall be thine when the sword is made. Amrac shall guard her for thee, and thou shalt have her as she came to me. Without there, the guard! Clear me this carrion away, and cover the faces of the cowards who ran from a single sword."

With that he rose from the throne, spurning the dead body of Zercal with his foot, and turning away from the girl without so much as a last glance at her. Amrac, bowing low as his lord passed him, made a sign to her to rise and follow him. Then, turning to me, he said, speaking for the first time since I had entered the throne-room:

"My lord has shown us many wonders in a brief space! A guard shall lead you to your tent that you may fetch the mail for my lord the king, and then, if it pleases you to honour me, we will eat the mid-day meal together in my chamber in the temple, to which the guard will escort you. After what I have heard I am all anxiety to hear more."

"I will gladly tell thee all I know, for to him who has no friends on earth courtesy and kindliness are doubly sweet."

I spoke in the ancient tongue that had been mine before I learnt the speech of Armen, for I remembered what old Ardo had told me in Armen about the hermetic language of the priests, and I wished to see if the ministers of Bel had preserved it. The ruddy face of the well-fed high priest of Bel turned grey as the curls of his carefully-trained beard, and, coming down to where I stood, he crossed his hands and stood with bowed head before me, saying in the same tongue:

"There are none here worthy to be the friends of my lord. It is honour enough for Amrac to be his servant. He who speaks the speech of the Gods as though it were his native tongue hath no need of earthly friendship. I will await my lord as I have said. Now I must go and do the king's commands. My lord's escort attends him."

I bent my head in response, and, with a backward look at the girl whom Amrac was leading away by the hand, said to the leader of a guard of twenty men who were awaiting me with eyes full of wonder and awe:

"I am ready. Lead on."

You will have guessed by this time that it was Ilma's coat of mail of which I had spoken to the king. Loth as I was to part with the dear relic, yet it was all I had to give if I would rid me of the hateful thought of her whom the Fates had fashioned in the form and image of my lost Ilma living as the slave and plaything of one who would amuse himself with her beauty for a season and then throw her aside like a faded flower or a jewel he had wearied of.

With a heavy heart, and yet with eager hands, I cleaned the mail and furbished it up and saw to all its trappings. I had found her helm of steel and gold also in the sand, but that I kept, for I could not bear the thought of crowning any other head but hers with the war-diadem she had worn as our Lady of the Sword. It was near mid-day when I had finished, and all the time my guard had stood outside my tent door, motionless, in the burning sun, so that there might be no interruptions or prying upon me. When I had prepared the mail I wrapped it in a strip of fine Tyrian cloth, and, with my bodyguard attending me as before, I carried it back to the palace.

Amrac met me in the throne-room, and said:

"The king will speak with my lord in his own chamber. Let my lord follow his servant."

Then he dismissed my guard with a wave of his hand, and I followed him through chambers and galleries, each one more splendid than the rest, till we came out into a vast garden which lay between the palace of the king and the towering Temple of Bel, that overtopped all the other buildings of the city. He led me through cool shady groves, protected by the trees, and made beautiful by the flowers of many lands, to a small palace of purest marble, every stone and pillar of which had been brought over a hundred leagues from the quarries of Elburz.

Tiglath awaited us alone. Amrac fell to the floor, according to the servile custom of the land, but I remained as before, standing, only bowing my head as I approached the couch on which the king was reclining. He rose as I entered, and greeted me with a frank friendliness, that seemed rather to come from one soldier to another than from a mighty king to a friendless stranger.

"Thou art faithful to thy bargain, thou strangest of all the strangers I have ever seen," he said in a friendly voice, and eyeing me with a curiosity that he was unable to conceal. "I see thou hast brought the mail, therefore thou hast but to ask Amrac for the maid and she is thine."

"The mail is here," I said, unfolding the cloth. "And if my lord the king wills, I will be his armourer, and gird it on him."

"So be it if thou wilt," he said, "But stay—the mail is not yet proved."

I smiled at the suspicion in his voice and said:

"Let my lord draw his sword and he shall prove it, but I warn him the sword will be broken."

"It is the best sword in Asshur, saving thine," replied the king as he drew his weapon, "and if it bends or breaks against the mail I will add ten talents of gold to the price."

I bared my right arm and laid the mail over it; then stretching my arm out towards the king, I said:

"Now let the king strike or stab as he chooses, and if my skin is scratched let the king slay me with my own sword."

He raised his untempered iron blade and struck with all his force. I braced my muscles to receive the blow, and as it fell the blade bent round my arm and broke off short at the hilt. Then I took the mail away and showed him that there was not a scratch on the fair skin of my arm.

"By the eyes of Ishtar, thou hast spoken truly!" he said, in a voice almost of awe, looking first at my arm and then at his bent and broken blade. "Quick, now, friend Terai, gird me the mail on that I may know that no weapon can pierce me. Then hasten and make me the sword thou hast promised, and thou shalt leave Nineveh with a score of camels laden with my bounty, and if ever thou hast need of a friend on earth send this ring to Nineveh, and all the hosts of Asshur shall go forth to help thee."

He gave me the signet from his own finger, and when I had thanked him in my courtliest speech I put the coat of mail on him and showed him the fastenings of it. By good luck it fitted him well and closely, and after he had given Amrac directions for my entertainment, and such service as I should need in the forging of the sword, we left him admiring himself in a long mirror of polished metal, pleased with his new armour as a woman with a new robe.

Amrac led me through the garden, which led to the foot of a broad flight of steps leading up to the lower terrace of the Temple of Bel. From this we passed under a great square doorway, surmounted by the winged circle, which, as you know, is the emblem of that

Supreme Deity of whom all the Gods of Asshur were but partial manifestations. From this gateway a broad straight passage led us into the heart of the pyramid, where there was a square chamber, and from this another flight of steps brought us to the end of yet another passage leading outward to the side of the pyramid, and when we had traversed this Amrac clapped his hands.

The heavy curtains which covered another archway were drawn aside by invisible hands, and he, standing aside and bowing himself almost to the earth, said:

"Let my lord honour the dwelling of his servant, and may the presence of the Son of the Stars bring blessing on the home of the minister of Bel!"

The chamber opened with wide, shaded windows on to the third terrace of the temple, and the half of Nineveh, with the fields and gardens beyond the walls fading away into the grey of the boundless desert. Yet I gave the splendid landscape but a glance, for there, cowering in a corner on a couch of furs, was the living, breathing image of her who had died beside me in the sand two thousand years before. Then earth had not held a fairer or a prouder queen than her we had loved to call our Lady of the Sword. Now she was a shrinking, trembling slave whom I had bought from her master for the corselet of mail that she had worn in our last battle. Had ever maid and lover confronted each other in such strange guise as this before?

So perfect was the illusion that deluded my senses that, do what I could, I could not refrain from going to her and taking her by the hand any more than I could keep her name from bursting from my lips:

"Ilma!"

The hand that I had taken was yielded to me limp and passive, the great deep eyes which, in the awful moment that had ended our last life, had looked love into mine even through the falling haze of death now stared up at me with the frightened look that I might have seen in the eyes of a dog that fears his master's lash. Her lips moved, and some sound came from between them, but whether it was a word or an inarticulate cry or fear or pleading I know not. I let go her hand, stricken to the heart with the dull chill of a deadly fear, and as it fell limply on her lap I turned to Amrac and said, as carelessly as I could:

"Who is this girl? Can you tell me anything of her history before Hiram of Tyre sent her to the king?"

"No more, my lord," said the priest with the ghost of a smile on his moving lips, "than I can tell why my lord hath taken such an interest in her. Five moons ago the king journeyed to Arvad, in the land of the Phœnicians by the shore of the Sea of the Setting Sun, and Hiram told him, among many other things, of the strange countries beyond the bounds of day which his mariners had visited, and yesterday, even as my lord arrived at the eastern gate, there came an embassy to the western gate from Hiram with this girl, and those who brought her said that she came from a far-off land in the north, on the outermost bounds of the world, and that she was sent so that the king might see how fair a flower could grow under the for-ever darkened skies of the north.

"Her name, they told us, is Gudrun, a strange, outlandish name for so fair a maiden, and yet no more outlandish than her speech, which is the strangest that ever came from such pretty lips. And that is all that I, or anybody else in Nineveh, can tell my lord about her."

"And therefore it must suffice," I said, "till I can learn her speech and she shall tell me more herself. And now thou wouldst learn something from me, and I shall be well pleased to make some return for thy friendliness. Ask on."

"That I will do gladly," he replied. "But first let the slaves bring meat and wine that my lord may eat and comfort his soul."

He clapped his hands and the shaven slaves brought in the best that Nineveh had to offer. When the table was set I called to Gudrun by name and pointed to a seat beside me, but she only looked at me dumbly and shook her head, and then threw herself down on her couch and covered her face with her hands.

"She will be more gracious with my lord ere long," said Amrac, with a smile that I could have strangled him for, "but it is ever thus with these captive beauties at first. When they have tasted the rod once or twice——"

"Hold thy peace, fool!" I shouted, in a voice that sent him leaping to his feet, and set him trembling with terror beside his chair, "or I shall forget that thou art a priest, and the dogs shall find thy carcase at the foot of yonder terrace. But there, there, sit down, man! I meant nothing. I forgot thou dost not know what I cannot tell thee; but, by the Gods, if thou didst know it thou wouldst bite thy tongue out rather than blaspheme as thou hast done."

He sat down, still trembling at the fury of my first words, and wondering at the strangeness of my last, and when he had somewhat recovered his composure, he began and asked me many questions, which I answered as I saw fit, and after that he told me that the king had given me a set of apartments in the Great Palace for my use while I remained in Nineveh, with servants and slaves and a guard of honour to attend me; and that further, he, Amrac, had caused a spacious chamber in the temple to be fitted as a forge for the making of the king's sword, where no eyes but my own could see the progress of the work.

"That is well," I said, when he had finished. "And now, Amrac, tell me one thing truly on the faith of a high priest of Bel—why has the Tiger Lord dealt thus with me when he might have killed me and taken all that I have for nothing? And when thou hast told me that, tell me also whether he will really let me leave Nineveh in peace, and, if so why, instead of seeking to compel me to serve in his army?"

"First," said Amrac, putting his arms on the table, and laying the tips of his fingers together, "because my lord the king hath passed his word, and that hath never been broken. If thou hadst quailed before the guard thou wouldst now be dying by moments on a stake outside the city gates, but the Tiger Lord was pleased with thy valour and called thee friend, and friend thou wilt be in his eyes for ever.

"Second, though my lord the king is the mightiest warrior in Asshur, he is less mighty than thou, my lord, and he knows it. Need I tell thee why a king of Asshur should not press into his service one who claims descent from the stars, and might, perchance, turn his soldiers' hearts away from him?"

"Wisely spoken priest of Bel, and faithful servant of thy master!" I answered, smiling. "I am satisfied. Thy reasons are as good as thy wine, and that is saying much. Now, I pray thee, let thy servants show me to my dwelling, for I have more to do than thou thinkest of before the sun sets."

"I will myself attend my lord if he will permit," said Amrac, rising with me.

I beckoned to the girl to follow me, and so we left the temple and returned to the palace, where I found my household already arranged for my reception, and myself lodged like a king. My first care was to select certain of the rooms for Gudrun's use, and to appoint slaves to wait upon her, and these I told to watch her and serve her as though she were a queen, for their lives should answer for the excellence of their service.

As for me, I determined, until some light was shed upon the mystery that bewildered me, to treat her as though she were in very truth my own Ilma risen from the dead. Her body was there, of that I was assured, and perchance it might be that the Gods would permit me to some day recall her soul to its house of clay from its dwelling in the stars.

That afternoon I shut myself up alone and recalled everything that I had learned from the smiths and armourers of Armen, who, under the direction of Ardo the priest, had taught me the mystery of their art, and when I had satisfied myself that I had forgotten nothing, I went back to the temple and inspected my forge, giving orders for such additions to its furniture as I thought necessary.

The next day I visited all the armourers' shops and forges, in company with Amrac, and then I went alone to the camp of the Phœnicians and made inquiries about metals, until at last I hit upon a trader who had come from Damascus, and had with him a small store of soft pure iron, which he had brought with him more as a curiosity than as merchandise, for, as he told me, it had been but newly discovered in one of the gorges of the Zagros. I bought all he had for its weight in gold, and carried it off to my forge, which was hidden away deep down in the basement of the temple, and on the fourth day from then I went with the sword in my hand, and asked an audience of the king.

He received me in the same room to which I had brought him the coat of mail, and when I drew the shining blade from its sheath, and held it before him, his eyes sparkled, great and mighty monarch as he was, like those of a child when it receives a longed-for plaything. He took it and balanced it in his hand, and swung it to and fro in the air, and then I, seeing him look about as though in search of something to try it on, picked up a buckler of leather studded with bosses of bronze and brass, and, holding this with both hands outstretched before me, I said:

"Let my lord strike at this, and prove the blade. If it is notched or blunted I will make him another, and ask no reward for either."

He swung the sword above his head, and brought the edge down with all his strength on the rim of the sheath, and with one clean cut clove it to the centre. Then he pulled it out and looked closely at the edge.

"By the Gods, this is in truth a weapon for a king! There is not even a scratch upon its brightness. Wilt thou still leave Nineveh, Terai?"

"Yes, lord," I said. "To-morrow at sunrise I shall claim the freedom that the king has promised. I am not ungrateful, but my purpose is set, and more than that, is it not better that there should be one blade like that in the army of Asshur rather than two?"

For a moment a flush of anger burnt red in his swarthy cheeks, and then he laughed like the good honest soldier that he was beneath his kingly robe, and, stretching out his hand, said:

"Even so, by Merodach thou hast hit it, for the Lord of Asshur must play second to none amongst his own hosts! Thou shalt go to-morrow, and I will speed thee like a prince."

So it came about that as the highest terrace of the Temple of Bel was shining white in the first rays of the sun, I and Gudrun sat on our horses in the western gate of the city at the head of a string of a score of camels laden with Tiglath's presents, and a guard of two hundred horsemen that he had sent to convoy us across the desert as far as Karkhemish, whence we should journey to Arpad and Hamath, and thence by Kadesh and Damascus to Tyre.

CHAPTER VI

WITH GUDRUN TO SALEM

We crossed the Euphrates at Karkhemish, and travelled southward over the burning sands of the Syrian Desert, through the lovely valley in which, in the midst of her palm-groves and rose-gardens, flanked by green pastures and watered by winding streams that sprang from the bosom of the earth, lay Palmyra that Tadmor of the Wilderness, of which there now remain but the mighty and desolate fragments amidst which the wandering Arab pitches his tent of camel hair, and stables his beasts in the broken chambers where the great Solomon rested from the cares of State and mused on the vanity of a world that had given him everything but content.

From the City of Palms we went southward to Damascus, and there I heard from a Phœnician merchant who had come last from Gabbatha, news so strange and perplexing that it speedily gave definite shape to the vague plans I had formed on hearing what Amrac had told me about Gudrun. He came to my lodgings the night I reached the city to ask the favour of my lady's inspection of some curious gold work that he had bought from a trader of Bozra, who had brought it by sea from a far-off land in the East which you now call India.

I called Gudrun, with whom by this time I could speak comfortably in her native tongue, into the room where the trader had spread his wares, and bade her choose such of the trinkets as caught her fancy. But when the Phœnician looked upon her face, for in those days women only veiled themselves when travelling or walking the streets of towns, he started and turned pale, and then bowing very low before her he said:

"Thy servant knew not that the City of Sweet Waters was honoured by the presence of the Queen of the South and the friend of the Great Solomon, else I had come into the house of my lord with more fitting reverence. I pray you, let my lord and the Queen look with favour on their servant, and forgive the presumption of his ignorance."

He spoke in the Hittite speech, and so Gudrun did not understand him. As for me, full of wonder at his words, I said:

"I will forgive thee that, and more, if thou wilt hold thy tongue and sell thy wares quickly. After that I will speak with thee alone."

"The will of my lord is the law of his servant!" he said, raising himself and bowing down again, this time before me, and so we got to business, and when Gudrun had gone away with her trinkets to her own chamber, I said to the Phœnician:

"Now tell me what is this talk of thine about a Queen of the South and a friend of the Great Solomon? Solomon I have heard of, but the lady thou hast called Queen has, to my knowledge, never worn a crown, and comes not from the south, but from the north."

"The words of my lord are full of marvel, for they cannot be anything but the truth, yet, as the Thirteen Gods shall judge me, I tell my lord that in Jerusalem, whence I have come straight by way of Succoth and Gabbatha, I saw but twelve days ago the Queen of the South sitting before the throne of Solomon, listening to the wisdom that fell from his lips, and, unless the Gods have made the two fairest women on earth in the same image, then the Queen of the South is the lady of my lord and no other."

There could be but one explanation of the riddle. This Queen of the South whoever she was, must have a marvellous likeness to Gudrun and therefore to her whose soul I still looked for in vain in the clear depths of Gudrun's eyes. But unless the story of her origin was false, it was well-nigh impossible that there should be such resemblance between this Queen of the South and the girl that Tyrian pirates had torn from her home in the distant and unknown North.

From Gudrun herself I had learned nothing, either of her home or her past life, for to my first questions about them she replied with such sweetly earnest pleading that I would ask her no more till she should tell me of her own accord, that I had wondered and consented, for how could I refuse a prayer that came from lips that had once been Ilma's?

I determined to start for Jerusalem at sunrise the next day, and to take good care that, until I could set Gudrun face to face with the Queen, neither man nor woman should see her unveiled. Though she knew of no reason for such precaution, she did my bidding in this, as in all things else, save as to my question about her past, with a sweet and gracious submission that won me closer to her every day that we journeyed together,

At first she had had fits of smothered anger, and hidden, silent weeping, for there was a proud spirit in her that chafed and rebelled against the great wrong she had suffered at the hands of the Tyrian pirates. But when day after day went by and showed her that, though I had bought her as I might have bought a slave in the market-place at Nineveh, I had no intention of making of her either a slave or a plaything; the wild frightened look died out of her eyes, the frowns fled from her brows, and the smiles came back to her lips, though, even as we grew better acquainted, she still looked upon me with a puzzled wonder that was perhaps not altogether free from fear.

We travelled south-westward by Gabbatha to Sennabrin on the lake that is now called Gennesaret, and from there along the westward bank of the Jordan, through Succoth and Jericho, whence we crossed the hill country of Judæa westward to Jerusalem. We reached the top of the ridge of hills where the road from Bethany slopes down and winds round to the north of the city, just as the sun was nearing the tops of the western hills, and, though I have seen many cities in many lands and ages, I have beheld no fairer sight than Salem seated on her hills in the fulness of her pride, with those sunset rays shining upon the unspeakable splendours of the newly-finished Temple, resplendent with snowy marble, yellow gold, and ruddy bronze.

You may be well assured that we did not enter the streets, thronged as they were with idlers and sightseers unnoticed. At the head of fifty desert horsemen that I had hired when the Assyrians left me at Karkhemish, and my long string of camels, bearing the bounty of the Tiger Lord, I rode on a great black horse that I had found after much seeking and bought for his resemblance to Tigrol, blazing with gold and steel and jewels, with a white ostrich plume nodding from my helmet, and a cloak of Tyrian scarlet hanging from my shoulders on to my horse's back, and with my long golden locks streaming down on to it from under my helmet. Beside me the veiled Gudrun sat upon a milk-white Arabian mare, decked out in all the bravery of gold and jewels, fine linen, and bright dyed stuffs, that women loved three thousand years ago every whit as keenly as they loved them to-day.

The crowd made way for us with prompt respect, for rumour had already noised it abroad that I was a prince and warrior of Assyria, and had come with gifts and greetings from the Tiger-Lord of Asshur to the king who was mighty in wisdom even as he was in war, and as I rode along under the fire of their curious glances I thought how swiftly their curiosity would change to amazement if the veil were to drop for an instant from Gudrun's face, and then of what would happen when the time came for me to bid her remove it in the presence of Solomon and the mysterious Queen of the South.

All the inns and caravansaries in and about the city were full, but it was not long before the Phœnician, whom I had hired in Damascus to act as what you would now call my courier, brought a Jew to me, who, after many salutations and politenesses, begged the honour of placing his house and all that it contained at my disposal—not without price, you may be sure.

As my errand was important, and as, before all things, I was determined that Gudrun should be suitably housed, I let my Phœnician first bring the Jew to something like reason—and a rare battle of bargains it was, I can tell you—and then paid half the price down as earnest-money, and took possession of the house, and, after placing the most precious of my possessions in safety in it, I sent my men to make their camp across Kidron on Olivet, among the other retainers of the great and wealthy folk who were visiting the city.

My host had sent his family into his brother's house, and remained himself to act as major-domo, and, as he was full to the lips with all the news and gossip of the city, I had not been master of his house very long before he had told me all that was worth knowing of the great doings that were following the dedication of the Temple. Of course, I questioned him narrowly about the Queen of the South, and learnt that she was the Queen of the Sabæns, a people inhabiting the country called Araby the Blest, which was that portion of South Arabia bordering on the Red Sea, part of which is now known as the Province of Yemen.

He told me, too, that she was the most beautiful woman that had ever been seen in Salem or the world, and that even Nitetis, the daughter of Pharaoh and the wife of Solomon, fair as she was, looked plain as a country wench from the hills beside her. All Jerusalem—nay, he said, all Judæa—had gone mad about her beauty, and as he told me this, anxious and perplexed as I was at heart, I could not restrain a smile when I thought of how great a marvel would be wrought if what the Phœnician merchant had told me in Damascus proved true of Gudrun.

But that other mystery that had wrapped itself round Gudrun was now destined to be but short-lived, for I was scarcely afoot the next morning before she herself came to me and asked me to send away the Jew who was with me, so that she might speak to me alone. And when he had gone she dropped her veil, and to my amazement fell on her knees beside me, and taking hold of one of my hands with both hers, looked up at me with anxious pleading eyes, and said with lips that trembled with the stress of her emotion:

"My lord has been very good to me. He has saved me from a fate that I would have killed myself rather than endure. Though he bought me as he might have bought a chattel in the bazaar, he has used me with honour and kindness, and granted all the wishes of my heart that I have spoken. Let him now grant the prayer that I shall ask, and I will be his handmaid till death!"

I took her by the hands and raised her from her knees and said:

"I am no lord of thine, Gudrun, and if thou could see thyself with the eyes that I see thee thou wouldst understand that which I cannot make plain to thee. Nor is it fitting that thou shouldst kneel to me, thou whom the Gods have fashioned so that I should rather kneel to thee. Now call me by my name and ask thy request as though I were not only thy friend but thy brother, and if I can grant it thou shalt not ask it twice."

"I thank thee—Terai. How strange thy name sounds on my lips, and yet it seems as though this was not the first time they had spoken it! Where was it? In my dreams or in some other world than this of which our teachers tell us in my Sabæan home towards the sun?"

"What!" I said, catching her by the arms and drawing her close to me—and, by the Gods, I could have sworn that in that moment some glimmer of Ilma's soul was shining at me out of her frightened eyes. "What say you? Your Sabæan home! Are you then from the same country as this Queen of the South who is visiting Solomon here in Salem, and is the story the Tyrians told of you a lie?"

She dropped her eyelids and the light was quenched. I felt her shiver in my grasp and saw her bosom heave and fall, as though with a quick choking sob. Then she looked up at me again, and said:

"Yes, it was a lie—a lie that they were well paid to tell, paid by her who took my share of my father's throne from me, so that she might reign alone and be the fairest woman in the land. Take your hands from my arms, I pray you, for they hurt, and I will tell you in a few words the fate that has befallen me, and then you shall hear my prayer."

I released her, flushing red to my eyes for very shame for forgetting my own strength and her tenderness, and then I led her to a couch and seated her beside me and bade her say on. She was silent for a moment or two, and sat with downcast eyes, as though wondering how she could begin, and then she shot one swift, shy glance up at me and dropped her eyelids again, and told her tale.

"This Queen of the South is my twin sister, and co-heiress with me to the throne of Sabæa. Her name is Balkis and mine is not Gudrun, as those Tyrian barbarians called me, but Zillah, and the Gods have made us so alike that if Balkis stood here beside me now, attired as I am, not even you would be able to tell which was the queen and which was your purchased handmaid."

"Say that again," I said, smiling and laying my hand gently upon hers. "And you shall ask your prayer in vain. Now say on, for I am all impatience for the story."

She smiled and looked up at me again. this time for just one brief instant longer, and then she went on:

"My father, the king, left us his throne as a joint heritage, believing we should live and reign together in all love and harmony; but no sooner did our rule begin than Eblis entered into Balkis' soul, and told her that but for me she would be, as men had said, the fairest woman in the world and sole queen of Sabæa. And so, fearing perhaps the vengeance of the Gods if she killed me with her own hands, she gave me a potion one night, and when I woke I was sailing far out at sea in a Tyrian galley.

"The captain told me, in answer to my prayers and tears, that the queen, as he called her, had determined to rule alone, and so had given him a talent of silver to take me out to sea and tie me in a sack and drown me. But he was too good a Phœnician for that. He had got Balkis' talent of silver and me too, and he said that if he knew anything of the worth of woman's beauty in the market of Tyre, it should become a talent of gold before he had done with me.

"So I was carried up the Red Sea and through the canal of Rameses into the Great Sea, and so brought to Tyre, where they changed my name to the barbarous one you learnt to call me by, and told that lying story which Amrac the priest repeated to you. But at Tyre the Gods befriended me, for, before there was time to expose me in the slave market, a report of me was carried to Hiram the king, and he commanded me to be brought before him, and bought me from my captors for the talent of gold that they asked.

"When I saw the fate that was before me I held my peace for very shame, and allowed the story about me to pass as true. Hiram kept me in his palace so that I could rest from the weariness and suffering of my voyage until a caravan was started for Nineveh. Then, as you know, he sent me as a present to the King of Assyria. I had but just been brought before him that morning when you slew the guard in the throne-room, and he was pleased with me, and had bidden me sit at his feet as you found me. And then you came, and the rest there is no need to tell you."

"That is a strange story, Zillah, although so simply told. So—you are a queen in your own right. Did I not tell you that I was no lord of yours, and only fit to kneel before you? Now let my lady make her request that her servant may grant it."

She caught the tone of my banter, and looked up laughingly at me, and, as there was blood and not water in my veins, I verily believe that the next moment I should have forgotten myself, and taken her in my arms and told her all the marvellous story of Ilma and my other life if she had not slipped gently and swiftly to her knees, and, resting her clasped hands upon mine, looked up with such sweet winsomeness that it sent me in an instant half crazy with love and longing for her, and said:

"Thou art the master of my life and —and the lord of my soul, and my prayer is that thou shalt take me away from this place, it matters not where, for I would rather serve thee in a tent of goats' hair in the wilderness than go back, if that were possible, to reign with Balkis in Sabæa. Nor would I for all the wealth of Solomon have her know that I am here in Salem, for she would surely find means to slay me, and I would not die, for the life which my lord gave back to me has become very dear to me. Balkis is welcome to our throne and my father's realm, since I learned that the Gods had better gifts in store than rule and riches. Speak now, my lord, and tell me that thy handmaid has not made her prayer in vain."

Zillah had risen, and was standing before me with downbent head and downcast eyes, and milk-white hands crossed over the gently heaving bosom in which the holy flame of love had been burning unseen for many a day—as dear a vision of sweet maidenhood as ever eyes of love and longing looked upon.

Alas! Had I but loved as she did—nay, had I but even known how priceless was the treasure that lay there within my grasp, I might have learned the long lesson in a flash, and this might never have been written; but to me in those days the love of woman was but as a precious jewel to adorn the diadem of empire. I started to my feet, my blood aglow and my eyes aflame, and caught her unresisting to my breast. Then, as she looked up in startled amaze, I stooped and kissed her lips and said:

"Nay, by the shining Sword of Armen, and for thine own sweet sake, thy prayers shall go ungranted! Instead, I will give thee justice and thy rights, and this very day this proud sister of thine shall confess thy rights before the judgment-seat of Solomon, or, there shall be but one queen in Sabæa, and she shall rule with me! What! dost thou not remember, sweet, how two thousand years ago we rode side by side to victory through the broken ranks of Asshur, in the days of the mighty Nimrod? Hast thou not seen him go down under my spear, and dost thou doubt that I can take thy throne back, and guard it and thee against all the tyrants of the earth?"

She slipped out of my grasp and sprang back a pace, and stood with her hands pressed to her temples, and staring at me with wild, frightened eyes and parted lips. For a moment she gasped for breath, and then cried:

"My lord—Terai—what are these strange and fearful words that thou hast spoken? Two thousand years ago! What art thou, and who am I? Yes; surely I remember—and yet, no! it can be but a dream, for such things could not be. I never saw thee before that day in Tiglath's throne-room. Armen? Nimrod? Nay, the riddle is too hard for me, and I want no throne save a seat at thy feet. Yet what am I but my lord's bondmaid? Let it be to me even as seems good in his eyes."

And so saying, she crept back dazed and frightened into my arms, and stood there trembling, her new-awakened heart fluttering against my mail.

At that moment I heard a hand-clap outside the curtain that covered the doorway of the room in which we were standing. As I opened my arms with a curse on the untimeliness of the visit, Zillah sprang away from me and replaced her veil. Then I called out "Enter!" and in came Ben-Hamah, my landlord, who with many salaams and apologies for disturbing my lordship's peace, told me that one of the royal heralds was waiting in the house-court, wishing to speak with me.

I bade Ben-Hamad bring him in, and, to be brief about a small matter, the herald brought a message from the king, who plainly thought that I had come as an envoy from the Tiger Lord, bidding me to an audience in the Judgment Hall of the House of the Forest of Lebanon. I soon undeceived him as to my character, but, determined not to lose the opportunity, I sent him away with a present, for in those days you got nothing for nothing, just as you do in these, and bade him ask an audience for me, since I had a matter of deep perplexity on which I sought the light of Solomon's wisdom.

In little over an hour he was back with another message which bade me most courteously to the presence of the king. Meanwhile I had summoned a guard of twenty of my men, all well armed and mounted, and my horse and Zillah's stood ready for us in the court. Zillah, too, at my request, had attired herself in the richest raiment and the most costly gold and jewels that my fond lavishness had supplied her with, and, as we rode on our way to the palace, there were no two more splendid figures to be seen that morning in the streets of Salem.

The king's house stood outside the city, on a ridge to the westward, over against Mount Zion, on which stood the smaller palace of his father David. A broad, straight sloping road led out of the valley to the porch, and, just as we reached the bottom of the slope, we heard a loud ringing of silver trumpets, and the cry ran along the crowd that lined the way:

"The king, the king; way there for the king!"

I looked back and saw a troop of the king's guards coming at a canter up the road that led from the country palace of Edmah. I shouted to my escort, and they ranged themselves at the bend of the road, ten on either side of Zillah and me, and presently the royal troop swept by. First came two hundred horse, dressed and armed in Tyrian purple and bronze and gold, with the thickly-sprinkled gold dust on their long flowing hair glistening in the sunlight.

Then came two small troops of outriders, and then two chariots abreast. The one nearest to me was of carved and polished cedar, floored with gold and covered with a canopy of purple upheld on pillars of silver; and in this, drawn by three milk-white horses of purest Arabian breed, sat Solomon, splendidly robed and crowned with a gold tiara, on the front of which rose three short golden horns. In the chariot beside him, a car of ivory adorned with gold and also canopied with purple, and drawn by three bright bays, reclined on a seat of ivory, cushioned with purple, the very image and counterpart of her who sat, veiled and trembling, on her horse beside me.

As Solomon and the Queen of the South passed I drew my great sword and saluted with it, as we were wont to do in Armen. The sun flashed on the white gleaming blade till it looked like a bar of light in my hand, and I saw the king and queen start as the unwonted flash caught their eyes. They both looked up and I saw the queen shade her eyes and look curiously at me and the veiled woman beside me, and in a moment more the procession had swept on up the hill.

We followed at a slower pace, and dismounted at the porch to wait our turn. My bribe had served its purpose, for the heralds called out my name first, and so, taking Zillah's cold and trembling hand in mine, I led her through the porch and into the audience hall. At the end of the hall, surrounded by his brilliant court and envoys from half the kingdoms of the world, sat Solomon on his famous throne of ivory and gold, flanked by two great brazen lions. Six steps of cedar overlaid with silver led up to it, and at the end of each stood two other brazen lions. In a chair of ivory, placed beside the throne sat, radiant with beauty and bewildering in her perfect likeness to Zillah, that Queen of the South who, for all the world has known until now, flitted across the stage of history like a nameless shadow in the midst of the glory of Solomon.

We were led to the foot of the throne, and made our salutations, and as I raised my head again I looked up at Solomon and saw before me a man with a goodly length of limb, though of a somewhat slender build, reclining on the throne with an air of listlessness which was almost languor, and according but ill with the earliness of the hour.

A languid flash of curiosity gleamed transiently from his eyes as he looked down upon us—upon me, clad in my strange white mail, and with my steel and gold helmet towering a good span above that of the tallest of his guards, and upon Zillah, the only veiled woman in the hall, standing beside me shining with gold and jewels, and yet with her greatest adornment concealed, for by my advice she had hidden her glorious wealth of red-gold hair for the nonce under her linen coif.

As for the queen, she sat upright on her throne, her hands clasping the ivory arms, in just the same attitude that I had seen Ilma in on that ever memorable day in the hall of the citadel of Armen, staring at me with fixed, wide-open eyes from under the broad white brow that was now knitted in a frown, as though the wondrous riddle of our presence there was afflicting her, too, with its unearthly mystery. But soon the king spoke in a voice that was the sweetest I had heard till then, save from a woman's lips, and he said, speaking in Assyrian:

"The stranger from the court of the Great King is welcome, for Benaiah has told me that thou wishest to see my face and hear my judgment upon a matter that has proved too deep for thy understanding. And so, too, is thy companion welcome, She is seemingly from a far country, of which I have not heard, and in which it is doubtless the custom for ladies to appear veiled before kings. Say on, now, and if my poor wisdom, of which well-meaning courtiers have given an over-good report, can serve thee, it is at thy service."

"O king, live for ever!" I said, saluting him again, and using the form of greeting that was then common in such a case, and which, though he knew it not, had such bitter meaning from my lips. "The matter concerning which I would hear the voice of thy wisdom stands thus:

"Ishtar of Arbela, Goddess of Love and Beauty, sent her image to the earth in mortal form, and the woman that she made was beautiful beyond all the daughters of men. Now seeing her, Eblis, the Father of Evil, being jealous of the handicraft of the Goddess, and fearful lest the hearts of men should be turned away from him by the sight of such transcendent beauty and perfect purity, made another woman so like the daughter of Ishtar, that the moon and her own reflection in a calm lake at midnight are not more alike than these two women.

"And into this fair body of hers he caused a portion of his own vile essence to enter; so that the good in the one should be annulled by the evil in the other, and men should still say that evil may dwell in as fair a shape as goodness. Now I would ask my lord the king how he who should find himself, by any strange chance, in the presence of these two women should decide which of them was the evil, and which the good?"

There was a brief pause when I finished, and in it I looked at the queen and saw her sitting, still rigid and upright, and staring at Zillah with eyes so burning bright, that it seemed as though she would wither away the veil that hid my companion's face. Then the king, smiling at me and waving towards Zillah the hand on which shone the mystic ring which, as men said, revealed all secrets to him, said in his smooth and gentle voice:

"There never was a riddle yet, nor ever will be, of which woman is not in some measure either the mystery or the answer. In the form of a parable thou hast told me the story of her who stands beside thee, and of some other, but thou hast not told me all, nor will I essay to answer thy question till I know more. Say on, and tell me who and what these two women were in mortal form."

"Those who have told me of the king's wisdom have spoken truly. Now I will say more if the king's ears are open," I said, speaking this time in the hermetic speech which I had first spoken on earth.

Solomon's eyelids lifted sharply, and a slight flush rose upon his cheeks as he replied in the same tongue.

"The ears of the king and priest of Salem and of the Lord's anointed must ever be open to words spoken in the holy speech! Once more say on, for now I know thou hast something of importance to impart."

Then, in as few words as I could, I told him the story of Zillah and Balkis, and also my own story so far as it affected Zillah. When I had finished he said, without looking at either of them;

"Thou wouldst have been wiser to have taken thy Zillah's advice and fled with her into the wilderness. But thy heart is hot and thy blood is young, and thou hast not yet learned the vanity of earthly pomp and riches. Thou wilt brave dangers to share with her the half-rule of a little tract of earth when she has given thee an empire wider than the whole world. So thou hast chosen, and no words of mine will turn thee aside.

"Now the Queen of the South, who sits beside me, does not understand the Assyrian speech, and so the meaning of thy parable has not reached her. Therefore I will tell thy story again in the Hebrew tongue, that she and all may understand, for her speech and ours are much akin. "But I will say only that her sister-queen was stolen and carried away by pirates of the Arabian shore and sold as a slave in Tyre, as thou hast said. Then let Zillah the Queen unveil—and then there will be no need for me to tell thee whether or not thy parable is true, and what the answer to thy question is."

So he told the story as he had said, and as he told it I watched Balkis' face, and, though she strove bravely and well to hide the storm of passion and anger that was raging within her, I saw, with how much horror you may well guess, rage and hate and disappointed evil gleaming out of eyes which would have been Ilma's had they not been Zillah's, too, and the tinge of shame rising to the fair brow that seemed made to be the very throne of purity itself.

At length the king finished, and, at a word from me, Zillah raised her trembling hands to her head, and the next moment veil and coif fell to the ground, and she stood revealed in all her loveliness, facing the only other woman on earth who was as beautiful as she was.

"By the glory of the Lord, this is such a marvel as no man's eyes have ever looked upon before!" cried Solomon, half rising from his throne, and for the moment utterly startled out of the languor of his world-weariness.

But he and all of us were fated to see in the next instant a marvel far greater even than this, for, as Balkis rose to her feet and stood with her hands behind her on the arms of the throne, swaying ever so slightly to and fro, and striving to make her stiff, pale lips utter some words that should not reveal her hatred and her sin, Zillah left my side, and, ascending three of the throne-steps, dropped on her knees before the woman who had sent her to death and sold her to slavery, and, stretching out her hands towards her, said in her own tongue:

"Balkis, wilt thou forget as I have forgiven and let there be peace between us?"

I had never seen an injury forgiven before, and I doubt much if any one in that hall had seen it either, for in those days the only justice was revenge. I, blind as I was, saw only that Zillah had asked for peace for my sake, but the Wise Man saw more than any of us, for as Balkis stooped to raise her sister up, and kissed her on the brow—as she did with those sweet, false lips of hers—Solomon turned to me with long-unwonted tears glistening in those world-weary eyes of his, and said in a voice that trembled with an infinite pathos:

"Friend! thou hast shown me, who never thought to look with eyes of interest again on any earthly thing, two miracles to-day, and, of the two, this, the second, is the greater, for in after days the glory of the Lord shall reveal itself in such a guise as this, and in it thou hast, as I have told thee, the answer to thy question."

CHAPTER VII

LOVE DEADLIER THAN HATE

When Solomon had said this to me he summoned two of the heralds and bade them conduct us—I and the two living likenesses of my lost and, as I believed, re-found Ilma—out of the Judgment Hall and into the private apartments of the palace, for he saw that our drama had been played up to a point past which it was no longer desirable that the public eye should watch its course So we passed from the foot of the throne through the parted throng of wondering and admiring guards and courtiers, through courts and corridors, until at length we were ushered into one of the king's own rooms, and there left to ourselves.

Balkis had not spoken a word on the way, but no sooner had the attendants left us to ourselves than she burst into a flood of passionate tears, and, throwing herself at Zillah's feet, began to implore her forgiveness for her unnatural crime, which she swore again and again she had committed under the direct inspiration and possession of Eblis himself.

But she had not gone far with her entreaties and protestations before Zillah, her own dear eyes streaming with far purer tears, raised her from the ground and kissed her, vowing that she had never brought herself to believe that she could have done so vile a thing in her right senses, and that she had ever been certain that the blame of it was not rightly hers, but due only to the evil arts of Eblis.

When she brought her to me, their two faces still wet with tears, and bade me take her by the hand and join my forgiveness to her own, I stared for a moment dumbly from the one to the other, for the more closely I beheld them the more wondrously and bewilderingly alike they were, and when she saw how wonder-stricken I was, Zillah laughed through her tears, and, taking hold of my hand and putting Balkis' into it, said:

"Truly my lord must look with favour on us both, since it is plain that he cannot tell which of us is Balkis and which is Zillah, and even as I have forgiven so will he forgive, too."

"Nay, Zillah," I said, "for thy forgiveness leaves me nothing to forgive. Who am I that I should bear malice for the wrong that all these loving tears have washed away? Even as thine enemies would have been mine, so thy sister, now that thou hast found her again, shall be mine also."

"And from what my lord has said," chimed in Balkis, smiling, too, now, and with Zillah's own smile so exactly counterfeited that I was straightway lost again in a maze of wonder, "it would seem that we shall have ere long, not two queens, but a king in Sabæa, and so will the Gods punish me justly for my fault, for thou knowest, Zillah, that, according to the testament of the king, our father, our joint throne must be yielded to her who first finds a lord worthy to rule in his place. Now thou hast found such a lord, and the Gods have led thee to him through the sin that I committed against thee. Thus I am justly punished, and yet too lightly, for my repentance and thy forgiveness have filled my heart with such joy and content, that in your happiness I, too, shall be happy beyond my best deserts."

Thus saying, Balkis took Zillah by the hand, and in her turn drew her towards me, and, laying her right hand in mine, said yet more sweetly than before:

"My words need no better confirmation than that tell-tale face of thine, Zillah. Now let me make the last atonement for my fault that I can, and let this be done in witness of your betrothal and my surrender of that which according to our father's will is now no longer mine."

"Is this, in very truth, the fact?" I said, putting my arm round Zillah, and drawing her close to me. "And thou hast told me nothing of it!"

"Yes, it is true," she murmured, almost in a whisper. "But how could my lips have told my lord when no words of love had yet passed between us? Nay, even now I do not know——"

"Nay, Zillah," I laughed. "Thou shalt not stain those pretty lips of thine with a lie, however innocent. They were made for better use than that."

And, so saying, I stopped them with a kiss, and when I raised my head again Balkis had vanished.

We stayed a full week after that as the guests of Solomon in his palace, and our betrothal was celebrated with feasting and revelry that kept all Salem busy with wonder at our strange story, and rejoicing at the happy issue of Zillah's misfortunes, and on the seventh day Solomon bade us a stately farewell in the porch of the House of the Forest of Lebanon, and we set out in the midst of a long and splendid cavalcade over the hill-road that led from Salem to the seaport of Joppa, where the Queen's fleet was lying waiting to receive us on board.

From the hills above Joppa I first beheld the sea, that glorious field of green and azure, that wondrous world of changing calm and storm, which in many an after year was destined to be my home and my battlefield, and, as my eyes opened wide to receive the splendours of the sight, and my breast swelled with a deep draught of the strong salt air, a new rapture filled my soul—prelude to other and wilder raptures to come—and I shouted aloud in my ecstacy like a very boy.

"It is beautiful," said Zillah, who was riding beside me, "but its blue is dull compared with that of the bright waters which wash the green shores and golden sands of Sabæa. Think not that thou hast seen the true beauties of earth or ocean till thine eyes have feasted on the loveliness of Araby the Blest."

"To me it will be Araby the Twice-Blest, sweet Zillah!" I replied, looking from the blue of the sea into the deeper brighter azure of her eyes, "and all its loveliness, however fair it be, will be but a reflection of thine own."

We embarked at Joppa, and favouring breezes filled the many-coloured sails of our stately galleys, and sent us merrily on our way over the smooth bright waters till we reached Pelusium, the eastern outpost of Egypt, that wonderland of yore which even then was hoary with an untold age, and, with the ensign of Solomon floating from our masts in token of peace and friendship, passed the forts of the great Rameses, and entered the Pelusiac arm of the Nile.

Thence we coasted down the wild and silent shore of the wilderness of Sinai, and so on ever southward, till at length we came to the smiling land of palms and orange groves, of verdant valleys and stately mountains, where, as I so fondly and so vainly dreamt, I was to find at once a kingdom, a crown, and a queen.

I could write pages, did the length of the task still before me permit, striving —I doubt not vainly—to describe the loyal warmth of our welcome in Sabæa, a welcome made doubly warm by the return of the twin-queen, who had so long been mourned as lost; the long public revels and the thousandfold sweeter private converse that led up to the thrice-blessed, thrice-accursed day on which the priests of the stars invoked the blessing of the Gods on my wedding with the dear re-incarnation of my long-lost Ilma, the sweet and radiant queen I had bought in far-off Nineveh for a sword and shirt of mail.

The last feast was ended, the music and song of the last revel had died down into silence. Balkis had taken my blushing Zillah away to her chamber to prepare her for the last rite that was to crown her life and mine with that supernal bliss which is the one remnant of Paradise that the Gods left to man when they forsook the earth. The white-robed priests had conducted me to the curtained portal of my bridal room, and the last notes of their epithalamium were dying away down the long corridor, and I entered with beating heart and silenced tread—and here, even as the curtains fell together behind me, so must the veil of silence fall between you and me for a space.

The flame in the golden lamp had burned low, and the sunbeams were stealing in through the curtained lattices of the room when I opened my still half-dreaming eyes and looked about me, and, wondering whether I was not still dreaming some sweet dream of Paradise, I sought to make sure by waking Zillah with a kiss.

"Thou pretty fool! Didst thou then think that I had really yielded my throne and thy stately lord to thee? Nay—what! already awake, my lord? Ah, what have I been saying—surely I have been afflicted with some evil dream that Eblis hath sent to mar my happiness. Kiss me again, my lord, my love Terai, that I may be sure it was but a dream."

She stretched out her white arms towards me as she spoke, but I, with the cold grip of a deadly, nameless horror clutching at my heart and pressing the life-blood out of it, leapt to my feet and shrank away from her as though she had been some loathsome reptile that had stolen in the darkness into my bridal couch.

"Zillah," I cried, half choked by a sob that rose from my breast and almost strangled me: "Zillah, where is she? Thou art not Zillah, for that pure soul of hers was never stained by such a foul vision as that. If thou art in truth Zillah, then rise and come with me to Balkis and set my soul at rest. If not, if thou refusest, then, by the sweet love that thou hast outraged and defiled, I will slay thee where thou liest."

"Then slay!" she cried, with a wild mocking laugh, whose weird echo I can still hear ringing across the gulf of centuries. "Slay, for I am not Zillah but Balkis! Zillah lies dead since yesternight in my bed, and I have sold my body and my soul for love of thee, my lord, and one taste of the bliss without which life would have been worthless to me. Now death is welcome—get thy sword and slay me, for I have lived!"

The naked blade was already in my hand ere the last of those withering words had left her false, smiling lips. She bared her white bosom to the impending stroke, still smiling at me and looking with unflinching eyes upon the approaching steel—but the Gods in their mercy spared me the deed, for, even as I drew back my hand for the justly vengeful stroke, my arm stiffened and my eyes glazed over with a mist through which I saw—not hers, but the lovely face and radiant form of my own Ilma, fading away ever fainter and farther into an infinite distance, and then the dark curtain of oblivion fell over the memory of my bliss and my woe, and, like a man who stumbles blindly through swiftly-gathering shadows, I reeled from the past of the things that had been into the future of the things that were to be.

CHAPTER VIII

CLEOPATRA

By The Nine Gods he lives—or soon will live! Truly, Lady, the great God Amen-Ra hath worked a miracle by the hand of his servant for thy pleasure, and, perchance, also for the better working out of thy destiny—thou brightest Hope of Egypt!"

"Had Egypt bred such men as this, my sire Auletes would not have gone, an exile and a beggar, to crave protection from the haughty Senate and pledge his kingdom for a loan, and I—I, Cleopatra, lawful Queen of Egypt, and daughter of the royal line of great Alexander, should wear the Serpent Crown worthily and alone and with ten thousand such as he I would make a wall round Egypt and my throne which not even the phalanx of Rome could break, though the great Caius himself were to lead it. "By Apis, what a man he is! I wonder what race of giants he was bred from. There are no men in the world like this now. Hast thou ever seen a man, Amemphis, who would not go down, though mailed in triple brass, under a stroke from that right arm of his, wielding that terrible sword which was brought from Arabia with his mummy?"

"Nay, Lady, I do not think that such a man lives. The Gods forfend that he should strike at me or any dear to me, for the man he struck would find himself in the Halls of Osiris in the next instant. But, with thy pardon, Lady, thou art mistaken in calling his body a mummy. Most strangely and miraculously was it preserved in the sepulchre where we found it, but it is a perfect body, and hath never passed through the hands of the embalmers.

"See again how, as I chafe it, the smooth, fair skin warms with the returning glow of life. That bath of warm oil and essences hath worked wonders—wonders that we shall not dare to speak of if the work of this night be crowned by the Gods with success, as I believe it will be, But now, Lady—if thy servant may advise thee—will it not be better that thou shouldst retire before I make the final trial? Thy fortitude hath been sorely tried already, and what is to come may be more dreadful yet.

"Thou mayest see the struggle of a soul returning to its earthly tenement, perchance only to rend it asunder in some awful convulsion, and then depart again. Thou mayest have to look upon the face of a man awakening from the death-sleep of uncounted years, and hear from his startled lips some hint of that awful secret which belongs alone to those who have passed through the shadows. It may be that——"

"Nay, nay, good Amemphis, enough, enough! I see thou knowest but little of Cleopatra yet. Go on with thy work, I pray thee, lest what thou hast gained shall be lost, and the flame that thou hast fanned into life be quenched in death again. Now see how I will help thee! His lips are soft and growing warm. Thus, then, I will lend them more warmth from mine, and the first breath he draws shall be a portion of my own. See, with a kiss I will recall his errant soul!"

"Ah! by Bel, where am I? Balkis! Murderess, have I not slain thee yet? Where is my sword? Have I been sleeping that thou hast stole it as thou hast stolen Zillah's sweet life away from her and me? Quick, take me to her and show me that she lives, or, by the eyes of Ishtar, I will strangle thee, were that milk-white neck of thine thrice as fair and soft as it is!"

The answer came in a hoarse cry of terror from the lips of a trembling old man cowering against the wall of a small stone-built chamber, and in a short, sharp shriek from a woman I had caught by the shoulders and lifted from her feet in the same moment that I had sprung, full of life and peerless strength once more, from the low pallet bed on which I had been lying.

The woman, or the girl, I should more justly say, for her loveliness was rather that of the girl than the woman, was Balkis—or was it Zillah, or Ilma, or what weird trick had the vengeful Fates played anew upon me? No. Ilma's dust still drifted about with the desert sands beyond Nineveh, and Zillah lay dead in the palace of Sabæa, for had not those mocking lips of Balkis told me so but a moment before?

A moment? By the Gods, where was I? In what new age or clime? This was not my bridal chamber in Sabæa. It was more like a tomb, and yet that perfect face, those eyes of living sapphire, those glorious tresses of long rippling hair, gleaming dusky golden in the light of the lamp—whose could they be but hers? Had the Gods fashioned another woman in her image to lure me on to fancied happiness and then dash down the cup that held the golden wine of bliss just as my lips kissed it? She called herself Cleopatra—for what

I have written here I heard as in a dream, before the blood began to move in my veins and the strength came back to my limbs.

"Who is Cleopatra?"

I spoke the words, spoke aloud, and as I uttered them the terror faded out of the eyes of the girl I held aloft, the blood came back to her cheeks and her lips, and she smiled down on me, and said in the voice that I had last heard on that awful morning in Sabæa:

"Set me down, friend, for thine is no woman's grip, and thou art bruising my flesh. Set me down, I pray thee, and thou shalt soon learn who Cleopatra is. Come, Amemphis, and soothe this fierce giant whom thou hast called back from the Halls of Amenti. What! Art thou afraid of thine own handiwork? Nay, nay, there is nothing to fear save this terrible strength of his, for he is no wraith or spectre, but very human flesh and blood and muscle, as these poor bruised arms of mine can testify."

He came towards me, bowing low, and still trembling somewhat with the remnants of his first fear, and said:

"I scarce know whether I should address thee as man or more than man, for thou comest in godlike shape out of the shadows with the speech of the Ancient Gods in thy mouth—that speech which is known only to those initiated into the holy mysteries of our Mother Isis—and yet ——"

"And yet, good friend, who ever thou art," I said, breaking in upon his speech somewhat hastily—for not only was I both hungry and thirsty, but very nearly naked to boot, and though in the earlier days of the world we had little if any of the false shame, which is now the fashion, for that which was made in the glorious image of the eternal Gods, yet, if only for the sake of company, I wished to be better clad than I was—"I am in very deed but just a man as thou art, so there is little need to stand on ceremony with me. If thou hast food and wine and a garment at hand, believe me I shall prize them more just now than many courtly speeches, and then when I have had a bite of bread and a draught of wine we can talk if thou wilt, for I have much to ask of thee."

"And we have still more to ask of thee, thou strangest of all comers into the world of living men," chimed in she who had called herself Cleopatra, as the old man left the chamber to return very shortly with a plate of bread and fruit and a silver flagon of good red wine, to which I did full and speedy justice, while he covered me with a long linen cloak as I ate and drank and looked with infinite wonder into those fatal eyes which were to lure Antony from the throne of the world, and, in the hour of her own fall, look Destiny unshrinking in the face.

"And now," I said, when I had eaten a little and drunk more, "where am I, and how goes the world since this maiden, who now calls herself Cleopatra, was Balkis, twin Queen of Sabæa with my sweet Zillah, whom she slew for love of me, and since the life ebbed out of me just as I was about to slay her for her sin? Is Solomon still king in Salem, and did the Tiger-Lord of Asshur come back with the wreath of victory on that sword I gave him as part of Zillah's price? Is Nineveh still mistress of the world, or has upstart Babylon disputed the place of empire with her?"

The more I spoke the more the wonder grew in their wide-opened eyes. When I had ended my questions Cleopatra nodded to the priest, and said almost in a whisper, so awe-stricken was she:

"Tell him, Amemphis, thou art better versed in these things than I am. Gods, what a marvel is this that we have chanced upon!"

"Stranger—nay, tenfold more than stranger as thou art, since thou comest, not only from other lands, but from far distant ages as well," began the priest in such a voice as he might have used in addressing his Gods, whoever they were, "it is plain that the web which the Hathors weave on the loom of time hath grown much, and that many generations of men have been called to the Halls of Osiris since thou didst fall into that mysterious sleep out of which, for some dark purpose known only to the Gods, I, by my simple arts, have called thee.

"Nineveh is but a name and a heap of ruins, lost in the desert sands, and that Tiger Lord of whom thou speakest is forgotten. As Nineveh fell Babylon rose, and she, too, hath fallen in her turn. The Mede humbled her to the dust, and the Macedonian conquered the Mede—that Macedonian whose descendant sits before thee, and who, three hundred years ago, founded the city of Alexandria, now the chief in the land of Egypt.

"So men come and go, so empires rise and fall, and so the slow flood of the ages sweeps on, impassive as the stream of our eternal Nile, submerging all things save the mighty fanes of Khem, which were old when thy Nineveh was young, and which shall endure unto the end of time itself."

I was silent for a while, thinking of many things, then I woke from my dream and said:

"Now, tell me, I pray you, how came I into this Egypt, which I remember sailing through from Pelusium, as it was called then, to the Red Sea, when Solomon was king in Salem?"

"Most marvellous, nay, incredible, as I should call it, did I not know that the soul of man is a spark of the Eternal Fire, and that to the Gods nothing is impossible!" replied Amemphis, slowly shaking his head as though his mind were wandering in a maze of perplexity. "But thy coming here is easily explained, and may be told in a few words.

"More than a hundred years ago, as it is written in the book of my great grandfather, Amenophis, a fleet of Egyptian galleys, returning by way of the Red Sea from India, were driven by a sudden storm to seek refuge in an old, half-ruined harbour far away to the south of Arabia. Anati, the nephew of Amenophis, who commanded one of the galleys, landed with some of his men, and behind the harbour found the ruins of a deserted city, and among these they began to search for treasure, as sailors ever do in such a case. Only one building of those which had once made a great city remained standing and entire. This was a vast mausoleum built in the form of a square, with the corners pointing north and south, east and west.

"After great labour they succeeded in breaking into it, and in it they found three sarcophagi of black polished stone. They broke them open and found in each a coffin of pure silver hermetically sealed. These, too, they opened. In two of them lay jewels of gold and precious stones and a few bones, which crumbled to dust as they looked on them. In the third they found thee, resting as in a deep sleep, untouched by the hand of time, clad in armour of steel and gold, and with a great sword, on the hilt of which thy hands were crossed, lying on thy breast.

"So life-like didst thou look that for long they feared to touch thee, but in the end they brought thee, coffin and all, back to Bubastis, where Amenophis heard of the marvel through his nephew, and bought thee. From him thou hast descended to me as a heirloom, surely the most marvellous that man ever had, and I, after many prayers from the royal daughter of Auletes, my pupil in the mysteries, have done that which hath, by the help of Amen-Ra, restored thee to life."

We talked long that night, speaking in what was then the lost tongue of Khem, known only to the priests of the ancient faith of Isis, now far declined in the apostasy which was leading men away to the altars of Greece and Rome. Saving myself, Cleopatra was the only one not an Egyptian born who ever spoke this speech, and Amemphis had taught it to her in exchange for a solemn oath which he took of her, making her swear that, when she became queen in fact as well as in name, she would banish Serapis and the false Gods of Greece, and restore the Queen of Heaven to her place throughout the upper and lower lands of Egypt.

Then at length Cleopatra took her leave and Amemphis, rising from his seat, said:

"I am weary with long watching, and thou, too, hast come from a long journey, and mayest well be weary also. Follow me and I will lead thee to a better chamber than this, where thou mayest sleep in peace; and when the stars that are now paling grow bright again I will come and wake thee."

I followed him, and he led me through many dim passages, whose rock-built walls seemed as though they had been reared to stand till the end of all things, into a large and airy chamber, where I laid me down thankfully enough on a soft couch spread with whitest linen, and there, even before he had left the room, sleep came to me, and all the marvels of the night were forgotten. When I woke he was standing beside me with a little silver lamp in his hand, for it was now night again, and as I looked up, blinking at the light, he said:

"Thou hast slept long, and I hope well. Now, if thou wilt rise, a bath and food and fresh raiment await thee, and then when thou art ready to see strange things we will go."

"Where to?" I said, rising from the bed and stretching my still sleep-laden limbs. "To Cleopatra?"

"Yes," he replied, smiling. "To Cleopatra, who will await thee before the altar of Isis in the great hall of the Temple, and as the time is short I will pray thee to make all convenient haste."

Hearing this, as you may believe, I made no needless delay, and half an hour had not passed before I had bathed and dressed myself in a woollen vest and tunic of fine white linen embroidered with many-coloured silks, and over these I put my shirt of mail, and girded my sword on, and set my helmet of steel with its circlet of gold upon my head, and bound a pair of sandals to my feet, and hung a cloak of white linen embroidered with purple and gold over my shoulders.

Then I ate a hasty meal with Amemphis, who evaded all my questions as to what we were about to do with true priestly craft, and when that was finished I followed him from the chamber, passing, as before, through a labyrinth of gloomy corridors until we came out into the star-lit night before a great pylon, or outer porch, built of such huge blocks of dark polished stone that it seemed as though only giants could have raised them to their places.

Here we were challenged by guards armed with spear and sword, and clad in armour whose white sheen told me that I was no longer the only man on earth who possessed the secret of steel. At a whispered word from Amemphis the crossed spears in front of us went up, and we passed through. Behind the pylon was another porch, and beneath this was a square doorway closed completely by a single block of dark grained granite.

"How now!" I said, stopping short before it. "Surely there is no way in here, or hast thou some magic that will find a way through this solid wall of stone?"

"A moment's patience and thou shalt see," said Amemphis, going in front of me.

I saw him put his foot in the right-hand corner of the doorway, and press with his hand on a lotus flower carved in the massive stone door-post. Then to my amazement the great mass of granite sank silently into the ground, and as we stepped across the threshold a low, sweet chorus of unearthly song welled up from the lips of invisible singers, and I found myself in a great gloomy hall, whose invisible roof was supported on long rows of great fluted pillars of black stone.

A score of golden lamps hung by chains out of the darkness above, and by their light I saw at the far end of the hall Cleopatra, sitting on a throne of silver, with her feet resting on a couchant sphinx of black stone. On her head was the vulture cap and the horned disk of Isis. The Serpent Crown of Egypt was twined about her brows, the sceptre of Menes was in her left hand and the Scourge in her right; behind her rose an altar of white stone, surmounted by the winged emblem of the All-Mother, and to right and left of her stood a double row of priests clad like Amemphis in long white linen robes.

That morning I had left her a girl, all innocence and youthful wonder. To-night I found her a queen, seated on the oldest throne in the world, and wearing the emblems of a royalty compared with which all other insignia were but as the toys of yesterday. As we advanced up the hall the priests on either hand bowed low to us, murmuring:

"All hail Amemphis, High Priest of Amen-Ra, Master of the Holy Mysteries of Isis! All hail thou who comest from the Halls of Osiris and the Shadowland of Amenti! Welcome to Egypt in the hour of her need!"

They set a seat for me opposite to Cleopatra at the other end of the two lines of priests, and Amemphis, standing in the midst, and facing her, raised his hands towards the emblem above the altar. As he did so every priestly head was bowed, and for the space of many minutes there was silence so utter and so solemn, that I scarce dared to breathe lest I should break it. Then, dropping his hands, Amemphis went and took his place at the right hand of the throne, and said:

"Priests of Isis and initiates of the Holy Mysteries—you who are still faithful to the cause of the Ancient Gods and our Holy Mother Isis, to whom we have prayed in that silence in which the heart speaks when the lips are closed—I have told you the wondrous story of him who by the permission of Osiris returned last night from the Abodes of the Dead, and was led by my all too honoured hand back into the world of the living.

"Wondrous as is his advent, it is yet not unexpected either to me or to you, my brothers, for the stars, in whose golden letters are written the fates of men and empires, have told us that the world is fast approaching a turning-point in the history of Man. We, to whom their lore is as plain as the hieroglyphs on our temple walls, know that the world is all unconsciously awaiting the coming of one who shall break the might of the Oppressor, and take his yoke from the weary necks of the subject nations.

"And whither should such an one come but to the Ancient Land, whence all that the world knows of arts and arms and wisdom has ever sprung? The fate of Egypt is hanging in the balance. Shall it not be that the miracle that was wrought yesternight has its meaning for us and this holy land of Khem?"

He paused for a moment, and again the solemn silence fell upon us. Then, turning his eyes, aglow with the fire of prophecy, upon me, he went on:

"And for thee, O Stranger from a distant land, surely that meaning shall not be far to seek. Here, in our Lady Cleopatra, thou hast found, as thou hast told us, the living image of her who was thy warrior-queen in Armen, and of thy Sabæan bride, whom the murderous hand of her false counterpart snatched from thine arms in the very hour of thine elusive bliss. Who shall say that the Gods have it not in their hearts to give thee here in Egypt that which they took from thee in their inscrutable wisdom amid the desert sands of Asshur and in thy bridal chamber in Sabæa?"

Again he ceased, and again there was silence. All eyes were turned on me, but I saw none save those two glowing orbs that looked at me from under the Serpent Crown. Then some spirit loosed the bondage of my tongue, and I rose to my feet and drew my sword and kissed the golden hilt, and said:

"If that be so, as well it may be, then by this sacred steel which the Gods gave into my hands in Armen, and which was hallowed by the holy lips of her whose later self now seems to sit before me, I swear that, once drawn for Egypt and for her, I will never sheathe it again till I shall do so in victory, or death shall strike it from my hand!"

Then I raised it aloft, and, as I held it there flashing in the lamp-light, Amemphis turned to Cleopatra and spoke again:

"And for thee, O Queen, peerless among women and the last hope of the Sacred Land! doth it not seem to thee that the Gods have sent thee at once a champion and a worthy mate out of the Halls of Amenti, a hero newsprung from the bosom of Osiris? Where among all the kings of the earth wilt thou find one whom the Gods have honoured with a destiny such as his—one who was never born of woman, and who may justly claim descent from the stars? Who shall be stronger than he to win back thy rightful throne with that good sword of his, and seat thee on it, not as the vassal of Rome, but queen in thine own royal right, and by the right that he shall win for thee in battle?"

He ceased, and yet again that awful silence fell upon us, standing there before the altar amidst the gloom of the vast temple, and then out of the silence came a voice so softly sweet, and yet so clearly penetrating, that it might have been the voice of the Goddess herself speaking to us from the stars:

"It is not for me to know that which is in the hearts of the Gods, yet did I but know their bidding clearly I would do it, though the doing of it should cost me all the joys of earth and all that mortals hope for between the cradle and the grave. The Gods have voices. Let them speak and I will obey."

Ere the whispering echo of her words had died away amidst the pillars, a pale haze of light dawned on the gloom at the other end of the Temple. It grew and brightened till the flames of the lamps grew dim and wan before it. Then moving shapes appeared in the midst of it, and these soon took definite but swiftly changing forms.

Once more, before the wondering eyes of the priests and of her who had asked for a sign, I charged at the head of the horse of Armen through the broken hosts of Asshur, and Ilma swept in her chariot like a shining angel of destruction down that broad red road that I had cleared for her three thousand years before. Once more Armen and Asshur faced each other under the walls of Nineveh. Once more the Tower of Bel rocked to its base and reeled thundering to the earth. Once more I stood by Zillah's side before the throne of Solomon, and once more with the naked steel in my hand I faced Balkis in my bridal room.

Then the vision vanished silently as it had come. I turned and looked at Cleopatra. She had risen, white as death, from her throne, and was staring with darkly burning eyes into the empty gloom. Then she turned, and, stretching up her arms towards the emblem over the altar, she said in a voice that trembled sweetly on the silence:

"I thank thee, Holy Mother Isis, for the sign! Thou hast made the path of destiny plain to me, and I will tread it to the end, and if I falter or turn aside then may all my hopes of happiness on earth be blasted, may I die by my own hand in the supreme hour of my despair, and may the Divine Assessors find me wanting when I stand in the presence of the Invisible in the Halls of Osiris! Thus do I swear, and as my faith is, so let thy mercy or thy judgment be, O Holy Mother Isis!"

She ceased, and, as the unearthly chorus that had greeted us rolled forth again as though to chant Amen to her oath, she sank to her knees before the altar, and, covering her face with her hands, knelt there white and still, the most sweetly solemn figure in all that solemn scene.

CHAPTER IX

BOW AND SWORD ONCE MORE

I MUST pass lightly over the events of the three months which followed the taking of our joint oaths before the altar of Isis in the temple of Ptah, for I spent them almost wholly in retirement, under the care of Amenphis and his brother priests, who instructed me in all that was necessary for me to know for the playing of the part that I had taken upon me.

But I learnt more than all they taught me from the lips and from the eyes of Cleopatra herself. She, girl though she was in years, was yet the very heart and soul and brain of the insurrection that was brewing against the Court party in Alexandria, who, when she had refused to obey the will of Ptolemæus and the orders of the Roman Senate, had conferred a spurious sovereignty on the lad Dionysius, her brother, and Arsinöe, her sister.

You have read how the great Pompeius came with a single tall Roman galley, a defeated fugitive from the fatal plain of Pharsalia, to Alexandria to seek a refuge from the victorious Cæsar, and how Pothinus, the vile Theodotus, and the false Achillas, put off in a boat, from the flat shore by the temple of the Casian Amon, to bring him to the land; and how, in the shallow water, Achillas stabbed him under the eyes of the stately Cornelia, his wife, who stood wailing and wringing her hands on the deck of the galley.

It was this foul murder which brought matters to an issue. Achillas led his troops to Pelusium, and I and Amemphis, and others of the leaders of our party were at Gaza with Cleopatra, when news was brought to us by a Syrian galley in our service. Now, if ever, was the time to strike the decisive blow which would scatter the forces of the usurpers, and rouse Egypt to one last struggle for independence.

We had a fleet of fifty galleys at Gaza, and—beside the three thousand men they carried—we had a force of two thousand lying in camp to the east of Pelusium, and it needed but little skill to see that Achillas would direct his first attack against these. Here he must be met and crushed, Pelusium must be stormed, and then the way to Alexandria would be as open as a caravan track through the desert.

So, at sunrise one glorious morning, we boarded our galleys, the flutes sounded, and the double rows of long oars dipped into the water, and sent the spray flashing in long lines astern. Outside a fair breeze was blowing from the east, so we hoisted our great square sails of gaily-coloured cloth, and went bowling away merrily over the smooth sunlit sea, on an expedition which but for a woman's weakness or a woman's falsehood—the Gods alone know which it was!—might have changed the history of the world.

I was with Cleopatra on her galley, the *Golden Ibis*, a great two-banked craft with high stern and forecastle, a golden ibis head on her prow and beneath a triple beak of brass, half in the water and half out, projecting a dozen feet beyond the stem.

I had so far been kept out of sight of all but Cleopatra's most trusted advisers, for it was wisely deemed better that I should come on the scene, as I did, full armed and on the eve of conquest, than that busy tongues should have time to gossip about the strangeness of my coming, for if victory crowned our arms it was the intention of Amemphis and his brother priests to boldly proclaim me a reincarnation of the great Rameses, returned to earth to wrest his ancient dominion from the talons of the Roman eagle, and to lead the sons of Khem to the conquest of the world.

As I crossed the boarding-plank and took my place by Cleopatra's seat under the azure silken awning on the poop the murmurs of amazement that had followed me broke into open speech, and the soldiers and sailors began to ask each other aloud if this was Menes or Rameses, Herakles or Merodach—according to their faith or speech—who had come back to earth to fight the battles of the new Isis, as men were already beginning to call Cleopatra, for the sake of her more than human beauty and her more than royal dignity.

This was not an opportunity to be lost, and so Amemphis, who was with us, sent a glance of intelligence at Cleopatra and then at me, and then went to the front of the poop and, raising his arms for silence, said in a loud, clear voice that could be heard on board the galleys on either side of us, for we were sailing in the centre of the line:

"Soldiers and mariners of Egypt, and those who are our faithful allies! I see you gaze, as well you may do, with eyes of marvel upon him who stands by the seat of your Queen, and I hear that you are asking yourselves whence comes this Godlike shape of a strength and majesty more than human. It is not lawful for me to tell you now, for I may not anticipate the designs of the sacred Gods, but a time is near at hand when you shall see for yourselves, and judge whether or not our holy Mother Isis has sent, in the hour of Egypt's need, a worthy champion to clear the way to victory for her living image on earth, our peerless Lady Cleopatra!"

He ceased, and the answer to his words rolled up from the deck in a mighty shout of delight and welcome, which was taken up by the ships on either side of us, ringing along our line to right and left, fast followed by the rumour that one of the old heroes had returned to earth to do battle for Egypt and her Queen.

We sailed on all that day and the next night without meeting friend or foe upon the waters, but the next sunrise showed us a great fleet of galleys, outnumbering us by two to one, stretched out in a long line in front of us, and behind them the low-lying land on either side of the Pelusiac mouth, crowned by the forts and houses of Pelusium.

Cleopatra came on deck from her cabin just as we sighted them, and as I looked at her, clothed in shimmering silk and snowy linen with the serpent fillet of gold round her hair, my thoughts went back with something like a pang of sorrow to Ilma as she had gone forth to battle on that far-off morning when I made my first charge into the Assyrian host, and I contrasted almost bitterly Cleopatra's luxurious raiment with her helmet and corselet of steel. Yet very sweet and lovely did my dear Egyptian look, standing on the poop shading her eyes and gazing towards the hostile fleet as I pointed it out to her.

"There are many of them!" she said, and I detected just a little quaver in her voice as she spoke these words.

"Yes, they are more than we, therefore there will be the greater glory to-day and the greater plunder to-night."

"Spoken like a good warrior! Those words should be a good augury for the day's fortunes," she replied, laying her hand slightly on my bare forearm, and sending the magic of her touch thrilling along my nerves over my whole body.

"Yes," I said. "They shall be! I have little faith in auguries, save those which men shape for themselves with sword and axe. But this deck will be no place for you, Cleopatra, clad like that. Why, a stray shaft would pierce that soft raiment of yours like a lotus leaf! Had you not better go below and arm yourself in shelter?"

"Arm myself?" she said, looking up at me in almost childish wonder. "What mean you, my champion? Ah, I see—nay, or do I remember—that Ilma of yours went to battle with you clad in steel and armed with bow and sword, and you think that I should do likewise. No, no, Apollodorus, the days of warrior-queens are over, and our weapons are other, yet no less deadly, than those of the battle-field. Still, I shall not go into shelter, for, though I am no warrior, you shall find that I am no coward. I will stop here and watch the assault and see my champion fight his way to glory and to victory. Now, tell me, who is to strike the first blow?"

"I shall," I said, "for if my hands have not lost their cunning you shall see that I can strike farther, as well as harder, than any other in the two fleets. But, believe me, you are rash almost to foolishness to remain exposed. Think what would happen to us and to Egypt if a shaft should strike you!"

"Nay! nay!" she interrupted, with a shake of her head. "My fate is in the future, not here, and I shall stay."

So she stayed and had her way then as ever, and I, seeing that remonstrance was of no use, ordered up her body-guard to protect her with their shields when the fight began, and then, calling to my weapon-bearer to bring my bow and sheaves of arrows, I went and took up my station on the high forecastle and strung my bow.

We steered more to the south, so as to get between them and the sun. Then we hauled down our sails, the slave-drivers got out their whips ready for the wretches who were toiling on the benches below, the flutes sounded, the oars splashed into the water, and the *Ibis* sprang forward with the rest, carrying me swiftly into my first sea-fight.

When the nearest of the Alexandrian galleys was within about six hundred paces of the *Ibis* I took an arrow from my bearer and fitted it to the string. He stared aghast at me, for half the distance was more than an Egyptian bow would slay a man at. I drew the shaft to the head and sent it soaring away far over the masts of the galleys till it was lost to sight. A low cry of amazement went up from the group of warriors standing on the forecastle, for the strongest of them could not have drawn the arrow half way to the point.

I, as you may see, had sped the shaft only to try the power of the bow, but now I was satisfied that it would stand me in good stead, so I took another shaft and, seeing a great galley flying the purple-blue flag, the royal banner of Egypt, coming on at us, I took a steady sight and sent it hissing into the midst of a group of gaily-dressed warriors who stood brandishing their weapons on her prow. Then, by the Gods, you should have heard the shout that went up from all our line as one of them sprang a yard into the air and dropped back on the deck with an arrow through his heart.

Soon now the bowmen and slingers on both sides got to work, and clouds of arrows were hissing through the air, and the stones and balls of lead and iron came rattling and pelting about us in ceaseless showers. With every yard of space that vanished between us the old battle-fury burnt up hotter and hotter within me. I had laid aside my bow, for my last shaft was spent. My bearer had strapped my buckler of brass and tough bull-hide on to my left arm, and in my right hand I swung my double-bladed battle-axe, like a pendulum counting the moments which still had to pass before I could give the signal to board.

Our ship's captain steered the *Ibis* to a marvel, and at last the quarter of the Alexandrian admiral lay exposed, and the longed-for moment had come. I waved my axe. The slave-drivers shouted, and the cruel thongs whistled down on to the backs of the sweating, breathless slaves, the great oars bent, and the *Ibis* leapt forward as though she would spring from the water. Then, as we braced ourselves for the shock, we heard the crashing and snapping of the Alexandrian's oars, and a yell of anger mingled with the shout of triumph as our triple beak bored into her side.

Our lofty forecastle towered over her deck, I measured my distance, and, with one mighty spring, leapt clear of the points of the pikes that lined the bulwarks, and, as I landed on the deck, the old battle-cry, which the walls of the throne-room of the Tiger Lord had last echoed, rang loud and fierce from my lips, and the blade of my axe crashed down through shield and helm and skull of a stout Roman warrior, who had shrunk back aghast at my wild leap.

A brief ten minutes of it was enough for them. Shame on them, they broke and ran like sheep, and I, tossing my buckler to my bearer, who by this time had followed me with a party of boarders from the *Ibis*, took my axe in both hands and chased the cravens up and down their deck, laughing and shouting at them to stand and fight like men, but I might as well have shouted at a pack of dogs in the street.

At last I heard a feeble shout of "Achillas!" behind me and I turned and saw the Greek, gorgeous from head to foot in splendid armour, holding his great shield in front of him, and stealing on me with his sword. Three swift strides brought me to him, and my red, dripping axe went up, but, ere it descended, the craven's heart melted within him, sword and shield went clattering to the deck, and he threw up his hands, crying with his trembling lips:

"Quarter! quarter! Men cannot fight with Gods, I yield."

"Thou cur!" I said, dropping my axe in front of me, blade downwards, and resting my hands on the haft. "Thou murderous cur and craven! Where is the knife that pierced the neck of great Pompeius? Thou couldst strike a king from behind. Take up thy sword and shield and let us see thee strike a foe in front!"

But the coward made never a movement towards me. He stood there trembling in his splendid armour, and at length found voice to say:

"Nay, I have yielded, lord; I and my ship are thine."

"Then," I said, "if thou art mine, tell thy captain to signal to the fleet to yield with thee, or, by the eyes of Ishtar, I will hang thee to thine own masthead, and so make the signal myself."

So to save his miserable life the coward made the signal, although, as it proved, there was but little need for it, for all this while the fight had been raging hotly all along the line, and that which we had counted on had come to pass. Our own men, strung up to a triumphant frenzy of enthusiasm by what they had seen me do, fought as they had never fought before, and all through the Alexandrian ships there had flown the rumour that some God had come down to-earth and was fighting for Cleopatra.

When they saw the signal flying from the admiral's masthead, they believed that their leader was dead, and that we had taken his ship, as in very truth we had, and many of the galleys put about and ran out of the fight to gain the shelter of the forts in the river. Seeing this, I told our men to tie up Achillas, and bring him on board the *Ibis*, and leave the slaves to get his sinking ship to the shore if they could. When I got back to our own ship, I took him on to the poop where Cleopatra, all unharmed, but white and quivering with excitement, stood awaiting me.

"Here is my first present to thee, O Queen!" I said in a voice hoarse with shouting and the battle-madness that was still burning in my veins. "Here is Achillas, Admiral of Egypt, and murderer of Pompeius. What wilt thou do with him, for he is thine to kill or keep alive?"

"Such a dog is hardly worth the hanging," she said in a voice so cold and pitiless that it sent a chill through me like a blast of frozen air. "Let him be of some use before he dies. Take him and chain him to one of the oars, and let him help to row us into Pelusium."

It was a bitter lot for one who but an hour ago had been the admiral of a hundred galleys. Even I pitied him for the moment, but the Queen had spoken, and so they took him away crying and cursing, and stripped his warlike finery off, and chained him naked to an oar-bench, in the place of a slave who had died under the lash. Then Cleopatra turned to me as I stood there on the poop, smeared with blood from head to foot, like a butcher fresh from the shambles, and with my axe red from blade to haft still in my hand, and said:

"By the splendour of Osiris! that was gloriously done, my godlike hero, for never was such fighting seen since Herakles himself went to Olympus. But tell me, have you taken no wounds in that terrible half-hour yonder?"

"Wounds!" I laughed. "I have a scratch or two on my legs and arms, I believe, and that was about all these cravens with their puny weapons could achieve. By Merodach! if there are no better fighters than these in the world now, I will soon set you on a throne to which all the nations of the earth shall bow."

"Ah!" said Amemphis, who was standing by, "these were but mercenaries and Alexandrians, with their mixed blood thinned with riot and excess. Thou hast yet to meet the Roman legions and measure swords with Cæsar, yet methinks even they would break before such an onslaught as thou madest on the galley of Achillas, for, by the glory of Isis, nothing like it was ever done in the world for one man to clear the deck of a great galley like that with his own weapon!"

And now, as the galley gathered way and went rushing through the water into that river mouth through which I had sailed with Zillah and Balkis a thousand years before, I took up my place on the forecastle again and sent shaft after shaft into the crowded decks of the flying Alexandrians. The battle outside was over now, for the ships that had not been sunk or captured had surrendered, their crews panic-stricken by the fate that had befallen the admiral, and dreading lest the strange War-God should come and swing his battle-axe among them, too.

So we, who had come into the battle but fifty strong, now swept into the mouth of the river nearly a hundred strong, and one by one we overtook the fugitives and sank them or drove them ashore, showing no quarter to any save those that surrendered. As we passed the forts they saluted us with showers of stones and darts from their catapults and other war-engines, but these did little damage, for the range was too great and we swept past them too fast. And so at last we came into the harbour of Pelusium itself.

Here on the quays we found the troops that Achillas had left drawn up to bar our way to the town, and soon the merry game of cut and thrust began anew. Despite all the showers of arrows and javelins, and the rain of stones and bullets from slings that they poured upon us, we brought our galleys alongside, ran out the boarding-planks, and then went at them with axe and sword and spear.

I had given my axe to my bearer, for my fingers were itching to grip the hilt of my dear old sword once more, and so for the first time the steel of Armen flashed again in battle in the light of an Egyptian sun. Yet I am fain to say that it was but sorry work, for of all the puny cravens I ever met in fight these miserable Egyptians and degenerate Greeks were the least worthy of good steel and honest blows.

We had among our mercenaries a company of about five hundred men—fine, tall, stalwart fellows, every one of them, with fair skins, blue eyes, and ruddy cheeks, and thick yellow hair that almost rivalled my own golden locks in brightness. Amemphis had told me that they were of a people called the Goths, who came from some country in which the Romans were ever fighting, far away to the north. They were armed with short swords, bows, and heavy axes, and I had noticed during the sea-fight that they were always the first on an enemy's decks and the last to leave them.

So, as we were working our way into the harbour, I had sent messages to the other ships to tell these Goths to come to me when we landed and fight beside me.

You may guess how eagerly they seized upon the honour, for, as one of them afterwards told me in his barbarous Latin, they believed, to a man, that I was Odin—Gods! how familiar that long-forgotten name sounded in my thrilling ears as he spoke it!—who had come back to earth to break the might of Rome and restore his own empire on earth.*

With the very first slash of my glorious blade I had shorn a slim Egyptian in half at the waist as he stood above me on the quay, disputing my way up the boarding-plank. As the two halves of him dropped on either side of the plank, I let out with the point and drove it through the skull of the man behind him, and then, wrenching it out, I sent a third sprawling into the dock with a backward blow of my shield, and the next cut I made with my sword was at the empty air, for every man of them had shrunk back out of reach, leaving a wide semicircle about me.

It was now that I had shouted for my Goths. Some had come swarming up the plank behind me; others had swung themselves ashore on ropes and chains, and so about two score of us made good our footing, and went to work while the others were coming up. It was short, sharp, bloody work at first, and then they broke and ran. We hunted them down as wolves would hunt a flock of sheep, but I was ashamed to use my sacred steel in such mean work, and so I took my battle-axe again from my bearer and laid on merrily with that.

My Goths fought and slaughtered like the untamed demons that they were, and I saw in them the makings of a troop whose name should be a word of terror thoughout the Inland Sea.

They fought with their short swords in their left hands and their battle-axes in their right, and better butchers I never saw. Street after street we cleared, and within a couple of hours the town was ours. Meanwhile, too, the news of our victory had been carried to our camp, and all our men had come flocking in from there to finish what we had begun. That night, as I had promised, Cleopatra and I feasted with our Captains in right royal style, for we had won two victories in one day, and had good cause to make merry.

Many was the flagon of the red wine of Cos that we emptied to the glory of Egypt and her future Queen, and many more than these we might have emptied to other toasts had it not been that, just when our revels were at their height, a light, swift galley came flying into port, bringing the fateful news that the great Julius, with 2,500 veterans, all triumph-flushed from the glories of Pharsalia, had cast anchor off the Mole of Alexandria.

* One of the oldest Norse legends makes Odin a hero who conquered large territories about the Black Sea, just before the time of Christ, and afterwards migrated across Russia and founded the Norse kingdoms of Scandinavia.

CHAPTER X

AVE CÆSAR!

THE news of Cæsar's coming through half expected, was, as you may believe, anything but welcome to us. Two days more would have seen us masters of Alexandria, and a week would have been enough to make the city impregnable. But now, as ever, the great general had moved with unexpected speed, and instead of wasting his time or strength upon outposts, had struck straight at the key of the position in Egypt, and, perhaps, captured it without a blow.

About half an hour before the news came to us, Cleopatra had retired to rest in the Governor's palace, which had been prepared for her reception, and I sent the tidings to her by Iras, a Greek waiting-woman of hers, who, as Amemphis afterwards told me, had ever hated and scorned Egypt, and looked upon the Egyptians as fit only to be the slaves of their Greek and Roman masters. The next morning she and Cleopatra had vanished, and so had the Syrian galley which had brought the news to Pelusium.

There is little need for me to tell you that which we learnt to our shame and rage soon afterwards. You know how she went to Alexandria; how wrapped in Syrian carpet, the Egyptian Straton bore her on his shoulder like a bale of merchandise by night into Cæsar's palace, and laid her on his couch; how the stern warrior of fifty-four years, the battle-hardened master of Rome, and the greatest warrior the world ever saw, yielded to the subtle witcheries and omnipotent beauty of the girl of nineteen summers; how she sold herself and Egypt for Cæsar's favour and protection, and so incurred the penalty of the oath that she had sworn to Isis on the Temple of Ptah.

But we on that fatal morning knew nothing of this. We only knew she had gone—that our Queen, the idol of the army and the fleet, had deserted us, or been stolen from us, which, in good truth, had been well-nigh impossible; that our victory had been annulled at a stroke, and that the future, which had seemed so full of fair promise, now held nothing but perplexity and uncertainty. It was hopeless for us to seek to keep the evil tidings secret, for already the fact of her going was known, and rumours of every sort were rife in the fleet and camp.

We spent the whole of that day repairing the damages that our own fleet and the captured galleys had received, and in making our troops ready for the march on Alexandria, for, Cæsar or no Cæsar, I had determined to try the venture of a combined sea and land attack, if the men and the ships would follow me. But towards evening Amemphis came to me in the cabin of the *Ibis*, and, instead of answering my greeting, stood before me, shaking his head and wringing his hands, and looking dumbly at me with eyes from which the tears were welling fast down his furrowed cheeks.

"What is it, Amemphis? What is it?" I said. "If you bring news it must be bad, as I can see, so tell me not that it is news of the Queen!"

"Of the Queen—of the Queen!" he cried, suddenly flinging his arms apart. "Nay, it is not of the Queen, for, by the glory of Isis, there is no Queen in Egypt now, nor ever will be again till her name is forgotten. Alas! alas! What have I done? The sin was mine and thus she has repaid it. I, a priest of Egypt and Chief Minister of Amen-Ra, have been tempted by the witchery of that bright intellect of hers to reveal to her the mysteries that are forbidden to all save those of the blood of the priests or of the ancient royal line of Egypt. I have sought to set on the throne of Menes one whose veins were defiled by Macedonian blood—I thought to betray Egypt to her, and she has betrayed both me and Egypt. Yet the Gods know that my heart was pure and that I did it for the best!"

"But what has she done, Amemphis? What is this betrayal thou art bewailing? What is it that Cleopatra has done?"

"Terai of Armen, my wonder and my hope," he said, coming to me and taking my right hand between his two cold and trembling ones. "The news that has come to me will be well-nigh as grievous to thee as it has been to me. Thou hast looked love into those fatal eyes of hers, and with me thou hast dreamed a dream of a throne which thou shouldst share with her. And now, alas for the bright hopes of yestermorn! thou hast to learn that last night, guided, I doubt not, by the evil counsel of that false-hearted Greek maid of hers, she went secretly to Alexandria and let herself be borne on the shoulders of an Egyptian traitor into the palace of Cæsar."

"What?" I cried, wrenching my hands from between his and recoiling a pace. "Into Cæsar's palace! Nay, nay, Amemphis, thou art dreaming: this cannot be true. It is too horrible for belief."

"Nay, but I tell thee it *is* true," he replied in his poor, thin, quaking voice. "And not only into Cæsar's palace, but into Cæsar's chamber—and she who yesterday might have been the Queen of Egypt is now a harlot, self-sold to Cæsar, the bondmaid of the most pitiless of our masters. It is, as thou sayest, too horrible for belief, but—may the Gods have mercy on us and judgment on her!—it is true, too true! Alas for Egypt and for us!"

While he was speaking his voice rose into a shrill, wavering cry that was almost like a scream of pain, and then it died away into a low, wailing moan, and he sank down on a seat and, with his face buried in his hands, sat rocking himself from side to side, while I, with clenched hands sore and angry heart, paced to and fro in the narrow cabin, wondering by what guilt I had incurred so grievous a blow, and seeking to plan how I might avenge it.

Truly, the fiat of the Gods had gone forth against that ancient land, for no sooner was Cleopatra's treachery known than our men began to fall away in hundreds, cursing her name and praying to the empty skies for vengeance upon her, but with no thought of taking vengeance for themselves in their fickle, coward hearts. While victory was with us all was well, and they would have followed us anywhere. But now their Queen had betrayed them to the Roman, and the fear of the great Cæsar's name lay heavy on their craven spirits.

So our regiments melted away, either scattering southward to their own homes or else going to Alexandria to wait the turn of events, and see whether Cæsar, or Pothinus, Cleopatra or Arsinöe, would come out the victor in the end. I saw that there was no time to be lost if anything was to be saved. Cæsar, I knew, was shut up for the present, but I had no knowledge of the strength of the army and fleet which, by this time, would be besieging him, or how soon a detachment of it might fall upon our craven-hearted and dwindling forces in Pelusium.

What was Egypt to me now? as I said in my anger to Amemphis, when I had found for myself how matters were with us. Why should I fight for a land whose degenerate sons were cravens and weaklings, who lacked the courage to take their necks from under the heels of their foreign masters? Was not the sea open and the world wide and fortune somewhere to be had for the taking?

What mattered it to me whether Cæsar or the eunuch ruled in Alexandria? or whether that pretty sinner who had betrayed us was Cæsar's harlot or Egypt's vassal Queen? Truly it mattered nothing; so that night I sent Amemphis back on a well-manned galley up the Nile to his home amidst the half-ruined temples of his vanished Gods, and set about saving what I could for myself out of the wreck of what we had won.

"Farewell, Terai," he had said, as I embraced him for the last time on the deck of the vessel. "Yet we shall meet again ere this new life which the Gods have given thee by my hand is ended. I go to endure the penalty of my presumption in long, weary years of repentance and waiting for that which is to come. But for thee there may be many happy years between then and now, so fare thee well, and may the Gods give thee glory and fortune according to thy deserts!"

And so I left him to meet him again as you shall see. Then I went back to the harbour where the galleys lay, and calling Hatho, the leader of the Goths, whom I spoke of before, to me, I told him straightly, and in a few words, how matters stood, and asked him if he and his fellows would help me to take the best of the galleys and follow me fortune-hunting on blue water.

"Follow you, my lord!" he said with a great, hearty laugh. "Ay, that we will, to the edge of Hades itself, and besides us there are five or six hundred stout fellows, Scythians, Gauls, and Iberians, in the army and the fleet who will come with us; stout sea-dogs and hungry war-wolves every one of them, who will follow you with us wherever there is a skull to be split or a pouchful of plunder to be won.

When we had satisfied our contract at the expense of the cellars of Achillas, we took ten of the fastest and strongest galleys in the fleet, and filled their benches with the sturdiest slaves that we could find, and, after that, we rifled the rest of the ships without scruple of the arms and provisions and warlike stores that we found in them to furnish our expedition.

For my own ship I took the *Ibis*, the stoutest and fastest craft of them all, as I had proved, and, when I had renamed her the *Ilma*, in memory of her in whose cause my sword had first drunk blood, and manned her with a picked hundred and twenty of the Goths, we pulled out of the river mouth; and so I, who had fought Nimrod for the crown of Asshur, and had been the friend and guest of the Tiger Lord and the great Solomon, and the wedded husband of the Queen of Sabæa, bade, for a time, farewell to thoughts of crowns and royal dignities, and set forth with my ten galleys and my thousand odd sea-wolves to seek, as a simple freebooter, such good or evil as Fortune might have in store for me.

My first order was to hoist the sails to the favouring south-east wind and steer for Alexandria, for I was determined not to leave Egypt without a sight of that famous city, and, if possible, of Cæsar himself, for I had heard so much of his greatness and his conquests that it seemed a pity that I should be within a night's sail of him and yet go away without seeing the greatest man that the world had yet seen born of the ever-fecund womb of time.

As soon as it was broad daylight we went in cautiously past the promontory of the Lochias until, on the other side of the Mole, guarding the private harbour of the palace, we could see the hulls of twelve great Roman triremes towering up out of the water, a fleet which, as Hatho told me, could have run us down and broken our ships to pieces like so many egg-shells, for the Roman trireme of those days was what the English three-decker was in Nelson's time or the steel-clad battleship of these days—a foe not to be lightly encountered, save by equal or superior strength.

So we turned aside from here and pulled out towards the Pharos till we opened the Great Harbour, and saw lying inside the Poseidium and along the great embankment of the Heptastadium a huge swarm of craft of all sizes, from two-bank galleys to the light pleasure craft in which the Alexandrian lovers took their evening sails by moonlight.

We had not been watching these long when we saw an opening cleared among them, and out of this came a big galley, flying the royal blue standard. It was also floating from the flagstaff on the Lochias, for there was both a king and a queen just then in Alexandria, and each flew the flag in defiance of the other. The galley was followed by a long string of others, forty of them in all we counted, and as they formed up and swept out round the Poseidium and across towards the Mole of the private harbour we saw that we had just arrived in time to watch, and perchance take part in, the doings of a busy day.

But what you would now call our armed neutrality was not fated to last very long, for, seeing us lying there and neither making any signal nor flying any flag, a light galley was sent out from the Great Harbour to ask our business, and I, keeping out of sight myself, bade Hatho tell them that we were neither Greek, nor Roman, nor Alexandrian; that we were there for our own pleasure and meant to stay as long as we pleased and to go when we thought fit.

This seemed to have agreed but ill with their mood, for when the galley took the message back a fresh fleet of fifteen ships, double and single banked galleys, put out from the harbour behind the breakwater which ran southward from the Pharos and came at us with flags flying, trumpets blaring, and flutes squealing, plainly meaning to capture us or chase us out of the harbour.

As I knew that my men were itching for a brush with an enemy of some sort, I was well pleased to see this and told my bearer to bring my bow and arrows up on to the forecastle. My first shaft went hissing into the heart of a tall fellow who was steering the foremost galley; the next I sent into a group of archers on her forecastle and pinned two of them together, and then as galley after galley came within range I picked off its steersman and those who showed themselves most conspicuously about the decks.

They were not long in learning from the effects of my far-flying shafts that their enemy was none other than the victor of Pelusium, and as the wildest of stories had been carried to the city about my exploits, the vigour of their advance plainly slackened as they came near to us.

My sea-wolves were not slow to see this, and when I gave the word to charge they burst out into a yell of exultation so fierce and savage, and our ships sprang forward at such a furious speed, that six out of the fifteen Alexandrians turned tail and ran for the harbour with all the speed they could make, followed by the curses of their commanders and the shouts of laughter which mingled with our own war-cries.

We swept down upon those that were left, raining storms of arrows upon them as we went; and then dashed into them and carried them by the board. I picked out the biggest of them as the victim of the *Ilma's* ram, and as the triple beak tore its way into her splitting timbers, Hatho and I sprang side by side on board of her, followed by fifty of our starkest Goths, and then the battle-axes went to work like hammers in a forge, and Greek and Egyptian, Nubian and Syrian, went down before us like children playing at soldiers.

In half an hour all that was left of the fleet was ours, no great achievement, I grant you, for, of all the men of the many nations that I have fought with, these mongrel Alexandrians were the worst cravens and most pitiful weaklings in a fight. But there had been this use in their attack. It had decided me which side to take in their quarrel, and so gave me the chance, as you will see, of paying my false sweetheart back for her treachery and apostasy in such fashion as she but little expected.

As soon as the last galley was taken we unchained the slaves and pitched them overboard, to give the poor wretches a chance for their lives, and then, as the wind was blowing dead into the Great Harbour, we hoisted the sails of the eight galleys that remained afloat, built up great fires on their decks, and sent them roaring and blazing and crackling into the crowd of shipping that was lying huddled under the Heptastadium, and then, by the Gods, you should have seen their crews run as the fire-ships reeled in amongst them, and the hungry flames sprang out and licked them up, ship after ship, till the whole line of the great breakwater was one vast smoke-crowned wall of fire.

The forty galleys which had set out to attack the palace harbour were now left with no choice but to go on, for there was but that roaring furnace to retreat into, since to gain the open sea they must have passed through the jaws of my own sea-wolves, and that, after what they had seen, was a journey they had little relish for.

But we were there, and, willing or unwilling, they had to fight us, for as soon as the Romans saw what we had done, and reckoning on us as good, if unknown, allies, they drop the chain that barred the entrance to the harbour and one by one the great stately triremes moved out, churning up the water with their huge sweeps, and gathering way with every stroke as they bore down upon the Alexandrian swarm. It was a gallant sight to see those mighty ships rushing on to their prey, their decks crowned with the shining helms and armour and the glittering weapons of the stern soldiery of Rome, and, as we watched, my men danced and shouted with delight, and watched me with fiercely eager eyes till I judged the right moment to be come and gave the word that let their furious valour loose again.

As we bore down upon the Alexandrians' flank a score of their galleys faced about to meet us. Then the storm of arrows and hail of javelins burst forth again until, amidst the ripping of timbers and the crashing of oars, we burst into the midst of them, and went to work with axe and sword. Yard by yard we fought our way through them until we joined the main battle, and then for the first time I looked upon the grim, orderly grandeur of the Roman phalanx.

A big trireme near the *Ilma* had just forced her way between a pair of Alexandrian two-banked galleys; her decks were filled with men, but every man was in his place, and the ranks were as perfect and as silent as though they had been drawn up on a parade ground. The great boarding platforms hinged to the sides were slung by ropes to the mast, and as soon as the grappling irons had been made fast in the Alexandrians' bows and sterns, I heard a short, sharp word of command, the great platforms fell with a crash on to their decks, and over them marched with swift, even tread two triple files of plumed warriors, a wall of brass and steel bristling with spear points.

The Alexandrians rushed at them once; I saw them entangled for a moment among the spear points; the moving wall halted for just that moment, and then surged on again, treading the dead and wounded under foot. Then it broke in the centre, the two halves wheeled outwards and cleared the galleys from amidships to stem and stern, leaving no living creature on board, save the slaves who were chained to the oar-benches below.

I had never seen fighting like this, such grim, silent, terrible work it was, and, as I stared in wonder at it, I saw the secret of Rome's mastery revealed. She had wedded order with strength and valour, and had made herself irresistible.

But my dream was soon broken by the rush of an Alexandrian galley which came tearing through the water, and drove her beak into the stern of the trireme. A man, whose armour was covered by a cloak of scarlet cloth, was standing on her high stern directing the battle, and when the shock came he lost his balance and plunged headlong into the water. A shout of "Cæsar!" rang out from a hundred Roman throats, and a Syrian archer on the Alexandrian galley uttered a yell of delight, and drew an arrow to the head, and stood waiting for the scarlet cloak to come up.

It came, and he drove his arrow through it, but the man who had been in it rose three yards away, and by this time the *Ilma's* beak was fast in the Alexandrian's side.

A grey, close-cropped head came up a second time, just beyond the blades of our oars, and I saw an Egyptian on the Alexandrian's deck pull out his sword and put it between his teeth, and then make as though he was going to jump in on to the swimmer.

Near me on the deck lay an axe whose owner had no more use for it. I picked it up and flung it at the Egyptian with such force and lucky certainty that it drove his own sword blade into his skull, and as he dropped dead I shouted to Hatho to follow me with a rope, and, pulling off my helmet, ran to the stern and jumped in beside Cæsar, who was now bleeding from a wound in the head from a stone which had been flung at him, and was swimming feebly and half stunned.

I gripped him by the arm, and as I did so Hatho dropped into the water beside me with a mighty splash. He had a rope in his teeth, and this he made fast under Cæsar's arms, and the three of us were dragged back till we could pull ourselves up on to the oars, and so climbed back on to the *Ilma's* deck amidst the joyful shouts of the Romans who were swiftly clearing the decks of the Alexandrians. We took Cæsar into the cabin and bound up his wounds and gave him a drink of wine which speedily brought him back to himself.

"There is no need for me to ask the name of him to whom I owe my life," he said, as he stood up and held out his hand to me. "Thou art Terai of Armen, that strange visitant to the world, of whom Cleopatra has told me. I will not ask now why thou hast saved the man to whom she fled when she forsook thee. It is enough for me to say that thou hast made a friend of Cæsar and therefore of his mistress, Rome."

"Yet not for the sake of Cæsar's mistress, Cleopatra," I laughed as I returned his hand-grip, "for to tell the truth, noble Cæsar, it was in my heart to let thee drown for her sweet sake, but then came another and a better thought—a thought of the shame which would be mine if I suffered the fate of the world to be changed for a wanton woman's sake, and so with Hatho's help I saved thee."

He looked up at me, and smiled—it was a smile as sweet as a woman's—and said:

"Nevertheless, for that second thought I thank thee in the name of Rome, and when the fight is over Cleopatra shall thank thee, too; and now let us go and see how fares the battle."

When we reached the deck the battle was already over, and only a score or so of shattered wrecks lay floating about the harbour and a few galleys flying seaward, with my own sea-wolves in hot pursuit, remained out of the Alexandrian fleet. Cæsar at once went on shore, and I soon followed him when I had performed such toilet as was necessary after the battle.

There was a guard of Prætorians waiting for me on the quay to conduct me to the palace, and when I joined them my war finery was as smart and my helm and sword and mail were as bright and spotless as those of a knight on the morn of his maiden fight. But the battle-glow had died out of my blood now, and I followed my guard in silence and cold and bitter angry, thinking only of the shame that had been brought upon me and Egypt by the treachery of the fair wanton to whose base-bought throne I was going.

When the bronze doors of the audience-hall swung open, and I strode in, attended by my guard of honour, I saw nothing of the splendours of the chambers, nothing of the brilliant throne that stood on either hand, watching me with all its eyes.

I saw only Cleopatra, crowned and throned in her mock-royal state, and Cæsar her lover and her master—by the Gods! he might better have been her father, with his grey hair and thin furrowed face—sitting in a chair beside the vassal-throne she had bought with her honour.

As I approached, with my eyes fixed on that fair, false face of hers, I saw it flush from chin to brow with the scarlet hue of shame, and then grow pale and grey as the ashes of a burnt-out fire. But she mastered herself, and her proud spirit rose again under the goad of all those eyes that were staring at her, and, holding out her hand for me to kiss, she said, as a queen might have spoken to a favoured servant:

"We thank thee in the name of Egypt, my Lord Terai, for the great service thou hast this day done to us and our noble ally."

I only touched her hand with mine for an instant, just long enough to feel that it was cold as the hand of a corpse, nor did I raise it to my lips, for sooner than have kissed it I would have crushed it out of shape in my grip, and, in answer to her greeting, I said, looking full into the shrinking, staring eyes that I held captive the while:

"The graciousness of Royal Egypt is too great. I am but a poor, homeless rover, and I and my sea-dogs did but join in the fight from love of battle, and because the Alexandrians attacked us first. As for the noble Cæsar, Royal Egypt does not need to be told that a service to him can win no higher reward than the honour of doing it, even though the service hath little honour in itself."

She was quick to read the hidden meaning of my smoothly-spoken words, for she blanched again and her eyes fell. Then, after a little silence, she spoke again, and said:

"Then, if that is so, as it surely is, may we not hope that my Lord Terai and his gallant followers will join us in the fight which our disloyal subjects compel us to wage for our rights and our throne? Such stout hearts and strong arms would be welcome to us now, would they not, my Julius?"

"Nay, Royal Egypt, that is as impossible as it is needless. I have no part or lot in the Land of Khem, for the oath that I swore is dissolved, and she whose ally is Cæsar needs no other champion. I will but stay till my ships are refitted, and then I can no longer hold my sea-dogs in the leash."

"What speech is that?" asked Cæsar, looking up sharply. "It is one I have never heard before."

"Then," said I with a short laugh, "thou hast a great pleasure in store, noble Cæsar, for thou wilt learn it hereafter in thine hours of leisure from the fairest lips that ever made human speech into music."

I was lodged that night in the palace, and I had not slept long before I was awakened by a light hand laid upon my shoulder. I looked up and there stood Iras.

"From the Queen," she said, laying a little roll upon my breast. "I will await my lord at the door."

I unrolled the scroll and read by the light of my lamp:

"*Come to me for I have that to say which could not be said in Cæsar's presence, or while the idle ears of the Court were listening. Iras will conduct you. Cæsar sleeps.*

"CLEOPATRA."

Had I obeyed that message, as my first impulse was to do, and succumbed once more, as I might have done to the fatal charms of her who sent it, the whole story of Rome and the East from that day might have been written otherwise than it has been. But my next thought was one of wrath, deep and bitter, and then of cold scorn for the shamlessness of such a letter sent at such a time. So, sending the slave who had been sleeping across my doorway, for a reed pen and ink, I wrote on the same scroll beneath her writing these words:

"*Terai of Armen and Cleopatra of Egypt will not meet again till Isis demands the penalty of the oath that was sworn in the Temple of Ptah.*"

I gave this to Iras with so sternly spoken a command to take it back to her mistress that she shrank away from me shivering and frightened, and when she had vanished into the gloom of the long pillared corridor, I dressed and armed myself and went down to the quay where my galleys were lying, for I knew Egyptian ways well enough by this time to be sure that after such a message I could no longer sleep safely in the Lochias.

CHAPTER XI

FROM ACTIUM TO CALVARY

According to your reckoning, it was the morning of the second of September in the thirty-first year before the coming of the Christ. On the coast of Epirus, by the Ambracian Gulf, Octavian was encamped with eighty thousand footmen and twelve thousand horse covered by a fleet of five hundred galleys, large and small, of which I and my sea-dogs were the eyes and ears. On the Acarnanian shore to the south lay Antony with a host of a hundred thousand foot and twelve thousand horse, protected by a fleet of great galleys commanding the narrow strait between the gulf and the sea.

Octavian had embarked in the morning, and our fleet lay in two divisions to the north—one commanded by the Imperator and the other by Agrippa—while I with my sea-wolves howling for battle and plunder, lay off the right wing watching our chance. If you could have seen the two fleets as those mighty galleys of Antony's came out, you would hardly have thought victory possible for us; but mere strength is not always power, as we proved before that deadly day's work was done.

We had on our side a swarm of light Liburnian galleys, which were then the swiftest craft that floated, and when the battle opened they went at the great slow-moving wooden castles like wolves at a herd of cattle. Then our two divisions bore down while the Liburnians crashed in among the big galleys, splintering their oars and raining showers of arrows into the crowds of soldiers that swarmed on Antony's decks.

As the two fleets met, and the battle-engines on their decks began to hurl their storms of stones and leaden bullets and javelins into bach other's decks and sides, I led my sea-wolves round to the south, where I saw the royal banner of Egypt flying.

"The wind is coming from the north," said old Hatho—who was still my well-loved lieutenant—as we neared them, and I made out in the midst of the Alexandrians a stately galley whose bulwarks were plated with gold and on whose deck I saw, standing by the mast, splendidly robed and crowned with the diadem of Isis, the woman who had called me back to life to teach me anew the bitterness that is worse than death.

"What if the Queen should lose heart, and those galleys—a good three score, are they not?—should fly with this north wind out of the fight? What would happen, then, my Hatho?" he said.

"We should win the day quicker, but lose some glorious plunder," replied the old sea-dog with a grin that showed half his fangs.

I made no answer, but went into my cabin and took a strip of parchment and wrote on it in the hermetic character:

"*From Terai of Armen to Cleopatra, the harlot-queen, greeting:*

"*The eyes of Isis are upon thee. As thy faith is so shall her mercy or her judgment be, according to thine oath. The Hathors wait in the halls of Osiris, and the words of doom are written in the Book of the Dead.*"

This I bound tightly round an arrow, and then I went up on to the forecastle and fitted the shaft to my bow. The splendid figure still stood beside the mast. We were much nearer now, and I could see Cleopatra as plainly as she could see me. As I raised my bow three men sprang before her to cover her with their shields. I drew the shaft to the point, and sent it singing on its way. It struck the mast a foot above the shields and stuck there quivering. I saw them pull it out, and then I gave the unwelcome order to rejoin the main battle.

Our oars had scarcely carried us a furlong before we saw the great purple sails of Cleopatra's galley hoisted and hauled round to the north wind. She swept out with ever-increasing way on her to the southward, and then up went every other Egyptian sail, and the whole fleet of three score mighty galleys with their cargoes of craven hearts cleared themselves from the press of the battle, and bore southward out of the bay after their flying Queen.

Then there went up from Antony's fleet such a howl of rage and dismay as drowned all the roar of conflict for the moment. A moment after it was answered by a great shout of triumph from the Roman fleet, and then I gave the long-awaited order to my sea-wolves, and let them loose at their prey. As we closed I saw a light, swift galley clear itself from the press and go speeding away after Cleopatra's fleet. By the Gods! I would have given half my own fleet to have known then that on board it was that besotted wretch who was fleeing from the field on which he might still have won the empire of the world to seek more shame within his wanton's arms.

But I knew nothing of this till we had been at it with axe and sword for well-nigh an hour, and then the cry ran through the fleets that Antony had fled. After that our work was easy, for we were fighting men without a leader.

Yet what were left of Antony's veterans fought well and stubbornly enough defending the great galleys which none of ours were heavy enough to sink, until Octavian and Agrippa loaded a score of rafts with combustibles and sent them blazing down the wind into their midst. So, with the fire to the north of them and us to the south, boarding their great castles one after the other, and setting their decks running with blood too good for the base cause it was spent in, they fought on till at last, as night fell and the flames spread from ship to ship along the great curve of their northern front, they threw down their arms, and called for quarter.

We saved three hundred of the galleys that had been Antony's that morning, but more than half of our own fleet had been destroyed in the taking of them, so you may think what would have happened if those sixty galleys, the greatest and strongest of them all, had not deserted when the battle-tide was at its flood.

All that night Actium shone bright with the blaze of the burning galleys, and when morning dawned Octavian was master of the world.

The news of Actium was just eleven months old when I, standing on the forecastle of the *Ilma*, led the van of the Roman fleet as I had led Cleopatra's between the forts of Pelusium, and I and my rovers disembarked to march with the legions of Rome on Alexandria, there to play out the last act of that shameful drama which Cleopatra had begun when her false heart bade her choose the shame of treason and the mock splendour of a vassal throne to the glory that might have been hers—ay, and mine, too—had but Ilma's heroine soul animated that fair counterfeit of hers, and she had kept the oath which she called Isis to witness that night in the Temple of Ptah.

Pelusium fell before us almost without striking a blow. It was an even easier conquest than I had made for Cleopatra seventeen years before, and when the news of its fall was carried to Alexandria, the last embers of heroism that remained in the breast of Antony burnt up into the semblance of a flame. He took courage from his despair, and sent Octavian a challenge, which surely must have been born of the madness of some drunken dream, to decide the dispute, which the Fates had already decided, by single combat under the walls of Alexandria.

But Octavian would have none of such grim fooling, for he was a man who had learned the priceless secret of never throwing away an advantage, and so he sent the messenger back to tell Antony that it was not Octavian, but Rome that he must master, and within an hour he had set out with the vanguard, leaving me and my Goths, grievously against our will, to come on with the main army. You may think how sorely I regretted this when, during the march, we learnt that Antony had sallied forth with the flower of the horsemen that were left to him, and inflicted a defeat on Octavian's cavalry.

But that was only the flare of a dying candle, the last of Antony's triumphs, for the next day he fought a battle under the walls which ended in the destruction of his mercenaries and the desertion of his last remaining legionaries to Octavian. To my sorrow, Antony was not in this fight. He was on the seaward side of Alexandria, preparing a fleet, the same in which Cleopatra had fled from Actium, to take him and her to some distant land, where, according to his last vain dream, he might live with her beyond the power of Rome.

Then came the last and vilest of Cleopatra's treacheries. From Antony she had nothing more to hope, but Octavian was a man, and so she dreamed that she might conquer him as she had conquered the great Julius and the miserable Antony, anl when, on the day after the land battle, our fleet was brought up from Pelusium to storm the harbour, she had already corrupted the captains of the galleys, and every plank of them was delivered without a struggle to the conqueror.

From so foul an act as this, it was but a short step that took her to the feet of Octavian, only to be spurned, as I had spurned her long before in all the pride of her youthful beauty, and to be told that the price of her life was the yielding of her treasures in Egypt and her own presence in Rome to adorn the triumph of him who was now doubly her victor. Then at last her pride revolted, and, more honourable in her death than in her life, she resolved to accept the penalty of her oath, and die by her own hand in the supreme hour of her despair.

You know the pitiful story of what followed. All I have to tell of is that which I saw with the same eyes which are now looking down, misty and dim, upon this written page. When Antony fell, I was just entering the palace at the head of a hundred of my Goths to take him alive or dead into the presence of Octavian in the palace of the Ptolemies on the Sebasteum. We had just forced our way into the little portico on the Street of the King, whither Antony had fled, when a slave came running out with streaming eyes, crying;

"Great Antony is dead! Let me go, that I may tell the Queen."

I caught him by the throat and turned him round, saying:

"Where lies he? Take me to him or I will break thy neck and send thee after him."

But just then a deep moan of pain came from a hall that opened out of the vestibule where we were. I ran in, and there on the marble pavement lay Antony, bleeding and writhing, with his sword in his breast, and moaning.

"Cleopatra! Take me to her, that we may die together."

"Ay!" I said. "Thou besotted craven! I will take thee to her, for I can carry thee, big as thou art, and thou shalt die in fitting company."

With that I lifted him up and swung him on my back, and, bidding the slave lead the way, I bore him, followed by my Goths keeping off the crowd that swarmed in the streets, to the mausoleum, which, at the command of Cleopatra, had risen from the earth like some magical structure in front of the Temple of Isis.

The strong hands of my Goths tore open the great brazen doors of the lower chamber, and I ran through and up the stairs which led to the death-chamber.

A blow of my hand sent the door flying open, and I strode in and faced Cleopatra once more and for the last time. She was reclining on a couch, robed, in the pride of her last blasphemy, as Isis, and crowned with the Uraeus diadem. Iris and Charmain stood beside her, and near her couch was a basket of figs. She sprang to her feet with a wild cry as I entered, and I, without a word, laid Antony on the silken sheets, which still bore the impress of her form. Then I rose and faced her, saying:

"Here is thy lover, Royal Egypt. Look to him, for he needs thy fondest care."

For one brief moment she stared in maddened silence at me, then, with a scream that rings in my ears even now, she flung herself on Antony's body, and, dragging the sword from the wound, pressed her lips upon it as though she would staunch the bleeding with them. I saw Antony's eyes open slowly, and, with the last effort of strength left in his once mighty frame, he raised his hand and laid it on her head, and then, with his bloated lips parted in a horrid smile, he died.

As the last sigh left him Cleopatra raised her face, hideous now, distorted with grief and passion, and with the lips that had once been so sweet all smeared with her lover's blood. She babbled something that was hardly human speech, and then she thrust her right hand into the basket of figs, and with her left tore the thin silken robe from her bosom. The next moment her right hand came out of the basket, and I saw something wriggling in it.

The next she had pressed it to her breast, and then I saw the flat head of the Uranus snake raise itself for an instant and then fall upon the fair white flesh. Without a sob or a cry she reeled back and fell dead across the body of the man she had first lured to his ruin and then betrayed to his conqueror. And so died the fairest and the vilest of the daughters of Woman.

When I reached the street again, a young priest came out of the crowd and accosted me, saying:

"Art thou he who was not and who is?"

"I am Terai, once of Armen, now of Egypt," I said, looking down into the eyes that were gazing half-frightened at me. "Thou canst come only from Amemphis with such a greeting as thine. Thou canst tell him that Cleopatra has paid the earthly penalty of her oath, and even now stands in the Hall of the Assessors."

"That the Master has already read in the stars. From his hand came the Uranus snake which, as my lord tells me, has already done its work. This, then, to thee from Amemphis."

As he spoke he slipped into my hand a little roll of papyrus, and before the last word had well left his lips, he had vanished in the crowd which pressed about the entrance to the mausoleum. I made my way quickly out of the vulgar press, and then, unrolling the scroll, read these strange words, written in the hermetic character:

"Amemphis, the unworthy minister of Amen-Ra, to Terai, the Stranger, greeting! In the blindness and the presumption of my half-knowledge I betrayed thee into false hope, which has gone the way of all such. That which is awaited is not yet come, but it is written that neither thou nor I shall see the dusk of Amenti till together we have beheld the revelation of the Invisible. When thou art weary of wandering and fighting, return to the Temple of Ptah, and there thou shalt find me waiting for thee, and in that time shall my last spoken words to thee be fulfilled. Till then farewell!"

Many a long year passed before the snows of my first life-winter on earth whitened and thinned my once thick golden locks, and so made true the words which Amemphis had spoken on the deck of the galley which bore him back to solitude.

For me they were years of fighting and feasting, of wandering and wondering amidst strange lands and seas, and still stranger peoples. Now I was feasting, garland-crowned, amidst the splendours of Imperial Rome, when Octavian went back to receive the title of Augustus and the diadem of the world. Now I was fighting for life or plunder, as the case might be, on the rock-bound shores of the Northland, which, in a far distant day, were to be my country and my home, and now I was wandering over trackless wastes of ocean to unknown lands, once towards the setting sun, and thrice to the eternal summer of the South, and through that to the Indies and the far-off islands of the Southern Orient, which the eyes of the West were not to see for nearly two thousand years to come.

It must suffice me to tell you how, after nearly thirty years of wandering and slowly-growing life-weariness, I came back at last to the well-remembered shore of Egypt alone in the wave-worn, worm-eaten hulk that had once been the stately galley in which the long dead Cleopatra and I had sailed out of Gaza, and how, as the last breath of a summer's day breeze filled her tattered sails, I beached her on the shelving sand, and made my toilsome way to Memphis with nothing left from all my years of toil but the shirt of mail, which now hung so loosely on my shrunken form, and the sacred steel which swung at my hip still bright and spotless as it had been when Ilma blessed it with her holy kiss in far-off Armen.

I found Amemphis waiting for me before the great dark pylon of the temple, as though only a week instead of more than three décades had passed since we had parted. I was old and grey and shrunken, but he, like one of the mummies of the Necropolis, had scarcely altered since my re-awakening eyes had first seen him and Cleopatra in that secret chamber in the temple. He greeted me with few but pregnant words.

"Thou hast been tardy in thy coming," he said, as he clasped my proffered hand, "yet thou hast come in time to see that which was awaited. Come and rest to-night in the temple, and to-morrow we must set forth on my last journey, and to the end of thy present pilgrimage."

We talked long that night of many things which may not be set down here, and at sunrise the next morning we set out in a sailing boat down the Nile to Pelusium. There Amemphis took places for us in a galley that was bound for Joppa, and from Joppa we fared overland to that city which I had last seen more than a thousand years before.

Guided by Amemphis, I traversed the winding, hilly road which led past the western wall of the city, and ascended the bare, bleak eminence which rises between the valleys of Kedron and Hinnom. On the summit of this stood three crosses, watched by a guard of Roman soldiers. Near them stood a little group of men and women, gazing with pale, drawn faces and tearful eyes upon the Shape which hung white and still upon the central cross. Along a path which led over the brow of the hill towards the city, wayfarers were passing to and fro, some of them stopping to look up at the crosses—which were not an uncommon spectacle in those days—and some to utter bitter words which since then have been graven deep into the history of the world.

"He saved others, Himself he cannot save!" scoffed one clad in the priestly raiment I had seen in Salem a thousand years before.

"Thou fool!" said Amemphis, in a low voice that only reached my ear, "and thou a priest of Salem! Alas for the city that once was holy and the people that once was chosen! But look, Terai, look and listen."

I looked up and saw the Shape on the central cross lift up its head, and heard a Voice that seemed to float down out of the darkening sky say in the tongue that Solomon had spoken:

"It is finished!"

Then the head fell again, and I saw a woman leave a little group and run to the foot of the Cross, and clasp her white arms about it. As she turned her face upwards a sunbeam shot through the fast gathering clouds, and, bathed in its radiance, I saw once more the vision of her whose presence haunted me through the ages. I sprang forward with her earliest name on my lips, but Amemphis stopped me saying:

"Not now nor here, Terai, for she is beyond thine or any other earthly love! Ay," he went on as though musing, "it is finished! In this hour the old order passes, and the Dream gives place to the Deed. The old Gods are dying, and the White Christ rises to reign in their stead on the throne that He hath reared to-day. Behold the night falls! We have seen that which the world awaited though it knew it not. Thou shalt see more, but I——"

Ere he could utter another word the lowering clouds closed over Calvary and the black pall of desolation descended like a curtain on the supreme Tragedy of the world.

The next moment I was alone in the midst of a waste of darkness. The earth reeled beneath me, and the very Heavens seemed to fall on it as though they would crush it and its guilt into nothingness, and I, with a crash of thunder and a wild, many-voiced scream of terror ringing in my ears, stumbled blindly forward and fell dead beside the woman who lay fainting at the foot of the Cross.

CHAPTER XI.

"THE SWORD OF GOD"

A SHEPHERD BOY watching his flocks of sheep and goats browsing on the scanty pasture of the valleys among the wild hills to the north of Mecca, the Holy City; a twelve-year-old lad, long of limb and strangely fair of complexion for a son of the desert and a child of the tribe of Koreish—such was I, who had been Terai of Armen, the friend of the Tiger-Lord of Asshur, of Solomon and Cæsar and Augustus, when I first began to peer vaguely and wonderingly through the mists of forgetfulness which lay behind me, parting me from my last life. As the years went on, the dreams grew longer and the visions clearer, and ere long there came another to help me to read them. This was Zoraida, a little maiden of the noble House of Hashem, and sister of my foster-brother Derar. I, in this new life of mine, was Khalid son of Othman, one day to be called the Sword of God. But that time was not yet, save in the dreams which Zoraida and I dreamt in our childish fashion, lying on the breezy hill-sides, under the shade of some great mass of rock which jutted darkly from the grey-brown sand.

Zoraida was fair like me, save that her hair was ruddy bronze, while mine was golden yellow, and her eyes were of sapphires' azure and mine grey-blue, like well-tempered steel. This difference from the rest of our folk was held to be such a prodigy that Abu Sophian, Prince of Mecca, and High Priest of the Kaaba, had predicted that mighty things should come of this marvel in the good time of the Gods, whose much nearer downfall had not been revealed to him.

For those were the days when he whose name was destined to rise to Heaven in the war-cries of ten thousand battlefields and in the orisons of many millions of worshippers was journeying to and fro with the camels of his mistress Kadijah, between Medina and Mecca, and Bozra and Damascus, and dreaming by the way even stranger dreams than ours—dreams which ere long were to shake the world and bring down in thunderous ruin those mighty empires of Persia, Byzantium, and Rome, which had been at the zenith of their glory when I, the Arab goatherd, had been captain of the fleet of Cleopatra and the ally of great Augustus.

In other dreams I saw myself standing in my shining mail on the high forecastle of a great galley, speeding such shafts as no mortal hand ever sped before through the shields and armour of other warriors on galleys into whose rent and splintering sides the brazen beaks of my own good ship bored their way, as I leapt on to their decks shouting my war-cry and swinging my blade at the head of my boarders.

So I, the Arab goatherd, dreamt on, day after day and night after night, until at length I came to know with the certainty of a perfect faith that I, Khalid the son of Othman, had lived in other ages on the earth before, and had done and seen those things of which you, who have followed me thus far on my strange pilgrimage, already know.

Then, as the years went on, I left my sheep and goats to go with the tribesmen to war and learn anew that grim trade which I had already plied in other times and ages. Now Derar and I, from being foster-brothers and playmates, became companions-in-arms, and many were the fierce forays and skirmishes with the hostile tribesmen in which we proved our youthful skill and valour. Nor was it long before, in all the tribes of Koreish—nay, in all the land that lay between the desert and the sea—there was none that could stand against us, lance to lance or sword to sword.

And now came the first tremors of that awakening storm which ere long was to sweep the world from the rivers of the Indies to the shores of the western ocean. Kadijah's camel driver had become her husband, and the dreaming trader had turned his back upon the Gods of the Kaaba and was calling the men of Mecca and Medina to worship a strange God we had never heard of, and to hail him as his prophet. You have read how we received the message—first with scorn and ridicule, and then with wrath, and how we took sides for and against him till Mecca and Medina were set one against the other, and at last the sword was drawn between us.

I was of the Koreish, and so, too, were Derar and Zoraida, and thus, when Mecca went to war, we, who were already the best of her warriors, went out to do battle for her and the ancient Gods, and it was not long before the first appeal to arms was made.

The Unbelievers, as we called them, had waylaid a rich caravan belonging to Abu Sophian, and we went out to relieve it. We marched southward from Mecca, and in the fertile vale of Beder, three stations' journey from Medina, we fought our first battle and suffered our first defeat. We avenged it—ah, how strangely!—afterwards on the hill of Ohud, and there my impious hand wounded the Prophet himself with a javelin thrust.

When I saw the blood flow I waved my spear and shouted:

"I have slain him! I have slain him! On, now, men of Mecca, and let us make an end of the Unbelievers!"

When my horsemen heard me they shouted for joy, and we rode down, yelling and swinging our spears, on to the little band that closed like a wall round the fallen Prophet. They gave us back cut for cut and thrust for thrust, till they went down to the last man where they had stood, and then to our wonder we saw the tall figure of the Prophet rise up from the ground in the midst of them, and in a voice as grave and calm as though he had been preaching in the Kaaba he said to us:

"O men of Mecca and Sons of Ishmael! why will you turn your spears against your brothers and seek damnation by slaying the Prophet of God? Behold, I am alone and unarmed! If it is the will of Allah that I should die let him that would slay me strike!"

Then in an instant every spear went up and every sword went down, and we looked at each other and at the wounded man standing alone in our midst, and there was not a man of us all who could strike the blow which would have changed the fate of half the world.

As for me, perchance seeing that which the others failed to see, I swung myself out of the saddle, and, dropping my spear to the ground, I tore a strip from my linen yashmak, and, going to Mohammed, I bound it about his brow and staunched the bleeding of his wound while he stood motionless as one of the senseless images of the Kaaba. Then, drawing my scimitar, I laid it across my breast, as I had seen those old warriors do in Armen, and cried to my followers:

"O brothers; it seems to me that this day we have been confounded by more than mortal strength. It is not Mohammed, the son of Abdallah, the son of Heshem, who hath thus defied our uplifted spears and stuck down our swords. Could Al Lata or Al Uzza have protected thus an unarmed votary from the weapons of such enemies as we are? Should we not have struck him down as we have struck many another down ere now? Think ye of it what ye will, but, as for me, from this moment I confess Allah as my God and Mohammed as his Prophet, and let him among you who would dispute that with me meet me now in the open field man to man, lance to lance, and sword to sword, and truly I will prove my faith on him or he shall prove my error upon me. Ye know me for I am Khalid the son of Othman, well known to you all; so now speak or for ever hold your peace."

Then there was silence for a space, and those swarthy warriors seated on their reined-in steeds stared at us—at the Prophet, still standing motionless and silent in the midst of them, and at me with my sword across my breast, making, as it were, a barrier of steel between him and them; and then, with one accord, every lance and blade was swung high above their heads, and one thunderous cry rang out at once from all their throats:

"*La I'laba illa Allah, Mohammed resoul Allah!*"

And as the shout died away the Prophet raised his hands outstretched above his head and said, still in the same deep, calm voice in which he had challenged us to slay him:

"God is victorious, and in His name ye shall march to victory! And thou, Khalid son of Othman, who hath stretched out thy sword before me, shalt henceforth be known in all lands and languages as the Sword of God, and in thy first conflict with the Unbelievers thou shalt find and win, by the strength of thine own arm, that sacred steel which in other ages and other climes that hand of thine hath grasped, and with it thou shalt hew a path to empire for Islam and for God!"

For an instant I stood before him stunned with amazement. It was the first time I had ever exchanged speech with him, and yet there, in his words, was the key to all my dreams and to the mystery of my being! I fell on my knee before him and, stretching out my arms with the palms of my hands turned towards him, I said, in a voice that was broken by the strength of the strange emotion that was stirring in my breast:

"Lo! now I know thee to be more than man, and gifted with a lore beyond human knowledge, for thou hast told me of that which is known to no other living man save to thee and to me. Whoso denies thee henceforth I will cleave him to the chin and tear the lying tongue from his throat, yea, though it were my own father or my own brother, for truly there is no God but thy God, and thou art the Prophet of God. Bismallah!"

Then he raised his hands above me again, and said:

"In the name of the most merciful God, I name thee, Khalid, henceforth Captain of the hosts of Islam, and these, thy companions, if they will follow thee shall go with thee to victory or to Paradise!"

"And, by Allah!" I cried springing to my feet and facing them, "I will lead them, as thou hast said, O Prophet of the Most High! and if there be any here who dare not or will not follow me let his face be covered with shame and the graves of his ancestors be dishonoured! Speak now; is there such a one among you?"

Then there was silence again for a space, and then Derar flung himself from his horse and came and stood beside me with drawn sword, and cried:

"I, Khalid, will be the first of thy followers! With thee I take Allah for my God, and Mohammed for His Prophet. Now, who is with us and who is against us?"

"We are with you, we are with you! Allah il Allah! Victory and Paradise!" came in another thunderous shout from the dark ring of warriors around us. "Lead on, and we will follow. To Mecca! To Mecca!"

"Nay, to Medina first," said Mohammed, "for there the Faithful await us, and we shall bring them tidings of a defeat and of a victory—nay, of the victory of victories, for from this hour the star of Islam shall not set till the will of Allah be fulfilled."

At Medina we were received as kings and conquerors and brothers, for in those first days of Islam, as ever afterwards, he who confessed the Faith, no matter how fierce a foe he had been before, became in that instant the brother of all true Moslems, and there Derar and I renewed our friendship, and once more clasped hands with Ali, the son of Abu Taleb a venerable chief of the tribe of Hashem, and uncle of the Prophet.

'Ali was then in his twentieth year, as both Derar and I were. It was he who, when he was but a lad of fourteen, had laid down on Mohammed's couch, wrapped in his green mantle, to wait for the assassins of the Koreish on that ever-memorable night when the Prophet fled with Abu Bekr from Mecca to Medina—the night from which two hundred millions of men now count their years.

In Medina we also found Amru, who but a few months before had been one of the bravest of my old companions in arms, a lean, swart-faced man of about twenty-five years, and as good a spearmen as there was in Arabia; and so we four, standing in the presence of the Prophet that evening, swore a bond of steel and blood, and witnessed each other's oaths never to turn our backs upon a foe, were he Arab or foreigner, and never to rest from battle till we had won the world for God and his Prophet, or the mercy of Allah had called us to Paradise.

And now the months went by swiftly and prosperously for the new faith. Every week brought its battles, its sieges, and its triumphs, until at last, at the head of the greatest host that had yet hailed the banner of the Prophet, we marched from Medina to Mecca to kindle those ten thousand watchfires on the hills about the Sacred City which warned the idolaters that the last hour of the worship of their Gods had come. Mecca, as you know, fell without striking a blow, and the haughty Abu Sophian himself laid the keys at the feet of Mohammed, and under my uplifted scimitar confessed the Faith of the one God and the apostleship of His Prophet.

Ere long all Arabia had but one God, and Mohammed was master of it from north to south and sea to sea, and soon envoys began to come in from Heraclius in Byzantium, and Chosroes in Persia from Egypt and Ethiopia, to seek the friendship of the Prophet in Medina. He received them in the market-place of the city, leaning his back against a palm-tree, just as he stood when he was preaching to us, and sent them back with gifts and exhortations to their masters to turn their people to the true faith and confess the Unity of God, and the mission of His Prophet—exhortations which ere long we were to preach in sterner fashion from the text of our battle-cries.

It was one of these envoys—a dainty, perfumed, silk-and-gold-bedecked knight from Byzantium—who caused the striking of the first spark of that fierce flame which ere long ran blazing from our northern confines up through Syria to the mountains of Taurus, and from the Inland Sea to the shores of the Caspian.

One day a party of his men, meeting Zoraida and me in the street, stopped and stared with all their eyes, wonder-stricken by the strangeness of her beauty; for I must tell you that by this time my little shepherd maiden had grown up as tall and stately and fair as my own Ilma herself, the very living image of her, as Zillah and Balkis and Cleopatra had been.

There was nothing much to take offence at in their stares, rude and all as finer manners might have found them, but one of them, letting his loose tongue outrun what little judgment he may have had, cried out in Syrian, which we understood as well as our own tongue:

"By the Saints! if the houris of Paradise are half as fair as yonder pretty barbarian, it would take but little to make a good Moslem of me."

I saw the fierce blood fly into Zoraida's cheeks, and an angry light kindled in her eyes as she looked quickly up at me and said:

"Khalid, wilt thou break me that Unbeliever's neck?"

"Ay, that I will!" I said, "and never was work better to my liking."

And with that I strode into the midst of the grinning Byzantines, and taking him swiftly by the throat, I shook him till his teeth rattled in his mouth, and said:

"Thou unbelieving dog! Who taught thee to yelp in the streets of the Holy City? Thou a good Moslem! thou a companion for a houri of Paradise! By Allah! there is not a girl in all Arabia that would not spit upon thee. Thou hast called a daughter of Islam a barbarian. Now come with me and lay thyself in the dust at her feet, and ask her pardon, or, by the mercy of Allah, I will wring thine empty head from thy shoulders and throw it to the dogs."

With every word I shook him anew, but ere I had finished the others crowded about me, some with their weapons already drawn in their hands, and of a sudden Zoraida cried:

"Thy sword, Khalid! Quick, or they will slay thee!"

I let go the fellow's throat, and, taking him by his belt and his thick hair, I picked him up from the ground and swung him round, so clearing a space about me. Then, seeing two of them coming in at me together with drawn swords, I lifted him high above my head, as I had done the false Zercal in the throne-room of the Tiger-Lord, and flung him at them, so that their two swords went through his body, and all three of them went reeling into the dust together.

"A life! A life!" the others shouted as they saw this. "He hath slain the servant of a Roman envoy. Down with the unbelieving barbarian!"

And they, too, came at me, four to one, two with their swords and two with short pikes; but my own scimitar was out by this time, and Zoraida, too, had drawn her blade, for you must know that in those days the noblest born of our Arab maidens were trained as we were in the use of arms, and, as you shall see, went to war with the best of us. She ran to my side, crying:

"Now, ye unbelieving dogs, ye shall see what welcome your pretty barbarian has for you!"

And with that she let out so swift and shrewd a stroke under the guard of the Byzantine opposite to her that she slashed him from brow to chin with as clean a stroke as sword ever made. He dropped blinded and howling in front of her, and I meanwhile had taken such a cut at the other's head that, as his sword went up to meet it, both his blade and mine broke to splinters, so, for want of a better weapon, I drove the hilt into his face and smashed it out of all human likeness.

Within an hour Zoraida and I were summoned before the Prophet to give an account of the affray, and there we found Sempronius, the envoy of Heraclius who had accused us of murder and breach of the law of nations, since we had slain five of the servants of his master when there was no war between us. But when we had told our story, and those of the bystanders who had seen the fight had told theirs, Mohammed turned to him, and said:

"It seems that thy men deserved their death, Sempronius, for to insult a maiden of Islam is what no man may do and live. What hath been sworn to on the oaths of Moslems cannot but be true, so with this thou must be content."

"Nay, but by all the Saints I will not be content!" cried the Byzantine, stamping his daintily-sandalled foot upon the ground. "Nor yet will Heraclius, my master, be content, and in his name I demand that this man and girl be delivered to me that I may do that which I hold to be justice on them."

"Now, by the glory of Allah, thou hast forgotten where thou art, and in whose presence thou standest!" said Mohammed, in his deep, musical voice, and turning upon him with the fire of anger in his eyes. Thou idolatrous slave of an Unbeliever! Dost thou dare to speak such words in the hearing of the Prophet of God? Knowest thou not that the life of a True Believer is worth more than all thy master's empire? Get thee to thy house, and see that thou art on thy journey betimes to-morrow, or I shall forget that thou art an envoy and thy life shall pay for thine insolence. Begone, and let my eyes be no longer defiled by the sight of thee!"

"I go!" cried Sempronius, white and shaking with passion, "but I will come back with a hundred cohorts behind me, and I will teach thee, false prophet——"

Ere another word had left his blaspheming lips, I had sprung forward and caught him by the throat. Then I slipped the fingers of my left hand into the neck of his steel and brass corselet, and, taking him with my right by the hair, I bent his head back till his neck broke, and then, flinging his body down at Mohammed's feet, I cried, so that all might hear me:

"Thus, O Prophet of God, will I break the necks of the Unbelievers, and silence the lying lips that dare to call thee false!"

"It was written, Khalid, and thou hast done it," he replied, gravely looking down at the dead Byzantine. "But this man was an envoy, and thy deed means war with him who but a month from now came back in triumph from Persia."

"Then war be it!" I cried, "O Prophet! Proclaim thou the Holy War, and fifty thousand swords shall shine at thy words. Send us to Syria, that we may teach these unbelieving dogs that there is no God but Allah and no Prophet but thyself."

"Syria" was now the word in every mouth, not only in Mecca and Medina, but in all the country round them.

At Mecca the proclamation was made and the last arrangements completed. First, five thousand horsemen were to advance to the banks of the Jordan to try the strength of our new enemy, and bring back tidings to the main army. The leader of this expedition was Zeid, who had once been a slave of Mohammed. You may wonder that we, who had already won renown in the home wars, and in whose veins the proudest blood of Arabia flowed, should have consented to follow such a base-born leader as this. Yet there was not a murmur among us when the choice became known, for that new faith of ours was a living thing. We not only professed it, but believed it; and so to us the word of the Prophet was as the law of God, and if he had told us to follow the meanest beggar that whined for alms at the gate of the Kaaba we should have followed him with equal obedience.

The night before we set out we camped on the level ground between the hills to the north of the city, and soon after sundown I went to Derar's tent to speak with him on a matter that lay very close to my heart; but as I drew near the tent I saw standing outside it, clad in all her war-like gear, her whom the matter most concerned, so I took the omen as a good one, and said to her:

"The peace be on you, Zoraida, fairest of the daughters of the desert! Is Derar in his tent?"

"The peace be on you, too, O Khalid!" she replied, with such a quick, bright flush on her pretty cheeks that I could have sworn she guessed my errand. "No Derar is in the city, and I, as you see, am here guarding his tent. Is your business with him for his private ear alone, or may his sister and companion-in-arms hear it?"

"Of a truth she may," I said, plucking up courage—which I needed more just then than I ever did in the face of an enemy—"for the business concerns his sister more than himself, and if you will forsake your trust for awhile, as you may without much danger, since none but True Believers are about, and come with me a little space outside the camp, I will soon make it plain for you."

"And if Derar comes back and finds that I have left my post, will you take the blame on those broad shoulders of yours, and stand between me and such anger as he may feel?"

I took good comfort from the archly-spoken words, and said, with a laugh:

"Ay, that I will, and with little fear, for I would almost brave even the anger of the Prophet at such a price; so come along, for yonder is the moon rising above the hills, and lighting a fitting lamp for lovers to guide their footsteps by."

She drew back half a pace at the boldly-spoken words, and for the moment I feared that I had spoken with more haste than wisdom. But then she came towards me again, and, after one swift, shy glance up into my eyes, she turned her face away and said:

"Now I know what you have to say, yet I will come and hear it so that you, too, may hear the answer which is already written on my heart."

If ever ardent lover walked on air I did so as we threaded our way in silence through the tents and took a path which led upward towards the base of the mountains. Neither of us uttered word or syllable till we were well beyond the camp, and alone together in the solemn moonlit stillness of the Eastern night. Then I took her by the arm, and in the strangest words that ever came from lover's lips, I told her the story of Terai of Armen and his love for Ilma, its warrior-queen of Zillah and Balkis and Cleopatra; and of the Woman who died beneath the Cross; and when I had finished my story I said to her:

"Now, in the wisdom and mercy of Allah, it has come to pass that we once more tread the ways of life together. To-morrow we set out to begin the Holy War, and you, with your sister-warriors, are going with us to nerve our arms and strengthen our hearts by your presence and your fair example. Yonder the Crescent floats in heaven above the hills that guard the Holy City—truly a good omen sent by Allah, who has given us the symbol of our faith to light us on the way to victory!

"Now, dear one, may it not be that you and I shall go to the war, not only companion-in-arms in the cause of Islam, but also in that still sweeter and holier companionship, which, if you will let me, I will ask the Prophet to bless to-morrow, and which, once accomplished, I swear by Allah and all the holy angels, shall be the only companionship of the sort that I will seek till we stand together before the gates of Paradise.

"Age after age we have met and been divided. Shall it not be that, now that we are one in a higher and a holier faith than we have known before, we shall join hands and hearts for ever here and hereafter till the mercy of Allah shall end our pilgrimage in Paradise?"

She heard me in silence to the end, walking beside me with slow, steady steps and downcast eyes.

Then she stopped, and I stopped too, and as she raised her head and looked at me, there stood Ilma's own self once more before me, beautiful with her own beauty, and pure as Heaven's light with Ilma's own stainless purity. Then she spoke and said, in the same soft accents that I had heard from Ilma's lips as we lay in our bridal grave in the sands beyond Nineveh:

"And whence have you learned, O Khalid, that this is the last stage of the journey which, by the will of Allah, we shall make together? Nay, do not frown—surely you would not frown on me, your oft-found and oft-lost companion, if such, in Allah's truth, I am—but listen even as I have listened to you.

"You say you have loved me in ages gone, and love me still in this new life of yours. Of your other lives I know nothing save what you have told me and what I seem to have seen in the dim visions that have flitted through my sleep. But in this life which is mine it has pleased Allah to put it into my heart to love you, and, since that is so, there is no shame in telling it. Yet all you have asked I cannot grant, for something tells me that it is not in the will of Allah that I should do so.

"You are not one who would take the fruits of victory before the battle has been won, and you and I have many battles to fight for the Faith before the time for love and resting comes, yet this much will I promise, on the troth of a maiden of Islam—I will be your battle-bride, and wed with you in the wedlock of war.

"I will go out with you against the Unbelievers and we will fight side by side in the sacred cause of Allah and His Prophet, and, if it shall be written that together we win the world for Islam and return to the Holy City in peace, then the least of your prizes shall be that for which you have asked me. But Islam must come first, for I have devoted myself soul and body to it, and you must conquer for the Faith before I can give myself to you without breaking the oath I have sworn."

"Then, Allah helping me, I will conquer for Islam and for you!" I said, drawing my sword from its sheath and raising it aloft till it shone whitely bright in the moonlight. "You shall keep your oath to Allah and your troth to me, and I will keep mine to you, and together we will win the world for Islam and for God, or together we will fall fighting for the Faith and go hand in hand to Paradise!"

Then I dropped my sword back into its sheath, and, taking her unresisting in my arms, I sealed our mutual oath upon her lips.

At the first hour of morning prayer the Prophet came out of the city, followed by all the citizens and the pilgrims, who gathered in a mighty concourse about the camp. When the prayer had been said and the myriad-voiced chorus had rolled up to Heaven confessing the unity of God and the mission of His Prophet, Mohammed ascended a little eminence, and there, surrounded by Abbas and Omar, Abu Bekr, the Companion of the Flight, and Abu Sophian, once Prince of Mecca, and all the notables of the Faith, he blessed our standards, and commended our enterprise to the mercy of Allah and dismissed us, and, amidst the prayers and exhortations of the vast multitude of people, we set forth on the first Moslem expedition that ever crossed the confines of Arabia.

For many days we journeyed on into deserts and mountains, and through pleasant countries, until at last our scouts, mounted on swift dromedaries, came in and told us that a large force of Romans and Syrians was drawn up at Muta, by the southern Jordan, little more than a day's march from us. It was then the hour of evening prayer, and, when we had done that which the faith required, we held a council of war, and decided to press on without delay with all our fighting force, leaving our beasts of burden and their drivers to come on more slowly, so that we might fall on the Unbelievers in the cool of the dawn.

The night was just melting into early morning when their sentries saw us, and our battle-cry woke them from their morning slumber. The Syrian light-horse were the first afield, and these held us engaged till the heavy troops were under arms. Therefore, by the time we had broken them by fierce charges, and sent them flying back to the camp, we found the solid ranks of the Roman phalanx like a wall of steel and brass bristling with spears, standing between us and the camp. Zeid was in the van, mounted on a great fierce war-camel. Recking nothing of the grim and formidable array which we now faced for the first time, he waved the sacred banner in one hand and his spear in the other, and shouting:

"God is victorious! Paradise! Paradise!" headed his beast at the centre of the Roman line.

At the first shock Zeid went down bleeding from a score of wounds. Jaafar, who was riding on his right hand, seized the standard as he fell. Then a great Roman, who might have been the twin brother of Mark Antony, gorgeous in gold and steel and scarlet, and mounted on a great black stallion, the sight of which brought the name of my old charger with a gasp to my lips, forced his way through the press, and made a sweeping slash at him with a long, straight, two-edged, golden-hilted blade, which I had but to see flash once in the sunlight to recognise as in very truth my own good sword, the sacred steel of Armen.

It fell, and with it went the right hand of Jaafar. He caught the falling standard with his left but a moment before that arm, too, was shorn through by a foeman at his side. Then he clasped the banner to his breast with the two bleeding stumps, still shouting his war-cry, until the great blade came down again, and cleft him well-nigh to the saddle. As he rolled over Abdallah made a dash to the front, and, stooping from his saddle once more, picked up the banner, and waved it aloft, shouting:

"Onward, True Believers, for Islam! There is victory or Paradise before us!"

Then he, too, went down, pierced and slashed by half a hundred spear thrusts and sword cuts, and then at last my turn came. I forgot everything at the sight of my matchless blade in the grip of an enemy. The long-forgotten battle-cry of Armen burst in a ringing shout from my lips. I spurred my horse forward over friend and foe as they stood transfixed for the moment at that strange wild cry of mine. Someone thrust the banner into my left hand as I passed.

Abdallah's body, and the next instant I was face to face with the Roman who had slain him.

As I went at him with lowered spear and buckler aloft, I heard a yell of exultation and triumph behind me, then a long, shrill, piercing scream, and after that came a rapid rush and the thunder of many hoofs. I saw the great black charger reach out his splendid head. His lips were drawn back like those of a snarling tiger, and with his strong white teeth he gripped my own horse across the neck, gave one shake, and then I felt my beast stop and shudder.

I dropped both spear and shield, and, grasping the Roman's horse by the mane, I vaulted over his head just as my own animal went down, flung my arms round the rider's waist as the great sword whistled through the empty air behind me, and with a mighty wrench I hove him clear of the saddle, and down we went together with a great clash of mail and weapons into the bloody, trampled mire.

For the next minute or two I was too busy to pay much heed to the battle about me. I knew only that somehow there must have been a space cleared about us, and that the great black steed was gone, else he would surely have taken me by the neck and crushed the life out of me by a single grip of his teeth.

From the manner of my attack I had the first advantage, for as the Roman went down he fell on his back and I on top of him, but as I was seeking to take him by the throat my hand slipped on his polished gorget and I lurched a trifle to one side. The next instant he had wriggled out from under me, and for a moment we lay on our sides, face to face, clawing and gripping at each other for the first hold.

In the scuffle a dagger had dropped out of my belt, and stood hilt up between our two bodies. I saw it and so did he, but he was quicker than I was, and with a swift snatch had it out of the sheath. I saw the blade go up in the sunlight, and then I played him a trick which settled the matter between us.

I loosed my hold of him and rolled over on my back with my eyes half closed, and he, thinking I had swooned, let out a short hissing cry of triumph, and brought the dagger down upon my neck. But ere it touched me my right hand went up and gripped him by the wrist with such a grip as he had never felt before. I felt the strong bones crack under it. Then with a slow, twisting wrench I screwed his arm round till the bones broke and the joints were loosened in their sockets. The dagger fell harmless on my mail, his face turned grey with the torture, his left hand loosed the grasp that it had sought on my throat, and with my own left hand I dealt him such a blow under the jaw that the bone broke under it, and he tumbled over senseless beside me.

Then I got up and shook myself, and wiped the sweat and mire from my eyes, and looked about me. The first thing I saw was the great sword lying on the ground a yard away. I picked it up, and as my fingers closed again on the familiar golden hilt I swung it high above my head, and once more shouted out that strange battle-cry whose unfamiliar sound had gained me the one moment of pause which had been worth all the battle to me.

Then I kissed the hilt with all the fervour of a man kissing the lips of his beloved for the first time, and as I did so Zoraida trotted her horse to my side, and said:

"The peace on thee, O Khalid! So thou hast found thine other mistress again! It was a gallant battle, and we kept the field clear for thee, so that thou shouldst win it to thine own honour."

"The peace on thee, too, O Zoraida!" I answered. "Yes, here is my battle-bride come back to me after many years. Now bless it once more, as thou didst so long ago in Armen, and then thou shalt see what manner of work it can do for Islam and for thee."

As I spoke I took it by the blade and held the golden hilt up to her, and she, taking hold of it with her right hand, kissed it, as Ilma had done ages before, and gave it back to me, saying:

"There, thou hast thy fancy! Now mount again, and let us see these Unbelievers scattered."

With that she beckoned to two of her troop, and they trotted forward with the Roman's black charger between them, for, as I learnt afterwards, it was Zoraida and her maidens who had charged past me, clearing the way as I made for the Roman, and they had captured his horse as I had flung him from it.

"Truly thou hast made me thy servant and thy debtor for ever!" I cried, as with one glance of love and gratitude at her glowing cheeks and shining eyes, I took the great beast by the mane and the crupper and swung myself into the saddle. They loosed his bridle as my feet found the stirrups, and the horse rose under me in one brief moment of rebellion; but he might as well have tried to rear out of his saddle girths as to unseat me, so much at home did I feel on his broad back once more, and when I had sent him prancing and curvetting once round the ring under the admiring glances of a hundred pairs of bright eyes, he had found his master, and then the ring broke.

Zoraida cantered up to my side. Those of our horsemen who were between us and the enemy opened a path for us, and away we went amidst a wild chorus of yells and shouts of triumph towards a body of Roman horse that was just then charging down upon a company of our footmen. It needed but a glance at me to tell them that their leader was either dead or captured, for there I was astride his great black horse with all his gay trappings still upon him, and there in my hand was the blade that he had taken into the battle.

They would have turned and fled if they had had time, but we were on them too quickly for that. We took them on the flank ere they had time to wheel, and the next moment I was among them shouting for Allah and victory, and sending man and horse down into the bloody trampled mire with every stride of my charger, and every stroke of my dear long-lost blade.

As soon as we had scattered the Roman horse, which we did in little more time than it has taken me to tell you of our first assault, we rode back to the main battle, and there we found Ali and Amru and Derar fast pressing the idolaters back, and breaking their array up into straggling, disorderly fragments, who, to give them credit, were fighting with more courage than hope. The glittering pride of the Roman phalanx was broken and gone. Only one cohort remained gathered round the imperial standard, and standing at bay with overlapping bucklers in a fashion worthy the days of the great Julius.

Before them lay a dark, ragged line of Moslem corpses, showing how grimly and well they were doing their last work, and behind these a couple of hundred of our best archers were raining arrows into them as thickly as the snowflakes fall on Lebanon.

As we rode up, Ali, who was now beside me, hurled a javelin with such truth of aim and strength of arm that it split the helmet of a man in the first rank and buried its point in the throat of the man behind him. Both staggered and fell forward at once, and for the moment the line was broken.

Ere the ranks could close I gathered my horse under me for a leap, and together we went crashing through the gap, flinging the others to the ground on either side of us, and I was in the midst of them, hacking my way to where the standard stood.

Ali and Derar followed hard behind me, and after them a column of our desert horse burst in like a swarthy torrent through the ever widening breach. The remnant of the phalanx melted away under our furious and now triumphant onset, and as I reached out to grasp the standard, Tigrol, as I had already renamed my sable steed, took the soldier who was holding it by the shoulder and lifted him off his feet, and as his white agonised face came up level with my arm, I drove my blade through it till the steel stood out two spans behind his helmet, and then, as he fell, I wrenched it out, and, waving the captured standard high above my head, galloped on through the now flying Romans, until I pulled up, laughing and panting, in the midst of what had once been their camp.

So ended the first battle in which the soldiers of Islam measured swords with the Unbelievers, and that same night laden with spoil and captives.

Darus, the big Roman from whom I had won back my battle-bride, died that night by his own order and the hand of one of his own men rather than be the prisoner and slave of a barbarian.

I was angry enough to have struck the slayer down when he told me of this, but the fellow was brave, and a captive, and his master had been a stark and a worthy foe; so instead I filled his helmet with gold out of my own share of the spoils, and bade him go back to Syria, telling him that he had wasted his master's life for nothing, for if he had told me honestly that which I wanted to know, I would have set him, too, free to go and get his arm mended, so that we might perchance have had another tuzzle some day in the wars that were to come.

He stared at me in no little amaze when I told him this, and said, with more respect than he had spoken with at first:

"My lord is as gracious as he is valiant and strong, and I would that Darus had lived to know thy generosity. Yet in return for thy gold and my liberty, if thou wouldst hear the story of the sword at thy side thou canst have it, according to what Darus has told us, from Sophronius, the Patriarch of Jerusalem, for it was in the Holy City that it was found, and there, too, as they say, hangs in the Church of the Sepulchre a most wondrously-fashioned coat of mail, which, as I have heard say, was found with the sword on the dead body of an aged man on Calvary the day that the Lord was crucified."

You may think how cold a chill those bluff, plain-spoken words of his sent through me as I listened to them. For a moment I closed my eyes, and saw again what I had seen as the darkness fell over that awful hill six hundred years before. Then I went to the soldier, and, laying my hand upon his shoulder, said to him in the old Greek tongue I had learned in Alexandria:

"Get thee to Jerusalem with what speed thou mayest, and tell Sophronius that he who has won back his sword is coming to seek his mail. Tell him, too, what thou hast seen and heard at Muta, and bid him beware for himself and his city if my armour is missing when I come. Now go, and the Peace be on thee!"

He gave me one frightened stare, and then, making the sign of his faith, he muttered something that might have been either a curse or a prayer, and, clasping his helmet full of gold to his breast, ran away into the darkness as terror-stricken as though he had seen some spectre from the nether world—the which I may, in very truth, have seemed to him when he had grasped the full meaning of my words.

CHAPTER XIII

THE HOLY WAR

When we reached the Holy City again we found the whole country between Mecca and Medina ringing with warlike preparations, and alive with auxiliaries who were pouring in from all parts to take their share in the Holy War.

We four, who were now honoured with the titles of Champions of the Faith, were appointed to leaderships of five thousand in the army that was assembling, and Mohammed, when he heard the story of my duel with Darus the Roman, once more named me publicly in the Kaaba the Sword of God, so giving me the title which for more than a thousand years since then has never been severed from my name.

I well remember, too, how, on the evening of that same day, I went to his house, as he had bidden me do, in order that I might tell him the story of the great blade which was now the admiration of all the host of Islam. As I entered the humble chamber where he was sitting in company with Ayesha, the best beloved of his wives, saving only the dead Kadijah, I found him weeping, with his left hand covering his face, and, in my amazement, I stopped short upon the threshold and said:

"The Peace be on thee, O Mohammed! What is this I see? Can it be that the Apostle of God weeps with the weakness of a man?"

"Nay, O Khalid," he replied, raising his tear-stained face to the lamplight. "It is not the Apostle of God that thou seest weeping, but a man who weeps for the loss of the friends that are no more. Zeid and Abdallah and Jaafar, the heroes of Islam, are already in Paradise, and need no tears of mine. Still, they were my friends, and so as a friend I am mourning them. Now sit and tell me the truth of this story which I have heard concerning that new-found blade of thine."

"Truly, the ways of Allah are mysterious and unfathomable as His mercies," he said, when he had heard me to the end in silence. "Thine hath been a strange destiny, O Khalid, and who can tell but that it shall be even stranger yet. But now listen, and I will tell thee that which perchance will seem to thee more wondrous still, and which thou shalt never tell, no, not even to the dearest of thy fellow-mortals, until the unerring voice within thee shall bid thee speak.

"I know that thy story is true, though, perchance, no other on earth would believe it, for I was he who, with the lips of Ardo the priest, showed thee a portion of thy fate, and faintly foreshadowed that which was to come to thee. I spoke to thee in Salem with the voice of Solomon the Wise, and in the shape of Amemphis, the last of the priests of Isis and Initiates of the Ancient Mysteries, I stood beside thee on Calvary when Issa hung upon the cross, and told thee that with His last words the old order of the world was ended, and the thrones of all the Gods overturned.

"Since then men, clinging too fondly to their old idolatries, have blasphemed His name in the worship of their images, and have dared to make to themselves idols of wood and stone and painted baubles of things that they called pictures in the likeness of the Invisible and the Unnameable, and for this purpose I have come back to earth for the last time, the last of the Incarnations of the Divine Message to man, to proclaim to the world that Allah is One and that there is no God but God, and that truth thou, too, Khalid, and thy Companions in the Faith shall teach to these dull-witted idolaters with the sword, since they will not hear the voice of truth and wisdom.

"For this your names shall never be forgotten while the Faithful confess Allah as their God and Mohammed as His Prophet, and that they shall do while the world endures. It may be that thou shalt live other lives after this, as thou hast lived others before it, and in them thou shall perchance see the triumph or the failure of Islam, according as the generations that come after us shall hold the Faith in singleness ot heart and unselfishness of purpose, or pollute it with their own lusts and vain imaginings.

"Not yet, it may be, but nevertheless, in Allah's own good time, the truth shall dawn upon them, and men shall confess that there is not, nor ever hath been through all the ages, but one God Who hath revealed Himself to men according to their intelligence; and when that time comes, O Khalid, whether thou art living some new life on earth or art standing at the gates of Paradise awaiting the end of thy pilgrimage, remember what Mohammed, the son of Abdallah, hath told thee this night!"

The next day the Prophet reviewed his army outside the city, and ten thousand horse and twenty thousand footmen sent up their thunderous shouts to Heaven as the great banner was unfurled above his head, and he proclaimed his purpose of leading us in person into Syria.

Yet even then and there were traitors and faint hearts among us, for scarcely was the order of march set than Abu Sophian—who, to my mind, had ever been a traitor to the Faith and a secret enemy to the Prophet—came at the head of fifty sleek and comfortable traders of the town, and prayed him to put off the expedition till what they thought a more fitting season.

I was seated hard by on my horse at the head of the Prophet's body-guard as they came up, and I can remember as well as if it had happened but yesterday, instead of more than twelve centuries ago, how Abu Sophian approached him with clasped hands, and said in his false, fawning voice:

"O Prophet, great as is thy wisdom, yet it seems to us that thy zeal is even greater, and it would be better that thy march should be deferred till the cool of the year, for the harvest is at hand, and the fields are unreaped, and our people will find the way weary and the sands of the desert waterless and hot."

"Ye will find Hell hotter!" cried the Prophet, breaking in upon his speech with such accents of wrath as made him stagger back as though he had been struck. "Who asked ye to come? Get back to your houses, ye faithless ones, and await our return in triumph. Ye are not worthy to fight for the Faith. Get back, get back, that my sight may be no longer polluted by you!"

And then, amidst the jeers of the whole host, the faint hearts slunk away to hide their shame in their houses, and we, shouting for Allah and His Prophet for victory and Paradise, formed up our ranks and set out on our march to Syria.

I, with three thousand of our best horsemen, scoured the country in advance of the main army as we went on, but nowhere did we find a trace of the legions of Heraclius; and, at length, ten days' journey from Damascus, Mohammed made his camp in the fertile vale of Tarbuc, and there he, who but eight years before had been a fugitive in the desert, with but a single follower and not half a score of friends in his own country, received the submission of all the tribes and cities, from the banks of the Euphrates to the shores of the Red Sea. There, too, the Prophet proclaimed for the last time in his life the Holy War against the Idolaters; but to all the followers of Issa in the region that had owned his sway, who preserved the ancient purity of their worship, he gave peace and security, and never while Islam remained pure were his commands violated by any soldier of the Faith.

So the last days of the Prophet were full of peace and prosperity. He had now almost reached the limit of three score years and ten, beyond which the life of man was in those days not often prolonged. I was standing amidst the saddened, speechless throng which filled the Kaaba when he ascended the pulpit to deliver the last charge that his lips ever gave to the Faithful, and well do I remember the last words that fell upon our strained and listening ears.

"If there be any man," he said, "whom I have unjustly scourged, let my own back bear the penalty of my injustice. If I have belied the reputation of a true Believer, let him now proclaim my faults before the face of this congregation. If I have despoiled any one of his goods, what I possess shall pay the debt and the interest."

"Yes," said one, stepping forward and holding up his hand, "thou owest me three drachms of silver, O Apostle of God."

My hand was already raised to strike the wretch to the earth, when Mohammed bade Othman, who was his secretary, pay the debt instantly, and then, turning to the man, he said, with a tremor in his voice and tears in his eyes:

"I thank thee, friend, that thou hast accused me here rather than at the bar of God."

Thus, at the end of his life and at the zenith of his power and glory, spoke the man whom the liars of after ages have called an imposter and a charlatan.

A few days after this last sermon he set out from Mecca to Medina, for, as he told us, he felt that death was very near, and he chose to die in that city, which, in the dark days of the Flight, had opened its gates to him when he was a fugitive from the city of his birth.

Borne in a litter surrounded by all his family and friends and escorted by five thousand horse of the victorious army of Syria, the Prophet of Islam made his last earthly journey.

When he reached his house his first care was to set his household in order, to free all his slaves, and settle the last of his earthly affairs. Then, in a plain chamber in a house that was no better than any other citizen might have owned, the giver of a new faith and the undisputed lord of millions laid himself down to die on a Syrian carpet spread upon the floor, with his head resting in the lap of Ayesha, his best beloved.

Derar and I stood guard at the open door of the chamber, striving hard not to break the silence with the sobs that shook our labouring breasts. Inside, Ali, his kinsman, and Abu Bekr, the Companion of the Flight, watched the fading life-spark and listened for his last words, and outside the streets and squares were thronged with silent crowds, stricken dumb by the coming calamity which men in their worship of him had come to believe impossible.

We heard his laboured breathing, broken by a few short gasps of pain, and then Ali came to the door, treading softly, and beckoned to us to come in. As we went and stood at his feet, with crossed hands and downcast head, he opened his eyes and looked at us, and made a faint sign as though of farewell with his right hand; then we saw his lips move, and strained our ears to catch what we all felt must be his last words on earth. Like an echo from the world to which his mighty spirit was already taking wing they came:

"Allah, pardon my sins! Farewell! I go to meet my fellow-citizens on high. Be true to the Faith—Paradise—Paradise!"

The last word—the watchword of a thousand victories since then, came clear and strong from his lips, and as it left them his head fell back in Ayesha's lap. And so died the greatest man that ever was born of woman.

We buried him in the same spot of earth on which he died, and there to-day you will find his tomb where once stood his dwelling-house. Though he had named no successor, our choice fell, as you know, on Abu Bekr, the venerable Companion of the Flight, and scarcely was he proclaimed Khalif than the injunctions of the Prophet were followed, and the Holy War was begun in deadly earnest.

First I was sent at the head of 5,000 horse and 10,000 footmen into Irak, beyond the great mounds of ruins where once Babylon, the twin-sister city of ancient Nineveh, had stood in all the pride of the arrogant glory which now lay humbled beneath the desert dust, and there, as you may read in your histories, we fought many battles and won many victories for the Faith against the Magians and other idolaters, and, by the grace of Allah, came back with much glory and profit.

When we reached Medina we learnt that Heraclius had at length awakened from his sloth, and was making ready to sweep us from the earth. The Khalif had already sent messages to all the lands of Islam, and in answer to his call more than 50,000 warriors, horse and foot, set forth one glorious morning in spring from Medina to Damascus.

I have no space to tell you of the minor battles that we fought on the way, or how the strong city of Bozra fell, sold into our hands by Romanus, the traitor—may his name be for ever infamous!—for deeds more worth the telling were soon to be done under the walls of Damascus, and on the fields of Aiznadin and Yermouk.

The twentieth day from Medina saw us encamped amidst the verdant fields and vineyards and palm-groves surrounding that ancient City of the Sweet Waters, and when I rode forth from our camp in the early morning with Zoraida, who—as I have little need to tell you—had come with her war-maidens to share our glory, and saw the fair city lying before us surrounded by its lines of trees and triple walls, I found it so little altered that I turned and said, laughing, to her:

"This is not the first time thine eyes or mine have looked on this sweet city, Zoraida. Dost thou find it much changed since the time when Terai of Armen and Zillah, the twin-queen of Sabæa, journeyed through it together—ay, through those very gates and along that very road between the cypresses down yonder from the court of the Tiger-Lord to the throne of Solomon in Salem?"

"It seems that I have seen some such city in my dream, O Khalid!" she said smiling back at me a trifle sadly. "Yet to me it is but a dream. But to thee, doubtless—Ah! look yonder, now dost thou remember something older than that? Dost thou remember thy fight with Nimrod beneath the walls of Nineveh? Dost not yonder Roman, in all his gallant finery at the head of his troop beneath the gate-tower yonder, remind thee somewhat of the Great King?"

"Ay, to look at him he does!" I said, laughing again, and so in truth he did at that distance, with his gold bedecked armour, his shining helm, and flowing plume. "Stay thou here, Zoraida, within reach of our outposts, and thou shalt see a pretty fight if he will come out and meet me."

"Well said, Sword of God; go forth and prosper for the Faith!" she replied, bravely enough, yet with just such a pallor on her cheeks and just such a smile on her lips as I had seen when Ilma bade me good-speed as I rode forth to meet that mighty warrior of old, between the hosts of Armen and Asshur.

I was armed with sword and spear and buckler, and as I went I shook my spear aloft, and presently one of the troop rode out to meet me, and asked me if I had come to parley.

"Parley!" I said, laughing at him in my scorn. "Dost thou think that a True Believer comes to parley with idolaters? Get thee back and tell thy master, yonder dainty knight in the golden harness, that if he hath the heart to break a spear for his faith a simple soldier of Islam awaits him here."

"Yonder knight," said the fellow, haughtily, "is John of Damascus, a knight and captain of the Roman Empire, and such as he do not accept single combat with such as thee."

"With such as me, thou fool!" I shouted, my ever-ready blood all aflame at the insult. "Then go and tell him that Khalid, the Sword of God, is here, and holds himself equal to the best knight in all the empire of Heraclius."

At the mention of my name, which was already a word of terror through all the land of Syria, the fellow shrank back and crossed himself as though he had met one of the demons of his faith, and without another word turned his horse and galloped back to the gate.

I saw him hold a brief parley with his leader, and then, to his honour, that gaily-harnessed, white plumed, golden knight rode forth to meet me. At five hundred paces distance we saluted with our spears, and then down went his long steel-tipped shaft, his plumed head was lowered almost to his horse's neck, and his brazen buckler shone like a golden sun in the morning light as he came thundering on towards me.

I waited till he was within a hundred paces of me, and then a twitch to the rein and a touch of my heel sent Tigrol with a single bound some half-dozen paces out of his path. It was too late for him to turn his heavy war-horse, and he pounded past me, shaking the earth as he went, while I cantered round behind him, laughing at him as he sat back in his saddle with his feet thrust out in front, striving to rein in his charger before it took him, as it well nigh did, into the midst of a swarm of my men, who had turned out to see the fun.

Yet he had but little cause for alarm, for seeing what was going on, not a sword nor a lance would have been raised against him even if he had galloped through the midst of them. As it was he pulled his horse round and rode along their front, and they stood silent, watching him with that respect which no difference of creed or nation can destroy in the heart of one good soldier for another.

But before he could come round and get his horse into the charging stride again I was on him, and he had only time to get lance and shield in place and make a forward dash at me before we met with a crash and a clash that burst our two shields asunder, splintered our lances to the hafts, and flung our two chargers back upon their haunches. There we sat for a moment staring and laughing at each other as a great shout of praise for him went up from my men, for they had never seen a horseman before who had taken my charge and kept his seat.

"Well ridden, Roman!" I cried. "Are there many more like thee in Damascus, for, if so, we shall have a right merry time of it?"

And even as I spoke my long sword was out, and as Tigrol recovered himself I lashed out at him with a sweeping stroke that would have taken his head from his shoulders had it but reached him fairly.

He saw it coming, and dropped his head just in time to save it, so that the sweeping blade shore the crest and plume of his helm away, but did him no further hurt. At the same instant he let out at me with the point, and I, swerving aside in my saddle, took the stroke between my arm and my side, holding the sword there for just one instant, and then as he wrenched it out my own blade came swinging back. His guard went up to save his head, the steel of Armen and of Damascus met with a ringing clash, and the next instant the fragments of his blade were scattered on the earth beside us.

"Magic! Magic!" he cried, as the battle-flush died out of his face. "That blade of thine was forged by demons, for no honest steel could have done that."

"Magic or no magic, good knight," I laughed, a trifle grimly, "the time has come for thee to yield or have thy head split, so say which shall it be."

"I never yielded to Christian or Infidel yet, nor will I now," he said, looking me full in the eyes. "So strike!"

My sword-arm went up, but my blade remained poised aloft in mid-air. I dropped the point and sent it rattling back into the sheath, for he was too brave a man to slay unarmed.

So, while he was sitting wondering at me, I sent Tigrol with a bound against his horse's flank, and as he staggered I reached out and flung my arms about his waist—in no gentle clasp, I can tell you—and then, putting forth all my strength, I hove him clear out of the saddle, flung him across my own saddle-bow, and bore him kicking and wriggling and cursing into our own camp amidst the laughing shouts of my own men.

There I left him in safe keeping, the most crestfallen man in Syria that morning, and, taking a new lance and buckler from Derar, made ready to ride out into the open again to seek another foe.

"But surely thou art fatigued with wrestling with that dog, O Khalid!" he said. "Stay thou here and get thy breath back, and let me go and meet this next one."

"Nay, O Derar!" I said, as I took the weapons from him. "That was but a gentle bit of sport, and we shall all rest in the world to come. Let me meet this one and thou shalt take the next."

And with that I rode off to meet the second champion who had already ridden out from the walls against me—a fine, burly warrior, splendidly dressed and armed after that pretty Byzantine fashion which gave us such dainty spoils in combats such as these. He was warier if no braver than John had been, and for a good half-hour by the sun we wheeled and dodged and circled about each other in the open space between the now crowded walls of the city and our own camp, out of which thousands had come to see the sport.

At last my horse stumbled on a loose stone and broke his stride, and like a flash the warrior was upon me. I dropped my spear and jumped from the saddle just as Tigrol, with a savage scream, swung round on his haunches and fixed his great teeth in his charger's muzzle, and then down went the rider and the two horses, and all you could see for the moment was a cloud of dust, a gleam of armour, and writhing arms and legs and kicking hoofs.

I, like a fool, stood laughing at the sight, and loth to slay a man in such a sorry plight. And while I was standing there leaning on my sword, he played off on me as neat a trick as ever was seen in the merry game of war. Tigrol was on his feet first, and, as I live, he had scarcely snorted the dust out of his nostrils before that Unbeliever had vaulted on his back and was careering away, waving his sword in triumph above his head.

You may think of the foolish figure I cut, standing there staring after my own horse with my enemy on his back, and with the shouts of laughter and yells of derision upon the city walls ringing in my ears. But I had short space in which to curse my folly, for the Unbeliever soon pulled Tigrol round, picked up a lance that one of his men had galloped out to give him, and then came at me where I stood, armed only with my sword.

He knew that I should be loth to slay my own beast, as I must have done to bring him down, and so I doubt not counted on an easy victory; but here he reckoned without that sweet friendship that there ever was between the Arab horseman and his charger.

When he was fifty paces off I jumped aside and whistled my familiar call to Tigrol. Obedient as a dog, he stopped and came trotting to me, bearing that blaspheming Unbeliever on his back, a picture of helpless rage and bewilderment for Gods and men to laugh at. In vain he drove his cruel spurs into the brave beast's flanks; in vain he tugged at the bridle and sawed at the bit. Not a foot did he swerve to right or left, nor by a single stride did he increase his pace.

I dropped my sword into the sheath, and, watching my chance, took Tigrol by the tail, and then shouting to him to stand still, I vaulted on his haunches, and the next instant my two hands were round the Unbeliever's throat choking the life out of him. It was in vain that he tried to turn and pierce me with his sword, for it was too long for such close quarters. He kicked at me with his spurred heels, gashing and scoring my legs with the rowels, and fiercely did he strive to fling himself to the ground and drag me with him.

I held his throat till his face went black and his head dropped forward and his struggles ceased. Then I shouted again to Tigrol, and he trotted off to the camp amidst such a storm of yells and laughter and such mingled shouts of rage and triumph as the grey walls of Damascus had never heard before. I flung my second captive to the earth when we got in, and jumping down beside him, I said to those who came thronging about me with their praises:

"Nay, by Allah! that is Tigrol's victory and Tigrol's prize, for if he had been as great a fool as his master, he would have been the servant of an Unbeliever, and my head would have paid for my folly by this time."

"Nevertheless, if I have such good fortune as thine I shall be well content," said Derar, as he rode past me out into the open space to seek game for his sword and spear.

But there was no more fighting that day, for, though he rode six times up and down before the gate, swinging his lance and shouting his defiances, there was not a knight in all Damascus hardy enough to come out and fight him after what had been seen. So at last he rode back, the angriest man in all our camp, swearing all the oaths that our Arab tongue could give him, and that, I can tell you, is not a few.

A few nights after this we were roused by a great ringing of bells and shouts of jubilation in the city, and, while we were wondering what it was all about, one of our men who had been taken prisoner in a sally dropped from the walls at the risk of his neck, and came to tell us that news had been received in the city that Heraclius was sending a great army from Emessa to the relief of Damascus. To have stayed before the walls would have been to have placed ourselves between two fires, so Abu Obeidah summoned a council forthwith, and by morning we had broken up our camp, and our main body was already moving towards the east, for it had been decided to stake the fate of Syria upon a single battle.

Then the gates of the city were flung open, and long streams of horse and foot came pouring out amidst waving banners and clanging bells and exultant shouts, believing that Damascus was already delivered, and that we were about to be crushed between them and the army of Heraclius. So we faced about, and that day we fought as bitter a battle as blood was ever shed in, for we were fighting for all that we had won and all that we hoped to win, and when it was over not ten out of each hundred Unbelievers were able to crawl back to the city to tell what had befallen them.

But for all our victory we were greatly weakened, and many a True Believer went that day to Paradise; so, knowing that our next fight must decide our fate and Syria's, I sent an urgent message to Amru, who was on the borders of Palestine, bidding him come with all speed and all his men to meet us at Aiznadin, and then, leaving Damascus weeping and trembling behind us, we pressed forward to that famous field where, as it was written, the Roman and the Moslem were to meet in the sternest struggle that had yet tried their strength and valour.

CHAPTER XIV

THROUGH STRIFE TO REST

WHEN the sun of the 13th of July, in the year 633 of your reckoning, rose over the broad, bare plain of Aiznadin, it shone upon the two greatest hosts that had yet faced each other to do battle for the supremacy of Cross or Crescent. Under our standards nearly sixty thousand Moslems—horse and foot and camel riders—were ranged in long, open files of footmen and ever-moving clouds of cavalry, and over against us was the great army of Heraclius, well nigh a hundred thousand strong, shining bravely with gold and brass and steel, and gay with nodding plumes and flaunting banners.

We had determined not to attack till the cool of the evening unless, indeed, the Romans attacked us first; but this delay was too much for the wild spirit of Derar to bear, for he was still burning with generous longing to outdo that which he had seen me do under the walls of Damascus, and—by the glory of Allah! I write it with more pride and joy than I have written of my own poor doings—he did that which was in his heart, and achieved that day the greatest feat of arms that was done in all our wars.

In the face of all that mighty host he rode out alone, armed with his single spear, and galloped up and down the front counting the cohorts and regiments as though he were their own general. Presently a troop of thirty Roman horse rode out to surround him, I doubt not, meaning and honestly thinking to take him in, whether dead or alive. As soon as he saw them his long spear went down, his buckler went up, and, like a shaft from a well-strung bow, he charged fairly into the midst of them.

One after another he picked them out and rode them down, the rest labouring after him vainly on their clumsy chargers, until seventeen out of the thirty that had come out to take him lay stark and still upon the plain. Then the others felt their hearts turn to water, and, amidst the jibes and laughter of all our host, made the best speed they could back to the shelter of their own lines.

When Derar came in laughing and panting after his glorious work, Abu Obeidah gently chided him for so rashly risking so valuable a life to Islam, and he replied, humbly, for he was as modest a warrior as ever thirsted for a foeman's blood:

"Nay, Companion of the Prophet, it was not my fault. I went out but to see what their strength was, and those dogs came out and attacked me first, so what could I do but strike back, for surely thou wouldst not have had a True Believer show his back to the Infidels?"

At which old Abu stroked his beard and laughed, as, indeed, none of us who heard him could help doing, and sent him to the rear to have his wounds dressed, and, since Zoraida dressed them with her own hands, I soon caught myself envying him his wounds even more than I did the glory he had won.

But I soon had other things to think of, for what Derar had done had stricken such terror into the hearts of the Unbelievers that they sent an embassy out to us, headed by an aged Greek, which sought to bribe with gold and the fineries of Byzantium to return to our homes and leave them in peace. And to them old Abu replied:

"O ye unbelieving dogs and cowards to boot! Is your host smaller than ours that you come with such offers as these? Know ye not that ye have but three choices—the Koran, the tribute, or the sword? Know ye not, too, that we are a people whose delight is in war rather than in peace? Get ye back to your master, and tell him that we despise your pitiful alms, since before morning we shall be masters of your wealth and all ye have."

So they went back silent and crestfallen, and when the last hour of prayer had come and gone we moved out to the battle.

First we threw out to right and left swarms of lancers and mounted archers, who galled the foe with an incessant rain of arrows; and then our footmen charged their front—that front which still preserved the name and shape of the Roman phalanx—flinging themselves heedlessly on the spears, and, as the front ranks went down, those behind climbed up over them and tore the bucklers apart with their hands, and then, with sword and axe and javelin, and the short Arab spear that our foes had long since learned to dread, hacked and hewed their way foot by foot and yard by yard through the breaking ranks, ever followed by fresh swarms of the furious death-defying tribesmen until soon a good half of our infantry were fighting in the midst of the vast unwieldy mass of men which at sundown had been the Roman army.

All the while our swiftly-moving clouds of horse hurled themselves in charge after charge on broken front and flank and rear; and so we fought on, hand to hand, foot to foot, and horse to horse until morning dawned over the red field of Aiznadin, only to behold the flying remnants of the mighty host of Rome being ridden down and slaughtered by our horsemen, while the footmen were collecting such a booty as had never fallen to our swords before.

Then we returned to Damascus, and for seventy long and weary days we kept our beleaguering camp about its gates and before its walls, till at last famine came to fight for us, and the stubborn gates were opened. Yet it was the will of Allah, that the Unbelievers should pay some price of blood for their obstinacy, for it so chanced at the very hour the embassy came from the southern gate to treat with Abu Obeidah that Derar and I, with five thousand of our starkest veterans, had scaled the walls to the north, and burst, sword in hand, into the streets.

We fought our way in a straight line through the heart of the city, and, just as we thought that Damascus was at last the prize of our swords, there in the Gate of Abraham, we came full on Abu Obeidah in the midst of a mob of priests and monks, who were imploring him to stay our arms. The city was ours, but, alas! only half won by the sword. Never was I nearer disobeying the commands of a superior than I was then, for my heart was ablaze with the lust of battle, and the savage blood-hunger was strong upon me.

But in vain I raged and entreated by turns, until at last the venerable Companion of the Prophet reduced me to silence and submission by raising his arms above his head, and crying:

"O Khalid, knowest thou not that the word of a Moslem is sacred? Behold Allah has given the city into my hands by the surrender of its governors, and I have given my pledge for its safety. If thou shouldst break that pledge, then all the glory thou hast won would be covered by a greater shame, for only over my dead body couldst thou continue the way of blood!"

At that my hot heart cooled, and I bowed my head abashed, so we made an agreement which divided the citybetween us, and by virtue of that compact there has been a Christian colony in the Moslem city of Damascus dwelling at peace under the banner of the Prophet from that day to this.

For a month we rested in the City of Sweet Waters, and during that month we heard that Allah had taken Abu Bekr to Paradise, and that Omar reigned as Khalif in his stead. After this came the stirring news that the Emperor was about to make one last struggle for the province that we had almost wrested from his grasp, and was pouring troops into Syria by land and sea from Europe and the countries to the south of the Euxine.

We moved out with every man we could command, and at our old camp in Emessa we were joined by a fresh force of ten thousand Moslems whom Omar had sent to strengthen our hands, and thence we marched to Yermouk, scattering a force of six thousand idolatrous Arabs of the tribe of Gassan on our way. Hard by Bozra, where the streams of Mount Hermon descend in their swift courses to the Plain of the Ten Cities, the last army of the Romans was drawn up on the banks of the Yermouk, not far from where it flows into the lake of Tiberias.

On the eve of the battle Abu called me to his tent and gave the supreme command into my hands, for he was old and sick, and no longer fit to take the field, and so he had piously determined to devote himself to praying for our arms and tending the wounded.

I took my place with my own troop in the van, with Derar on my right and Amru on my left. In the centre was the main body of our footmen; behind these Zoraida had taken her place with her war-maidens, so that those who would retreat would have to do so under the fire of their eyes and the lashes of their scornful tongues; and in the rear of all stood the venerable Companion of the Prophet, flying the yellow banner which had been borne before the Prophet in the fight of Chiaban; and about him were the wives and children of many a hundred True Believers. The line they made was a barrier such as no man with the heart of a soldier in him could pass.

There was little time for talking, so, as I rode along the ranks for the last time, pointing to front and rear with my sword, I shouted:

"Victory and Paradise are before you, shame and the fires of Hell are behind you. Remember that, and forget not that you are fighting under the eyes of Allah!"

Scarce had the thunderous shout that greeted my words died away, when the Roman trumpets sounded and the grim, bloody work began. Five cohorts of the heavy Roman cavalry came forward at a swinging trot, which soon broke into a gallop, and like an avalanche of steel and horse-flesh they burst upon our right flank, riding down horse and man by sheer weight, and driving those that were left in upon the main body.

Thrice that terrible charge was repeated, and thrice by weight of horse and man and armour they forced us back, broken and bleeding in spite of all our utmost valour could do. But thrice also the fierce reproaches and bitter scorn of Zoraida and her maidens sent us back as the Romans retreated, rolled back in turn by the fury of our desperation.

The third time Zoraida, her eyes aflame with anger and shame, swung her sword aloft, and crying out:

"After me, maidens of Islam; let us show these men how women can fight!" forced her way through the loose ranks, and at the head of her troop charged full upon the Roman centre.

A cry of rage and agony burst from my lips as I saw my darling going to what must be her certain death, and in that instant the same fury that possessed me blazed up in the heart of every Moslem who saw that glorious example of fatal daring. I raised myself in my stirrups, swung my great blade round my helm, and shouted, I know not what, for it was drowned in such a roar of mingled rage and shame for forty thousand throats that the air shook with it as though a tempest had broken loose.

Then, seeing nothing, thinking of nothing but that gallant little troop of heroines charging down the slopes with Zoraida at their head, I shouted to Tigrol, and away I went at a gallop, followed by all that mighty flood of rage and valour seething behind me, and, forty thousand strong, we burst in one wild charge upon the solid ranks of Rome.

What followed I know not, saving only one thing. I saw the white plume that Zoraida wore in her steel cap floating hither and thither like a snow-flake on the dark, roaring battle-tide. The shock and the crash of our irresistible onset came and passed, and I felt myself being borne towards it by the press of the crowding warriors behind me.

I reached it, and for a moment I and my darling fought side by side, slowly hewing our way through the deadly press about us. Then suddenly it opened, men and horses pushed their way to right and left in front of us, a blare of trumpets rang shrill above the din of war, and down the lane that was made a fresh body of Roman horse came thundering full tilt at us, with levelled spears, three abreast,

"Get behind me, Zoraida!" I shouted, driving Tigrol in front of her, and bracing myself in the saddle to receive the shock. I took one of the first three spears on my buckler, and dashed it aside. A second I shore through with one desperate cut of my big sword, but the third passed me. I would to Allah it had rather pierced me to the heart, for the next moment I heard a shrill, gasping cry behind me that smote me like a dagger of ice to the heart. I dared not look back, knowing all too well what I should see, but, with a cry more like that of a wild beast than a man, I shouted:

"The curse of Allah on thee, thou dog! Get thee to thy companions in Hell!" and then down came my vengeful blade with such a stroke as I had never made before on the head of him who held that fatal lance. Helm and skull spilt asunder like a severed orange, and as he dropped I caught his lance, and, careless of the charge that swept past me, I looked back along the shaft.

Alas! Zoraida's hands grasped the other end of it, and she sat swaying in her saddle white as death—nay, already half-dead, for the point was well-nigh buried in her breast.

One last look of love shone at me through the battle-dust out of her glazing eyes, her lips moved in one last smile, at once a greeting and farewell, and then her dear head drooped forward, and, just as she was falling from her saddle, I snatched the accursed spear from the wound, flung my left arm about her, and lifted her on to the saddle in front of me. In vain my tears and kisses fell thick on the cold loveliness of her upturned face as it lay upon my tortured breast. She was dead—dead as she had been when my hand had driven her dagger through her heart in our desert grave beyond Nineveh, and once more she had gone to the stars before me.

Clasping her dear dead body close to me with my left arm, swinging my great sword fiercely and fast with my right, and guiding Tigrol with my knees, I fought my way out of the battlepress, careless in the cold fury of my despair whether I came out of it alive, or whether one of all the thousand lances and swords that were thrusting and waving about me struck me from the saddle and flung us both down, to be trampled out of human shape by the stamping hoofs and feet that were churning up the bloody mire of the battle-plain.

Then I rode back to the front with but a single thought in that heavy heart of mine. I found Derar and Amru gathering the flower of our remaining horsemen together to take a dear and deadly vengeance for the loss that had befallen us. The Romans had drawn back into the angle between the river and the hills, and on our side the hour of evening prayer had been sounded, and Abu, with the banner of the Prophet in his hand, had recited the prayers, and was bidding us avenge the blood of the True Believers who had fallen.

So our prayers rose up into the still evening air, mingled with the songs of the Unbelievers; but ere these last were finished there rang out from thirty thousand Moslem throats the long-drawn, screaming battle-cry:

"*La I'laba illa Allah—illa Allah—Allah—hu——!*" and down the slope we swept, rank after rank, wave after wave, in one fierce, fiery, torrent of passionate valour and burning vengeance.

Never did the good steel of Armen do such fierce and bloody work as it did in that brief stormy hour of sad triumph and bitter-sweet revenge. I fought on in mad, blind desperation, with gallant Derar at my side, his own heart hot, and his own arm nerved by just such savage sorrow as mine were, and with the same thoughts burning in his brain to kill, and kill, and kill until the last Roman left alive had paid for that dear life, whose quenching had robbed Islam of its brightest earthly light.

The night was far spent when the triumph of the Yermouk was complete. Every Unbeliever that had not fled was slain, for we knew that we had broken down the supreme stand of the legions of Heraclius, and we meant that he should never take the field again—as in good truth he never did—and when the snowy peaks of Hermon began to redden in the light of dawn Syria was ours, all save Antioch and Aleppo, and Salem, the Holy City.

After Mecca and Medina we revered Jerusalem as the holiest city in the world, for the memory of Moses and Solomon and Issa; so it did not take us long to determine that it should be the next and greatest prize of our arms. We returned to Damascus for a month of rest and leisure, and to await reinforcements from Arabia and Irak, and then we advanced on Salem.

From the same hill by Bethany whence, riding by Zillah's side, I had seen the Holy City shining in all the glory that Solomon had shed upon it, I beheld it again, hoary with the added age of seventeen centuries, and shorn of nearly all its ancient splendours, yet grey and grim and stern, throned on its rugged hills, and beleaguered on all sides by the mighty host that we had brought against it.

It was not till many weeks had passed and famine and pestilence had begun to fight for us in the streets and houses, the gate at the end of the street which was once called Beautiful opened, and Sophronius the Patriarch came forth at the head of a double line of priests and monks to treat with Abu Obeidah for its surrender. He gave him the inevitable conditions—the Koran, the sword, or the tribute—and, as you know, he chose the last, yet himself adding to these a fourth, that the most holy city in the world should be delivered to none other than the Commander of the Faithful himself.

This was accepted, for in truth it was a worthy one, and swift messengers were at once despatched to Medina acquainting Omar with what had happened. Ten days after that we heard that he was coming, and I, with a thousand horse, rode out to meet him, tricked out in all the finery that we had won from our enemies; and lo! to our surprise and shame, we found the successor of the Prophet and the sovereign lord of Arabia and Syria and Persia riding alone, save for the escort of half-a-dozen horsemen, on an old red camel, with a bag of corn, another of dates, a wooden dish, and a leathern bottle of water slung across his saddle.

When he came in sight of the city, he raised his hands aloft, and cried:—

"God is victorious! O Allah, give us an easy conquest!" And then he rode down and pitched his tent of camel hair before the gate, and sat on the ground in front of it waiting for the Patriarch to come forth. What remained to be settled was soon done. Sophronius came out and laid the keys at his feet, and Omar, after greeting him courteously, mounted his camel and rode back with him into the city, discoursing quietly on the great deeds of which it had been the scene, as though he had been an honoured visitor and guest instead of a conqueror.

Not a life was taken, not the value of a piece of gold was stolen, when Salem passed from the dominion of the Cross to the rule of the Crescent, and so rigidly did Omar observe the terms he had made that, when he and I were standing that evening with Sophronius on the steps of the Church of the Sepulchre as the hour of evening prayer was proclaimed, he turned and said to me:

"Come, Khalid, we will pray yonder in the street."

"Why should not my lord pray here?" said the Patriarch, bowing before him. "Is the street a holier place than this?"

"Nay, by far less holy, Sophronius!" replied Omar with a smile. "But did we pray here might not the Moslems of a future age take from our example an excuse to break the treaty?"

And with that he went down into the street, and I followed him.

When we had done what the Faith required, I went back and said:

"Did that Roman soldier, the follower of Darus, bring my message to thee, O Sophronius, and does my mail still hang on the walls of thy church?"

"It is even so, O Wanderer through the Ages," he replied, speaking slowly and steadily, and yet like one in a dream. "Thou art he who died yonder on Calvary in the same hour that the Lord died on the Cross. Now thou boastest thyself as the victorious champion of another faith, yet thy lesson is not all learned. Follow me, and thou shalt learn more."

So I went with him into the dim interior of the church, and there, hanging before a crucifix on the wall, he showed me my long-lost, oft longed-for shirt of mail. He took it down and gave it to me, saying:

"There, thou hast that which is thine again. Now, listen to me, Khalid, so-called Sword of God and soldier of Islam.

Thou hast been a scourge on earth to those who call themselves by the name of Him whose lowliness they have mocked with their pomps and vanities. In the days to come thou shalt wear thy mail again, and over it on thy breast thou shalt wear that holy Symbol which now thou dost deride and blaspheme, albeit in the honesty of thy ignorance. Ay, thou mayest hear with wonder now, yet when next thou seest the walls of Jerusalem remember what I have said, and keep my words fresh in thy heart!"

I looked down into his steady old eyes as I took the mail from him, and, though what he had said was rankest blasphemy to my Moslem ears, I thought of all the faiths that I had seen rise and fall, and the fierce words I would have spoken to another died ere they reached my lips.

So, bending my head in an impulse too swift for me to control it, I said quietly, and humbly:

"The will of the Invisible is inscrutable, yet what is written shall be done, and so may thy words come true. Fear not, I will remember!"

Then I turned and left the church in silence, and the next day I set out, with my breast once more covered by my own dear mail, at the head of the army of Syria northward to Antioch. And by the mercy of Allah we subdued not only Antioch and Cæsarea and Aleppo, but Tripoli and Ancient Tyre herself were delivered into our hands, and then all the cities of the coast submitted, and there was no town in all Syria and Palestine that did not own our sway.

But to me the swift succeeding triumphs brought but little joy, for the brightest gem in the diadem of victory was no longer within my reach. For the fourth time the cruel hand of my bitter fate had snatched the full cup of love from my lips, and poured its sweet wine on to the thirsty earth at my feet.

For such sorrow as mine there was but one anodyne—the fierce blood-drunkenness of ceaseless war; so when Syria was subdued I joined the army of Persia, and after the sack of Ctesiphon feasted with Derar and Said and Ali in the White Palace of Chosroes.

Later on I fought half-naked, seeking death in a thousand welcome perils, in the great fight of Nehavend, that "victory of victories," which gave us all the lands of Persia from the Tigris to the Oxus, and then, with the wound in my heart unhealed, and the thirst of my soul unquenched, I followed Amru into Egypt, and there, like a shadow on a wall, I who had been Khalid, the Sword of God, the Victor of Damascus, Aiznadin, and Yermouk, the Conqueror of Syria, and the most brilliant figure in all the bright pageantry of that glorious war—I, the paladin and hero of Islam, vanished so utterly from the sight of my comrades, that, knowing not where I had died, they built my tomb at Emessa beside the grave of Zoraida.

After a siege of seven months we stormed the strong town of Babylon and the Roman camp which protected the eastern end of the boat-bridge across the Nile to Memphis, carried the island of Rhouda in the centre of the river in one day of furious fighting, and drove the Greeks and Egyptians into the water.

That night, impelled by what I thought was only curiosity to see once more that ancient city which I had seen in the days of Solomon, and which had been my home when Cleopatra was Queen in Egypt, I crossed to the western bank and wandered away amidst the mighty maze of ages-old ruins of temples and palaces that I had beheld in all their pride, until I found myself standing before a great dark pylon which in an instant I recognised as the entrance to the Temple of Ptah.

I passed through, and there, in the grey cliff-like wall before me, perfect as it had been seven hundred years before, was the low square door closed by its smooth granite slab. I remembered what Amemphis had done to open it, and the fancy took me to try and do the same. I put my foot where his had been, and my right hand found the lotus flower, whose secret was now perchance lost for ever.

I pressed, and the mighty stone descended, the hidden machinery working as perfectly and silently as it had done in the remote ages when it was first set up. I stepped over into the cool dark space beyond. My foot touched a stone and it moved beneath me, and ere I could turn back the door had risen behind me.

In an instant I was as utterly lost to the outer world as though I had been buried fathoms deep beneath the everlasting rocks of Elburz, yet I cared nothing for the fate that was so near, and which might have been so appalling to another. I had sought death too often and too eagerly to trouble about the form in which it came, so with even, steady steps I went on towards where I thought the inner hall lay.

Then—it might have been but the effect of my dreaming fancy, or it might have been one of those things which it is not given to man to explain—I saw a dim, white misty light hovering in the midst of the darkness before me. I went on towards it, and as I approached, it grew until I could see in the midst of it the altar of Isis and the throne in which Cleopatra had sat the night she had taken that oath whose breaking was her own shame and Egypt's ruin.

"Why should not Khalid the Moslem sit in the throne of the Pharaohs?"

The words came unbidden to my lips, and their echoes whispered weirdly around me in the gloom and the silence. I obeyed the impulse that had spoken, and sat down with my feet on the Sphinx. I was weary with hard fighting, and the throne-seat was easy and comfortable as a couch, so my head went back against the faded dusty cushions, and my eyelids drooped, and I slept.

Then, for the fourth time, the curtain of oblivion fell across the portals of my senses, and I drifted sleeping down the Stream of Time which flows out of the afterglow of the evening of the Past into the foreglow of the Future's dawn.

CHAPTER XV

THE SEA-WOLVES' GUEST

A STREAM of strong, warm light slowly flowing over my brow and face awoke me. I opened my dazzled eyes, and saw dimly a long, thin beam of sunlight, outspread like a fan, falling from a slit high up in the roof of the temple, down on to the throne-seat where I was resting, half sitting, half reclining.

I stretched out my aching limbs, shaking the dust of my crumbled garments from them as I did so, and then rose, stiff and stumbling, to my feet, with a low, groaning cry, rather of sorrow than of wonder, for my heart had been heavy when the welcome sleep had come to my eyes, and it was heavy still, weighed down by the sad though still-living memory of all that I had lost, and oppressed by the dumb, vague apprehension of that which, perchance, I was to win and lose again, and the mystery of the doom which still held me in its invisible toils.

I looked up at the light-beam still falling bright athwart the gloom of the great chamber, and, as I gazed at it with blinking eyes, I remembered that Amemphis had told me—alas! how many years or centuries before?—that there was such an opening as this which pierced the great roof-stones of the temple in such a fashion that once in a cycle of five hundred and fifty years the moon and sun alternately sent a beam of light through it on to the throne-seat of Ptah.

After this I remembered the white light that had shone before me as I entered the temple—which could scarcely have been anything else but the moon-ray keeping its appointed watch, and, by some mysterious decree of the Powers which ordain the destinies of men, guiding me to my resting-place. Therefore the coming of this sunbeam marked the passage of at least the half-cycle of five hundred and fifty years.

Now I had entered the temple in the Year of the Flight 18 according to the Moslem reckoning, which was the year of the Christian era 640, and, therefore, by the reckoning of the West this must be the Year of the Lord 1190. Thus, if this were so, a space of time had passed very nearly equal to that which had elapsed from the day I had laid down to die on Calvary to the day when my first vision of recollection had come to find me a goat-herd on the Arabian hills.

I shook the dust from my limbs and looked at myself and found that I might well have begun the world again in worse plight. The centuries had passed but lightly over me, robbing me only of that which could easily be replaced. My mail was whole, and, but for the dust between its links, as bright as ever. I pulled my sword out of the sheath, and let the sun-ray fall along the glorious blade, and found its lustre undimmed by a single speck of rust.

Then I sent it back into the sheath, and graver thoughts came to me. I was hungry and thirsty, and I was a prisoner in the temple, for, though I could open the door to come in, I neither knew how to open it from the inside, nor was there any light at that end of the temple by which I could seek for the secret. Had I, then, but awakened from the death-sleep to perish anew of hunger and thirst in the great gloomy temple like a wolf in a pit-trap?

Surely not, and yet how was I to escape from this mighty tomb of age-enduring stone, this vast gloomy maze of endless chambers and galleries, surrounded for all I knew by yet vaster wildernesses of ruins? As I stood thinking of this, and striving to recollect whether Amemphis had not given me some clue to the opening of the door by which I had entered, I watched the sunbeam climb slowly up from the back of the throne-seat till it rested on the carved symbol of Isis over the altar, and just under the horned disk I saw two lotus leaves carved in relief on the stone, and between them in the hermetic character a chiselled tracing, which read:

"*Over the altar is the way to light and the means of life.*"

There were two meanings in this, as any one might see that had eyes to see. I sprang on to the throne-seat, and, kneeling on the altar, I pressed on the lotus leaves just as the sunbeam vanished and left me in utter darkness. Then as I pressed harder, I felt the wall in front of me swing back. I stretched out my arms into the void beyond, and felt nothing on either side. Then I put them down and they rested on a smooth, sloping surface of stone.

Here was the way, but where was the light; for all was pitchy darkness in front of me, though the air of the gallery, or whatever it might be, was cool and fresh, and I felt a faint stream of air blowing on my face as I leant into the void. I groped about with my hands till I found that behind the altar there was a square chamber of some considerable size. I crawled in, still feeling about me, and soon to my pleasure put my hand on what it recognised as an old-fashioned Egyptian tinder-box.

With the help of this I soon got a light, and lit one of two or three wax torches lying on the floor of the store-room, for such in truth, it appeared to be. In one corner were some green glass bottles and a flagon, and a little heap of dried dates and nuts. I was not long knocking the neck off one of the bottles, and washing the dust of centuries out of my throat with a draught of the true old mellow wine of Cos, such as I had pledged Cleopatra in more than a thousand years before. This done, my eye next fell upon a large roll of papyrus, on which, written in the hermetic character, I saw the first name I had borne on earth.

Wondering not a little at this, I took it up and opened it and read in the same writing on the inside of it as follows:

"To him who have slept and awakened, Greeting!

"The Priests of Amen-Ra, taught by Amemphis the Son of Seti to await thy return, have watched over thy slumbers in the seat of Ptah till I Mnesthenes, the last of them left alive, being old and sick unto death, write this for thine information against thine awakening. The old Gods are dead, and the once lovely land of Knem is a waste of tombs and ruins. The temple of Ptah has been buried and forgotten by all save us for centuries. Steps under thee will lead thee to the light. The rolls of wax-cloth contain all that is left of the treasure of Pepi, who was Pharaoh in Egypt many ages ago. To the high Gods it is of no service, and the last of their servants is dying, so it may well serve to cheer a portion of thy pilgrimage. Farewell!"

In the roll of papyrus there had been three other rolls of wax-cloth. One of these I took and slit with my dagger, curious to see what Fortune had sent to speed me on my way. As I unfolded the cloth it revealed to me line after line of great diamonds, embedded in the wax, and blazing in the torchlight with dazzling scintillations. With hands that trembled now, I unrolled the other two, and when they all lay outspread before me I sat and stared breathlessly at such a priceless hoard of gems as not even I had seen before—I, who had seen Tiglath and Solomon in their splendour, and had loaded myself with the spoils of Damascus and the treasures of the White Palace of Chosroes.

The other two were filled with rubies and pearls and emeralds even yet more inestimable than the diamonds, so perfect were they in size and shape and colour. I took a few of the smallest out of each roll, and put them into a little leathern bag that I found containing a few worn gold coins.

Then out of a little bale of linen cloth that seemed to have been left for my use, I made myself as well as I could a rude turban and cloak, tied the precious rolls of Pepi to my body under my mail, took the two remaining bottles of wine and the nuts and dates, and, so equipped to meet the world again, I found and lifted the trap-door in the floor, at which the old priest's words had hinted, and descended a long flight of steps.

At the foot of these I found a narrow passage, along which I went until it ended in a smooth wall of stone. My torch soon showed me a tracing on this which gave the charm to which the monolith yielded, and as it swung to again behind me I found myself once more in the open air. From here I made my way like a spectre among the ruins to the riverside.

I must have walked a good two leagues when I came on a fair-sized boat moored in the stream near a little cabin of reeds and mud. A sudden desire to smell the strong salt breath of the sea once more took possession of me, so, tying in a white rag a ruby worth ten such craft, I stuck it in a cleft in the morning-post, got in, cast loose, and drifted away out into the stream unseen. I paddled a little way, then hoisted my ragged brown sail, and trusting the rest to Fortune, lay down in the stern and went to sleep, for, like one who has slept long, I was still drowsy.

I was awakened by a crash and a shout. I sprang up to find that it was broad daylight, and that the gilded beak of a big galley was cleaving my frail boat in two under my feet. My hand went up and caught something, and closed on it. It was a boarding-grapnel hanging over the bow. I caught hold of another prong with my other hand, and scambled up, helping myself with my knees and feet, till I got one hand, and then another, on the bulwarks, and then I swung myself aboard just as a big fellow—who might well have been my old Hatho's other self—came running forward with a double-bladed axe uplifted, evidently in the intention of splitting my skull for coming aboard his ship in such unceremonious fashion.

I had no time to draw a weapon or defend myself, so as I scrambled to my feet I flung off my linen turban and steel cap, and stood facing him with my long golden locks, which were brighter and fairer than his own, flowing about my uncovered head.

He stopped with axe uplifted, staring open-mouthed at me, and I, laughing, went to him with outstretched hands, and said in good old Gothic:

"Was hael, friend! Thou hast a rough but ready welcome for thy guests, but as I come unbidden I can hardly grumble at it, yet methinks thou art too good a sea-wolf to strike a head that has been bared before thee."

He dropped his axe and shifted it from his right hand to his left; then he stretched his right out and took hold of mine, and said in a speech that was near enough to mine for me to understand it:

"Thou art right, friend, whoever thou art and wherever thou comest from. I have split many a skull, but never yet an unguarded one. But who art thou? Thy speech and thy long, yellow hair, proclaim thee a Northman, though the one is somewhat strange and the other would be none the worse for trimming and combing. What is thy name and country?"

"I have neither name nor country at present," I replied. "But I have that in my pouch which will buy me land, and that at my hip which will win me a name. As for where I come from—well, from the river last, for I was asleep in my boat drifting down the stream, when your galley ran me down and sank her. And now, whither are you bound, and why so fast? Are you flying from yonder two galleys astern of you?"

"As thou seest!" he said, looking round and laughing at a dozen or so of the crew that had come forward to see who the stranger was. "We have been looting all night up the river, and we have more booty under the oar-seats than we would willingly give back to these black-faced sons of Mahound, so we are making the best of our way to sea, where we have a dozen stout long-ships waiting for us off the river-mouth, and, by Odin's hammer, if these heathens will but follow us far enough, their voyage will end in the slave-market of Tyre."

"And since when have the sea-wolves of the North learned to fly from any foe or through any cause?" I said, laughing half scornfully, and remembering how old Hatho and I had thought nothing of charging with a single galley into the midst of a squadron, and fighting away merrily till help came or victory made it needless. "By the Gods! were I but captain of this galley——"

"Well, friend, and if thou wert what wouldst thou do?" said a stark-built, long-limbed young warrior, who came striding forward just as I spoke. "I am Ivar Ivarsson, and this is my ship. Now, what wouldst thou do if thou wert me—thou who swearest by the Gods in the tongue that our forefathers spoke?"

"Whatever tongue I swear in," said I, looking not without some love and respect into his fair, handsome face, "I have seen more fights of this sort than thou hast ever dreamed of, and if I were in thy place I would bid the rowers slack their speed, and row with one hand on the oars and the other getting their weapons ready, so that the Egyptians yonder would think that they were getting tired.

"Then they would come up, one on either side, foot by foot, until they could cast their grapnels, and, when they did that and the grapnels were fast, I would raise the weapon-song, and at them with axe and sword and every man on board, and, by the bright eyes of Baldr, neither axe nor sword should rest till the last of the Egyptians was flung in pieces into the river."

"Egyptians!" he laughed at me in reply. "Why, what age hast thou awakened out of, that thou talkest of

Egyptians? Dost thou not know that Saladin the Moslem is Lord of Egypt, and that yonder galleys are crowded with the best sailors and warriors in the Eastern world?"

"And what is thine own good longship filled with?" I said, wondering who Saladin might be, and what sort of fighters I should find these Moslems of a later age. "How many men hast thou on board that can wield axe and sword?"

"Six score," he said, hastily. "But wherefore dost thou ask, and by what right?"

"Let us talk of right and reason when the fight is over, friend," I said, tearing my linen cloak from my shoulders, and pulling my big blade out of its sheath. "Look yonder," I went on, pointing with it over the bow. "There is the open sea. In an hour you will be on the waves. There is not another war-galley in sight, for it seems that this is not the mouth of Alexandria, else in good truth thou wouldst run into a hornet's nest. Do thou take three score men, and bid the other three score follow me, and, when your two galleys come up with us, do thou take one and I the other, and let us see which of us will clear his deck first."

Those who stood about us greeted my words with a shout, for it was just such a proposition as suited the hot blood that boiled in their veins, and when Ivar heard their shouts he stretched out his right hand and said:

"Give me handfast on that, and by the beauty of Brenda the Lily, our Queen of the Sea——"

"Hold there!" I cried, seizing his hand in a grip, which, stark and hardy, as he was, made him wince. "Brenda! Who is she? Where and when have I heard her name before? No, no; it was in the ages that are forgotten. Say on, good Ivar, say on. I was but dreaming."

"Dream or no dream," he said, breaking loose from my grasp, and coming close up to me and laying his two hands upon my shoulders, and looking into my eyes with a new-kindled light in his, "hast thou ever borne the name of Valdar—or dreamed that thou hast—for in Odin's truth thou art liker to all we have heard of him yonder in the Northland than any other son of woman could be? Speak, and if thou art he thou shalt not need twice to bid me turn the ship about and head her back—ay, though there were a hundred galleys after us, instead of two."

For a moment I stood mute and confounded by the question, for this name, too, like that sweet sounding-name of Brenda, though it awoke dim, strange memories within me, and set my pulses beating harder and my blood flowing faster, yet told me nothing of any of those lives that I had lived on earth. I could not say yes with any certainty, and yet I felt that to say no would be lying; so, for want of a direct reply, I said:

"It may be that in some age I have forgotten I bore such a name, and that age may be the one in which thy lady's name was as familiar to me as my own. But tell me thou in turn—hast thou ever heard in thy Northland any talk of one like me who came with ships from the South filled with just such gallant sea-dogs as these about me, one whose name was then Terai, and whose lieutenant was one Hatho the Goth, in the days when Cæsar was lord of Rome and master of the world?"

"Yes," he said, and as he spoke I saw his eyes droop, and the warm flush fade in his cheeks, "we have a saga of such an one, and I have often heard the skalds sing it at the Yuletide feasts."

"Then," I said, "since the time for talking is growing short, thou mayst call me Valdar for the present, and I will lead half thy men and thou the other, and when the fight is over we shall have leisure to talk more of these things. Now give me a helm that will fit me, and the heaviest war-axe in the ship, and bid the rowers slow their oars, for the river banks are sloping away and we are close upon the sea."

"It shall be so, Valdar, and, if thou art worthy of thy name, thou at least will join the fleet in victory though I go to Valhalla before thee. If not——"

"If not," I repeated after him, "thou canst flay, living or dead, what is left of me after the battle, and make buskins of my skin for better men. Now let us get to work, friend, and talk afterwards."

"Spoken like a true man," he said. "Now come with me and choose thy helm and axe, and do you, Wulf, tell the rest what's afoot."

I followed him aft into the cabin under the high poop—for the Norse galleys of those days were bigger and better furnished than any whose remains have been preserved to these times—and soon chose for myself a helm of steel like his, with golden wings, and as pretty a double-bladed axe as ever I swung, saving it might have been a few pounds heavier to suit my taste perfectly. Then I loosened my belt, and pulled up my shirt of mail, and took off the three rolls of gems and gave them to him, telling him to put them away in his chest, and if I fell and he survived to take them home with him, and give them to Brenda as a keepsake from Valdar.

Then we went out of the cabin again, and found the sail down, and the rowers just keeping their oars moving with their left hands, while their right were busy making their weapons ready.

The two pursuing galleys were now drawing close up to us, and as they came on I heard the shrill beating of brazen kettledrums, and the shriller screaming of the war-cry that I had last heard yonder up the river on the island of Rhouda, when Amru and I stormed it together. The nearer they came the louder and the shriller they yelled, for they had swallowed my stratagem, and believed us weary with rowing and too worn out to fight. But their tune soon changed, for, as they shot alongside and threw their grapnels, every oar came in at once, every Northern mother's son sprang up full armed upon the oar-benches, and, Ivar to the right and I to the left, we leapt on board their crowded decks, I shouting my old war-cry of Armen, and Ivar chanting the battle-song of Odin, which his men and mine took up in such a thunderous chorus that the yells of the Moslems sounded above it like the screaming of sea-birds in a storm.

They met us first with long pikes, and from behind the rank that held these their archers sent flight after flight of arrows and javelins into our faces. But the Northmen had doubtless seen this kind of fighting before, for they put their round bucklers up over their heads, dashed the spear-points aside with swinging blows of their axes, and sprang, leaping and shouting, into the midst of the Moslems as though the work were but the veriest child's play to them.

Then in the heat of battle there came back to me like a flash the memory of what the Prophet had said to me, and I saw that, if such as these were the masters of the Moslem world, then the worst and not the best of his prophecy had been fulfilled, and that the sceptre of Islam had passed from the House of Hashem into the hands of the barbarians. This thought kindled so fierce a fire within me that for the moment I forgot where and what I was, and, as a whole crowd of them recoiled before the sweeping strokes of my battle-axe, I raised my voice anew and shouted in Arabic:

"The curse of Allah and his Prophet on you, degenerate dogs and sons of unbelieving mothers! What ban hath fallen on Islam that such as ye pipe the Tecbir in your squealing women's voices? Have ye never heard of the Sword of God? Now, by Allah, ye shall see and feel it."

With that I swung my axe round my head and hurled it into the midst of them with all my force. Like a stone flung into a patch of reeds, it dashed them backwards and to right and left, the one flinging the other down as nine-pins do under a well-aimed ball; and then my great blade flashed out, and I went at them, hacking and hewing, cutting and thrusting, and all the while shouting the old battle-cry of Islam in mockery at them, till they broke and fled, flinging themselves one after another over the bulwarks into the river, screaming to each other that Allah had let Shaitan himself loose upon them for their sins.

By the time we had finished with our own ship, and stood panting and laughing at each other on her bloody decks, Ivar and his fellows had done much the same on the other, though their work was not yet quite finished. But as soon as the Moslems that were left saw what had befallen their comrades, and saw, too, that we were ready, if needs be, to take our part in the merry game that was being played on their own decks, they lost heart, and soon cries for quarter began to mingle with the battle-shouts.

"Was hael, Ivar?" I shouted across to him. "If thou hast need of a few more axes or swords thou canst have them, for ours are idle already."

He waved his axe to me in greeting, and shouted a great laughing shout of battle-joy, and then his axe came down, splitting a steel-capped skull as it fell, and the next instant he fell, too, for a wounded wretch on the deck, who was not as near dead as he thought him, caught him round the legs and tripped him up on the slippery, blood-smeared deck.

My jest was good earnest now, and I sprang forward, followed by a score of my own fellows, to his aid. We cleared bulwarks and oar-seats in our long leaping strides, and just as the crowd closed round him we were upon them. There was neither time nor room to use a weapon in the press, so, opening my arms, I picked the pigmies up two and three at a time, and pitched them back over my head and shoulders under the feet of those who came after me; and so I tore my way through the crowd till I came to where Ivar lay, now sorely wounded by the showers of blows that had been rained on him while he was down.

One yellow-skinned knave was just stooping over him to drive a dagger into his neck as I reached him, and him I picked up by the ankles and swung him round my head like a flail, till his head and arms and shoulders were smashed out of shape against the weapons and mail of his fellows, and his blood and brains spattered them from head to foot in such a ghastly shower that they fled screaming and half-blinded out of reach, only to be cut down by the axes and swords that were rising and falling in a ring outside them like hammers round an anvil.

Then, with a good ringing Arabic curse, I flung what was left of him at their heads, and, throwing Ivar over my left shoulder, I pulled my sword out and soon cleared a way back to his own ship, and laid him in his cabin, where I stripped off his armour and clothing and set myself to wash and bind up his wounds, which were many and deep enough to have let the life out of any but a man made in hero mould. Here old Wulf found me when he came to say that the last of the Moslems was either dead or a prisoner, and that the two great galleys were ours.

When he saw what I was doing, the honest old fellow came to me and held out his hand, saying, with tears in his eyes and something very like a sob in his voice:

"Friend Valdar! I see that thou art a true warrior—as gentle after the battle as thou art savage in it. By Thor and Odin, it was well for us that I didn't break thy head as I meant to in the bow yonder. Thou hast given us the victory when we were flying from our foes—shame on us!—and, if Ivar lives, thou wilt have given him his life also, and I tell thee that sooner than have gone back without him to his father, who is out yonder with the fleet, and to our Lady Brenda, who waits for him in the Northland, I, for one, would have found a fight somewhere and died in it, so that I might have gone with him to Valhalla."

"He will live, never fear," I said; "but the sooner we have him back to the fleet the better, so get us under way again as quickly as maybe. You see to that, and I'll stay and watch by Ivar. If you have any good wine on board bring it to him, for he will be all the better for it when he comes to himself again."

He brought me the wine—good, red, strong stuff it was, too—in a big silver flagon, out of which I took a mighty draught by way of toll, for that noonday fight had made me as dry as the sands in the Vale of Siddim. When I went on deck again, leaving Ivar sleeping quietly in his bed, I found that we ha already cleared the river mouth, and with our two prizes in tow, were gliding over a smooth sea towards a fleet of some dozen and a half great stately long-ships, whose gay-striped sails and golden beaks and dragon heads were glittering merrily in the light of the evening sun.

We ran alongside the biggest of them, as trim and lovely a long-ship as ever bore the sea-wolves of the North to victory and plunder, manned, I could see, by as gay and gallant a set of sea-robbers as ever made might right, or found a good title to their neighbours' goods in the strength of their own right arms.

On board of her they took me to clasp hands with Ivar's father, a stately, stalwart veteran, bronzed and battle-scarred by many a hot sun and bitter fight, yet still as strong and supple as the best of his men, and as royal an old sea-king as ever sailed out of the North. When they told him how I had fought and what I had done for Ivar—and you may believe me that the tale lost nothing in the telling—I saw the tears come into his fierce old eyes, and he said to me in a voice that rang like a deep-toned bell:

"Blood for blood, and life for life, Valdar Starkarm, as thou art well worthy to be called! That is our war-creed, and while one of our long-ships floats, or there is a man of us left who can fight beside thee, thou shalt never want a friend or a brother-in-arms; and to-night, if thou wilt, we will swear the blood-troth, and thou shalt be a brother among us, and fare home with us to the Northland, where perchance thou shalt find better things awaiting thee."

"That I will," said I, "and right willingly, for it seems to me, I know not how, that in some fashion, and after long wanderings, I have come back among my own people. Henceforth, or till I again pass into the shadows out of which I came but yesterday, the Northland shall be my home, and the sea my country, and you and your gallant sea-wolves my brothers and my kindred—for others I have none in all the world.

"That is a strange speech, Valdar," he said, gravely and slowly. "Strange enough for thee to be that very Valdar of whom the saga tells. Have they already told thee what the skalds have sung of one like you?"

"Yes," I said, "they have, and I should love well to hear that same saga sung."

"Then to-night thou shalt hear it," he said, "for my youngest lad, Harald, yonder, has the sweetest harp and the clearest voice in all the fleet, and to-night he shall sing it for thee when the wassail bowls go round."

Later on that night old Ivar kept his promise. The whole fleet was sailing north-westward for the Adriatic, bound to Venice, in those days the market of the world, where merchants and sea-robbers alike could find purchasers for their wares, whether won by the trickery of trade or the rougher but, perchance, more honest methods of war.

The captains had come on board at old Ivar's invitation, and, according to the manner of the ancient time, we had each one of us pricked his arm and let a few drops of his blood fall into a great flagon of red wine, and this had been passed round from lip to lip till the last drop had been drained. So we had sworn the blood-troth, and henceforth I and they were brothers to the death.

Then Harald, a fair haired, white-faced lad who had yet to see his fifteenth birthday, brought out his harp and tuned it, and, with us seated on the broad deck about him, and his brother Ivar lying on a couch of skins beside him, he struck the first opening chords, and then, through the silence of the moonlit sea-night, to the accompaniment of his own music and the soft splash of the oars and the ripple of the water along the vessel's side, he lifted up his sweet clear voice, and sang the saga of Valda the Asa, son of Odin, who brought the Nornir from Totunheim to read for him the Sacred Runes which none but the Gods might read, and was for this over-daring sin driven forth from Asgard of the Gods to wander through many climes and ages till his doom should be complete, and told how his true love, Brenda, the daughter of Hela, had sworn that for love of him she would share his doom, and prove to Gods and men that Love is stronger than Fate itself.

Then he told how Valdar came naked and alone to the stronghold of a people who in the ages that were forgotten dwelt in a land of mountain and forest and swift-flowing torrents far away towards the portals of the morning, and how he found there a warrior queen of peerless beauty who went to war with him against the king of a mighty nation who had made himself as a God upon earth, and how they had overcome the great king's armies and marched in victory to the walls of his city.

Then he told how, as the ages went on, the land whose name had been forgotten was invaded by mighty armies, from the south, and how family after family and tribe after tribe had forsaken their homes and had wandered northward over mountain and valley and plain, and round the shores of a great inland sea, and then over boundless plains traversed by great, slow-flowing rivers, journeying ever towards the north, till, after many centuries had passed, their descendants had come to a land of green fields and dark, forest-clad hills, of deep, rock-bound creeks and bays, and long, smooth, shining sea-reaches, and there had made their home, worshipping Odin and Thor and Frigga and Freya, the Gods of battle and thunder and the Goddesses of love and beauty, until Olaf Tryggvasson had come with the sword in one hand and the cross in the other to banish the old Gods and preach the faith of the White Christ who died for men on Calvary.

Then, in a last burst of triumphant song, he sang, as though inspired by some gift of prophecy, of the times that were to come when Valdar should return, and a people sprung from the seed of the Northmen should go forth armed with thunder and flame to do battle for the empire of the world, and rule it from north to south and east to west.

A strange new spirit stirred within my breast, and under its impulse I sprang to my feet. The sacred steel of Armen leapt from its sheath and flashed white in the moonlight above my head, and then I, too, lifted up my voice and sang, as I had often sung to my old sea-dogs of a thousand years before, in quaint old rugged Gothic stanzas, the story of Armen and Ilma, of Nimrod and the fall of Nineveh. I sang the might and splendour of the Tiger-Lord of Asshur, of Solomon and his glory, and of the great Cæsar and Rome the mistress of the world; of Cleopatra and her world-wide shame; of Calvary, and the falling of the curtain over the past of the ancient world: of the Prophet of Mecca and the early glories of Islam.

There I stopped short as one whose tale is told, and then they leapt to their feet about me, their swords sprang out with one sharp, rattling ring, and my name went up into the calm, bright sky in such a thunderous shout of full-toned, deep-voiced melody as I had never heard since I stood in the throne-room of the citadel of Armen amidst their ancestors of four thousand years before.

Young Harald threw his harp aside and swung his blade with the rest, and even Ivar, weak and wounded as he was, waved his hand above his head, and shouted with all the breath that was left in his body.

CHAPTER XVI

THE LILY OF THE NORTHLAND

THE next morning old Ivar told me the story of Brenda the Lily. How a were-witch had found her floating to the shore of the fjord by which his own burgh stood, a lovely, laughing girl-child lying wrapped in silk and fine linen on the cushions of a wondrous cradle fashioned like a longship, and had brought her up to his hall and laid her on his knees as he sat in the high-seat feasting among his jarls and berserkers, and had prophesied that she should grow up under his care the fairest woman in all the Northland, and told how a warrior should come from distant seas to claim her for his own, and should fare forth with her to accomplish his fate and hers under suns that shone over far-off lands.

"And that man, perchance, art thou, Valdar!" he said, when he had ended his tale. "Yet if so, I warn thee that thou wilt have to pass through stern ordeals, and do great deeds of valour, ere Brenda the Lily will lay her hand in thine, and follow where thou shalt lead."

"If Brenda in truth be she whose fate so far hath been so strangely linked with mine," I answered, "then there shall be no ordeal that man can pass, and no deed that man can do, that I will leave undared or undone to win her now as I have won her before in the ages that are past, and the days that are forgotten!"

"Well said!" he replied. "And mayest thou find her all that thy heart desires! And now, Valdar, what sayest thou? The summer is yet young, and when we have sold our cargoes in Venice our ships will be light, though our pouches will be passably heavy. Wouldst thou that we should seek more booty on the sea or shape our course with what speed we may to the Northland?"

"To the Northland!" I cried. "And that with all speed that oar and sail can give us; and if the ships' crews should demur on the score of booty, then, when we get to Venice, I will give them in good gold and silver coin, whatever the fashion of them may be in these new days, thrice to each man the value that he could win in a whole summer's fighting with sword and axe, and think it but a small price to pay for losing no time on the way to home and Brenda."

"Art thou then so rich," he asked me, smiling. "And hast thou found the secret of bringing thy treasures with thee from one age to the next?"

"Nay," I said. "Not that. I left many thousands of gold pieces yonder in Syria, and Persia, and Egypt, all good booty, honestly won by sword and spear, yet I am rich enough to do that which I say, as thou shalt see in Venice."

So, talking of this and many other things that were happening in the world, in which I was once more a stranger, we fared on with prosperous winds over a smooth sea till we came to that glorious City of the Waters, seated in all her pomp and pride and splendour on her thousand islands—such a marvel of beauty and strange grandeur as even I had never seen in all my wanderings.

There we sold our cargoes, and there I, too, found certain Jews and Lombards, who were the Phœnicians of those later days. I need waste few words in telling how these tried to cheat me after the manner of their kind, and how I swore at them in good old Hebrew and Augustan Latin, and told them such strange things of old Tyre and Rome, of Jerusalem and Alexandria, that at last I frightened them into some show of honesty, and among them they gave me such a price in good broad pieces and bars of gold and silver for a handful of my gems, that it took six stark fellows to carry the treasure down to our ships, and five hundred more as a guard to show the good Venetians that we were people who meant to take our own way without other tax or toll upon it than we could pay with axe and sword.

The next day another and a happy fancy took me. I had learned from what old Ivar had told me on the voyage, that the world was just as fond of fighting now as it had ever been, and that there were wars well nigh everywhere, from the rocky shores of his own Northland to the burning sands of Syria, where a great Christian host, led by puissant kings and princes, were striving to wrest back from Islam that Holy City which I had last entered riding by the side of Omar's red camel.

So I took another handful out of the treasure of Pepi, and went back to the city with five hundred of our starkest fellows, and there, by purchase and barter, I equipped them with the finest suits of Milan steel, and the best weapons that gold could buy, and then I marched them back to the ships, all splendid and shining in steel and gold and silver, the most magnificent troop of sea-robbers that the world had ever seen.

Then once again I returned to the Jews and the armourers, and this time I chose with loving care the daintiest suit of chain and plate inlaid with gold, with silvered shield and white-plumed, gold-plated helm and gorget to match, and the most sweetly-tempered weapons that the cunning artificers of Italy and Spain had ever made, not for my own wear or use, you may be sure, but for a purpose that is no doubt plain to you.

When we got to the sea again I obliged old Ivar, though much against his will, to add my gold and silver to the common treasure which, according to custom, was to be shared out according to rank and service when we got home, and this made all willing to make the utmost speed home without seeking further fight or plunder; so we sailed on down the blue Adriatic and along the Inland Sea quietly and prosperously, landing here and there as the fancy took us, or the beauty of the land invited us, now for a feast and now for a brush, just to keep our hands in, with such who thought they had a better right to their own than we had.

Then day by day we watched the sun sink lower, and night by night we saw the northern stars rise higher, till at length one morning, just as day was breaking over the smooth and almost windless sea, I went up on to the *Sea Hawk's* forecastle, and saw before me a long, dark coastline of black and blue-grey mountain masses, heaped together as though new-sprung from primeval chaos, shooting their sharp peaks and pinnacles of rock far into the calm, clear air, and high above the white snowy patches and green, gleaming ice-fields which lay flashing in the new-risen sun about their middle heights.

Now the glad cry of "Homeland! Homeland!" rang from ship to ship, and, after breakfast had been served and speedily disposed of, all hands were busy cleaning the ships down and getting them into their holiday trim, and when this was done weapons and mail were got out and burnished, and cloaks of silk and cloth of gold were made ready for the fair shoulders they were soon to adorn.

Then the white peace-shields went up to our mastheads, and every man who could get a seat on the oar-benches or a grip on an oar set himself to work in joyful earnest, and the home-race began. The oars groaned and bent, and the great long-ships sprang forward with well-nigh half their length out of the churned-up foaming waters of the fjord, and away we went, now one in front and now another, the rowers putting every ounce of strength in their mighty muscles into the blithesome work, and the captains and steersmen cheering them on, and shouting now in joy and now in rage as their ship forged ahead or fell behind her rivals on either hand.

So, in one long, straggling line we rushed on towards the smooth, sloping beach, where kerchiefs and weapons were waving their welcome to us. Nearer and nearer we came, and as every yard was passed the good *Sea Hawk* forged inch by inch ahead of the rest, her sixty oars smiting the froth-strewn water with a single stroke, and sending it flying in long streams of foam behind her, till old Ivar, who was standing beside me on the forecastle with Harald and young Ivar, who was now nearly well of his wounds, roared out one last shout to the rowers, and with a mighty leap the long-ship sprang half her length out of the shallowing water, and drove her keel deep into the shelving, sandy shore.

We sprang together to the land, and as my feet touched it and I pulled myself up straight after the leap, there before me stood a sweet and stately woman-shape, which no man had need to tell me was Brenda the Lily—the oft-lost re-found once more!

For a moment we faced each other without speaking, we two wanderers from afar once more so strangely met, I from a past age on earth and she from beyond the stars. For me there stood once more incarnate in that fair shape the sweet stateliness of Ilma, the gentle grace of Zillah, the haughty loveliness of Cleopatra, and the heroic devotion of Zoraida. All these and something more that I had yet to know—but for her I was only a stranger come back with her people from the distant wars, a nameless soldier of fortune who was no more to her than any other chance visitant to the shores of the Northland.

"Who is this?" she asked, turning away from me to greet Jarl Ivar and his sons.

And so, when their own greetings were over, they told her the circumstances of my joining them, yet saying nothing of my wondrous past, for Harald had added many new stanzas to the Saga of Valdar during the voyage, and was to sing them that night in the great hall of the burgh when we were all assembled at the feast of the home-coming, and so his father had no desire to spoil his story. Then she turned back to me, and holding out her hand said in her calm, sweet passionless voice, as though I had been, as no doubt I seemed to her, the veriest stranger:

"Welcome to Ivarsheim, Valdar the Strong, as they tell me thou art. Is this the first time thou hast come to the Northland? There is something in thy face or form that is half familiar to me. Where have I seen thee before, if ever?"

It was in my heart to answer: "In the battle-press at Yermouk, when the Roman's spear-head was buried in that white breast of thine!" But there was something in the distant coldness of her manner that was strange to me, and so taking her proffered hand—that hand which I had last clasped and kissed when it was cold and stiff in death—I bent low over it, and said:

"I have seen this Northland before and looked on a face like that of the fairest of its daughters, yet now for the first time I stand in Ivarsheim and see the peerless beauty of Brenda the Lily."

"A courtly speech, if somewhat strange-sounding in our rude Northern ears," she said, taking her hand from mine and turning her pretty head aside half smiling and half frowning. "It may be that some day, when we are better acquainted, thou wilt make it plain to me."

And with that she left me to go and talk to Ivar and Harald, and Jarl Ivar took me up to the burgh to find me quarters for the present. That night by sundown the great hall was all ablaze with torches of Northern pine and great wax candles that we had brought with us from the South. Jarl Ivar sat in the high-seat at the top of the great table, which was loaded with huge joints of flesh, roast and boiled, and great jugs and wooden bowls and silver flagons full of froth-crowned mead and wine red as blood or yellow as gold.

I sat in the guest-place on Jarl Ivar's right hand, and Brenda sat on his left, and young Ivar faced him at the other end of the table.

We ate, and drank, and laughed, and talked, and boasted of our great deeds, till the huge dishes were empty and our appetites of one sort were satisfied, and then the ale-cups and wine-flagons were filled up anew, and Jarl Ivar smote with his dagger-hilt upon the table to command silence, and bade Harald fetch his harp and sing the Saga of Valdar with the new verses that he had made to it.

Harald took his harp and sang as he had sung on board the long-ship in the Adriatic, and when he had finished the ancient saga that they all knew so well, and yet never could hear often enough, they sprang to their feet and waved their bowls and flagons, and shouted their praises of the singer and his song, thinking that he had come to the end.

Then Jarl Ivar rose and silenced them again with a shout of his deep, rolling voice, and in the wondering silence that followed Harald struck his harp again and drew forth so weird and sweet a strain from the answering strings that those rough warriors and wild sea-wolves bent their heads and sat them down again as orderly as chidden children to wait for the new song they saw was coming,

Then out of the silence that followed his prelude his clear, sweet voice uprose again, and as he sang, and the ringing stanzas followed each other, now loud and swift and now slow and plaintive, I saw that with that magic singer's art of his he had woven all that I had told them of my past lives during the voyage into his song.

I turned and watched Brenda's face as he sang, and on it I saw every change of the song stamped in quick succession as her heart, all unknowing, beat responsive to the strains. I saw her cheeks flush and her eyes flash when the battle-song of Armen or the fierce yell of the Tecbir thundered or screamed through the changing strains, and her bosom heaved and fell, now slow, now fast, as the singer told of the changing fortunes of my many loves.

At last the throbbing strings trembled into silence, and Harald's voice melted away into the fainting echoes of the great hall, and then there was silence again, and as I looked about me I saw the battle-fire flashed at me from a thousand eyes, and heard the deep breathing of many a breast that throbbed with longing to do such deeds as those of which the singer had sung.

Then, like the hoarse, croaking cry of a raven in the deep peace of a summer's night, there came a harsh, mocking laugh through the hush, and a great, broad-shouldered, hairy-limbed berserker, seated half-way down the table threw his hands up above his head and roared out:

"Ha! ha! ha! Well sung, young Harald, sweetest singer in the Northland, and a pretty tale as ever was spun out of the fancy of a lad sick for love and battle! Yet we could well have done without that old fable, that were-woman's tale of the White Christ on His Cross, which Olaf Tryggvasson tried to hammer into our grandsires' heads with his war-axes—as though Odin and his hammer and the Valkyries on their long-maned steeds were not worth a thousand Christs and twice as many of that virgin mother of His. When next thou singest thy song, Harald Ivarsson, leave that out, for it is only fit for the ears of children. Here's to Odin and Thor, and the bright hair of the battle-maidens who come after the fight to show us the way to Valhalla! Was hael! Was hael! to the good old Gods and the heroes of Valhalla!"

With that he sprang to his feet with a great wine flagon between his hands, and every reveller in the great hall save me rose with him, mead-bowl or wine-cup in hand, and, hailing the toast with a great thunderous shout, drank deep to the name of the Gods who were no more. Then the cups clattered down on the table again, and all, still standing, looked round on me, still sitting, silent and smileless, like a spectre at the feast amidst their noisy revel.

But of all the eyes that were turned upon me I felt but two, for Brenda also had risen, and had touched the rim of her golden wine-cup with her pretty lips, and she still stood with the rest staring at me as I sat. For a moment there was silence again, and then through it came the cold, clear music of her voice, saying:

"What, Valdar! thou in whose honour the saga was song—hast thou lost thy voice or is thy wine-cup dry that thou canst neither shout nor drink with us?"

"Neither, Lily of the Northland," roared Hrolf the Berserker again. "He hath but listened to the monk-magic, and it has taken the heart out of him. He comes from the East, and doubtless believes, as I have heard some women and children do, this tale of the shaven-pated liars—"

"Liar thyself!" I shouted, springing to my feet and flinging over the heavy chair in which I sat. "Liar thyself, whatever thy name or country. Dost thou think nothing possible save what thy nurse hath told thee or those drink-dimmed eyes of thine can see? I tell thee and all here that this is no lying tale, but the greatest of all truths that the ears of men have ever heard!"

Then they roared out laughing again, and shouted:

"The proof! The proof! Why should we believe thee, stranger as thou art?"

"For the reason that I have seen that of which I speak—for I have stood before the Cross of Calvary as I now stand before you, and with these eyes that look on you I have seen the White Christ on His Cross. That is the truth. He who next calls it a lie shall call me liar too, and take the penalty,"

"And what if I say that it is but an idle tale, and that thou, Valdar, art but dreaming when thou dost tell it to us?"

Brenda laughed out the smoothly-spoken words with a mocking smile on her pretty lips and a flash of mirth in her eyes that showed me that the tale had gained no more credence with her than it had with the roughest and stupidest berserker in the hall. They waited to see what my answer to her would be, and in the silence that followed her speech I turned and faced her, and said:

"Then, Lily of the North, I should tell thee that in the land beyond the stars, where thou hast been since then, there is no remembrance, for thou thyself wert lying weeping beside the Cross when the darkness fell from Heaven, and I lay down beside thee to die on that same hill of Calvary. Say now, dost thou not remember how that darkness fell as the voice of the White Christ cried, 'It is finished?' Dost thou not remember how the lightning blazed through the riven sky, and the earth quaked, and Nature veiled her face in the horror of that awful hour?"

She shivered as though stricken with a sudden palsy and turned white to the lips, but, before she could shape a word in answer, an angry shout burst out all round the table, and above it rose the fierce, harsh roar of Hrolf's voice crying, with a laugh more like the howl of a wild beast than the voice of a man:

"Liar! Liar! I will call thee liar and prove it on thee, though thou hast lived a thousand years, thou who canst frighten women with thy lying tales. Let us see what thou canst do with a man. By the bright eyes of Baldr thou shalt not steal the roses from our Lady's cheeks for nothing! Now what hast thou to say to that?"

"That thou hast found more courage in thy cups to-night," I said, "than thou wilt find in the morning in thy heart, and if thou wouldst hear more I will tell thee that I have fought and conquered warriors who could have wrung that bull-neck of thine, thick as it is, as they would have wrung a chicken's, thou misbegotten son of a heathen mother!"

As I spoke I left my place and strode down the hall towards where Hrolf was standing in the midst of a group of his fellow berserkers, stamping with his feet and waving his great hairy arms about his head, and foaming at the mouth in the height of his berserk fury.

Jarl Ivar called to me to come back, telling me that he could protect his guest, but it was too late. There was the same mad rage burning in my blood that had spurred me on to that last wild charge at Yermouk. I strode in amongst the crowd, flinging the stark Northmen to right and left with swift blows of my clenched fists as I went, and before Hrolf could draw a weapon, or fling his arms about me, I had taken him by the beard and the thick locks that hung down upon his neck, and with one swift wrench screwed his head round till the bones of his neck cracked and his tongue sprang out from his choking throat, and when I let go his neck was broken, and his great body tumbled on to the floor like a carcase of a stricken ox.

"There is one lying fool's tongue silenced!" I said, turning round on the others. "Now whose shall be the next?"

But the words were hardly out of my mouth before a dozen brawny arms were cast about me, fastening my arms to my side, and well nigh squeezing the breath out of my body. I wrestled with the utmost of my strength, but to no avail, and then down I went on Hrolf's body with half-a-dozen of those stalwart heathens on top of me.

The next thing I knew or heard was the deep voice of Jarl Ivar breaking through the din and crying:

"Up, up, there! He is my guest, and has the guest-right! Let him up, I say. What, half a score to one! Shame on you! Is that the way good Northmen fight?"

"Bind his hands and let him up," cried one of the crowd above me.

And then I felt my hands drawn behind my back, and tied together by the wrists. They dragged me up to my feet, and I stood in the midst of them, silent, and with clenched teeth and burning cheeks and blazing eyes, for this was the first time in all my life that I had suffered the indignity of bonds.

"He has slain my blood-brother, and I ask the blood-right upon him!" roared a great half-naked berserker beside me.

"He has given the lie to our Lady Brenda?" yelled another. "Let us take him to her feet, and let her tell him what his weird is."

"That is thy right, Brenda, since Hrolf got his death through speaking for thee. What sayest thou?" said Jarl Ivar.

"Hold there!" cried young Ivar, ere she could answer, making his way through the throng towards me. "I claim his life, for he saved mine, as you all know, when the Saracens had me down under their weapons. If he dies, I swear by Odin's glory that I will follow him to Valhalla, for never did a braver man draw sword than he, Christian or no Christian!"

"The Valkyries have not come for him yet, brother Ivar," said Brenda, in answer to him, still in the same sweet, cold voice that had goaded me to madness before. "Bring him here, and let us hear what he shall say for himself."

So they pulled the table away from before her seat and dragged me to her, and would have forced me on my knees before her, but she said:

"Nay, nay, not that; he is a man, whether mad or sane, so let him stand like a man upon his feet."

So they let me stand, one of them holding me on each side, and so once more we faced each other, she cold and calm and stately, and I red-hot with rage and shame, my blood boiling, and every muscle in my body trembling with the fury that possessed me.

"Now, Valdar, well named Starkarm, what sayest thou? Wilt thou go to the Stone of Sacrifice and pay the blood-guilt thou hast incurred, or wilt thou own thyself my bondsman, and pay such other penalty as I shall lay upon thee?"

"Though thy bonds were of silk and gold, and thy service the sweetest bondage that could fall to man, yet they should never make me serve thee. Take back thy bonds, for thou wilt need stronger than these to bind Valdar with!"

And with that I felt all the strength of my body flow into my arms, and with one mighty wrench I burst the cord that they had tied about my wrists, seized the two who had held me by the hair, and dashed their skulls together so that they dropped, stunned, to the floor.

Then I flung the broken strands of cord at Brenda's feet, and had already half-drawn my sword from its sheath to sell my life as dearly as might be, when a swift and wondrous change came over Brenda's face, and I saw that the soul that had known me of yore had awakened again, and was looking at me out of her melting eyes.

There was a hoarse roar of rage and a trampling of many feet behind me, but before I could turn Brenda sprang to her feet, and, spreading her arms out, cried in just such a voice that had rung from Ilma's lips in that old hall in Armen:

"No, no, stand back all of you! He is my man, and I claim him. You have given him to me for his weird and I will have my right."

"And I will slay the first man that lays his hand upon my guest!" shouted Jarl Ivar, drawing his sword, and setting his back to mine, while I stood mutely staring at Brenda, wondering what marvel was going to happen next.

"Put back thy sword, Valdar, and hold out those strong hands of thine that I may see them," she said with so sweet a smile upon her pretty lips, and such a merry light dancing in her eyes that I obeyed as a child might have done, and put out my hands towards her close together with the palms upturned. Then with a motion of her hand, so swift that my wondering eyes could scarce follow it, she plucked a long shining golden hair, finer than the finest silk, from her head, and wound it thrice round my wrists, saying:

"Now, Valdar the Strong, let me see thee break that as thou didst the cord!"

I gave but one glance up into her sweet smiling face, and then down I went on my knee before her, and, raising my clasped hands above my head. said:

"Nay, that I cannot, for thou hast taken from me the will to do it. I am thy bondsman, Brenda, and this sweet bond shall hold thee faster than fetters of forged steel could ever do, nor shall they ever be unloosed save by thine own dear hands."

"Then I will loose them now," she said, "for hands like these of thine look not their best in bonds, however light. So there, now thou art free!"

And with a touch so light that I could scarce feel it she took that slender thread of silken gold from my wrists. But before she could take her hands away I had caught them in mine; still kneeling I pressed them unresisting to my lips, and, looking up at her again, said:

"Nay, not free, Brenda! for that I can never be again till the memory of thee and thy dear graciousness hath faded from my heart. I am thy man, as thou hast said, and shall be until death shall part us once again, so lay thy commands upon me and let me taste the sweetness of thy service."

"Then stand up, Valdar," she said, with yet another swift change of voice and gesture; "stand up and tell all here once more that the Saga of Valdar is true; that thou art he who, by the will of the Eternal who is above all Gods that men have dreamed of, hast come here from other ages to bring His greatest truth to us, and that I am she with whom thou hast clasped hands in other climes and ages, for the soul that awakened in me at thy words is now speaking through my lips, and he who says the words are truthless shall with the same breath call me a liar."

"And he who does," I cried, plucking out my blade and facing them beside her, "let him stand out there in the midst of the hall so that I may prove the truth of thy words upon his body!"

There was silence for a space, and they all stood there in a great, crowded semicircle on either side of the table staring at us, dumb with the wonder of what they had seen. Then out of the crowd there came a roar like the bellow of a wild bull, and Hufr the Berserker, who had been Hrolf's blood-brother and had claimed the blood-right on me, sprang up on to the table, kicking the drinking vessels about him on to the floor, and began leaping and dancing and waving his big, bare blade above his head, and shouting at me out of his foaming lips.

"I am Hufr the Berserker, Hufr the Strong, Hufr the Valiant, Hufr the Unconquered! I have drunk the blood of better men than thee and torn out stouter hearts than thine. See, I spit at thee, thou lying teller of monk-tales. Come out and fight for thy White Christ and I will fight for Odin, and let us see which shall be worshipped henceforth in Ivarsheim."

"Thou drunken fool!" I laughed, not moving from my place, "go dip thy hot head in the sea and wash out that foul mouth of thine, and when thou art sober I will wring thy neck as I wrung Hrolf's, for a mad beast like thee is not worthy of good steel that has tasted the blood of kings and warriors."

"Beware, Valdar, beware! He hath the berserk fury on him, and that gives him thrice his strength. Get thy shield and helm ere thou meetest him."

It was Brenda's voice, and as she spoke I felt the light pressure of her hand upon my shoulder. I felt it tremble through my mail, and I put up my left hand and clasped it, saying:

"Never fear for me, sweet lady-mine! If his madness gave him tenfold strength I would beat him bareheaded and without shield, and cut his ugly carcase into shreds before he touched me. Clear away the table there!" I shouted to the crowd, "and give me room to let the madness out of that braggart's blood."

"Weapon-place! Weapon-place!" went up in a shout from a hundred throats. "Christ or Odin! Let them fight! Let them fight!"

And half a score of them seized Hufr and dragged him down from the table, still howling and foaming in his fury. Then the tables were flung aside and a clear space made for us half the size of the great hall's floor.

"Bless the weapon, Brenda, as thou didst before Old Nineveh and in that fierce fight at Muta, and thou shalt see what it will do for the White Christ and thy dear sake."

I held the golden cross-hilt up to her lips and she kissed it, and I kissed the place that had thus been thrice hallowed by her lips, and then, striding out towards the middle of the hall, I cried to those who were holding Hufr back:

"Let that wild beast go!"

They loosed him, and he came at me with a roar and a rush, his body bent half double, his head covered with his round brazen buckler, and his sword swung aloft. He made a swinging slash at me that would have well-nigh cut me in half if it had reached me; but I had fought too many fights for that. Ere the blade fell I sprang aside, and as he passed me I dealt him such a blow with the flat of my sword across his hindquarters that he roared with the pain of it, and all who were looking on yelled with laughter at him.

He pulled up and came at me again, madder than ever, but this time with more method in his madness. I stood still to receive him, and he began hacking and hewing and thrusting at me, but never a blow or a thrust reached me, for such rude work was but child's play to one who had learned swordsmanship in the stern school of the Syrian wars. Wherever his blade fell there was mine to meet it, until at last it was so notched and blunted that it looked more like a worn-out saw than a sword.

All the while I had not spoken a word, and he had been roaring and gasping and panting with the stress of his own fury and the weight of the work I had given him to do. At last he held his battered sword above his head just a moment too long, and I made a slash at it just above the hilt and sent the blade rattling to the ground.

"Get thee another sword!" I said, laughing at his bewildered rage. "That poor reaping-hook of thine is worn out."

"Monk-magic! Monk-magic!" he yelled. "His sword is charmed and flies of itself to a thousand places at once. Let us see if he will cut this through!"

With that he ran to one of his fellows who was watching the fight leaning on a great double-bladed battle-axe. He snatched it away from him, dropped his buckler, and, swinging the axe high above his head with both hands, rushed at me again. I heard a shout of anger from the crowd about me, and a low, short scream from the top of the hall, and then, ere he could bring the axe down, I made a sideward sweeping slash with all the strength of my sword-arm, and the next moment the axe tumbled to the floor, with his two severed hands still gripping the haft.

Then, as he stumbled past me, I made a backward cut at his neck and sent his great ugly head rolling along the floor like a skittle ball to within a yard of Brenda's feet. Then a great shout went up from every throat, shaking the pine rafters of the roof, and my name rang from end to end of the hall as though borne on a thunder peal, and when it had died away I stood out in the midst where Hufr's headless and handless body lay, and putting my foot on it and raising my sword aloft, I cried:

"Now, is the White Christ that lives or the dead Odin your lord? Is there any other of you, jarl or youngling, sea-king or berserker, who has still a mind to call the truth that I have seen a lie?"

Then the wild shout broke out again, loud and long and deep, weapons were swung aloft, and cheer after cheer rolled up to the shaking roof-tree, and so, in such rude fashion, yet faithful to the manner of their time and race, did the men of Ivarsheim first hail the name of the White Christ and the truth that I had expounded to them with that good blade of mine.

CHAPTER XVII

FOR THE WHITE CHRIST

THE next morning I gave to Brenda the suit of mail I had brought her from Venice, and, as I showed her piece after piece, and explained its use, I told her, in gentle, loving, words, how, in the days that were forgotten, she had ridden out with me mail-clad in her chariot at the head of the hosts of Armen, and how in a later age she had charged at the head of her war-maidens at Muta and Aizuadin and Yermouk; and then, taking her two hands in mine, I told her of the resolve which until then had remained unspoken, and asked her to do again that which she had done before, and go forth with me to the Holy Wars and fight for our new faith as together we had fought for Islam in the days of its newborn strength and purity.

She heard me in silence, but with flushed cheeks and brightly-sparkling eyes, and when I had done she put her hands in mine again and said:

"This is a weighty matter, Valdar, and I must have time to take thought on it. Leave us now, and by midday thou shalt have my answer."

"And the suit of mail?" I said. "What of that? Is my poor gift rejected?"

"Nay," she said, laughing and blushing yet more brightly than ever. "Thou foolish knight, dost thou claim to have known me all these ages and canst not see that, being a woman, I must first see how thy gift becomes me?"

And with that she pushed me towards the door, and so perforce I took my dismissal. From the guest-room I went to see Jarl Ivar, and told him what I had done, and also the reason for which I had bought the five hundred suits of mail in Venice, and he, like an old war-horse starting at the sound of a trumpet, put out his hand without more ado, and said:

"Well thought of, Valdar! By Thor and Odin, that is a good thought of thine! And so it was not alone to see the Lily of the Northland that thou hast made so much haste home? Yes, yes; it is not yet August, and there is time and to spare. There is no day like to-day, for to-morrow never comes. Our men are still all in Ivarsheim. In an hour they shall meet thee in the Thingplace, and thou shalt preach thy crusade to them, nor doubt that they will hear thee gladly if thou dost but tell them plenty of the loot that is to be found in Syria."

"Thou needest have no fear that I shall forget that." I laughed, as I shook his hand and left him.

The hour was scarcely sped before the Thingplace was alive with a great crowd of warriors all agog to hear the promised news, and when, with Jarl Ivar by my side, I strode into the midst of them and took my place on the mound in the centre, still clothed from head to foot in steel which blazed and glittered in the sunlight, weapons flashed out and hands went up, and cheer after cheer rang out, for it needed no words of mine to tell them that war was in the wind again.

Then Jarl Ivar made silence for me, and pulling off my helmet, which I had left unbolted, I told them my errand in a few plain words, and asked them to take the Cross in token of their new faith, and come with me to Syria. Then when the shouts which answered me had died away I told them of my Eastern wars, and the treasures that stout hearts and strong hands could win in the golden East.

And last of all I told them that if five hundred would follow me I would give each a suit of mail and lance and sword and battle-axe, and buy a horse for him whenever we came to a convenient market, and, in a word, that the whole war should be waged at my expense, and all the booty shared as usual.

It was a bargain after their own hearts, and instead of five hundred I might have had two thousand, and I had scarcely finished before some of them had nearly come to blows in the rivalry for a place in my troop.

But suddenly their shouts and the noise of their wrangling was hushed, and all eyes were turned and all hands pointed to the path that led down from the burgh. I looked round with the rest, and there coming down towards us was the daintiest shape of knightly beauty that mortal eyes had ever looked upon, all gold and steel and silver sheen from head to foot, with sword at hip and shining shield on arm. The shape came on, silent amidst the silence, and took its place on the mound beside Jarl Ivar and me.

Then two daintily-gauntleted hands went up and doffed the golden-visored helmet, and there stood revealed Brenda the Lily, the loveliest maiden-knight in all the ranks of chivalry, blushing and laughing and shaking her head till her long, thick tresses, released from the confinement of the helmet, rippled in bright shining waves of gold over the glittering steel of her close-linked gorget.

Then you should have heard the shout of wonder and worship that went ringing up into the sky as she put her hand in mine and said:

"Now, Valdar, does my answer please thee? Hast thou still a mind to take me as thy companion-in-arms to the Holy War?"

"Ay, that I have!" I cried. "And, if thou wilt let me, as something yet dearer even than a companion-in-arms."

"Nay, nay; of that anon!" she laughed, blushing rosier red than ever. "Thy wooing is too swift, Sir Valdar, and the maidens of the Northland are not won as easily as that. Now, tell me, how fares thy preaching? Will the men of Ivarsheim follow us to Syria?"

"All, all!" they shouted. "Weapon! Weapon! To the ships!"

And, like a pack of schoolboys let loose, those great stalwart warriors broke and ran, racing each other down to the shore, crew against crew, to get their long-ships first afloat, as though we were going to start for Syria that very day and hour.

The next day I taught them what little they needed to learn about their new armour and weapons, while Brenda and all the maids and matrons of the country-side made us white linen tunics with broad red crosses on breast and back to wear over our mail in token of our mission; and by the fourth day all was ready, and a fleet of fifty strong and stately long-ships lay on the rollers on the sloping shore, full-freighted and equipped, and needing but a thrust of willing hands to plunge once more into their element.

The morning of the fifth day had been fixed for sailing, and all Ivarsheim was out on the beach before sunrise making or watching the last preparations. As the sun rose over the great ring of Eastern mountains and his earliest rays shot over the grey waters of the fjord, turning them to gold and sapphire, Brenda, who was standing beside me already clad in her travelling gear, suddenly took me by the arm and pointed out over the Western fjord.

"Look, Valdar," she said; "what is that? Is it a happy and blessed omen for our voyage, or is it some real thing that is coming to us out of the West?"

I followed the direction of her pointing hand, and there, rising out of the water, I saw the shape of a great golden cross flashing in the rosy light of the sunrise. Soon the others saw it also, and a shout, half of awe and half of wonder, rolled along the beach in greeting to the holy sign. But as it came nearer we soon saw the reality of the apparition. It was a little white-painted galley, rowed by twelve oars, and, instead of a mast, there was set up in the bows a great cross of flat planks, covered with thin plates of burnished brass, and it was this that we had seen blazing in the sun.

As it came on we saw that the rowers were monks with shaven crowns and coarse grey woollen smocks. They stopped rowing some fifty paces from the shore, and then there uprose in the bow beside the cross the tall figure of a monk, with the cowl thrown back from his grey-fringed head and a long white beard flowing down upon his breast; and he, spreading his arms out wide, cried in a deep, rolling voice and in good monkish Greek and Latin:

"*Kyrie Eleison! Kyrie Eleison! Benedicite in nomine Jesu Christi! Benedicite! Benedicite!*"

"Who art thou?" shouted Jarl Ivar, going down to the water's edge. "Tell us thine errand, friend, in good plain speech that Northern ears can understand." And he paused for a reply.

Then the monk answered him in a tongue that differed but little from ours, and said:

"I am Anselm of Lindisfarne, an unworthy servant of the Lord, and bringer of his good tidings to you, which shall call you out of the darkness of heathenness into the glory of His truth."

"Then thou art welcome, Anselm of Lindisfarne!" shouted Jarl Ivar. "Come to land without fear. Thou wilt find us ready to receive thy teachings and take thy blessing."

"Kyrie Eleison! Kyrie Eleison! Christ is victorious! Blessed is he that cometh in the name of the Lord, even the humblest bearer of His tidings!"

And now there came to pass what all three took for a miracle of good omen, for no sooner were his feet down upon dry ground, and his eyes had rested upon me, than he made his way towards me through the press about him, and, standing half aghast before me, said:

"Thou art he whose vision in my sleep hath called me hither! I see the light of other ages in thine eyes. Who art thou?"

"I am called Valdar, who was Khalid the Sword of God, who was Terai of Armen, who came from the stars in the days that are forgotten," I said slowly and gravely, looking full into his eyes as I spoke. "Art thou another shape of him who stood with me on Calvary, for thy voice sounds to me like an echo of one that spoke to me there when the darkness fell and the thunder pealed the knell of the White Christ?"

"I know not, I know not!" he murmured, bending his head and making the sign of the Cross on his breast. "I have but dreamed what thou hast seen, thou highly favoured among men. Yet it may be—yes, it may be, for truly the ways of the Lord are full of mystery and beyond all fathoming."

"Yet the way of thy coming hither is plain enough," I said. "Thou hast a holy work to do, and here is the time and place to do it."

Then, to his wonder and delight, I told him the purpose for which we were gathered there by our ships on the beach, and when I had done he fell on his knees and, with hands outstretched and face upturned to Heaven, he cried, with streaming eyes and in a voice broken by sobs:

"Hosannah in the highest! Blessed be the name of the Lord, for He hath done marvellous things, and hath turned the hearts of the heathen unto His worship."

Then I mounted on the stern of one of the ships and told all there of the errand of the monk, and after that I put him in my place and bade him speak. And speak he did—till rude hearts melted in the heat of his burning words, and men shouted and women wept as he told in strong, simple speech the story of the Christ and the fate of His sepulchre.

When he finished there was silence, broken only by the plash of the little waves upon the beach, and men held their breath and looked at each other, with their hands gripping the hilts of their weapons.

Then a thousand blades flashed out at once, and a thousand voices shouted, fierce with new-born fervour:

"Hael to the White Christ! Hael! To Jerusalem! To Jerusalem!"

We did not sail that morning, for the coming of Anselm and His monks had given them and us much to do and think of, for the holy men would not rest until they had baptised every soul in Ivarsheim—man, woman, and child—and as there was some five or six thousand of them it was not done in an hour, albeit they knelt down in rows on the two banks of a little stream that flowed through the valley; and when Anselm had blessed the waters his brethren tucked up the skirts of their monkish garments, and went up and down in the stream sprinkling them with the water, and making the sign of the Cross on their foreheads.

When this ceremony was over I took Brenda aside and asked her if she would not let me bid Anselm perform yet another of the sacraments of his Church, and join our hands in wedlock ere we went to the Holy War. But at this she shook her pretty head, and chid me in such sweetly solemn fashion that, sore as her refusal was to me, I loved her all the better for it; nor could I find it in my heart to seek to persuade her further when she laid her hands upon the cross on her breast, and told me, even as in another tongue and for the sake of another faith she had told me centuries before, that as a maiden-knight she had vowed herself to our holy enterprise, and that as a maiden-knight she would come back from it in victory and peace, or give her life for it again as she had given it before for Islam.

That night, as was fitting, we feasted long and merrily in the great hall of the burgh, and Anselm told us many strange stories of the coming of generation after generation of Northmen to the English shores, not only from the Northland itself, but from another land they had won in the South called Normandy, whence the grandson of a stark sea-king, Hrolf the Ganger, had led a great army to the conquest of England and reduced the Saxon churls of the South to slavery, winning for himself that name of "Conqueror" which, as you know, is his unto this day.

He told us also how Richard Lionheart, King of England, the great-grandson of this same Conqueror, was even then on his way to the Holy War. When we heard this, the name of Richard Lion-heart went up from every throat in a shout that shook both walls and roof of the great hall, and there and then we swore we would serve no other leader than him in whose veins the true blood of the sea-kings flowed.

When we put to sea next morning, Anselm of Lindisfarne sailed with us, and as we cleared the fjord his brother monks stood up in their little galley round their great brazen cross and bade us a pious farewell, singing the "Te Deum" in their sweet, sonorous monkish Latin, as our long-ships swept past them on our way to the South.

In Italy and Cyprus we bought horses for our troop, and at Larnaka I had the good fortune to find a charger well worthy to bear once more my old warhorse's name, a coal-black stallion strong enough to bear Richard Lion-heart himself; and there, too, I found a bright Cyprian bay, on whose back Brenda, armed *cap-a-pie*, looked the daintiest knight that ever went to war even in those days when many a noble dame and maiden donned the knightly mail, and rode with her liege lord or plighted lover wherever honour called him.

From Cyprus we went on to Syria and landed a few furlongs to the north of Acre, round which just then the whole war was raging.

Behind the city the Crusaders had drawn a beleaguering camp from sea to sea, and behind this again to the landward side the hosts of the great Saladin were drawn up against us. As our good fortune willed it, we came with our well-laden ships in the nick of time to save the camp from famine, for to such sore straits had the Crusaders been reduced that the knights were slaying their chargers to get meat.

While the last days of the siege were drawing to a close I took out my Northern knights into the plain and practised them in the needful evolutions, and ere long proved their skill and strength in many a brisk skirmish with the Turks. Then Acre fell, as you know, worn out by famine and the grim hardships of a two years siege. But hardly was this first and greatest triumph accomplished, than they who had won the prize fell out among themselves, and brought ruin and failure on the enterprise in the very hour of success

Until the siege was over, and the city had fallen, I had neither seen nor spoken with Richard of the Lion-heart, "goodliest knight of Christendom," as all men called him, for a lingering sickness had kept him to his litter and a hut from which he had directed the siege. But at last, it was on the twenty-second day of August, in the year following that in which I had awakened in the seat of Ptah, the news flew through the camp and city that the King had given orders to march the next day on Ascalon.

The order of the march was southward along the coast of Hiafa and Cæsarea and Joppa, with the fleet protecting our sea-flank a little way from the shore, so, as Jarl Ivar and I, like most of the other leaders, followed our own counsels as we thought fittest, we settled that he should take command of our galleys, while Brenda and young Ivar and I led our troop of horse on ahead of the main army to keep the road for it; and it was in the performance of this office that the fortune of war first brought me face to face with Lion-heart.

Towards nightfall we entered a level grassy plain, flanked landward and seaward by low, rounded hills, and narrowing towards the south. I knew enough of Eastern warfare to see that this was just such a place as Saladin would choose to make a night attack, if he could once get the heavy-armed Crusaders penned up within it. So I sent out scouts along the western hills, and soon, as I expected, they came riding in to tell me that the whole country beyond them was swarming with the Moslem soldiers.

I drew my troop off the head of the plain to where a low spur of hills ran out almost across it, and then, placing sentinels along the height, and sending a couple of light-armed, well-mounted horsemen to skirt the eastern hills and take the news to Richard, I waited for the moment of battle to come.

The sun went down, and the full harvest moon climbed slowly up behind the eastern hills, and just as its disk rose broad and red against the ridge I saw it shining on line after line of glittering steel, gleaming in thousands of points of light like ripples on a moonlit sea. It was the vanguard of the Crusaders, and from what I had been told in the morning I knew that Lion-heart himself was riding at the head of it.

The Soldiers of the Cross came on in bright and orderly array, rather as though they were on the tourney-field or parade-ground than in a hostile country and the near neighbourhood of a vast host led by such a leader as Saladin.

As they reached the middle of the plain, still riding at ease in loose, open order, as though thinking of anything rather than the grim work of war, there burst out without warning all along the line of the Eastern hills that long, shrill, screaming battle-cry of Islam which my ears knew so well; and over the hills swept the swift-footed horse of Saladin, wave after wave in innumerable ranks till I thought the mighty flood would never cease; and, like a storm-driven ocean that had overswept its coast, they rolled in a furious tide of hate and valour across the narrow plain.

The front rank of the Crusaders stood like a solid rampart of iron with their long lances in rest and a hedge of spear-points a dozen feet from the mailed breasts of their chargers, and between each pair of knights was an archer or a cross-bowman. The first and the second and the third ranks of the Moslems swept up with their wild shouts, and went down under the terrible spears and the ceaseless rain of bolts and arrows, and the crushing blows of mace and falchion which fell on those who passed the spear-points. But for every rank that went down another and another came on, till the Crusaders looked like an island of iron in the midst of a vast tossing sea of white burnouses and turbans, lit up with the gleam of mail and weapons.

At length the last rank came over the hills and went down on to the field of Death. And now our time had come. I drew my sword, and waved it once in the moonlight, and before I had sent it back into the sheath every man was in the saddle, and our long shining line streamed up from behind the hill where my troops had lain hidden, and halted on the summit. There was no need for words of command, for every man already knew what there was to be done. I pointed with my lance to where the thickest masses of the Moslems were swarming against the Christian front, and then dropped my visor and trotted to my place in the middle of the line. As I reached it Brenda and Ivar rode out. Brenda took her place between us, and then we moved down the slope.

A thousand paces from the crowded flank of the Moslems we formed in close order, two deep, for the charge. Then I waved my lance aloft again and put my charger to the trot, and like a moving wall of steel we went on, silent as night and terrible as death. The trot quickened to a canter, and the canter broke into a gallop, then down went every spear and up went every shield, and we swept in an irresistible torrent of destruction through the thronging swarms of the light-armed, light-horsed Paynims. Then our two flanks swung back till we formed a wedge, and then mace and battle-axe went to work, and yard by yard we drove our way into the heart of the host, leaving a broad red road behind us strewn with the crushed and mangled dead, who but a few moments before had been so full of life and valour.

We had almost reached the Crusaders' front, when of a sudden it broke and melted away, and for a moment it seemed as though the chivalry of Europe was flying before the half-savage hordes of Saladin. The Turks yelled with triumph and dashed after them at full gallop, waving their spears and scymetars, and shouting that Malech Ric, as they called Lion-heart, had at last turned his back to them.

So he had, but not for long, for, as the Crusaders galloped off Northward, the footmen drew up into solid squares, pikemen in front and archers in the middle, and against these the waves of light horse broke in harmless fury while Richard and his knights rode out into the open plain, forming into close lines as they went. Then one by one these lines wheeled round, and we, too, in the meanwhile had fought our way clear of the press, bursting our way through the crowd that swarmed about us by sheer weight of man and horse and armour.

Then we, too, formed our double line again, and as the Crusaders charged the hastily-formed Moslem front we thundered down once more upon their rear, and crushed them in between us and Richard's lines till their ranks were broken up and they were nothing better than a rabble, fighting each one for his own hand and his own life.

With bridles interlaced and her sword dealing stroke for stroke with mine, my sweet maiden-knight and I hewed our way through the battle-press, close followed by Ivar and our gallant Northmen, until at length we reached a place where a single knight on foot was standing by the dead body of his horse, laying about him with a great two-handed sword in such fashion as I have never seen steel wielded before or since. But one against many is hard work, and as he made one sweeping stroke that sent a tall emir reeling from his saddle, the Moslem fastened his death-grip upon the blade and dragged it down with him, biting at the steel in the madness of his dying agony. He only held it for a moment or two, but it was long enough for a great Nubian to swing his iron-spiked mace aloft and aim such a blow as no helmet ever made could have stood.

I was close behind him as the mace went up, and, standing up in my stirrups, I brought my great blade down on his shoulder with such a savage stroke that it bit its way through flesh and bone and mail well nigh to his middle. As I wrenched the blade out again and he rolled over, the knight on foot turned to me and shouted in a deep, manly voice that rumbled like thunder in the hollow of his helmet:

"That was a shrewd stroke, friend, and well sped, and Richard of England thanks thee for it, and perchance for his life also!"

I waved my blade in reply to him, for there was other work on hand just then than the exchange of compliments, and we fell to again on what were left of the Moslems till my Northmen closed in on all sides to my rallying cry, and made such short, sharp work with their swords and axes that they left not a man or horse alive within the circle, in the midst of which King Richard stood with visor up, leaning on his great sword, and laughing at the grim sport that he had had.

Then I swung myself off my horse, threw up my visor, and, dropping on one knee before him, there and then thanked God that He had let me save the life of the greatest knight and the most gallant king in Christendom, after which, laying my sword at Lion-heart's feet, I proffered him the allegiance and service of my troop till the Holy Sepulchre should be won.

"By St. George," he said. "I would to God I had five thousand instead of five hundred of such gallant fighters under my banner, and then I would hunt these false French traitors and mongrel knaves of beer-swilling Germans and Austrians into the sea, and with you and my own brave English clear the road for ever to the Holy Sepulchre. And now, who art thou, friend, and what is thy rank and country? Stand up, that I may see thy face and grasp the hand that saved me."

I stood up and faced him, and as I did so I saw a look of wonder flash into his eyes, for, though he was the tallest man in all the Christian host, my helm overtopped his by a good two inches.

"By the saints!" he said, as our hands met in a grip that would have crushed the bones of some men, "she was blessed indeed who bore so stalwart a son as thou art. Thou art the only man who yet returned my grip with good interest. Who art thou?"

"I am called Valdar of Ivarsheim in the Northland, whence the fame of the Lion-heart has brought me to Syria to fight under his banner. And these, my fellow free-lances, have come with me. As for lineage, I have none, yet my blood is older than the blood of the oldest and the noblest line on earth."

"And right noble blood, too, I warrant me, whatever thy reasons for hiding thy true parentage under such strange words. Never did I see a better charge than that of thine, and never were goodlier blows struck for Christ and His Holy Sepulchre. Give me thy sword."

I picked it up and gave it to him, and, as his fingers closed on the golden hilt, he balanced it in his hand and looked at it narrowly, and said:

"By my faith, a goodly weapon, curiously fashioned, and not forged yesterday, I warrant me. How long hast thou carried it?"

"More years than thou wouldst believe were I to tell thee, Royal England," I answered, laughing. "Yet if thou wouldst hear the story of it I would tell thee when better occasion offers."

"So, so," he laughed, in reply. "Then I will hear it right gladly, for no one loves a story of martial deeds better than Richard of England. Now kneel down again and I will thank thee for what thou hast done."

I knelt down, and he drew the flat of the blade across my shoulder, saying in his deep, rolling voice:

"Rise, Sir Valdar of Ivarsheim, Knight of the Holy Cross and a peer of Christian chivalry, and as such take back thy blade, never to draw it without just cause, or to sheath it without honour. Come to-morrow to my tent, and thou shalt have thy golden spurs and baldrick, and the heralds shall proclaim thy name, and honour, and this, our act, to thy peers in arms."

I rose to my feet again amidst the shouts of my Northmen cheering for Lion-heart and me, and then a company of English knights, who had been anxiously seeking for the King, rode up, and Richard, after telling them who I was and what had passed, took one of their horses and rode off, bidding me not fail of my appointment in the morning.

The main army had now come up, and we made our camp in the plain and on the hills about it; and soon after sunrise I did as Lion-heart had bidden me, and right royally, I can tell you, did he perform that which he had promised, in the presence of the greatest nobles on the roll of English chivalry, with many a gracious act that I would fain tell of did but the space remain to do so; and when we broke camp again I and my Northmen rode out with English pennons on our lances to take the station to the front of the vanguard which Richard had given us.

Then began that long, weary march over the parched soil, and under the pitiless heat of the blazing sun, past Haifa and Cæsarea, along the coast to the Dead River, of which you have read in your history. Day after day we met and repulsed the incessant attacks of the hosts which swarmed on our flanks, until on the sixth of September we pitched our camp on the River of the Cleft, some five leagues southward of Cæsarea. Here we fought that famous Battle of the Cleft in which, as you may remember, the Grand Master of the Hospitallers and gallant Baldwin DeCarew, opened our way to victory by charging alone into the ranks of Saladin's chivalry. Hard on their heels we Knights of the Northland spurred, shouting above the battle-roar:

"Way for the Cross! On to the Holy Sepulchre! On for St. George and England, on! Have at them! Have at them!"

The cry rang out loud and fierce behind me, and I knew that the whole weight of the English chivalry was bursting into the gap that we had made. Then somehow we shaped ourselves into a wedge, and with axe and mace and sword hewed and drove our way foot by foot and yard by yard through the breaking Moslem ranks, and hour after hour we kept the grim game going, wheeling and charging through the ever-thinning masses about us till the battle became a rout and the rout a pursuit; and we rode them down or chased them in between our converging lines of pitiless steel till the shores of the River of Death sent rivulets of blood into the well-named stream, and the mighty host that Saladin had brought out against us was rent and torn into flying fragments, and only the darkness of night saved its remnants from destruction.

With this the fighting ended, and the Third Crusade was over, and I was at length free to fulfil my ancient vow and the prophecy of Sophronius by making a pilgrimage with Brenda and Ivar and the good Father Anselm to the Holy City and the Sepulchre of the Christ. Richard himself rode out with us; but on the summit of the last ridge of hills overlooking the city he stopped, and, covering his face with his hands, bowed himself to his horse's neck, and with his great deep voice broken by a sob, he said:

"O Jerusalem, now thou art, indeed, helpless! Who will protect thee when Richard is away? I have seen thee for the first and the last time; nor will I enter thy gates as a pilgrim, since I cannot enter them as a conqueror."

And with that he reined his horse about, and rode back alone down the road to Joppa. We never saw him again, for when our own pilgrimage was done and we got back to the coast we learnt that the fever had struck him down again, and that he had sailed for Europe—to find a dungeon in the castle of one of the traitors who had betrayed him and the holy cause, and to meet his death in an obscure fight for a paltry treasure.

As for us, we boarded our galleys once more and fared back to the Northland, leaving many a score of our gallant Northmen on the Syrian battlefields, but carrying with us good fat cargoes of Syrian spoil and coffers well filled with ransom gold. But what glory and booty we had won had but small value for me, for we had been but a few days at sea when signs of the deadly Eastern fever began to show themselves among us, and on the sixth day Brenda fell sick of it.

From ship to ship it spread like the plague that it was. Then came driving rains and bitter storms, and every sun that rose saw some of our fleet missing, till at last, out of sixty gallant ships that had sailed from Ivarsheim, only three storm-tossed and wave-battered galleys won their way through the North Sea storms and came at length to rest on the beach of Ivarsheim.

But Brenda, though she knew she had but come home to die, still loved me with the faithful love that had been renewed again and again through the centuries, and when, on the morning of the fourth day after the home-coming, Anselm took me to her chamber to say farewell, she put her thin white hand in mine and sweetly told me that now she would keep the promise she had made before we sailed, and so, ere she became once more the bride of Death, for the first time she gave herself to me.

All that day and through the next night I watched her dear life ebb away so slowly that I could hardly mark the passing of it until, as the first ray of the sunrise shone from the cold, clear winter sky across a window that looked to the south, and fell on her face, I did not know whether she was dead or sleeping, so white and still it was. Then she opened her eyes and looked at me. Her lips moved in a smile, and as I cast myself on my knees beside her a faint whisper came from them and said:

"Farewell, Valdar, once more—kiss me good-bye, dear—till we meet again."

And as our lips met she died, even as she had done on that far-off day when we died together in the sands of the Assyrian desert. I let no one touch her dear dead body but myself, and I dressed her in her knightly mail and built a funeral pyre on the deck of my own long-ship and laid her on it. Then I took farewell of Ivarsheim and Anselm, who stayed to do his Master's work or die in the doing of it, and hoisted my sail and steered out into the Northern Sea for three days and nights, and then one midnight, alone with my dear dead on the black waste of waters, I lit the pyre, and as the flames roared up round the still, shining form in the midst of them, the hand of my fate smote me once more with the chill of death and I sank to the deck, and the burning ship drifted on with its dead through the night.

CHAPTER XVIII

IN THE DAYS OF GREAT ELIZABETH

Lying full-clad in my crusading mail, just as I had set out on the death-voyage from Ivarsheim with Brenda, saving only that my helm had been unbuckled and stood beside me on the narrow couch spread with faded tapestry on which I lay, and that my sword lay along my breast with my crossed hands folded over the hilt, and that my shield stood at my feet—so I, who had fallen asleep before Brenda's burning pyre in the black and dreary midnight on the Northern Sea, woke to new life again at the beginning of another stage of my long pilgrimage.

For awhile I lay still, my thoughts wandering unchecked by any will of mine over that misty borderland which lies between the twin dreamlands of sleep and waking, now with closed eyes looking back over the long expanses of the past which returning memory made ever plainer and plainer to me, and now gazing lazily and dreamily about the little tapestry-hung, crypt-roofed chamber in which I lay.

As the blood began to flow quicker and stronger through my kindling veins I rose from my couch and stretched my stiffened limbs, and then, as the first act of my new life, I drew my blade from its sheath to find its blue-grey lustre still undimmed, and the faithful steel whole and bright and keen as ever. My baldrick, adorned with gold and gems, still crossed my breast from the right shoulder to the left hip, and the belt of knighthood that Lion-heart had given me on the far-off Syrian battlefield was still buckled round my waist. My mail and shield and helm were as brightly burnished and as speckless as my own hands had made them on that sad morning in Ivarsheim, and every rivet was as sound and every joint was as supple as it had been when I first bought the mail from the armourer in Venice.

How had this come to pass? By whose loving care had I been tended through the years of my death-sleep—years which I might well guess had been counted by hundreds?

The unspoken question was soon answered, and that in the sweetest fashion the memory of my lost love could have made me wish for, for, as I stood there wondering, with my naked sword in my hand, I heard a key turn in a lock, a door opened, the tapestry was pulled aside, and there, clothed in strange yet dainty fashion, with the light of life in her eyes and the flush of health glowing in her cheeks, stood she whom I had last seen lying cold and pale in death, clad in her knightly mail on her funeral pyre on my long-ship.

But the next moment the flush died out of her cheeks, a short, low cry broke from her half-open lips, her eyes dilated in a stare of wonder and affright, and then, like a flash of light fading out of the darkness it has illumined, she vanished just as with outstretched hands I took a long swift stride towards her.

Dumb with amazement, yet with my pulses beating high with new-born delight and hope, I stood motionless as a statue of steel till the door opened again. The tapestry was flung hastily aside, and a tall, stalwart young fellow, whom I guessed at a glance could be none other than the brother of her who now wore Brenda's shape, strode into the room, and, after one brief backward start and the passing of a swift pallor over his face, held out his hand to me and said, in a tongue that differed but little from that sweet, strong English speech that I had learned on our voyages from the lips of Anselm of Lindisfarne:

"Welcome back to the world, Sir Valdar of Ivarsheim! You have slept long and, it seems, well, for never did I see a man of your years look so hale and youthful."

He laughed as he said these last words, and I, returning his hand-grip with interest, laughed too, and said, in my older speech:

"How long I have slept I know not, yet it is not the first sleep of the kind that I have awakened from, as thou perchance knowest, since thou knowest also my name and the rank that Lion-heart gave me after the Battle of the Plain. Now let me thank thee for thy kindly welcome and for the loving care that thou hast lavished on me while I have lain asleep. But first tell me thy name, that I may know to whom the debt is due."

"Nay, nay, there is but small debt due to me," he said, "since ten generations of Carews have passed on to me that wondrous legacy from old Sir Baldwin of which it seems I am to reap the pleasure and the profit."

"What!" I cried. "Is, then, thy name Carew, and was he thou speakest of that brave Baldwin de Carew who so gallantly charged the Turks with the Marshal of the Hospitallers—two against two hundred—and fought side by side with me in that great Battle of the Cleft, where we so broke the Soldan's power that, but for the foul traitors who hindered us, we could have taken all Syria from him, and maybe Egypt as well?"

Before he could answer me the door opened again very slowly, the tapestry was gently drawn aside, and the sweet face of the girl who had found me first, peered in timid wonder at us. Then, seeing us talking and laughing together like any other creatures of good, honest flesh and blood, her wonder got the better of her fear, and she shut the door and came in.

"Ah, Mistress Kate, so you have come back," said her brother, as I soon found he was. "I thought it would not be long ere your woman's curiosity conquered your woman's fears. Well, you see the marvel that old Sir Baldwin prophesied in his will has come to pass after all, and here is your Sleeping Crusader awake again, and longing greatly to know whose tender care, as he himself has put it, has watched over him while he lay asleep. So now come and shake hands with him. Nay, nay, there is no cause for fear. You will find his hand as living-warm as mine, and vastly stronger, too, for my fingers are still tingling with the grip he gave me."

While he was speaking he took her by the hand, and led her, half shrinking half eager towards me: and, as he put her little fluttering hand in mine, I dropped in knightly fashion on my knee before her, and, raising it to my lips, kissed it, saying:

"As in the past so in the present and the future I will be thy true knight, sweet lady, and he who does not confess thee peerless among the daughters of this or any other land shall have the truth proven on his body."

"What is that Sir Valdar?" cried her brother in amaze. "In the past? Would you tell us that you, who have been lying sleeping here for full three hundred and sixty years, have seen and served my sister Kate before as her true knight in the days of chivalry?"

"Ay," I said, rising to my feet and facing them both, "I would tell you so, and tell you truly, though I can scarce hope you will believe me. But that is a long story, and I crave your pardon for having broached so strange and terrible a theme with such rude suddenness. Tell me dear lady, that I may hope to be forgiven."

"Yes, yes," she said, recoiling a pace from me and clasping her hand to her breast. Then she stood silently gazing at me for a moment or two, and then, with the same sweet smile that had gladdened my heart so often, she went on: "But there is nothing to forgive, and I, indeed, believe you, most wondrous as your strange words are, for you are the knight of my dreams—dreams that I will tell you of some day when you have told us again the story that has been a legend among us for generations. But now, fie on me! I am forgetting that I am hostess here, and that you, our guest, must be hungry and athirst after so long a fast. Come Philip, bring Sir Valdar out of this cheerless sleeping-room of his into the parlour, and I will go and see what there is in the larder."

Here soon we sat down, and Lady Kate, as I ere long came to call her in my old-world fashion, soon spread a plentiful repast for me with her own fair hands, saying the while that for the present she must be both hostess and housekeeper, since old Marjory, their serving-woman, would surely die of fright at the sight of me. Then, when I had eaten and drunk my fill, with an appetite that would have been no shame to a starving wolf, I prayed Sir Philip again that he would tell me how I came to awake in such pleasant company.

So he began and told me my own story as follows:

"This house is Carew Manor," he began, speaking, I thought, somewhat sadly, "and it stands on the remnant of what was once one of the fairest estates in Northumberland, and that little chamber in which you have slept your long sleep is in a poor half-ruined tower, which is all that is left of the strong and stately castle to which our gallant ancestor, Sir Baldwin de Carew, came home from the Holy War, after the Crusaders had made that truce of which you know far more than we do. The castle keep stood up yonder on that little hill, on which you can still see a few remnants of the outer ramparts. On the night of the day that he came home the warder on watch at the top saw a blaze of light out at sea, for I should have told you the coast is only a bare half a mile from here, and when the report was carried to Sir Baldwin he ordered one of his galleys to put out at once, for there might be lives to be saved on the burning ship, for, as you doubtless know, the good old knight was as kind of heart as he was strong of arm. So the galley went out with all speed, and found a knight of mighty stature, clad from head to foot in splendid armour, lying prone in the stern of one of those dragon-ships in which the old Northmen went to war. The fore part of the ship was almost burnt away, and the water was already pouring in through the opening seams, and hissing against the fire as they lifted up the knight from the deck and bore him to the galley. And scarcely had they done this when the flames blazed up through the deck amidships, and the vessel broke in two, and went down."

"Alas, poor Brenda! And yet thou didst find a grave worthy of a sea-king's daughter."

"And who was Brenda, Sir Valdar?" asked Kate, with a flush on her cheeks and a tremor in her voice. "Was she, too, with you on that burning ship?"

"Nay," I said, "for that sweet soul which is now looking at me out of those eyes of yours, dear lady, had already gone back to its home beyond the stars; but all that was mortal of her—ay, and of you, too—lay on that blazing pyre which I had built for her and lighted with my own hand. But that is only a little part of that longer story which I must tell you, for you must hear the whole before you can understand a part."

She shrank back in the deep window-seat where she was sitting, and for a moment covered her face with her hands, as though to shut out some fearful vision, and Sir Philip, glancing first at her and then at me, went on:

"Methinks, Sir Valdar, that this tale of mine is but a dull and trifling thing to be told before all the wonders that you will tell us of, so I will make it as brief as maybe, so that the less may the sooner give due place to the greater.

"When the galley brought you to land and you were carried into the castle, Sir Baldwin instantly recognised you. And when there was a talk of burying you, he swore that you had but fallen into a trance, and vowed that, until his own eyes should see the signs of decay upon your body, the graveyard mould should never touch it. When, twelve years after, his last sickness took him and no trace of change had come over you, he made a will, and, after appointing masses to be said for the repose of your soul in case it should never come back to your body, he left that part of his estate which forms this manor to the heir of his house for ever on the condition that you should be left to rest in peace in your chamber till either the decay of death set in or you awoke from your trance. Further, he provided, as you will see in the will when I show it to you, that nothing appertaining to you should ever be taken away, and that every day the lord of the manor, or, in his absence, someone whom he could perfectly trust, should visit you and see that your armour and weapons were kept bright and your chamber in order—an office which, I may tell you, Mistress Kate yonder took on herself six years ago, when our mother died and she was but a little maiden of twelve years; so, you see, you are already old friends."

"That you might have well left out, Philip," cried Kate, blushing anew, and trying with but indifferent success to keep her eyes from meeting mine. "What has that to do with Sir Valdar's fate?"

"More, perchance, than your dear modesty would confess, fair lady," I said, smiling at her sweet confusion. "As we may prove ere long."

"That well maybe," said Sir Philip, with a laugh that quickly died out of his voice as he went on with his tale.

"But let me finish my story, of which there is now not much more to tell. As the generations rolled by and you slept on, the fortunes of our House passed through many changes, ever for the worse, till the Wars of the Roses left us with only a ruined castle, our own unsullied name, and this one manor which old Sir Baldwin's will had kept for your sake, and, fortunately for us, beyond the reach of the usurers who have taken all else, for if a Carew had tried to sell it, then by the conditions of the will it would have passed at once to the Abbey of Alnwick, and thus you may see, Sir Valdar, that we owe all that is left of our possessions to you."

That same night, after supper, Sir Philip told me of the growth and glory of his own people, of that strong, strenuous English race, which, as I knew, might have traced the best and strongest strain of its blood back through the stalwart Northmen and their many migrations of that primeval hero-folk whose queen had been my first earthly love, and whose armies I had led with her to victory against the ancient might of Nineveh.

When at length he had finished, there was silence among us for a moment or two, and then the old battle-fire burnt up in my breast again, fanned by the spirit of the brave story he had told me, and I sprang to my feet and, drawing my sword, I put the golden hilt to my lips and said:

"Then such a land as this heroic England and this gallant people, into whose veins has flowed through the unnumbered centuries the blood of my first companions-in-arms in long-forgotten Armen, shall be my land and my people, and I will fight for it and them so long as my fate shall let me, so help me God and this good blade of mine!"

"A righteous oath and sworn, as becomes a true knight and a good man!" cried Sir Philip, springing from his chair and coming to me with outstretched hands. "The Carews are poor enough now in worldly wealth, and I am the last man of their line, but I have still heart and hand to give to England, and with yours, Sir Valdar, I will give them. The time has come when every hand and sword is needed, and he is no man who holds back, for ere long England must measure her strength against the tyrants of the world, and overcome them or fall, never, perchance, to rise again. Here is my hand to thine, all unworthy though it be to clasp that which has felt the grip of Lion-heart, and when the day of Armageddon comes may thou and I stand together in the fight!"

And on that our hands clasped in a silence that said more than words, and then Kate came to us, and, laying her soft, warm hand on ours, said, with solemn sweetness:

"Amen to that, my brother and you, knight of my dreams, whose awakening I have so long and almost hopelessly awaited! No better oath was ever sworn in a better cause, and well I know that you will keep it. And now, Sir Valdar," she went on, looking up half shyly at me, her sweet gravity melting into a yet sweeter smile, "since you are now doubly one of us I may be bold enough to ask you once again to tell us your story and that of her whose soul you have called mine and whose shape you say I wear."

The night was far spent when I had finished telling them of our home-coming to Ivarsheim and Brenda's death, and the voyage that had brought me to England, and as the last words fell slowly and sadly from my lips Kate rose from her seat and came to me with outstretched hands, her eyes overbrimming with tears, and her fair face almost as pale as it had been on that last winter's morning in Ivarsheim, and said:

"Yes, it is so! You said we should not believe your story, yet we do, for you are the true knight of my dreams, and all that you have told us I have seen done and heard spoken—every deed and word of it, perchance not only in the night-visions that have come to me!"

I took her hands in mine, and, looking down into her melting eyes, I said, moved by some strange impulse that shaped the words without my will:

"Yes, sister soul of mine, it is true. And now you are alive again on earth with me, and I am your true knight once more, and——"

"And there the story ends, till Fortune's hand shall write it further, good Sir Valdar," she said, snatching her hands from mine, and starting back a good arm's length beyond my reach, as though she had known, as in good truth she may have done, that the next moment such an escape would have been impossible. For just an instant she stood looking at me, half laughing, half afraid, with such a pretty look of defiance in her eyes that my own grave mood passed from me like a drifting shadow, and I, too, laughed, and said:

"So be it sweet lady mine, that has been and that yet may be, and though Fortune may hold the pen, yet will I do all that in me lies to guide her fingers as they write."

"A fair challenge, on my faith, and given in right knightly guise," laughed Sir Philip, rising from his chair and looking from her to me. "And now, Mistress Kitty, there are but few hours of the night left for you to dream yet another of your strange dreams, so be off to bed, or we shall see fewer roses in your cheeks to-morrow. You can trust me to see to your good knight's further wants, so say good-night and get you gone."

Yet, late as it was, Sir Philip and I sat on talking of other things which demanded early settlement. First he helped me to put off my mail in which I had been for such an unconscionably long time. Then he went to the cellar and filled another flagon of wine, and when he came back he found me with the last of the rolls containing all that was left of the treasure of the long-dead Pharaoh spread out on the table before me.

When I had told Sir Philip, who, of course, already knew of the coming of the treasure into my hands, how, though I had forgotten it, the roll had been preserved to me, and showed him how the loyal faith of his ancestors, who, in all their poverty, had not even taken a jewel from my baldrick, had preserved not only my poor trance-bound body, but also a treasure that should restore the House of Carew to all and more than its former greatness, I picked out the finest of the gems, a glorious great diamond, whose matchless purity well befitted the dear destination I designed for it, and said:

"That no dealer's dirty hands shall touch; and these, and these," I went on, picking out four of the finest emeralds and rubies, "shall go with it, and the cunningest craftsman in England shall make them into a troth-gift against the decision of that gentle challenge which your sweet sister may perchance take up. But these, which are well worth a king's ransom, are yours and mine, Sir Philip. With your share, which is justly yours by the testament of old Sir Baldwin, you shall buy back the ancient lands of Carew, and from you and some sweet English maid that you shall take to wife the old line shall take new life, and flourish as it has never done before. With my share I will go back to my old trade, and buy ships and these strange new flame-and-thunder arms which you have told me of, and I will hire English crews with good sea-king's blood in their veins, and then you shall present me to this Virgin Queen of yours, this great Elizabeth, whom you, I doubt not justly, so much delight to honour, and I will go and fight for her and England against these dark-souled, bloody tyrants that you have told me of, and when I have proved myself by deeds of war worthy to enter the lists of love then I will essay that dearer conquest of which I spoke just now."

"Nor shall you go alone to fight the Dons, my good and generous Sir Valdar!" he cried, taking me by the hand. "I may speak frankly to you now, and tell you that nothing save my poverty and my duty to Kate, and that trust which has been a heirloom to us all these generations, has prevented me turning adventurer and seeking fame and wealth upon the sea and in the golden Spanish

Indies; for I have loved the sea since I first saw it, and my life's dearest dream has been of distant lands and the sunlit seas which one day shall be England's. So, if you will have me, we will go together, and the ancient lands of Carew can wait awhile."

"Right willingly!" I said, "I could wish for no better brother-in-arms. But what of this fair sister of yours? Can you find a safe asylum for her while we are away?"

"We will talk with her of that to-morrow," he said, with a laugh that raised a half-shaped hope within me. "I doubt not that she will have something to say for herself on such a matter as that."

The next day we laid our plans before her ladyship and asked her counsel on them. She heard them, as I knew she would, with bright-flushing cheeks and sparkling eyes all aglow with that heroic spirit which could not but be hers. But when Sir Philip spoke of leaving her behind she flamed out into the prettiest mock-anger, and told us roundly that she was as good a sailor as the best of us, that she had been born beside the sea, and knew and loved its every mood, and that we should take her with us or she would cut her hair and don boy's clothes and ship as cabin-boy in spite of us on one of our own ships.

We let but little of the dust of delay gather upon our resolves once they were made, and I had not been their guest a month before Sir Philip had shut the Manor up and pensioned off his few remaining servants, and the three of us went to Newcastle, where, with the price of two or three of the old Pharaoh's jewels, we hired a good stout barque of some two hundred tons well found and armed, and in her made a fair and prosperous voyage to London, I on the way learning with the help of Sir Philip and the ship's gunners, the use of those terrible new tools which had come to be used in my old trade of war.

Once landed there I got to work, and with the help of Sir Philip and certain merchant-friends of his and his father's I sold enough of my Egyptian gems to give us a sum of the value of more than fifty thousand pounds of your modern money, and with that we bought and manned and equipped four of the best ships that we could find in the Thames and the Medway.

All this gave us some two months of hard and busy work, and during the doing of it we kept pretty much to ourselves, and when at last all was ready and we were wondering how much longer Mr. Secretary Walsingham, whom Sir Philip had petitioned for our letters of marque, was going to keep us waiting, there came on the same day—it was the 25th of May, 1585—the stirring news that Philip of Spain had treacherously seized a greet fleet of English corn ships to feed his ever-growing Armada, and a summons to us to proceed without delay to the Court at Westminster to be presented to the Queen.

"That is good news, Sir Valdar," said Sir Philip, as he showed me the dispatch. "And doubly good news for you, for now you will see, not only the greatest Queen that ever ruled a realm, but also the greatest man that ever helped to make one, for Francis Drake himself is at the Court, and there will be great deeds done ere long."

And when the day and the hour of our presentation came this is what my old-world wondering eyes beheld.

A lean, sharp-featured woman, with coarse red hair, and small greenish-blue eyes, dressed in garments of splendid fabrics, yet of the grotesquest shape that ever insulted the fair form of womanhood, so appeared to me, as the ushers halted us at the door of the audience-room, the great Elizabeth, that strong-souled woman in whose hands the Fates had placed the English sceptre in those dark and troublous times when the fate, not alone of England, but of all Europe and half the world besides, hung trembling in the balance between freedom and slavery.

As we halted among the others who were waiting at the door, a little, thick-set, bull-necked man, with fair hair and clear, quick, laughing blue eyes, sun-bronzed skin, a brown moustache, and short, pointed beard which seemed to make his cheeks look even rounder than they were, came strutting with short strides down the hall, and shook hands with Sir Philip, bidding him in a deep, clear, ringing voice that would have become a man twice his size:

"Welcome to the maze of dark ways and crooked turnings."

When they had shaken hands, Sir Philip, with all the ceremony of the time, presented me to him, and then to my utter amaze I learnt that this was Francis Drake.

As I looked down upon him from the height of my own giant stature I thought of Nimrod and Tiglath, of stalwart Derar and mighty Lion-heart, and wondered what kind of figure he would cut beside them, and then I blushed for my own folly as I thought next of that little, spare, puny-looking man with the eagle eyes and strong square jaw who, fifteen hundred years before, I had seen on the utmost pinnacle of earthly glory, with his masterful grasp on more than half the world.

"So this is your friend, Sir Philip," he said, putting his head back and looking up at me. "And he has bought him a fleet and wants to go a-privateering with me to the Spanish Main, or where else the grace of Heaven and the wisdom of our mistress may send us. Well, well, he is a goodly man, if somewhat big for a sailor." Still, that is but my fancy and bad manners to boot, and the giving of unasked opinions is not presently my errand. Our Sovereign Lady has bidden me bring you and Sir Philip to kiss her royal hand, and methinks you need have little doubt of your reception, for with all respect, there is no better judge of manhood in the world. And now, an't please you, come along, for Her Majesty is also the worst waiter in the world."

There was but brief space for thought before we reached the foot of the throne, and Sir Philip and I fell in turn on bended knee before the Majesty of England.

She gave me her hand to kiss, and when she had bidden me rise she looked at me with a keen, searching glance that seemed to read my inmost thoughts—Gods, what would she have done had she in truth been able to do so!—and then she said in a high-pitched voice which, coming from a woman's lips, somewhat jarred harshly on my ears:

"Sir Valdar of Ivarsheim—a name and title both foreign, are they not? We, for certain, have never heard either of them before."

"Yes, Majesty," I replied, "both are foreign, yet I take both from the land whence sprang that great ancestor of thine, whom the world still calls 'Conqueror.'"

"A seemly answer," she said, "though given in a tongue that has a strange, old-fashioned ring about it. And your title, whence had you that—by inheritance, or as the reward of some brave deed performed with that strong right hand and arm of yours?"

"Royal England, the title that I bear was won with the sword, and is already ten generations old, since it takes its rise from the time of the Holy Wars."

"Then your name, Sir Valdar, is more honourable than is familiar to us, yet I doubt not that it has descended to a worthy scion who ere long will give us due cause to know it. We hear from our trusty Admiral, Sir Francis Drake, that at your own cost and risk you have equipped a squadron with which you crave our royal licence to put to sea on certain ventures to which you expect some profit to attach. Is that not so?"

"Yes, Majesty, it is," I replied. "Yet our aim is not alone for profit, but rather before that the protection of this ancient realm, the confounding of its enemies, and such increase of the glory of its gracious mistress as the favour of Heaven and the wisdom of Royal England may vouchsafe to us."

As I spoke I saw the eyes of the courtiers about her throne widen, while some brows frowned and some lips curved into smiles which were half sneers, but over Drake's face their spread such a smile as no true man could but love to see, for, as I knew afterwards, my speech was after his own heart, and, as with his own lips he told me, he loved me for it. What was even of more account, they found such echo in Elizabeth's soul that there and then the Royal licence was given to us, and were commended to the good care of him who, even in those early days, was beginning to be called "The Queen's Little Pirate."

Then other seekers of audience came forward with their introducers, and the three of us made downwards towards the door, where we turned and made our last obeisance to the Throne. As we came into the ante-room I saw amidst the crowd that was waiting for entrance a young fellow of some two or three-and-twenty years, whose face, clear cut in every feature and stamped in every line with that mysterious mark which Nature sets upon her chosen sons and daughters, arrested my glance and held it instantly, as though by some spell wrought by the soul that looked up at me out of his clear grey eyes.

"Who is that man, Sir Philip?" I whispered, taking him by the shoulder.

"I know not; but perchance you do, Sir Francis?"

"Nay, I know him no more than you do," laughed the great Admiral. "But here is one who doubtless does," he said, catching an usher by the arm and saying to him in an undertone: "Who is yonder lad with the handsome face and high white forehead, dressed in country garb, standing by Sir Thomas Fitzalan?"

"That, most noble Admiral," said the usher, bowing low before the greatest man in England, and taking a look meanwhile at a written list in his hand, "is one named William Shakespeare, of Stratford-on-Avon, in Warwickshire, a country lad who would fain follow in the footsteps of Her Most Gracious Majesty's sweetest of singers, Master Edmund Spenser, and he hath come hither to-day craving an audience that he may lay at the feet of the Queen's Majesty some idle ode or other doggerel, whose only recommendation can be that it is designed, however unworthily, to so duteous and laudable a purpose."

"Then, saving the presence of all here," I said, moved by that same impulse which many a time before had made me speak without my will, "there is that in William Shakespeare's face which tells me that in days to come no English name will stand much higher than his."

"My Lord is pleased to prophesy," said the usher, again bowing low, this time to the friend of Francis Drake, "yet this Will Shakespeare is but one of many others who come hither on like errands, and go away again to lose themselves amidst the meanness of their own low-born obscurity."

I turned my back on the smooth-spoken, fawning jack-in-office, and, taking a couple of strides across the room to where Will Shakespeare stood, I held out my hand to him and said:

"You are William Shakespeare, as I am told, a poet in search of royal favour. There is a hand that has grasped those of kings and conquerors. Unless your face belies your genius, as faces seldom do, it will be honoured if you lay yours in it. I am a soldier of fortune and you are a servant of the Muses, almost as fickle mistresses. So we may well shake hands, if you will."

He looked up at me with a swift, searching glance, that glance which was destined to read the inmost thoughts of human hearts as they were never read before and maybe never will be again, and then he put his hand in mine and said:

"No greeting can be kindlier than that which comes spontaneously from the kindly heart of one stranger to another. I thank you, sir, whoever you are, and if ever I can repay this kindness, poor though I be now, yet shall not the will be wanting to do so."

"Thou wilt do it," I said, "in this age or another, or I, who have talked Virgil and Ovid and Lucretius, have never seen a poet yet on earth."

This last was spoken in a whisper that only reached his ear, and ere the stare of blank amazement had faded from his face I had wrung his hand and turned away and left him—the greatest of the great that were to be in all the gallant times of Great Elizabeth. Yet as we left the ante-room I laid my hand on the great Admiral's shoulder and said:

"Sir Francis, if ever I shall earn a favour from you repay it to me by keeping a kindly eye on yonder youth, for some voice within me tells me that in the days to come few will do more for England's glory than he will."

"Why, that I will right willingly, Sir Valdar," he rolled out, with his jovial laugh. "It is a small thing to ask at most, for, though but a plain man myself, I ever loved a good poet."

That night Sir Philip and I went to supper with him at the Old Ship Inn, where he was lodging, and there I found myself one of as gallant and glorious a company as ever sat round a single board. Nay, I think it but good truth to say that if you hunted the world's history through you could find seated round one table no other company of men who, singly or together, have left so great a mark on the tablets of Destiny as did those with whom I supped as the guest of Francis Drake.

The next morning we dropped down the Thames on the ebb tide in our galley, and pulled up the Medway to Upnor, where our ships were lying snugly at anchor, and there we made the last of our preparations for the voyage that was now certainly before us. The next day a Queen's messenger, riding post haste, brought our letters of marque all in due order under the royal sign manual, and with them a letter addressed to myself, which ran as follows:

"*A boy's will, the winds of heaven, and a woman's whim have never yet been stabled since the world began, and, if the wind shall presently be favourable when this reaches you, it were best to sail lest a head-wind should come to-morrow. The trysting-place is Plymouth.*

"FRANCIS DRAKE."

Such words from such a man could have but one meaning, and one answer. That afternoon our anchors came up, and so, a fair wind behind us, we began that first cruise of ours, of which more skilled pens than mine have already told you; how we burnt Santiago in Cape Verde where the Dons had burnt young Will Hawkins alive five years before; how we fared through good and evil fortune till we reached the golden lands of the West; and how we stormed the strong cities of San Domingo and Cartagena, and came home—what were left of us—well-nigh sick to death, yet covered with glory and laden with the richest plunder that the Dons had ever lost.

But, in the meantime, Philip of Spain had been devoting all his strength to the building of such a fleet as the world had never seen before, and, though his agents at the Court of England and the traitors whose souls they had bought with Spanish gold lied hard and skilfully to the contrary, there was not a sailor in the English fleet or an honest man at Court who did not know what the true purpose of that great Armada was. With it Philip would join hands by sea with Parma by land, the revolting Netherlands would be crushed, and after that England's turn would come.

Was it any wonder, then, that we came back to a land of gloom and apprehension? Yet our anchors had not been lying in the mud a week before the news of what we had done flew like wildfire over England and across the narrow seas, and men saw that a new power had been borne into the world, for it was on that very day which saw us come back victorious that the first hour of Britain's empire of the sea struck. As for us, having done that which we set out to do, we were well content to leave the troubles of nations to the liars who made them, and so we took our ships round to Newcastle, where we laid them up to be refitted, while Sir Philip, with his share of what we had taken from the Dons, set to work buying back his ancient lands and restoring the fallen fortunes of his House.

But hardly was January out than Walsingham fired the train that was to set Europe ablaze by showing the Queen a letter from Philip to the Pope, stolen from His Holiness's own cabinet, in which the Champion of the Church, as he loved to call himself, declared in so many words that the true purpose of the ever-growing Armada was the invasion of England and the restoration of the Catholic rule in that last stronghold of religious liberty.

"*If you love me, and have any stomach for even better sport than we lately had on the Spanish Main, get your ships refitted with all possible speed and join me at Plymouth, for Her Majesty hath been graciously pleased to order me to the coast of Spain, where I hope to singe King Philip's beard with a torch fashioned out of such of his own shipping as I can lay hands on.*"

Words like these from Francis Drake, for you have already rightly guessed the writer of them, meant none could say how much, and the same day that the post-rider had brought his letter to me Sir Philip and I rode into Newcastle and gave orders that neither time nor money should be spared in getting our ships ready for sea as soon as might be. That was about the end of February, and by the middle of March the *Lady Kate*, spic and span from truck to keel, dropped down the Tyne with five tall ships in her wake, and shaped her course for Plymouth.

Her dear name-mother was shipmate with us on board her, but this time she was only bound for Plymouth, to be the guest of the Admiral's wife while we were away, and when at last, one mild, sunny day in April, we once more rounded into the familiar Sound and saluted the Admiral's flag flying from the masthead of his old ship, the time had already come for my Lady Kate and I to say good-bye, for the first news we got was a message to re-water and victual with the utmost haste, and be ready to sail at any moment.

That same afternoon Sir Philip and I took her ashore and presented her to her hostess, for the Admiral was all impatience to beg one, and dreading lest any hour should bring a messenger post-haste from Court to revoke his orders.

The next day at sundown the signal gun to weigh anchor boomed from the Admiral's forecastle, and, ready or unready, every ship had to make sail or be left behind. As our own anchor came up, Kate was standing beside me in the cabin of her stately namesake. I took her two hands in mine, and bending over her, half-whispered in her ear:

"Sweet Kate, I am going to war for England and for you, and war's chances are many since this vile gunpowder made any pigmy knave that can point a gun straight the equal of the starkest knight that ever swung a blade. All this time I have loved and served you as your own true knight, and never asked reward. Now have you not one little kiss to spare of all the hundreds those dear lips of yours can give? I crave but one—the first—which, in the hazard of war, may also be the last!"

She looked up at me half startled as I spoke, and I, seeing neither anger on her brow nor refusal in her eyes, took silence for consent, and she took the kiss with such half-hearted protest that I, with my eyes suddenly opened, and seeing how many such kisses I, perchance, had lost through blindness or over-diffidence, straightway picked her ladyship up in my arms, and there and then made up as well as time permitted for lost opportunities, and when I set her down again she faced me, blushing from brow to chin, and laughing and crying and frowning all at the same moment, and said, tapping her indignant little foot on the deck:

"So, Sir Valdar, my stalwart hero of a hundred fights, is that the way your old-world chivalry has taught you to use your strength to overcome the weakness of a helpless woman?"

"Not quite helpless, lady mine," I answered, "since a single word from those sweet lips or one forbidding glance from those dear eyes which now look laughing at me—ay, laughing in spite of your frowns—would have made this same strength of mine but as the weakness and fear of a chidden child. Surely now, your anger comes too late. If you had but chidden me before, as you did not—"

"Because I would not," she interrupted. "And because this is neither time nor season for any talk that does not come straight from a true heart. Good-bye, Valdar, for I hear the anchor coming up, and I know the Admiral will brook no delay. I would fain come with you as I did in those old wars we went to long ago, but since you will not let me, I can only stay at home and pray for your safe return. Good-bye, then, once again, and when you come back in victory—"

"Then," I said taking her unresisting in my arms again, "then I will ask you for that which I now have good hope you will not deny me. What say you, sweet, think you that I shall ask in vain?"

"That I will tell you when you come, for methinks I have made surrender enough for one day."

"Almost enough and yet not quite," I said, catching her close to me again as she made a motion to escape. "Come now, sweet Kate, just one kiss in return such as you gave me long ago that night outside the walls of Mecca, ere we went away to the Syrian wars, when I was Khalid and you were Zoraida."

"Just one, then, for those old times' sake," she said, and as the kiss was half-given, half-taken, she slipped out of my arms again, and made good her retreat to the cabin door, and, holding it half open, she said, with a saucy toss of her pretty head: "That was not the *first* kiss, Sir Valdar. Have you forgotten my sleeping crusader?"

Swiftly as I took two long strides to the door I was too late to catch her ere she had vanished up the companion-way, and when I reached the deck she was already bidding farewell to Sir Philip in such demure and sisterly fashion that I had perforce to hold back and make the best of my thoughts till they had embraced for the last time, and she came to me with outstretched hand and said:

"And, now, good-bye to you again, Sir Valdar. Give the Dons a right warm greeting for my sake and Merry England's, and let not your keels tarry on the homeward voyage. Strike hard and true, and every time you strike think of those who are waiting to welcome you home again."

"Farewell, again, sweet Kate," I said, almost in a whisper, as I led her to the gangway, "and when I do come back you shall tell me how you called me back to life, even as Cleopatra did in the Temple of Ptah. Farewell, once more!"

"Farewell, again, Valdar, my own good knight!" she murmured, her voice breaking in a tender tremor as I stooped and kissed the hand I would so willingly have exchanged for her lips, and then as the words "All clear" came in a hoarse cry from the forecastle, and the ship swung free from her moorings, I handed her down into the boat which was waiting for her, and sprang back on to the deck.

CHAPTER XIX

THE FLEET INVINCIBLE

FAIN would I tell you in loving detail of that singeing of the King of Spain's beard in Cadiz harbour where we lit a blaze that shone throughout the length and breadth of Europe; fain, too, would I trace our course along the coast of Spain storming and sacking, burning and plundering, from Cadiz to Finisterre, and thence to the Western Isles, and tell you how we took the great *San Felipe;* but that is familiar history to you and has little to do with my story, so I will pass it over with the bare mention and tell you rather of our home-coming and what followed it.

Hardly had my anchor plunged into the blue water of the Sound than my pinnace was alongside, and I dropped into it and pulled away to the Hoe. Kate and Lady Drake were there amidst a crowd of bright-faced friends to meet us, and scarce had I landed, than, in my old-world, hot-blooded impatience, I picked my sweet lady up in my arms and kissed her soundly before them all, stopping the very words of welcome on her lips, and bringing blushes to many a fair cheek that was only less bright than her own.

But I was not the only fortunate lover who came back to find his sweetheart waiting for him, for, though I have been too busy with my own affairs to tell you of it, Sir Philip had sailed with just such a promise from another fair English girl as I had taken from my Lady Kate, and Mary Sydenham, the younger sister of our dear little Admiral's wife, gave him a welcome which I have no reason to believe was less warm than that my own dear girl accorded me when the occasion was at length favourable.

That night we feasted in the old Town Hall right royally, with all Plymouth ablaze with lights, and vocal with sweet carillons and thunderous salutes in our honour, and the next day came the settlement of higher and more important matters. There was no hanging back now on my dear lady's part, for that which she had promised and I had fairly won was mine at last to take it when I would. One condition only she imposed, and that was such that I should have been less than man had I not yielded to it. She would marry me nowhere else than at the old Manor, and in that little chamber in the old castle tower in which old Sir Baldwin had laid me and she had tended me with such loving care while I was yet her Sleeping Crusader and the knight of her maiden dreams. So, though my well-loved companion-in-arms won and got his bride in Plymouth, I had to wait awhile for mine. Yet it was not for long, for, three days after, Mary Sydenham had come back from church, the *Lady Kate*, a fine new Bristol ship that I had bought, was lying in the Sound with loosed sails, ready to take us to the North Country; and with fair winds and over sunny summer seas we sailed away, as gay a company as ever English oak carried over English waters.

And so, in due course, Sir Philip brought his bride home, and he and she stood side by side with us when the dearest of all my many days at length came, and Kate and I stood hand in hand before the little altar that had been set up in the newly-consecrated chamber, already concentrated for us by such strange and loving memories.

There are things which may not be written, since to write of them were desecration, even if human words could truly paint the bliss and rapture of them; and of such things that wedlock of ours—the strangest that had ever joined the hand and heart of man and wife together—was surely one, so here for a space my pen falls from my fingers, and I lean back in my chair, dreaming awhile of all that true love means to him who has loved and won, and lost and found, and lost again, until through my long dream of that bright autumn and love-warmed winter and the sweet spring that followed it more than three hundred years ago there breaks once more the boom of cannon echoing along the English shore, and through the mist of tears that gathers in my dreaming eyes I see the glare of the warning beacon-fires springing from cape to cape from Mount Edgcumbe to the Forelands, and leaping from peak to peak and spire to spire over all the awakening English land on that ever-memorable night of the 19th of July, to tell us that the war-cloud had burst again, and that Philip's oft-baffled and long-dreaded Armada was drawing near the inviolate English land at last.

Then came that long, bitter fight up Channel from the Lizard to the Nore. Four times the shifting winds, traitors to their Ocean Queen, had baffled us and helped the Spaniards on to hoped-for victory. Human strength had done its worst. The greatest sea-captains of the time, the most heroic sailors that ever manned a ship, had done all that valour and skill could do, and, in spite of all, there was the great Armada, brought safe through a thousand perils, and still invincible. There was not an Englishman afloat or ashore who in that hour did not feel his heart grow heavy, and who did not think that now there was nothing left for it but to await the end and fight till the death, when it came, and then, even at the eleventh hour, the miracle was wrought and the Armada anchored.

It was madness inexplicable, but it was true, though so far were we from guessing at the truth that we almost ran them down before we knew what they had done. So close were we upon them that we barely saved ourselves and the weather-gauge by dropping anchor scarce more than a gunshot to windward of the myriad lights which showed us where they were. Seymour and Winter joined us with the Dover squadron, and a council of war was summoned on board the *Ark Royal*—a council on whose decision, as one of your greatest chroniclers has truly said, the fate of mankind depended.

When the council was being held I was pacing up and down the poop of my ship, watching the lights of the Spanish fleet, and as I did so there came to me out of the far past a vision of that awful day and night's work which I had seen in Actium Bay more than sixteen hundred years before.

I closed my eyes, still standing facing the anchored Armáda, and out of the darkness I saw rising the lurid blaze of the fire-ships, drifting with wind and tide down on the swarming galleys of Antony's feet. I saw them plunge in among them, and watched again the wreck and ruin that followed, and once more I led my shouting sea-wolves in the last attack on that broken and panic-stricken array.

It was enough. Not in vain did that blessed vision come to me in that supreme hour of England's fate.

The *Revenge* was lying anchored two cables' lengths from the *Lady Kate*, and when I opened my eyes again I saw a pinnace sweeping through the gloom towards her. I hailed it, and Drake's own voice answered me. I shouted again, asking him to come alongside, and the pinnace swung round under my quarter.

"What now, Sir Valdar?" asked the Admiral, in a voice that told me he was but ill-pleased with something. "Have you seen aught? Do the Dons show sign of moving?"

"If you can make time to come aboard, Sir Francis," I replied, "or if you will take me to your own ship, I will tell you of something that I have seen which might have some bearing on to-morrow's fight, if fight we do, but I must have your private ear to tell it."

"Then the sooner it is told the better," he growled, as he came clambering up the side. "And may it be more to my liking than anything I have heard yonder by my Lord Admiral's council-table."

"That I doubt not it will be," I said, as I went with him into the cabin, and shut the door behind me. Then I told him of that old-world sea-fight at Actium, and how we had made the flames do battle for us. And when I had done he brought his fist down upon the table with a blow that made the dust jump from it, and said:

"By the Lord of Hosts thou hast hit it, Sir Valdar! and it shall be done if I fire my own ships to do it. Thou knowest there is much idle talk nowadays about such means not being fit for Christian men to use, as though, forsooth, there were any difference in burning ships at anchor as we did at Cadiz, and sending fireships into an enemy's fleet. Yes, on my faith, it shall be done, and thou and I, Sir Valdar, will do it, if the Dons will but wait till the ships are ready. I have four or five craft that I can well spare to send on such a goodly errand, and I doubt not that we can find others."

"I will find the rest," I said, "if I devote every ship I have but this one to the flames."

And so it was settled. That was Saturday night. All Sunday we toiled hard preparing for our master-stroke, and when the night fell, moonless and cloudy, we had eight ships crammed and heaped high with combustibles, and each with half-a-dozen barrels of powder snugly stowed beneath her deck.

Then the word was given, the ships were fired and with rudders lashed and yards braced square we sent them loose. The flames roared and leapt higher and higher as they drifted swiftly on their way, and then we heard shrieks and screams of fear and hoarse shouts of command come pealing across the water from the affrighted Dons.

There was no time to heave up anchors or to make sail. Cables were slipped, and we could see the great floating castles, reddened by the glare of the fire-ships, drifting helplessly away, crashing into each other, fouling each other's spars and rigging, and locking together in wild and irredeemable confusion, as the relentless tide swept them away towards the Flemish sands; and all the while the fire-ships bore down upon the entangled mass, pitiless as fate and terrible as death with their blazing cargoes of fiery ruin. Then one by one the powder barrels caught and one after another the eight ships burst asunder, scattering sparks and blazing splinters high into the air and far and wide among the Dons.

Now was the time to strike if the Armada was to be scattered and England saved. Every anchor was already up, and under every sail that every ship could bear the English fleet sped in to take its long-awaited vengeance. The great *San Martin* had somehow got under way, and some half-dozen other tall ships were forming about her. Howard turned aside to capture a big galleasse, already entangled with another galleon and so half helpless. It was foolishness for him, but fortune for us, for it left Drake to lead the line.

The hour and the man had come. In a moment Howard with his idle tactics was forgotten; Drake was our leader, and him we followed in grim and dreadful silence till there was only half a pistol shot between us and the ring of ships about Sidonia. Then like one gun our broadsides thundered out. It was the roar of the Sea-Lion leaping on its prey, and with it sounded the knell of the Sea-Empire of Spain. We swept on through clouds of smoke and flame, swung round, and loosed another tempest on the huddling Dons. Then from northward came the answering roar of Winter's and Seymour's guns, and, when we had been at the grim, glorious work for three hours of as hard and bitter fighting as ever set hot hearts aflame, Howard came up with his laggards.

The English lion was at bay at last, and with fangs and claws he rent and tore those giant hulks to splinters, flinging them aside to settle and sink, and charging on to seek new prey; and so we loaded and fired and pounded away, giving the Dons what they had come so far to seek, and mile by mile we drove them, in a huddling, tangled mass of wreckage and confusion, through the narrow waters past Dunkirk, all that night and the next day: till all that was left of the mightiest fleet that had ever put to sea was drifting away, shot-shattered and helpless, and the fight had become a chase.

With the afternoon came rain and freshening winds blowing dead on that Netherland shore, which we believed would be ere long the once Invincible Armada's grave, and we, well on the weather quarter of the labouring galleons, watched the big seas breaking over them, hemming them in and driving them on so that none might escape.

Three hours more of that good wind and Sidonia would never more have sat beneath his orange-trees at Port St. Mary. But yet it was not to be. Once more the wind shifted, and once more the Dons were spared. Right round to the South it swung, and then down went every Spanish helm, and out went every shred of Spanish canvas, and, with an open sea before them and the freshening breeze behind, the great ships staggered on their way to the North with *El Draque*, shot-riddled and out of powder, following helplessly behind them.

We chased them up the North Sea, until ship after ship they faded from our sight into the mist of the days and the darkness of the nights, and then Sir Philip and I, thinking that we had done all that true men could do for England's safety and her still unsullied honour, put our two storm-tossed and battle-worn ships about and shaped our course for Newcastle.

But how shall I tell you of that which greeted us instead of the sweet warm welcome we expected. We landed and took horses, and rode hot haste in our true lovers' ardour to the Manor of Carew, and there we found, in place of our expectant brides, only poor old Marjory, wringing her hands, and weeping in the empty rooms of that desolate home, and telling us between her sobs how but the night before a Spanish caravel and pinnace had come in under cover of the darkness, seeking water and provisions, and had sacked the Manor from roof to basement and put to sea again, taking with them those who were dearest of all on earth to us—all the booty that Philip's mighty fleet had won, and yet, alas! how priceless!

Back we went hotspurred to Newcastle, with but a single thought in our two sore-aching hearts, to snatch our darlings out of the power of the Dons ere it was yet too late, or to take such vengeance for their dear sakes as should be told for many a day if any were left to tell of it.

Our own two ships were, as you may well guess, far past such work as we had now in hand. But, as I said to myself in my old heathen fashion, the Gods were good to us in the hour of our need, for when we got back to Newcastle we found a fine new ship just launched and ready for sea—a gallant frigate of close on eight hundred tons that had been built for privateering on the Spanish Main.

Money then, as now, could work miracles, and we spent it without stint, and powder and shot, victuals and water went on board as if by magic, till from keel to hatches the *Sans Merci*, as we renamed her in our bitter anger, was crammed with them, and in two days from the time of our landing we dropped down the river again and put to sea in the wake of the flying Spaniards.

For four days and nights we held on our northward way, racing the long green seas as they rolled abreast and astern of us, until on the morning of the fifth day we sighted a caravel, half-waterlogged and with tattered sails and tangled rigging. There were no cautious tactics for us now, no admiral's orders to curb our hot, fierce hate. She was a Spaniard, and that was enough for us.

With our gun-muzzles almost touching her sides we drove a broadside into her, which, big as she was, sent her heeling over as though a tempest-blast had struck her; and then we gave the word to board. Clad in my old matchless mail, and with my dear old sword fast gripped in my right hand, I was the first man on her deck, with Philip hard behind me, and after him a hundred of our gallant Englishmen swarming up the sides.

The Spaniards stared aghast at us, thinking El Draque was on them again in some new shape, but we gave them little time for pause or wonder, but went at them with shot and steel and such fierce, furious rage that, storm-worn and half-starving as they were, the wretches fled before us like panic-stricken sheep; and before we had been ten minutes aboard I had her captain by the throat, and was bidding him under pain of a split skull tell me if he knew aught of those we were seeking.

Alas! we were just a few priceless hours too late, for she was the very craft which had landed off the Manor, and done that which had brought us on our errand of rescue or revenge. Only that morning she had surrendered her two dear captives to the *San Miguel*, a great carack which, as her captain told me on his craven knees, we should know by the figure of the saint with his flaming sword blazoned on her foresail,

Then I split his skull in payment for his crime, and when we had got on board the *Sans Merci* again we sent broadside after broadside into the caravel till her sides gaped open and she sank; and then we made sail again, with the northern land of Scotland on our quarter and ahead of us, between us and the watery setting sun, scattered far and wide over the wind-lashed sea the distant hulls of the remnant of the Armada, among which, if she was still afloat, we had to seek that argosy which bore for us the most precious freight that ship had ever borne across the treacherous sea.

All that night we kept their cresset-lights in sight, watching anxiously lest one might disappear into the darkness, and that one be the argosy which carried at once our hopes and our fears.

Ninety-six of them we counted before the chill dawn broke over the grey, foam-flecked sea. A hundred and forty strong the great Fleet Invincible had passed into the jaws of death between the shores of the Channel, well found and water tight, glorious in pride and strength, and lured on by the brightest hopes that ever were brought to naught. Now shot riddled and leaking, stricken with the deadly sickness of the sea, wind beaten and wave buffeted, with a pitiless heaven above, the deep treacherous sea beneath them, hostile coasts ribbed with adamantine granite on their lee, and in their wake the *Sans Merci* hate-laden and merciless as Fate itself, the poor remnants of it staggered on, despairing and almost defenceless, towards the refuge which lay so far away and past so many perils.

When morning came we made sail, which we had shortened during the night so as not to overrun them and then ran up to begin our search for the *San Miguel*. As they saw us come racing through the water with every rope ataut and our sails white and well-fitting, as though we had but just come out of harbour, their signal-guns boomed out, and they began to huddle together like some frightened flock of sheep when they hear the howl of a wolf on the hillside.

The third morning dawned grey and cheerless as before, and we found ourselves far too northward of the fleet, and, as we thought, alone upon the waters. But as the light increased our look-out saw an open boat some three miles to the westward full of men who were making signals to us. We bore down on her, hoping against hope that we might get some news of our lost ones from her, and found her full of sorry-looking wretches, who hailed us in English, and when we had taken them on board they told us that during the night the galley slaves on board one of Hugo de Moncada's galleasses had revolted, broken loose, and seized the ship, and after killing every Spaniard on board her or driving them into the sea, had run her for the land. They had been among the mutineers, and had seized the boat and pulled out to the northward in the hope of finding us.

Happily for them and for us their venture had been successful—for them because it gave them a good chance for revenge upon their captors, and for us because among them was a Scotch fisherman named Donald MacIvor, who was able to give us the tidings which confirmed our most terrible fears.

Donald, with four of his companions, had been captured five days before by the *San Miguel*, and forced to pilot her through the perilous passage of the Pentlands. This he had done to save his life, as most other men would have done in like plight, and this, too, accounted for the carak having been able to take so good a course amidst the treacherous currents that she had kept to windward of the rest of the fleet and far outsailed it. But when he had been three days on board of her, he discovered that two English ladies were being held captive on board, and there and then he up and told the captain, like the true man that he was, that sooner than pilot the *San Miguel* another mile with such a freight on board he would stand to be hewn in pieces on her deck, and the Don, having tried bribes and threats in vain, at last put him into irons and sent him and his fellows on board the galleasse, promising them they should be galley-slaves for life.

But Donald told us more than this—of women's screams that he had heard from the cabin under the poop where he steered, and of vile jests that he had seen rather than heard passing among the officers on the ship.

No sorer or bitterer tidings than these could mortal lips have brought us, and instantly they quenched alike our burning impatience and the hot anger that had so far possessed us. In their place came the cold, pitiless rage of despair, for now we saw all too clearly that our poor darlings were lost to us for ever. The hope of rescue had gone, and only the deep and quenchless thirst for revenge was left. I looked into Philip's eyes and he looked into mine as Donald told his story to us in the cabin. There were tears in mine and in his, and in the eyes of strong men tears meant agony too deep for words. We clasped hands in silence, and in that silence each swore in his own soul that so far as in us lay all that was left of the great Armada should pay the price of the more than blood-guiltiness that had been incurred.

Then we went out on to the poop and had the crew called to quarters, and we told them in plain, straightspoken words what we had learned. There was no cheer or cry in answer, but hands and teeth were clenched and two hundred honest English breasts heaved with one deep gasp of silent rage and sorrow, for then, as now, the most sacred thing on earth in the eyes of Englishmen was the honour of an English woman.

They looked at each other from under their frowning brows, and then our old master-gunner stepped out of the ranks, and touched his cap and said:

"Noble sirs, we wait your orders. We want no more plunder after what you've told us. Sink, burn, and destroy is the word for us, if you'll but give it. That's it, lads, isn't it?"

A low, deep growl ran through the ranks and answered him, a sound that would have made any Spaniard's heart quake to hear it, and I, pulling my sword out of its sheath, held up the cross hilt before them and kissed it, and said:

"Then sink, burn, and destroy it shall be so long as a Spaniard floats, or the timbers of our good ship hold together! We have called her the *Sans Merci*, and, by the Lord of Hosts, Whose justice will permit our vengeance, without mercy we will be on small and great till this deep guilt is wiped away!"

At this they cheered, a cheer so fierce and savage in its deep-toned fury that I knew every man of them would fight to the last gasp of breath had left his body in the doing of that which we had now resolved to do. Then we set about our preparations.

Hardly had the Armada cleared the north-western point of Scotland than the wind went round and blew a gale from the north-west, and in the teeth of it we saw the long line of labouring hulks go staggering away to where the granite shores of the Hebrides awaited them. With our light sails in, our top-gallant masts housed, and our courses reefed, we rode along to windward of them, hanging just within shot of our long brass guns, and whenever a fair mark showed itself sending home the vengeful iron into hull, or masts, or bulwarks.

In vain they tried to make reprisals. Half waterlogged, storm-shattered, and crowded with sick as they were, they had all they could do to keep afloat and stagger on, while we, snug-housed and tight, and with every man hale and hearty and nerved with the one dire purpose, held on and pounded them with shot and chain and bar as relentlessly as the waves themselves beat upon their straining timbers.

Thus we rounded Lewis, and then we had them between us and the hungry granite rocks upon their lee. Ship after ship we crippled and watched as mast or bowsprit was shot away, and the rigging fell in tangled ruins on her decks, and she fell off the wind and reeled helpless to destruction.

We hunted on them past Donegal and the wild shores of Connaught, ever aided by the good north-west gale, sinking and crippling and driving upon the rocks carack and galleon, galleasse and caravel, as the justice of Heaven gave them into our hands, until at last the Islands of Kerry were passed, and then, out of the ninety-six ships that we had counted in the Pentlands, a bare three score spread their worn and tattered sails to the now favouring winds, and bore away southward for the shores of Spain.

But now we had to be more wary, for our storm-friend had left us after having done us right good service, yet our purpose was as firmly fixed as ever not to let a ship get home that we could sink or cripple. So we held off on their weather quarter, tacking and wearing and dodging about them, getting in now a shot or two at long range, and now a lucky broadside, and so, league on league and day after day, we harried them without mercy, yet never once in all our long busy voyage getting a sight of the *San Miguel* and her painted foresail.

At last fifty-three storm-wearied and shattered hulks, carrying some ten thousand men "stricken with pestilence and death," as their own chroniclers say, rounded up in Cadiz Bay with the *Sans Merci*, pitiless and full of fight as ever, sailing to and fro in the offing still hungry with unsatisfied revenge.

Then, while we were debating whether we should leave them there and rest content with the havoc we had wrought, or whether we should do as Sir Richard Grenville was soon to cover himself with immortal glory by doing, and sail into the midst of them and fight the whole half hundred of them, our look-out spied a great carack coming down full sail upon us from the north-west. We put about and ran to meet her, and, as we neared her, there we saw in all the blazonry of white and scarlet and gold the great figure of St. Michael with his flaming sword shining on her foresail. It was the *San Miguel* at last, and it was easy to see that, as we had supposed, she had out-sailed the rest of the Armada and got to St. Vincent or Lagos and there refitted.

There was no need to ask our brave sea-dogs whether we should run or fight, for no sooner had her name leapt from lip to lip than every man went to his place without bidding and stood expectant for orders. To the rest of the Armada we gave never a thought as we sped along towards our long-sought foe, and never a ship of it put out to hinder us, as indeed there was little fear of their doing, for they were no longer battle-ships, but only floating plague-dens and shambles, and the Don's only thought was to be towed into Cadiz Harbour and set foot on the welcome land once more.

More than that the wind was blowing a fresh breeze dead into the harbour, and there was not one of them that could have worked a mile to windward for all the wealth of the Indies. So alone and unmolested, we held our way for the *San Miguel*, and, as we came within gunshot, Philip took the helm, as was his wont, for he was the most skilful steersman on board, and I passed the word to the gunners to aim high, and let her have it in the masts and shrouds. First the twenty-fours roared out their thunder from their brazen throats, and we saw the good shot go plunging through the lofty bulwarks, hurling the splinters far and wide; and then the carack's broadside burst into smoke and flame, and a storm of shot went whistling over our heads.

Before she could load again our yards came round, and we went about, and again our iron hail crashed into her. Another broadside roared out from her towering sides, but we were round again just in time to avoid it, and the shot churned up the water harmlessly astern of us. Then I bade the gunners train all their pieces on her waist, and Philip brought the *Sans Merci* up, with sails shivering in the wind, that they might take the more careful aim. I waited until the master-gunner said "Ready," then I gave the word, and as, like a single gun, the broadside thundered out, we held our breath and watched and saw a great ragged hole torn in her midship bulwarks. The great mainmast swayed to and fro for a moment or two, and then down it crashed over the side into the sea, with all its cloud of canvas and maze of rigging, and after it went the fore and mizzen topmasts. tumbling down on deck; and there lay the proud *San Miguel* crippled.

Once more her batteries roared out, and a hurricane of shot swept down upon us —this time aimed all too well, for when it had passed our fore-topmast was hanging down on to the forecastle, and our bowsprit was dragging in the water by the stays. The next moment we heard a shrill cheer from the Spaniard, and saw six galleys clear the harbour mouth, and with swift-swinging oars come striding over the smooth water towards us.

Before the Spaniards could load their guns again our forward guard had sprung aloft with their boarding-axes and cut away the wreck. Then the *Sans Merci* righted, and her after sails with the wind full astern drove her ahead of the *San Miguel*. Our foremast still stood, and when it was clear of the wreck of the topmast we soon had the foresail in working order again, and the frigate, though crippled, under some control.

We worked our way round the carack's bow and drew off on her starboard side, over which the great mass of wreckage was still hanging, masking the guns of her battery. The Dons were doing all they could to clear it, but we soon gave them something else to attend to, for with guns double-shotted, and at less than musket range, we poured so fierce a hail of iron and lead into the cumbered side of the carack, which could scarcely reply to us with a single gun, owing to the sails and cordage which hung over the muzzle, that we swept away every man who showed himself above cover.

This we did with our lighter ordnance and small-arms, for the big guns on the lower tier were doing other and deadlier work. With muzzles converged on one spot at her water-line, the twelve well-served guns rained in volley after volley, of which every shot struck true within a space of some two yards along the water-line. We watched the rendering timbers split and gape, and at every volley the great ragged wound grew wider and deeper, and the water poured in faster and faster till, just as the first of the galleys showed round her stern, the great *San Miguel* gave a mighty heave, and, reeling over towards us, went down into her ocean grave.

We waited till the galley was within pistol shot, and then we let her have it, and straight from stem to stern the shot-storm swept her, and she stopped death-stricken and lay like a huge wounded spider on the water as we sheered off again to make ready for the others.

If these had been our only foes, we should soon have made an end of them as we had done of the carack; but scarcely had the *San Miguel* vanished in the midst of the swirling eddies that swept over her grave than we saw four more galleys, with a frigate in tow, coming out of the harbour towards us.

So we waited, some eight score smoke-grimed, blood-and-sweat-dappled men, with our guns loaded, and the last of our powder and shot upon deck, saving it in silence till we could use it to the best effect.

They came on warily, like hounds about a stag at bay. Four times they tried to take us with a rush, and four times we drove them back with such a storm of lead and iron as they had but little stomach for, and had our magazines but been full not all the ships in Cadiz could have taken us. But soon from broadsides we came down to single shots, and then at last the good guns that had served us so well lay silent and useless about us, and with shrill cries of triumph the Dons came at us once again, now, alas! only too well assured of victory.

They took us on bow and stern and broadsides, and, as they swarmed in over our bulwarks, our gallant fellows met them with pike and pistol, boarding-axe and sword, and as fast as they came over we struck them down or hurled them back into the sea, and so for three long hours of fierce and furious fighting we held their ever-growing swarms at bay with ever-lessening numbers till they stared in marvel at us, wondering whether we were men or demons like El Draque

One by one our gallant sea-dogs dropped where they stood, fighting to the last gasp of life that was in them, and closer and closer drew the ring of swart, fierce faces round us till at last we two were left alone of all the *Sans Merci's* crew. Then, out of the ring, there stepped forth a tall Don in complete armour, with a rapier in one hand and a pistol in the other, and said in good English:

"Surrender, Señors, for the love of God and your own lives. You have done all that men could do, but fate is against you. Surrender, then, and all honour shall be yours, for we would not willingly slay such foes as you by mere brute force of numbers."

"Get thee back out of reach, good sir," I laughed, wiping the battle-sweat from my brow with the back of my left hand, "lest that pretty plate of thine get scratched, or, if thou wouldst prefer it, bid thy fellows stand back a pace, and fight a bout with me; but say nothing of surrender, for we came here but for revenge or death, as the chance of war went. Revenge we have had, as Sidonia can tell you, and now, if needs be, we are ready for death. What say you, Philip?"

"What you say, Valdar," replied he with a laugh so merry that it made the Don stare. "As for me I could die in no better company than yours."

Even while he was speaking, the Spaniard raised his sword and I saw a score of muskets levelled at us. Like a lightning flash my blade leapt out and took him in the jaws. I drove it through flesh and bone and steel till the point stood out behind his neck, and dashed him back on the musket muzzles. Then the volley rattled out, I heard a groan behind me, and, turning for an instant, saw Philip drop to the deck bleeding from a score of wounds.

Then I wrenched my sword free and, still, by some miracle, unharmed, flung myself on to the Spaniards, and hacked and hewed my way into the midst of them until a crushing blow fell from behind upon my bare head, and, with my sword plunged up to the hilt in the breast of the last Don I slew, I stumbled forward blind and fainting upon his body, with half a score of his fellows on top of me—the last man to fall on board the lost *Sans Merci*.

CHAPTER XX

THE MARTYR—CROWN OF FLAME

I CAME to myself lying on a straw-covered stone pallet in a cell of the Holy Inquisition. As I opened my eyes I saw standing beside me a cowled Familiar, such as Philip had told me of in his stories of the dark and terrible deeds which had been done in England in Mary's reign, and which we had saved her from in that last glorious fight off Gravelines. All I could see of him was the dark grey habit and the black, peaked cowl, which covered his head and face completely like a mask of cloth, with two holes where his eyes should have been, and a gaping slit for a mouth.

I must have been dreaming of sea-fights, of Alexandria and Actium, or else I must have been back again in old Augustan Rome, for, as my senses came back to me and I sat up staring at the uncouth shape, I said in the old Latin tongue:

"By the Gods! where am I, and what art thou!—man or demon, or what? Take that mask from off thy face and let me see thee, or, by the glory of Bel, I will tear it off and wring thy neck to boot."

But still he stood there, crossing himself and muttering unintelligible words under his cowl.

"Nay; then by the eyes of Ishtar, if thou wilt not, I will do it for thee," I cried, this time in the old Assyrian tongue, staggering to my feet and making towards him.

He turned to the door, as though he would open it and fly from me, but I was before him, and taking him by the shoulder with one hand and thrusting him away from it, I tore the cowl from his head with the other, and there, as though we two had been standing together once more on the beach at Ivarsheim, was Anselm of Lindisfarne, feature for feature, just as I had parted from him more than three centuries and a half before.

I stretched my hand out to him as to an old friend that I was right glad to meet, and said:

"Welcome, Anselm, fellow-wanderer with me through the ages! What hast thou been doing since thou didst bring the Cross to Ivarsheim, and we went together to the Holy War when Richard Lion-heart was fighting Saladin in Syria?"

"The Saints have mercy on me and pity on thee!" he cried, shrinking back affrighted at my strange greeting, "thou art still raving with thy wound, my son, to talk such wild babble as that. True I have seen such face and form and heard such voice as thine in dreams that oft bewildered me, yet I have never seen thee in the flesh before, and that great Crusader thou hast spoken of is dead these three hundred and three-score years and more. Lie thee down again and sleep till thy right senses have come back to thee, for thou wilt want them anon, since it is my task to prepare thee for the question before the tribunal of the Holy Office."

"And have the Gods brought me to this after all my wanderings, and art thou, Anselm, my old friend, now a servant of this foul tyranny which mocks the gentleness of the White Christ with the countless crimes which it commits in His name? Shame on thee, once good servant of thy Lord! Better thou hadst died—but no, what foolishness am I talking? Thou hast died and lived again as I have, but thou, it seems, hast forgotten, while I have remembered."

"Peace, peace!" he cried, breaking through my speech, and crossing himself again; "mad or sane, thou art blaspheming. Already thou hast said enough to send thee to the stake, even wert thou not suspected of being the familiar demon of that for ever-accursed English sea-devil El Draque."

"Friend," I said, going to him and laying my hand heavily on his shoulder as he shrank back against the wall, crossing himself and muttering his Popish spells, "thou hast the face and the voice of one who, ere I died my last death, was very dear to me, else I would wring thy neck ere thou couldst cry for help, and then let thine infernal Holy Office do its worst, if it could, for I verily believe thou art but here to spy upon me and betray me as is the wont of such vermin as the Inquisition uses for its vile work. Yet, far as thou art fallen from thy former state, I will spare thee and forgive thee all that thou mayst do against me if thou canst tell me aught concerning two English gentlewomen who were brought captives to Spain by the *San Miguel*, on which, I thank God, we have done due vengeance."

His eyes dropped before mine as though in shame, and he was muttering something in his beard when, as though in answer to my question, the door was flung open, and, as I turned round to look, I saw four other cowled figures enter the cell, and after them came two more, half carrying between them so piteous a wreck of womanhood that even my love and hate-quickened eyes did not at once recognise it as all that was left of her who had once been my darling and my wife.

Ere the mad rage within me would suffer me to utter a word they loosed her and she came tottering towards me with trembling arms and white, drawn, haggard face upturned to mine. In an instant my arms were about her and her poor wasted form was clasped close to my breast, and my hungry lips were pressing hot kisses on those dry, drawn, bloodless lips of hers that had once been so soft and sweet. Then she drew her face back from mine, and, looking at me with hollow burning eyes, whose last tears were already shed, she said in a voice that would have shaken the hearts of any save such soulless brutes as stood about us:

"Nay, Valdar, once my own true knight and well-loved husband, do not kiss me, for I am no longer worthy of your kisses. Let me go, for I am not even worthy to be held in your arms. Let me go, for shame and torment have done their worst on me, and I am no more a woman or your wife. I was not so blessed as to die as Mary did under the torture of the rack, but to-morrow I shall pass through the fire, and after that we may meet again as we have done before, when the flame shall have purged my shame, and I am once more worthy of you; for I have not denied you or my faith, and the rest may be forgiven me. Let me go, dear Valdar, or kill me now again as you did long ago in the sands beyond Nineveh."

Heart-stricken by her piteous words, I, unknowing what I did, flung my arms apart, and let her fall prone to the floor. Then with a hoarse cry of more than human rage I sprang forward, gripped the two nearest of the cowled figures and dashed them together till I heard their skulls crack under their hoods. I dropped them, and, running at the others, caught three of them in my arms, crushed the breath out of them, and then, lifting them up, dashed them half-strangled on to the stone floor and stamped the life out of them.

Then I turned to wreak my vengeance on the others, and found the cell filled with armed men, who flung themselves upon me and dragged me down, though not till I had broken the neck of one, and smashed the face of another out of all human likeness with a blow of my fist. But they were a score to one, and so they had me down at last and bound my hands behind me.

Then they dragged me to my feet again, and drove me out of the cell, where my lost darling lay among the dead I had killed for her dear sake, and down a long, stone-walled passage, and into a gloomy, vaulted chamber where three cowled shapes sat at a black covered table, with the rack on one side of them and on the other the torture bench, the charcoal furnace with the irons already heating in it, the boot and mallet and wedges, and all the other engines of torment that these devils in human shape used to wring from their victims the words of madness which sent them from the torment of the Question to the last agony of the stake—the very same which they had used to make my darling that woeful wreck of once peerless womanhood which a moment ago I had held in my arms, and these cowled devils were they who to-morrow, as she had said, would send her to the fiery death of the Auto-da-Fé.

Those who had hold of me dragged me to the front of the table, and then he whose lost soul possessed the shape that had once been Anselm's came from behind me, and after he had bowed to the crucifix, which hung on the wall behind the table, said in monkish Latin so that I should understand as well as my judges:

"The accused hath confessed himself to be the familiar demon of the English wizard El Draque, and he hath moreover told me most strange and marvellous things which, if he be not more than man, prove most assuredly that he hath had direct dealing with Hell itself, and hath so procured the extension of his life far beyond the allotted span of mortal existence, for he hath told me——"

"Hold thy peace, knave!" I shouted. "I know my doom, and I can meet it, as I have met death in a thousand shapes ere the earth was polluted by such devil's-spawn as you ministers of this infernal Office miscalled Holy.

"I am he who fought with Drake in the Indies and at Gravelines. I am he who sent the fire-ships into the midst of your Armada, once invincible, and scattered it to the winds of Heaven, and I am he who chased its remnants through the northern seas, and, for the sake of that dear life which you have wrecked, drove ship after ship to death and ruin on the rocks and shoals. For her sweet life ten thousand Spanish lives have paid, though, could I take ten thousand more, yet would full justice not be done."

"Thou art as bold in speech as they say thou art in battle," said a voice, that seemed to come from under the hood of the centre figure at the table—a voice of such cold, passionless tone that I could have sworn that had the cowl been raised I should have seen the face of the Tiger Lord of Asshur beneath it—"and thine avowal saves us some trouble and thee some pains, for hadst thou not spoken so freely we had the means at hand to make thee speak. Yet the justice of the Holy Office demands that I should state the offences with which thou art charged so that thou mayest answer to them if thou canst. But first tell us how long hast thou lived on earth?"

"Thou poor fool, thou child of a few dark nights and fleeting days, what art thou that thou shouldst ask me such a question as that? Yet I will answer that thou mayest know how poor and mean a thing thou art to wield the power of life and death and mete out misery to those whose slave thou art not fit to be!

"Ages unremembered have passed since I drew my first breath on earth. I saw Babel fall and heard the speech of men confounded in the terror which overwhelmed that earliest Nineveh which is forgotten. I have stood before the throne of Solomon and heard the words of wisdom fall from his lips. I saw Rome in her glory when the might of the great Julius held the world trembling in its grasp, and I was on Calvary when the darkness fell from Heaven and the earth shuddered in the death-agony of the Christ.

"I heard the last words spoken by those lips which, in the end of earthly things, shall ask you here, and those who gave you your infernal power, for an account of all the blood and tears that you have shed in your foul blasphemy of His Holy Name and His Divine Mercy—the Friend of the poor and needy, the Healer of wounds, and the Forgiver of sins! I saw the reality of that effigy which you have made an Idol of——"

"Peace, blasphemer, peace!" he shouted, springing to his feet, and taking the crucifix from the table before him, and raising it high above his head. "Of thine own free will and uncurbed speech thou hast blasphemed the Holy Emblem of our ancient faith. It is enough. Get thee hence to thy cell, and prepare thyself, if thou canst, for that which awaits thee to-morrow. Take him away, for he is not fit for Christian eyes to look upon."

At his last words those who held me swung me round, and hurried me from the chamber ere I could reply to him as I would have done. When I entered my cell again I found it empty. They had taken my darling away to await that fiery fate which I now believed we should share together.

Yet this was not to be, for when, after a night of waking dreams more torturing than all the torments of the question-chamber, they led me forth from the prison-house of the Inquisition into the great plaza of the town, I soon saw that their malice had doomed me to a worse agony than this. They put on my shirt of mail, and hung my sword by my side, and then they took me out, with my hands bound behind me, to make a show of me full armed and helpless before the foes that I had conquered.

When I reached the plaza all the hideous pageant of the Auto-da-Fé was already prepared. Round it the guards stood in serried ranks three deep. On one side were two canopied thrones. On one of them sat Philip of Spain, surrounded by his grandees and courtiers and courtesans, and on the other sat John Torquemada, Grand Inquisitor of the Holy Office, with the Archbishop of Seville, and their attendant crowd of monks and priests.

Over against them was a long line of tall stakes, about which men were piling faggots, and, standing on little platforms half-way up their height, were men and women chained to them, but of these I saw only one—the shape of a woman with down-hanging head, death-white face, and closed eyes, and long, streaming, red-gold hair, chained to a stake just before Philip's throne.

A low, deep roar of vengeful hate rolled round the square as my guards led me out and stood me in the midst between Philip's throne and Torquemada's. Then two heralds came forth, and, after summoning silence with their trumpets, proclaimed the long list of my crimes against the Holy Church and the Catholic Majesty of Spain—at which I laughed aloud in my bitter wrath and fierce despair. Then Philip raised his hand, and they turned me round facing the row of stakes, and I saw men with torches begin from either end to light the faggots.

I heard the dry wood crackle, and saw the smoke and leaping flames mount upwards, and as they rose scream after scream of agony pealed shrill upon the slumbering air. At last I saw the torches thrust amidst the faggots about that stake to which was chained all that earth held dear for me.

On either side of her men and women were writhing and screaming in the first agony of their fiery torment, but on her the flames breathed their torturing breath in vain. She was dead—the mercy of Heaven had already raised her beyond the reach of the inhumanity of man.

Then the spell that held me was broken.

I prayed to all the Gods I had known on earth for strength to take the vengeance that was surely due, and then, as if they had been threads, I snapped the cords that bound my hands, and gave Philip and his people a different show to that which they had brought me out to make. My good sword flashed out of its sheath, the battle-cry of Armen rang fierce from my lips, I rained a swift hail of furious blows about me, my guards fled screaming with terror, and the next moment I had leapt on to the daïs where the Archbishop sat in his splendid robes by Torquemada.

A few more swift slashes of my sword cleared the platform of the howling monks about the Archbishop's throne. Torquemada sat rigid and motionless on his throne, staring at me with the same deep black eyes which, ages before, I had seen gleaming from under the diadem of the Tiger Lord.

"I will come for thee anon, Tiglath," I shouted at him; "but this one shall first show thee thy fate. He's better food for fire than thee."

Then I took my sword between my teeth, and, gripping the Bishop round the waist, I swung him, screaming with terror, over my shoulder, leapt from the platform and ran with him to the great fire that was roaring round my darling's stake.

I saw men running at me from all parts of the square, but I held him fast with my left hand, and with my sword in my right I cut down all who came within reach of the sweeping blade till I came to the fire, and then, like a faggot, I pitched the silken-clad cleric into the midst of the leaping flames, and then, sword in hand again, I turned about with the fire behind me and thousands of foes in front, to sell as dearly as might be the life I had now no further use for.

But ere they reached me or I could strike a blow the blackened firmament split from west to east in a great jagged gash of flame, and, like the very trump of God proclaiming the hour of doom, the thunder crashed out. The lightning blazed forth again through the darkness that had fallen over the noonday, the solid rock on which Cadiz sat reeled and shuddered as the earth had done by Nineveh when Babel fell, and still flash on flash, and peal on peal, the lightning streamed and the thunder rolled across the shaking sky, and through the riven darkness I saw crowds running to and fro, blind and terror-stricken, screaming to their saints in an agony of fear.

Out of the plaza and down to the harbour I ran through the dust and deluge of the storm, thinking how fine a blaze the remnants of the Armada would make could I but get on board one of the ships. But as I reached the water's edge Heaven did the work itself, for a flash of lightning struck a great galleon's mainmast, a stream of fire ran down through the splitting deck, then there came a roar and a crash which beggared the thunder itself, and the blazing fragments went flying far and wide.

A skiff with two oars in it lay at my feet. I sprang in and pushed off and rowed away down the harbour, drawn by my instinct towards the open sea. Through the terror of the storm and the blazing ships I passed unheeded amidst the fire-lighted gloom till I reached the stern of the *Sans Merci*, lying at anchor off the outer fort. A slash of my sword severed the stern cable, and then I pulled to the bow. Another cut her free, and then, as she began to drift out before the hurricane that was sweeping down from the land, I laid hold of the main-chains and swung myself on board at the waist.

There were a score of Spaniards on deck, watching the storm and crossing themselves and praying. In an instant I was among them, laying hard about me, yet not for long, for they no sooner saw me than, yelling with terror, they scrambled over the bulwarks and dropped to their fate in the seething sea. So I took back the *Sans Merci* again, and so before the tempest that had brought me deliverance I drifted away with her, once more alone in the world, towards the red glare of the sunset over the storm-lashed western sea, with a horror of a past fate behind me, and before me the dim promise of the days which, perchance, were yet to come.

Day and night that furious tempest raged, and on before it, over the seething sea beneath the low, fast-driving cloud-wrack, the poor *Sans Merci*, crippled and half wrecked by that last brave fight of hers, drove on ever westward. At last out of the grey seething waters ahead of me, I saw two black-pointed rocks rise up. Soon I could see the snowy surges foaming and tumbling about their bases. Between them yawned a deep dark abyss, into which the boiling ocean-torrent rushed foam-crowned and thundering. Dead ahead of the reeling *Sans Merci* it gaped black and deep, and straight for it I steered her, urged on by wind and wave behind me.

The twin rocks seemed to rush at me over the water, and the chasm yawned like a huge black, hungry mouth to swallow me and my poor half-sinking bark. Up under her stern rose a moving mountain of pale green, snow-capped water. I felt her heave under my feet, and then, as though endowed with life and motion of her own, she plunged forward between the black shining rock-walls. A roar of thundering waters burst upon my ears, wild voices seemed to laugh and shriek at me out of the echoes of the cavern, and then with a crash and a grinding, groaning shudder the good ship stopped, fast-wedged between the rocks; and I, cold and drenched, and bruised and weary, raised myself from the deck on to which the shock had flung me, and crawled into the cabin, and when, from long habit rather than any need, I had dried and cleaned my mail and sword, I threw myself down on a heap of sails on which some of our wounded had lain during the fight, careless in my utter weariness whether the *Sans Merci's* timbers held together till I woke again or not.

So, lulled by the thunder-song of the storm, I slept; while round me the winds screamed and whistled, and the surges hissed and roared, and night followed day, and calm followed storm, and the swift flight of the years sped on unheeded towards the day when the finger of Fate should touch my long-closed eyes and bid me wake to action once again.

CHAPTER XXI

ILMA OF ENGLAND

I WOKE with a dull, booming sound as of distant guns rumbling in my ears. There was fighting somewhere, and, like a trumpet blast, the sound of it roused the battle-lust within my slumbering soul.

My eyes opened on the world of real things once more, and I sprang to my feet and looked about me. The heap of sails on which I had lain down was now a few mouldering dusty rags. The curtains of the cabin windows and doorways hung in faded dusty tatters, the woodwork was all dry, rotted, and worm-eaten, and my mail and sword lay upon the table deep covered by the dust of uncounted years.

Across the after part of the ship lay heaps of stones and rubbish, and behind her, over the mouth of the cavern, stretched a high ragged wall, built up of rock-masses which had fallen, through the slow course of years, from the roof of the cavern, and so, as I imagined, built up that screen which had shielded her and me from the sight of passers-by in boats or ships, if, indeed, any came that way.

Over this wall I could see from the high poop of the ship the smooth blue sunlit sea, and drifting across it, blue fading wreaths of smoke—no doubt the smoke of the cannonade, whose roar had awakened me from my death sleep. There was war in the world still. So I armed myself, and dropped over the *Sans Merci's* side, and, wading through the shallow water that surrounded her weed-hung, barnacle-cumbered hull, I clambered over the rock-wall across the mouth of the cavern, and, making my way along a narrow rock-ledge that led round the cliff to my right hand, I got out on to the sandy beach of a little rock-ringed bay, and there I took my next look at sea and shore, and sky and sun, and drew a long, deep, sweet breath of the warm, pure air of Heaven.

Then I climbed on to a pile of rocks close by me, and looked out to sea. In the offing two ships of a strange rig that I had never seen before, not unlike those of the Elizabethan time, yet without their high poops and fore-castles, and seeming, as I thought, much simpler and more workmanlike, were lying close together. Puffs of smoke were rising from their decks, and faint cries came over the water from them.

"One of those ships is taking the other by the board," I said to myself aloud, and very strange did the sound of my own voice seem to me as it echoed round that lonely shore. "And I would give some of the golden ducats that should be yonder in the *Sans Merci's* hold for a place on board either of them, for I need nothing better than a good hot fight to warm these stiffened limbs of mine. Ha! who are they who come yonder—fugitives and beaten men it would seem. I wonder what nation they are of? Ah! that they were only Spaniards!"

This last was drawn from me by the sight of a boat which put off crowded with men from the side of the larger vessel which lay nearest to the shore.

They pulled straight into the bay, and as the boat touched the shore I ran down to have a look at them.

Surely my prayer had been granted, and I had seen something like those black beards and keen eyes and swarthy skins before. As the keel touched the beach a man sprang out with a rope in his hand, and then stopped, staring aghast at the strange figure striding out from among the rocks towards him.

He made the sign of the Cross, and gasped out a few broken words which my ears instantly knew for that hated Spanish speech which I had last heard in the most terrible hour of all my lives.

They were the last he ever uttered. He was a Spaniard, and so to me an enemy. My sword sprang out as I ran towards him. One swift slash clove him from the shoulder to the middle. and as he dropped on the bloody sand I shouted my old Crusading battle-cry: "St. George and Merry England," and sprang with one leap into the midst of the crowded boat, and went to work, laying about me with my swift sweeping blade, here cleaving a skull and there sending an uplifted arm flying into the water, till what was left of the affrighted wretches tumbled over the sides, and left me alone in the boat with those I had already slain.

The old battle-fury was strong upon me now, and the brief scrimmage had given me a good appetite for more, so I picked up an oar and pushed the boat off, and then sat down and rowed away to the two ships; while those that were left of the Spaniards, doubtless thinking they had been attacked by some demon, ran off to hide themselves in the rocks.

I had got about half-way to the two ships when a deep, muffled roar rolled over the smooth water towards me. I turned in my seat and saw a great blue-grey cloud lying on the sea with a bright red glare of leaping flames under it. Then these vanished and when the smoke cloud drifted away there was only one of the ships afloat. I pulled my boat alongside her and in a few moments more I was standing on her deck in the world of living men once more.

Her name was the *Sea Hawk*, and a right worthy namesake she ere long proved herself to be of old Jarl Ivar's dragon-ship. She was bound to the West Indies, seeking such fortune as might fall in her way, or trusting to find it when she reached her journey's end. Mark Vernon, her captain, I soon found to be a man after my own heart, and a worthy successor of those old shipmates of mine in the days of Drake and Frobisher. More than this, by the look of him, he might have been Philip Carew's own brother, and this of itself was enough to win my love.

We dined together in private that night, and as you might expect, exchanged our histories of the past and present; all of which talk you will understand sufficiently if I tell you that the day of my last awakening was the 20th of May,. 1805, since from that you will know that it was just about the time when Napoleon was perfecting his scheme for the annihilation of the British sea-power and the invasion of England from Boulogne.

On the eighth day after the battle we came in sight of a fleet of great ships, such ships as I had never dreamed of seeing, so stately and splendid were they with their towering tiers of guns and their vast spread of snowy canvas—a fleet of warships that could have sailed through the great Armada and scattered it in splinters over the water with a broadside from each battery.

"There are thirty of them," said Mark, who had been up in the mizzen shrouds counting them with his glass. "And that means that they are Frenchmen, for we have no fleet of that size in these waters. They are coming from the West Indies and they are bound for the Channel. Now I wonder what they've been up to, and what they are going to do on the other side. A big fleet like that isn't out here for nothing."

"No more than a squadron of the Armada was once, as I remember," I said, "when it made for the coast of Ireland to lead Drake astray and leave the Channel open."

"By the heavens above, you've hit it, Valdar!" he said, clapping me on the shoulder. "And it may be a good thing for England that we sighted that fleet this morning. They are French in build and rig, and they've got some serious work in hand, or there wouldn't be so many of them. I shouldn't wonder if that is Villeneuve's fleet which disappeared from Spanish waters last March. I wonder where Nelson is? I know he's in the West somewhere, and he must know about that fleet as soon as we can tell him. We'll try Barbadoes first, and now you shall see how the *Sea Hawk* can fly.

We had a fine, steady breeze from the north-west, with plenty of north in it, and to this the brigantine spread every stitch of canvas that her tall masts and long spars could carry, and before the Frenchmen had sighted us we were tearing away over the water at a speed which, to my old-world eyes, looked incredible. On the 2nd of June we made Barbadoes, which was now a British island, and there we learnt that Nelson was expected on the look-out for a French fleet within the next day or two.

We kept our own counsel about what we had seen, and, after taking in fresh stores and water, stood off and on about five miles out to sea waiting for the fleet. On the morning of the 4th it hove in sight from the northward, and we, with British flags flying, ran out to meet it. We found the Admiral's pennant flying from a stately battleship, on whose broad, lofty stern I saw, as we ran round it, emblazoned on a golden scroll the word "*Victory*," a name soon to be written beside that of the *Revenge* in the chronicles of the sea.

Mark answered the hail as we swept up alongside the flagship at a speed that made more than one on board her stare. Then we shortened sail so as to keep abreast of her, and Mark, after telling who he was and what errand he had come on, was bidden to go on board the *Victory* and give his message to the Admiral; so we dropped our gig into the water, and made fast the rope that was thrown to us from the flagship, and soon Mark and I were standing on that deck where Nelson was to take his death-wound ere many more months were passed.

We were taken at once to the Admiral's cabin, for, as you know, Nelson never took his news at second-hand if he could help it. As the door opened I saw seated at a table a spare, fragile, sallow-faced, one-eyed man, with the empty right sleeve of his coat pinned across his breast. This was Nelson, the greatest of all the great English sea-captains from Drake's time to his own. Yet when I looked at him I thought great as he was he would have cut but a sorry figure beside the jovial round face and sturdy form of my own dear little Admiral, now, alas! sleeping in his sea-bed these two hundred years or more.

He asked for and took our tidings with quick, quiet decision; then he held a brief, whispered conversation with an officer who was sitting at the table with him, then he looked up at Mark, and said:

"Your tidings may prove most valuable, and I thank you heartily for your promptness in bringing them. That is a fast craft of yours. I understand that you sail under letters of marque. How long would it take you to reach London, do you think?"

"The *Sea Hawk* could do it in twenty-five days, my lord, with good winds," replied Mark. "As we thought we might be wanted for work that needed doing quickly we victualled and watered yesterday, so we can start for London this afternoon if your lordship pleases."

Nelson looked up at us with a twinkle in his eye and smile on his delicate, woman's lips, and said:

"Your foresight, like your promptness, is beyond all praise, Mr. Vernon, and it may be in your power to do your country a very great service. By the way, you have not introduced your friend yet. His face seems familiar to me, and yet I cannot remember where I have seen him before."

"This is Francis Valdar," said Mark, inventing a name for me on the spur of a moment. "Half owner with me of the *Sea Hawk*."

Then, as I exchanged salutations with the great Admiral I thought of Cæsar and Actium, while Nelson was wondering where he and I had met before.

We went back on board the *Sea Hawk* with orders to lie by the fleet until daybreak, and then a gig came from the *Victory* and took Mark on board the flagship again. He came back with a dispatch from Nelson to the Admiralty in London, and as he showed it to me said:

"Our orders are to take these dispatches straight. The Admiral has given three other copies to the three fastest craft in the fleet, a ten-gun brig and two sloops, and the four of us are going to race across the Atlantic for the honour of getting the news in first and a thousand pounds. The others are getting under weigh, but we can spare them an hour or two easily. I have told the men that if we get in first they shall have the thousand pounds among them, and that you and I will give them another thousand each, so I don't think they'll lose any time.

"They would lose less if you had said two thousand each," I said, "and we have plenty to spare, you know."

"True," he laughed, "but it doesn't do to make the British sailor rich too suddenly. He is a good fellow and a splendid fighter, but riches don't agree with him, and your old-world generosity might empty the ship for us when we get to London. Now, we had better get under way."

We crossed the Atlantic faster than any other craft had done before us, and just twenty-five days after he took them from Nelson's hands Mark delivered his dispatches to the Admiralty in London. That was the 9th of July, and, as events soon proved, we were just in time to confound Napoleon's plans and save England from invasion.

As soon as Nelson got back to Portsmouth he came out to Cadiz to command the blockading squadron, which was now twenty-nine strong. For nearly a month we kept the Frenchmen and Spaniards shut up, forty sail of them, in that harbour in which Drake and I had singed the King of Spain's beard two hundred and eighteen years before, and at last, in order to tempt the cowards to a battle, Nelson sent eight of his ships away, and when the report got into Cadiz that he had only twenty sail, Villeneuve came out with his thirty-three, still fearing, even now, to go too near to the claws of the terrible English sea-lion.

But at last, when day broke on that for ever famous 21st of October, Nelson had lured him out far enough to make fighting a certainty, and from the poop of the *Sea Hawk*, which was still attending the English fleet as a scout and despatch vessel, I saw the thirty-three French and Spanish battleships, with their seven attendant frigates, away to leeward, their sails showing like points of snow against the blue-grey clouds on the horizon. Almost at the same moment a signal flew from the *Victory*, telling us to find out their position and formation, and so away we went to do it, and as we came well within sight of the mighty armament I caught Mark by the arm, and, pointing towards them, said:

"It is a good omen, Mark! See, they are sailing in crescent shape, one ship behind two others, and it was in that very formation that we saw the Armada pass Plymouth two hundred and seventeen years ago, on its way to destruction."

"They won't get as far as that, now," he laughed, in reply. "You have seen many a sea-fight, Valdar, but never such an one as you will see to-day if that fellow Villeneuve doesn't take to his heels again. You see that land down yonder to the south-eastward, that is Cape Trafalgar—a name which, if I mistake not, will be famous before another sun rises on it."

"Yes," I said, "I can well believe that, for these waters have too often borne English keels to victory to swallow them now in defeat. Yonder is Cadiz, where we burnt Philip's shipping and crippled his Armada for a year. Yonder are Lagos and Vigo and Bayona, where many a time we taught the Spaniards that an Englishman was worth a dozen of them, and what Drake did with his little ships Nelson may well do with his big ones."

There is no need for me to tell you whose fathers won it, how ended the last battle of the Titans on the sea. For the second time I had seen the Isle Inviolate saved in the crisis of her fate from the invasion of a foreign foe, and the grip of a foreign tyrant. Trafalgar broke the sea power of France and Spain. The Grand Army of Boulogne, which in a few more days was to have invested London, turned about to seek other fields of conquest, and to this day you may see the statue of Napoleon on its column on the heights above Boulogne with its back turned to that English land which the would-be despot of Europe was never to see again till he stood prisoner on the deck of a British battleship.

But for that swift voyage of the *Sea Hawk* there might have been no Trafalgar, and the statue of Napoleon might have been facing the other way.

We brought the news home, racing away before the gale which burst over the battlefield the next morning, and never did ship carry tidings at once of greater joy or sorrow than we did. Britain was saved, but the hero who had saved her had died his hero-death in the hour of victory and the supreme moment of his country's fate.

For five years after Trafalgar we kept the *Sea Hawk* busy till the British cruisers had swept the seas so bare that scarce a prize worth taking was to be found; so at length we returned to the lonely scene of my last awakening and took the great treasure which Philip and I had won from the Dons out of the hold of the poor *Sans Merci*, and, returning, paid off our crew.

But to me there was no pleasure in golden ease, nor any rest on land or sea till once more my life-way crossed that of her to whom I had said my last farewell in the Inquisition dungeon. So once more the quest of my oft-lost love became the moving passion of my new life, and once more I set out to seek her along the red pathway of war.

Half the manhood of England, as you know, had sprung to arms to meet the menace of Boulogne, and, since Mark and I had money to spend without stint, we were not long in raising a troop of five hundred horse, and with these, mounted and equipped with Spanish treasure and French spoil, we sailed to seek the fortune of war with Wellington in the Peninsula.

All Europe was now ablaze with battle, from end to end, and the Corsican adventurer who had made himself the tyrant of France was, as it seemed, marching fast to universal empire, like some new Moloch, through the flames of countless cities,1 and the blood of millions of men who died at the bidding of his accursed ambition. You know how he rose, and how he fell, only to rise again for that supreme struggle which in one day burst the chains that for nearly twenty years he had striven to rivet on the limbs of the nations.

It was the night before Quatre Bras. The clocks of Brussels had just chimed eleven as the Duchess of Richmond greeted with a welcoming smile the two leaders of the troop which was now known through the fame of many a fierce death-ride and many a desperate forlorn hope, and so not least esteemed even in that historic room which held the flower of Britain's chivalry.

The formal compliments of our presentation had been given and returned, and I raised my head and saw standing by her Grace of Richmond's side—the most beautiful figure in all that brilliant throng—her whom I had been seeking for ten long years through storm and strife on sea and land. Sweet and stately and lovelier than ever with the added grace of a new and more perfect life there, once more radiant in her re-born womanhood, stood she whose poor torture-wrung frame I had last held in my arms in the Inquisition dungeon at Cadiz, and whose white shape I had last seen blackening amidst the flames of the martyr-fire; and there, too, on her white bosom shone the great jewels I had given to her as a troth-gift when I wooed and won her as Kate Carew.

Our eyes met, and from hers to mine flashed a welcoming glance of such perfect recognition, that, all forgetting where I was, or how many eyes were on us, I took a stride towards her with hands outstretched and her earliest mortal name upon my lips.

"So you know each other already, do you?" said our hostess, all unknowing how strangely those commonplace words of hers sounded in our ears. "And I was just about to present Captain Valdar to you, Lady Ilma, for I protest you would make the handsomest couple in the room to lead a cotillon."

"There is no need, your Grace, as you see," said Lady Ilma—where had she got that old-world name of hers again?—"I met Captain Valdar some time ago in Spain—in Cadiz, was it not?"

"Yes," I said, taking assurance from her perfect self-possession. "It was in Cadiz, and if your ladyship is not better engaged I have not a little to tell you of what has happened since then to one whose fate you were once pleased to take some interest in."

"And how could I be better engaged, my Valdar," she said, looking up at me with the love-light already rekindled in her dear eyes—those eyes which for more than two hundred years had been darkened in death. "And yet," she went on, as we took leave of our hostess and moved away out of reach of too curious ears, "it may be that I have more to tell than you——"

"Whether more or less, tell it quickly, sweet Ilma," I interrupted. "For this, as no doubt you know, is but the calm before the battle-storm, and the summons to march may come at any moment. So say on, that I may not leave you with the mystery of this strangest of all our meetings unsolved. Those jewels, too, that I gave you so long ago, ere you and I were wedded——"

"Yes," she said, laying her hand on them, and looking up into my eyes again. "That is well thought of, husband mine that was——"

"And is," I said, "if true wedlock ever had the sanction of earth and the blessing of Heaven."

"And is and shall be, as you will, my own true knight," she said, bending her head in sweet acquiescence. "Now to my story, and first the jewels. You know that Sir Philip willed Carew Manor to Mary, and so, as she died before an heir was born, it passed to Lady Drake, and when the *Sans Merci* never returned, and Sir Francis took possession in her name, these were found with my other jewels in your own little chamber, where you remember I kept them. Lady Drake's first-born daughter married Lord Howard of Effingham's eldest son, and these jewels of yours were her mother's wedding gift. Since then they have been an heirloom, and, as I am her daughter in the sixth generation and the last child of our line, they have come through me back to you again."

"Not through you, but with you, dear," I said. "And now, how did you know me again?"

"Because I have never forgotten you."

She spoke the words, for me so full of wonder, in a voice that had no tremor in it, so strong was her sweet conviction.

"Because it has been given to me to attain through the lives I have lived and that last death I died for your sake and the truth's to see through the veil which encompasses the things of time."

"When my body was hanging dead upon the stake I saw you with other and clearer eyes, daring death in all its shapes for your righteous vengeance' sake. I saw you drift away alone through the storm and darkness. I watched you through your death-sleep in your cavern in the midst of the sea, and then there came rebirth for me, and with my new mortal life there grew another life in which, when the world was forgotten, I remembered all that had gone before, and all the reason of it was made plain to me.

"It is this that I have earned for myself and for you, and it shall be yours when, as you will soon have done now, you have fought the last of your many fights for truth and freedom. This is your work, and ere long it will be ended as mine is. Through the battle-clouds of your last fight a new age will dawn upon the world, and for you, as for many others, there shall come peace after long strife."

The sweetly solemn words had scarcely died upon her lips when an orderly entered the little alcove into which we had retired, and, saluting, handed me a little folded scrap of paper, and left us without a word.

I opened it and read:

"*The troops will march within an hour. By the Duke's order.*

"Gordon."

I gave it to Ilma, and she read it, and gave it back to me with untrembling hand. Then she put her two hands into mine, and said to me, as she had said ages before on the banks of the Tigris:

"Good-bye, Valdar, till you return in victory. The time for war has come. To-morrow or to-morrow's morrow, the time for love will come again."

"Nay, it is ever here for me, and ever must be while my heart holds a thought of you, sweet," I said. And then, as there was no time for long farewells, and my heart was too hot and full for more words, I took her in my arms and kissed her, and with her farewell kiss still warm and sweet upon my lips I left her, to find Mark and take leave of our hostess.

Before the hour had passed we were all in the saddle, and pressing forward with the long streams of foot and horse and artillery that were pouring along the road to Quatre Bras. There, as you know, we met Ney and drove him back on Frasne, while Napoleon was driving Blucher out of Ligny upon Wavre. Then we fell back to await the assault of the Corsican on the rising ground of Mont of St. Jean by Waterloo. There the night of the 17th found us camped on the sodden ground which was so soon to be a wilderness of bloody mire, seated by our spluttering camp fires under the ceaseless deluge which, in sober truth, was sapping Napoleon's strength with every drop that fell.

By nine the deluge had ceased, and still for more than two hours we stood and faced each other, silent and terrible, gathering each our strength together to deal and take those mighty blows which ere noon would be shaking the world. This was the respite that the rain had given us. But for that daybreak would have seen the batteries of Austerlitz and Jena raining storm and death into our ranks. But the wheels of the guns and the ammunition waggons were fast rooted axle-deep in mud, motionless and useless, till the ground was dry enough for them to be hauled out.

So the slow minutes, big with fate, dragged on, the village clocks striking the hours clearly through the lull before the storm, until half-past eleven chimed from Nivelles Tower. Then we saw a movement in the right wing of the glorious array which stretched its now shining lines along the crests of the slopes in front of us on the other side of that Valley of Death in which Freedom and Tyranny were so soon to be locked in the death-grapple.

A few more minutes and then we saw a puff of smoke, a flash of flame, and heard the short, sharp bang of a single gun. It was the battle-signal, and the knell of Napoleon and that great army which ere midnight was to be a broken rabble, flying leaderless and despairing from the scene of its last defeat.

Scarcely had the smoke drifted away than the roar of a whole battery thundered out, and then column after column of the Frenchmen rolled down the slopes on their left wing and flung themselves on Hugomont.

I have no detailed story of Waterloo to tell you, no history of the battle such as you have more than enough of already. I was but one man with a single pair of eyes, and a shipwrecked sailor clinging to a drifting spar sees as much of the wide expanse of the sea as I could see of that vast ocean of smoke and flame.

To me it was a chaos of charging squadrons, now rolling up on to the solid bayonet-hedged British squares, now reeling back withered and broken by the whirlwind of fire and the hailstorm of lead which burst out just as they reached striking distance; of movement and counter-movement, of long, sinewy lines of horse and foot swaying to and fro in the bitter struggle, like monsters writhing in their death-agony, bending now this way and now that, breaking to fragments and joining again, till at last stragglers would stagger out on one side, ever-multiplying, then the bending, writhing line would surge forward, and what had been a fight was a pursuit.

All this and more I saw in glimpses and the brief breathing pauses of our own hot work. Our first chance came when Napoleon made his first charge on the British left and centre. Eighteen thousand infantry, with a steel-fringed cloud of Kellerman's horse, swept down the slope from the main French line and up the next ridge, where seventy-four guns were planted ready to begin their work of death. They filed swiftly between these and down into the valley before us. Then the guns roared out, and over their heads hurled their storm of grape and solid shot into the thick of the British line.

In front was a brigade of Dutch and Belgians, and the French skirmishers had hardly opened fire than the cowards broke and ran like sheep. As they passed through the English lines, the Englishmen, half laughing, half cursing, opened out and gave them a volley to hasten them on their shameful way, and then turned to meet the Frenchmen, standing as coolly and orderly under that iron storm as if it had but been raining hailstones.

These were Picton's men, three thousand of them all told, as they formed up in two thin red lines. We were on their left, and on the high ground to their right was Ponsonby with his heavy horse. On the crest of the low ridge the Frenchmen halted and deployed, eighteen thousand strong against three.

It was a moment for a brave man, and Picton seized it. I saw him wave his sword as he shouted:

"Now a volley, boys, and at them!"

They were scarce thirty paces away when the three thousand muskets spoke like one. I saw the front of the French column shrivel together and collapse, and then through the screams of pain and fury the deep-toned British hurrah rolled out, the three thousand bayonets came down to the charge, and in two long waves of shining steel dashed at the run into the French front.

At last the French wavered, the line bent back, and we saw red coats among the blue. A bugle call rang out to the right and left of the long line. Never did sweeter music greet my ears. My big blade flashed out of its scabbard and swung high above my head. My well-proved veterans needed no other order, and we dropped our bridles on our horses' necks as we trotted forward. The trot quickened to a canter and the canter broke into a furious gallop, and, with pistol in one hand and sword in the other, we burst in a torrent of steel and flame on the Frenchmen's reeling flank.

At the same instant Ponsonby's Horse pounded in upon their left, the gallant red-coats drew back, re-formed, and plunged into the front again with the bayonet, and then the huge French column bent back upon itself, crushed in from either end, and with sorely wounded centre. For a few moments it fought inch by inch for standing-ground. Then the crowd at my feet parted—some trampled down, some hurled aside—and before me I saw two of Kellerman's Dragoons in front of a troop that was forcing its way through the struggling mass to get at us.

I pulled my gallant old charger to his haunches, and as I rose in the stirrups to lighten him he sprang forward with a bound that landed me between them. While I was in the air my sword went up. I brought it down on the neck of the horse to the right of me, and shore through flesh and bone and sinew so cleanly that the head dropped, and for the twinkling of an eye, hung by the bridle. Then horse and rider pitched forward, and rolled together to the ground.

But even as I made the stroke there fell a swinging blow on my left shoulder, and, strong as I was, I reeled under it.

Then the thrust of a blade took me in the side. But both times the good mail held true, and the blunted blades passed harmless from me. Then I dashed my pistol butt out and sent the dragoon to my left reeling back in his saddle, and as his chin went up I sent the point of my blade under it and out at the back of his skull a good span's length.

I wrenched it free just in time to make a backward slash at the other, who was making a thrust at my horse's side. As his arm came out I got it between the elbow and the wrist, and sword and forearm dropped into the mire. Then another sword flashed across his face, and as we rode over him I saw nothing but a great red splash of blood under his helmet.

"Hammer away, Valdar! They're giving. Let them have it hot and heavy!"

I looked round and saw Mark by my side. My answer was a slash that sent another dragoon's helmet rolling under our horses' feet with his head inside it. The cheers rolled up anew behind me, the French line bent back and back, and at last broke, and, as the ground cleared before us, away we went in a mad, glorious gallop down the slope, up the next, and into the midst of the guns that had wrought such havoc on us. The gunners fled screaming with terror, only to be cut down or trampled under foot. Then we cut the traces and killed the horses, and, when that brief deadly charge was over, France was the poorer by two eagles, two thousand prisoners, and seventy-four guns—the price that Napoleon paid for sending eighteen thousand Frenchmen against some five thousand British horse and foot.

While we were flinging back this first attack, Somerset's Dragoons had been fighting a glorious battle with the French Cuirassiers, who had ridden over the Germans that were holding La Haye Sainte, and by weight of horse and man had hurled the mail-clad Frenchmen down the slope and chased them back into their own lines.

Meanwhile, Hugomont was still a volcano of blazing ruins and bursting shells, ringed round with fire by the columns after columns that were launched against it, only to be hurled back shamed and shattered by the gallant few who fought behind the crumbling walls, and all the while under the shriller chorus of the clash of steel, the shouts of command, the screams and yells of rage and agony, rolled the deep diapason of the ever-thundering guns; and over all the thick, sulphurous battle-cloud hung dark as the frown of Heaven itself.

So the hours came and went, and the strife of the giants went on. The two greatest captains and the two greatest nations in the world were measuring swords, and the matter was not one lightly to be disposed of. As we came back from our pursuit. hewing our way through a column that had been thrown out to head us off, I saw through the breaks in the smoke the Cuirassiers of the French Guard sweeping in swift, succeeding waves of glinting steel and fierce and furious valour up the slopes behind which I knew the British squares of the centre were posted.

Then, as you know, Napoleon made his last struggle to wring victory from defeat. Over on the slope by La Belle Alliance I saw the two huge columns of the infantry of the Old Guard form up. To their right was a motionless figure on a white charger. It was Napoleon, and he was about to direct with his own hand the last blow at those stubborn British squares which lay between him and the mastery of Europe.

We watched the Cuirassiers cross the crest. The British guns roared once and were silent, and the steel-clad horsemen swept on. Then from behind the hill came another sound—the deep, continuous roll of musketry—and the Cuirassiers came rolling back from those bayonet-hedged, impenetrable squares. Again and again they formed, and again and again reeled back. Five times we saw them charge and five times recoil. Then I thought our time had surely come.

As they streamed over the crest for the last time, I leapt into the saddle, the troop mounting like one man, and away we went at the gallop into the midst of them, rolled them in irretrievable ruin down into the valley, and hunted the few that were left of them almost to Hugomont.

So charge followed charge, and attack was succeeded by repulse along the whole of the unwavering British line. La Haye Sainte had fallen, but Hugomont still held out, shot-shattered and smoking, but still impregnable, and the gloom of the afternoon began to deepen into the dusk of evening just as the deep continuous rolling of a new cannonade boomed out to the eastward, telling us that "old Marshal Forward" was at last coming to our aid with his gallant Germans.

Now Napoleon raised his arm, and a roar of cheers went up as the huge columns moved down into what in sober truth was to them the Valley of the Shadow of Death. Over their heads the French artillery thundered anew, and a hurricane of shot and shell opened the way for them through the thinning ranks of Britain.

Then the word was given, the Foot Guards sprang up four deep, and flames began to run from end to end and back again along their line. I saw the French front stop and crumple up, and then the British cheers rolled out, the bayonets flashed forward through the smoke, and away went the veterans of the Old Guard, for the last time reeling, broken and defeated, down that fatal slope.

The word was passed for us to charge, and down between the immovable squares we galloped, the Guards halted, and opened to let us through, and down we swept, laughing and shouting and cheering, on to the remnants of that once glorious brigade, which but an hour ago had been the pride of France.

All this time, saving only the squadrons of cavalry, not a British regiment had moved from its ground. For nine hours they had stood and fought under the ceaseless iron storm which long ago would have scattered any other troops to the four winds of Heaven—patient, dogged, and irresistible.

But now the long awaited moment was very near; the remnants of the Old Guard had reached their lines again, and Napoleon was making a last effort to rally them. Blücher and his Prussians were already thundering on the right French flank. There was a cloud of French cavalry about La Belle Alliance, and the order was sent to us to join Vivian's brigade of Hussars and charge with them.

"That's the beginning of the end," laughed Colonel Vivian as I took him the order. "The Duke's going to move at last. Come along, boys, we'll soon have those fellows out of the way."

Then he rode to the front, and away we went at a trot, with accoutrements jingling and scabbards rattling, and jests running from lip to lip. Then Vivian's sword went up, and the welcome words came sharp and clear:

"Trot! Gallop! Charge!"

And in we burst with a thunder of hoofs and a roar of cheers. For a few moments it was wild, hot work, and then the Frenchmen broke, and after that it was only riding them down and splitting their skulls as opportunity offered. Hardly had we begun to ride rough-shod through the rout of them when the clouds that had lowered all day over the battlefield broke. Out of the West streamed the broad red glare of the setting sun over a scene of carnage and destruction redder than itself. It was the very eye of Heaven looking down on the field of Armageddon to watch the brave sight of the last triumph of order and freedom.

At last the restraining grip of the Iron Duke had been relaxed, and the strength and chivalry of Britain was pouring in triumphant waves of exultant valour on to the ragged, broken masses of huddled up horse and foot, crushed in one upon the other in the stress of panic and the bitterness of defeat, the shattered remnants of that mighty host which the grey dawn had shown us eighty thousand strong, and ranged in matchless order waiting for Napoleon to lead it to the victory which would have meant the humbling of Britain and, perhaps, the conquest of the world.

I spurred on till I could see the French officers run out in front, and hear them shouting to their men to re-form and meet their fate like men. Here and there a few ragged groups took some shape and order, only to be dissolved again in the surging flood of panic that raged about them. Then, three hundred paces from me, I saw a troop of the Young Guard wrench itself out of the struggling throng about it, and to the right of it a man, bare-headed, smoke-begrimed, and blood-bespattered, with torn uniform, and death-white, haggard face.

It was Ney, "the bravest of the brave," the most gallant traitor that ever broke his plighted word. He had but half a sword in his hand. He waved it above his head, and shouted:

"Forward the Guard! Let us show them how Frenchmen can die."

But by this time we were within a hundred paces of them, and pitiless as Destiny we burst upon those gallant ranks, rode them down and scattered them, and the last stand of France was over. I saw Ney grasp the bridle of a riderless horse, and fling himself on his back. I could have ridden him down and killed him had I chosen, but I let him go, for I was loth to kill so brave a man; and yet it would have been better and more to his liking had he fallen under my sword than be shot to death by French bullets as a traitor.

But I was hunting higher game than he, and yet in vain. The little squat figure on the white horse had vanished, for the slayer of millions had turned craven in the hour of his fate, and was running for his life amidst the rabble that was streaming away southward to Paris.

The British lines swept on past Hugomont and La Haye Sainte up the heights to La Belle Alliance, and on past that to Blanchenoit, clearing the field of all but dead and dying before them, and the battle ended and the rout began. The Prussians were up now, and, with the memory of Jena hot in their hearts, they plunged, swinging their vengeful steel into the flanks of the flying rabble.

At Planchenoit the British regulars halted, but we had not had enough of it yet. Of the five hundred troopers I had taken into the battle scarcely three hundred now remained, and Mark was far behind, dead somewhere where the fight had been thickest; but our orders still held good, and so we went in with the furious Teutons to make sure that the wreck of the Grand Army should never be an army again.

Through Genappe and Quatre Bras,

past Sombreffe and Frasne, over Thuin and Charleroi, we kept up the mad carnival of slaughter and death, until all that was left of the conquerors of Austerlitz and Jena, of Ulm and Marengo, was chased across the frontier into France like a flock of panic-striken sheep, and the moon shone down on the living and the dying and the dead, on the victors and the vanquished, and a world delivered from as vile a tyranny as ever threatened the liberties of mankind.

EPILOGUE

IN A GARDEN OF PEACE

Now the tale is told and the dream has been dreamt. Yet was it but a dream or more? Beside me as I write this last of my many pages stands she whose presence tells me that it is no dream, but very truth—my love, ages-old, yet still in the first sweet flush of her re-incarnate womanhood, my four times wedded bride, whose dear sister-soul has kept its tryst with mine through all the changing ages that have passed since Valdar the Asa, son of Odin, was driven forth from his home in Asgard of the Gods.

The centuries have come and gone, empires have waxed and waned, and the very face of the heavens has changed since then, and yet the eyes that watch these words as I write them are the very same which smiled up into mine when I looked my last on the Plain of Ida, and the godlike kindred that had been mine.

This little hand which is resting so lightly on my shoulder is the same that was laid in blessing on my helm when I went to my first fight against the hosts of Nimrod ere Babel fell, and the fair face which is now so close to mine looked down upon me from the martyr-stake in Cadiz. The voice which chides me so sweetly for letting my heart stray into my hand as I write is the same that called the warrior-maidens of Islam to that desperate charge at Yermouk; and this soft, silken tress of red-gold hair which strays in such sweet wantonness across my breast once felt the touch of the Tiger Lord's hand in the throne-room of the second Nineveh.

This tale, too, which I began to tell three years ago in the New Babylon when the first corn was ripening on the harvest fields of death round Waterloo, is finished in a sweet-smelling English garden sloping down from the terrace of the old Manor House of Carew towards that northern sea over which Brenda and I made our death-voyage from Ivarsheim, and yonder is the little grey, moss-grown tower within whose walls I slept that sleep from which my Lady Kate's kiss awakened me, as Cleopatra's had done nearly two thousand years ago in Memphis.

How, then, could I doubt its truth, however strange the tale may seem; for, even though Odin's name and worship are now but an old-world myth, has not that dream of the Saga of Valdar been very truth for me?

Have I not lived and loved and lost and lived again, and found and lost again through many a changing age, and seen the fierce flood of human strife roll thundering down between the echoing shores of Time? Have I not seen Solomon, life-weary with all the world could give him; the White Christ crucified; the great Cæsar murdered in the city in which he had reared the throne of the world; the Prophet of Islam mocked and scorned and driven from his home; the faith and valour of Lion-heart brought to nought by the traitors of his own camp; and Christian men and women torture-racked and writhing in Torquemada's martyr-fires?

And yet, through all the storm and strife, has run unbroken that golden thread of Love which, dropping down from Heaven, leads like a God-given clue through the labyrinth of human things and back to Heaven again. Death has come, not once, but many times, and surely Love has conquered it. It may be that for me there are other conflicts yet to come, and that my long lesson is not yet fully learned. It may be that once more the death-sleep shall come to my eyes, and that they shall open again in some distant age of the world when the glories of to-day shall be the things of yesterday; but in that the men of the present can have no concern.

When two generations have passed away this story of mine shall go forth to the world that those who will may read it, and by that time belief or doubt will matter little to us whose eyes have scanned its pages with so many a fond recollection, for then either the long journey will be truly done at last, or we shall be waiting, as those old Egyptians used to say, in the Halls of Amenti for the hour of our next tryst to strike.

THE END.

www.ingramcontent.com/pod-product-compliance
Lightning Source LLC
Chambersburg PA
CBHW030342310726
48979CB00001B/143

* 9 7 8 1 4 3 4 4 8 8 8 7 9 *